Fantastic and Horrific Stories

Fantastic and Horrific Stories

Arthur Machen

MINT EDITIONS

Fantastic and Horrific Stories contains work first published from 1894–1924.

This edition published by Mint Editions 2021.

ISBN 9781513218311 | E-ISBN 9781513217314

Published by Mint Editions®

 **MINT
EDITIONS**

minteditionbooks.com

Publishing Director: Jennifer Newens
Design & Production: Rachel Lopez Metzger
Project Manager: Micaela Clark
Typesetting: Westchester Publishing Services

More in This Series:
Weird and Horrific Stories
Mysterious and Horrific Stories
Romantic and Horrific Stories
Scientific and Horrific Stories

Contents

The Shining Pyramid

The Hill of Dreams

The White People

THE TERROR

THE GREAT GOD PAN

I

The Experiment

I am glad you came, Clarke; very glad indeed. I was not sure you could spare the time."

"I was able to make arrangements for a few days; things are not very lively just now. But have you no misgivings, Raymond? Is it absolutely safe?"

The two men were slowly pacing the terrace in front of Dr. Raymond's house. The sun still hung above the western mountain-line, but it shone with a dull red glow that cast no shadows, and all the air was quiet; a sweet breath came from the great wood on the hillside above, and with it, at intervals, the soft murmuring call of the wild doves. Below, in the long lovely valley, the river wound in and out between the lonely hills, and, as the sun hovered and vanished into the west, a faint mist, pure white, began to rise from the hills. Dr. Raymond turned sharply to his friend.

"Safe? Of course it is. In itself the operation is a perfectly simple one; any surgeon could do it."

"And there is no danger at any other stage?"

"None; absolutely no physical danger whatsoever, I give you my word. You are always timid, Clarke, always; but you know my history. I have devoted myself to transcendental medicine for the last twenty years. I have heard myself called quack and charlatan and impostor, but all the while I knew I was on the right path. Five years ago I reached the goal, and since then everyday has been a preparation for what we shall do tonight."

"I should like to believe it is all true." Clarke knit his brows, and looked doubtfully at Dr. Raymond. "Are you perfectly sure, Raymond, that your theory is not a phantasmagoria—a splendid vision, certainly, but a mere vision after all?"

Dr. Raymond stopped in his walk and turned sharply. He was a middle-aged man, gaunt and thin, of a pale yellow complexion, but as he answered Clarke and faced him, there was a flush on his cheek.

"Look about you, Clarke. You see the mountain, and hill following after hill, as wave on wave, you see the woods and orchard, the fields of ripe corn, and the meadows reaching to the reed-beds by the river. You see me standing here beside you, and hear my voice; but I tell you that all these things—yes, from that star that has just shone out in the sky to the solid ground beneath our feet—I say that all these are but dreams and shadows; the shadows that hide the real world from our eyes. There is a real world, but it is beyond this glamour and this vision, beyond these 'chases in Arras, dreams in a career,' beyond them all as beyond a veil. I do not know whether any human being has ever lifted that veil; but I do know, Clarke, that you and I shall see it lifted this very night from before another's eyes. You may think this all strange nonsense; it may be strange, but it is true, and the ancients knew what lifting the veil means. They called it seeing the god Pan."

Clarke shivered; the white mist gathering over the river was chilly.

"It is wonderful indeed," he said. "We are standing on the brink of a strange world, Raymond, if what you say is true. I suppose the knife is absolutely necessary?"

"Yes; a slight lesion in the grey matter, that is all; a trifling rearrangement of certain cells, a microscopical alteration that would escape the attention of ninety-nine brain specialists out of a hundred. I don't want to bother you with 'shop,' Clarke; I might give you a mass of technical detail which would sound very imposing, and would leave you as enlightened as you are now. But I suppose you have read, casually, in out-of-the-way corners of your paper, that immense strides have been made recently in the physiology of the brain. I saw a paragraph the other day about Digby's theory, and Browne Faber's discoveries. Theories and discoveries! Where they are standing now, I stood fifteen years ago, and I need not tell you that I have not been standing still for the last fifteen years. It will be enough if I say that five years ago I made the discovery that I alluded to when I said that ten years ago I reached the goal. After years of labour, after years of toiling and groping in the dark, after days and nights of disappointments and sometimes of despair, in which I used now and then to tremble and grow cold with the thought that perhaps there were others seeking for what I sought, at last, after so long, a pang of sudden joy thrilled my soul, and I knew the long journey was at an end. By what seemed then and still seems a chance, the suggestion of a moment's idle thought followed up upon familiar lines and paths that I had tracked a hundred times already, the great truth burst upon me, and I saw, mapped out in lines of sight, a whole world, a sphere unknown; continents and islands, and great oceans in which no ship has sailed (to my belief) since a Man first lifted up his eyes and beheld the sun, and the stars of heaven, and the quiet earth beneath. You will think this all high-flown language, Clarke, but it is hard to be literal. And yet; I do not know whether what I am hinting at cannot be set forth in plain and lonely terms. For instance, this world of ours is pretty well girded now with the telegraph wires and cables; thought, with something less than the speed of thought, flashes from sunrise to sunset, from north to south, across the floods and the desert places. Suppose that an electrician of today were suddenly to perceive that he and his friends have merely been playing with pebbles and mistaking them for the foundations of the world; suppose that such a man saw uttermost space lie open before the current, and words of men flash forth to the sun and beyond the sun into the systems beyond, and the voice of articulate speaking men echo in the waste void that bounds our thought. As analogies go, that is a pretty good analogy of what I have done; you can understand now a little of what I felt as I stood here one evening; it was a summer evening, and the valley looked much as it does now; I stood here, and saw before me the unutterable, the unthinkable gulf that yawns profound between two worlds, the world of matter and the world of spirit; I saw the great empty deep stretch dim before me, and in that instant a bridge of light leapt from the earth to the unknown shore, and the abyss was spanned. You may look in Browne Faber's book, if you like, and you will find that to the present day men of science are unable to account for the presence, or to specify the functions of a certain group of nerve-cells in the brain. That group is, as it were, land to let, a mere waste place for fanciful theories. I am not in the position of Browne Faber and the specialists, I am perfectly instructed as to the possible functions of those nerve-centers in the scheme of things. With a touch I can bring them into play, with a touch, I say, I can set free the current, with a touch I can complete the communication between this world of sense and—we shall be able to finish the sentence later on. Yes, the knife is necessary; but think what that knife will effect. It will level utterly the solid wall of sense, and probably, for the first time since man was made, a spirit will gaze on a spirit-world. Clarke, Mary will see the god Pan!"

"But you remember what you wrote to me? I thought it would be requisite that she—"

He whispered the rest into the doctor's ear.

"Not at all, not at all. That is nonsense. I assure you. Indeed, it is better as it is; I am quite certain of that."

"Consider the matter well, Raymond. It's a great responsibility. Something might go wrong; you would be a miserable man for the rest of your days."

"No, I think not, even if the worst happened. As you know, I rescued Mary from the gutter, and from almost certain starvation, when she was a child; I think her life is mine, to use as I see fit. Come, it's getting late; we had better go in."

Dr. Raymond led the way into the house, through the hall, and down a long dark passage. He took a key from his pocket and opened a heavy door, and motioned Clarke into his laboratory. It had once been a billiard-room, and was lighted by a glass dome in the centre of the ceiling, whence there still shone a sad grey light on the figure of the doctor as he lit a lamp with a heavy shade and placed it on a table in the middle of the room.

Clarke looked about him. Scarcely a foot of wall remained bare; there were shelves all around laden with bottles and phials of all shapes and colours, and at one end stood a little Chippendale book-case. Raymond pointed to this.

"You see that parchment Oswald Crollius? He was one of the first to show me the way, though I don't think he ever found it himself. That is a strange saying of his: 'In every grain of wheat there lies hidden the soul of a star.'"

There was not much furniture in the laboratory. The table in the centre, a stone slab with a drain in one corner, the two armchairs on which Raymond and Clarke were sitting; that was all, except an odd-looking chair at the furthest end of the room. Clarke looked at it, and raised his eyebrows.

"Yes, that is the chair," said Raymond. "We may as well place it in position." He got up and wheeled the chair to the light, and began raising and lowering it, letting down the seat, setting the back at various angles, and adjusting the foot-rest. It looked comfortable enough, and Clarke passed his hand over the soft green velvet, as the doctor manipulated the levers.

"Now, Clarke, make yourself quite comfortable. I have a couple hours' work before me; I was obliged to leave certain matters to the last."

Raymond went to the stone slab, and Clarke watched him drearily as he bent over a row of phials and lit the flame under the crucible. The doctor had a small hand-lamp, shaded as the larger one, on a ledge above his apparatus, and Clarke, who sat in the shadows, looked down at the great shadowy room, wondering at the bizarre effects of brilliant light and undefined darkness contrasting with one another. Soon he became conscious of an odd odour, at first the merest suggestion of odour, in the room, and as it grew more decided he felt surprised that he was not reminded of the chemist's shop or the surgery. Clarke found himself idly endeavouring to analyse the sensation, and half conscious, he began to think of a day, fifteen years ago, that he had spent roaming through the woods and meadows near his own home. It was a burning day at the beginning of August, the heat had dimmed the outlines of all things and all distances with a faint mist, and people who observed the thermometer spoke of an abnormal register, of a temperature that was almost tropical. Strangely that wonderful hot day of the fifties rose up again in Clarke's imagination; the sense of dazzling all-pervading sunlight seemed to blot out the shadows and the lights of the laboratory, and he felt again the heated air beating in gusts about his face, saw the shimmer rising from the turf, and heard the myriad murmur of the summer.

"I hope the smell doesn't annoy you, Clarke; there's nothing unwholesome about it. It may make you a bit sleepy, that's all."

Clarke heard the words quite distinctly, and knew that Raymond was speaking to him, but for the life of him he could not rouse himself from his lethargy. He could only think of the lonely walk he had taken fifteen years ago; it was his last look at the fields and woods he had known since he was a child, and now it all stood out in brilliant light, as a picture, before him. Above all there came to his nostrils the scent of summer, the smell of flowers mingled, and the odour of the woods, of cool shaded places, deep in the green depths, drawn forth by the sun's heat; and the scent of the good earth, lying as it were with arms stretched forth, and smiling lips, overpowered all. His fancies made him wander, as he had wandered long ago, from the fields into the wood, tracking a little path between the shining undergrowth of beech-trees; and the trickle of water dropping from the limestone rock sounded as a clear melody in the dream. Thoughts began to go astray and to mingle with other thoughts; the beech alley was transformed to a path between ilex-trees, and here and there a vine climbed from bough to bough, and sent up waving tendrils and drooped with purple grapes, and the sparse grey-green leaves of a wild olive-tree stood out against the dark shadows of the ilex. Clarke, in the deep folds of dream, was conscious that the path from his father's house had led him into an undiscovered country, and he was wondering at the strangeness of it all, when suddenly, in place of the hum and murmur of the summer, an infinite silence seemed to fall on all things, and the wood was hushed, and for a moment in time he stood face to face there with a presence, that was neither man nor beast, neither the living nor the dead, but all things mingled, the form of all things but devoid of all form. And in that moment, the sacrament of body and soul was dissolved, and a voice seemed to cry "Let us go hence," and then the darkness of darkness beyond the stars, the darkness of everlasting.

When Clarke woke up with a start he saw Raymond pouring a few drops of some oily fluid into a green phial, which he stoppered tightly.

"You have been dozing," he said; "the journey must have tired you out. It is done now. I am going to fetch Mary; I shall be back in ten minutes."

Clarke lay back in his chair and wondered. It seemed as if he had but passed from one dream into another. He half expected to see the walls of the laboratory melt and disappear, and to awake in London, shuddering at his own sleeping fancies. But at last the door opened, and the doctor returned, and behind him came a girl of about seventeen, dressed all in white. She was so beautiful that Clarke did not wonder at what the doctor had written to him. She was blushing now over face and neck and arms, but Raymond seemed unmoved.

"Mary," he said, "the time has come. You are quite free. Are you willing to trust yourself to me entirely?"

"Yes, dear."

"Do you hear that, Clarke? You are my witness. Here is the chair, Mary. It is quite easy. Just sit in it and lean back. Are you ready?"

"Yes, dear, quite ready. Give me a kiss before you begin."

The doctor stooped and kissed her mouth, kindly enough. "Now shut your eyes," he said. The girl closed her eyelids, as if she were tired, and longed for sleep, and Raymond placed the green phial to her nostrils. Her face grew white, whiter than her dress; she struggled faintly, and then with the feeling of submission strong within her, crossed her arms upon her breast as a little child about to say her prayers. The bright light of the lamp fell full upon her, and Clarke watched changes fleeting over her face as the changes of the hills when the summer clouds float across the sun. And then she lay all white and still, and the doctor turned up one of her eyelids. She was quite unconscious. Raymond pressed hard on one of the levers and the chair instantly sank back. Clarke saw him cutting away a circle, like a tonsure, from her hair, and the lamp was moved nearer. Raymond took a small glittering instrument from a little case, and Clarke turned away shudderingly. When he looked again the doctor was binding up the wound he had made.

"She will awake in five minutes." Raymond was still perfectly cool. "There is nothing more to be done; we can only wait."

The minutes passed slowly; they could hear a slow, heavy, ticking. There was an old clock in the passage. Clarke felt sick and faint; his knees shook beneath him, he could hardly stand.

Suddenly, as they watched, they heard a long-drawn sigh, and suddenly did the colour that had vanished return to the girl's cheeks, and suddenly her eyes opened. Clarke quailed before them. They shone with an awful light, looking far away, and a great wonder fell upon her face, and her hands stretched out as if to touch what was invisible; but in an instant the wonder faded, and gave place to the most awful terror. The muscles of her face were hideously convulsed, she shook from head to foot; the soul seemed struggling and shuddering within the house of flesh. It was a horrible sight, and Clarke rushed forward, as she fell shrieking to the floor.

Three days later Raymond took Clarke to Mary's bedside. She was lying wide-awake, rolling her head from side to side, and grinning vacantly.

"Yes," said the doctor, still quite cool, "it is a great pity; she is a hopeless idiot. However, it could not be helped; and, after all, she has seen the Great God Pan."

II

Mr. Clarke's Memoirs

Mr. Clarke, the gentleman chosen by Dr. Raymond to witness the strange experiment of the god Pan, was a person in whose character caution and curiosity were oddly mingled; in his sober moments he thought of the unusual and eccentric with undisguised aversion, and yet, deep in his heart, there was a wide-eyed inquisitiveness with respect to all the more recondite and esoteric elements in the nature of men. The latter tendency had prevailed when he accepted Raymond's invitation, for though his considered judgment had always repudiated the doctor's theories as the wildest nonsense, yet he secretly hugged a belief in fantasy, and would have rejoiced to see that belief confirmed. The horrors that he witnessed in the dreary laboratory were to a certain extent salutary; he was conscious of being involved in an affair not altogether reputable, and for many years afterwards he clung bravely to the commonplace, and rejected all occasions of occult investigation. Indeed, on some homeopathic principle, he for sometime attended the seances of distinguished mediums, hoping that the clumsy tricks of these gentlemen would make him altogether disgusted with mysticism of every kind, but the remedy, though caustic, was not efficacious. Clarke knew that he still pined for the unseen, and little by little, the old passion began to reassert itself, as the face of Mary, shuddering and convulsed with an unknown terror, faded slowly from his memory. Occupied all day in pursuits both serious and lucrative, the temptation to relax in the evening was too great, especially in the winter months, when the fire cast a warm glow over his snug bachelor apartment, and a bottle of some choice claret stood ready by his elbow. His dinner digested, he would make a brief pretence of reading the evening paper, but the mere catalogue of news soon palled upon him, and Clarke would find himself casting glances of warm desire in the direction of an old Japanese bureau, which stood at a pleasant distance from the hearth. Like a boy before a jam-closet, for a few minutes he would hover indecisive, but lust always prevailed, and Clarke ended by drawing up his chair, lighting a candle, and sitting down before the bureau. Its pigeon-holes and drawers teemed with documents on the most morbid subjects, and in the well reposed a large manuscript volume, in which he had painfully entered the gems of his collection. Clarke had a fine contempt for published literature; the most ghostly story ceased to interest him if it happened to be printed; his sole pleasure was in the reading, compiling, and rearranging what he called his "Memoirs to prove the Existence of the Devil," and engaged in this pursuit the evening seemed to fly and the night appeared too short.

On one particular evening, an ugly December night, black with fog, and raw with frost, Clarke hurried over his dinner, and scarcely deigned to observe his customary ritual of taking up the paper and laying it down again. He paced two or three times up and down the room, and opened the bureau, stood still a moment, and sat down. He leant back, absorbed in one of those dreams to which he was subject, and at length drew out his book, and opened it at the last entry. There were three or four pages densely covered with Clarke's round, set penmanship, and at the beginning he had written in a somewhat larger hand:

Singular Narrative told me by my Friend, Dr. Phillips.
He assures me that all the facts related therein are strictly and wholly True, but refuses to give either the Surnames of the Persons Concerned, or the Place where these Extraordinary Events occurred.

Mr. Clarke began to read over the account for the tenth time, glancing now and then at the pencil notes he had made when it was told him by his friend. It was one of his humours to pride himself on a certain literary ability; he thought well of his style, and took pains in arranging the circumstances in dramatic order. He read the following story:—

The persons concerned in this statement are Helen V, who, if she is still alive, must now be a woman of twenty-three, Rachel M., since deceased, who was a year younger than the above, and Trevor W., an imbecile, aged eighteen. These persons were at the period of the story inhabitants of a village on the borders of Wales, a place of some importance in the time of the Roman occupation, but now a scattered hamlet, of not more than five hundred souls. It is situated on rising ground, about six miles from the sea, and is sheltered by a large and picturesque forest.

Some eleven years ago, Helen V came to the village under rather peculiar circumstances. It is understood that she, being an orphan, was adopted in her infancy by a distant relative, who brought her up in his own house until she was twelve years old. Thinking, however, that it would be better for the child to have playmates of her own age, he advertised in several local papers for a good home in a comfortable farmhouse for a girl of twelve, and this advertisement was answered by Mr. R., a well-to-do farmer in the above-mentioned village. His references proving satisfactory, the gentleman sent his adopted daughter to Mr. R., with a letter, in which he stipulated that the girl should have a room to herself, and stated that her guardians need be at no trouble in the matter of education, as she was already sufficiently educated for the position in life which she would occupy. In fact, Mr. R. was given to understand that the girl be allowed to find her own occupations and to spend her time almost as she liked. Mr. R. duly met her at the nearest station, a town seven miles away from his house, and seems to have remarked nothing extraordinary about the child except that she was reticent as to her former life and her adopted father. She was, however, of a very different type from the inhabitants of the village; her skin was a pale, clear olive, and her features were strongly marked, and of a somewhat foreign character. She appears to have settled down easily enough into farmhouse life, and became a favourite with the children, who sometimes went with her on her rambles in the forest, for this was her amusement. Mr. R. states that he has known her to go out by herself directly after their early breakfast, and not return till after dusk, and that, feeling uneasy at a young girl being out alone for so many hours, he communicated with her adopted father, who replied in a brief note that Helen must do as she chose. In the winter, when the forest paths are impassable, she spent most of her time in her bedroom, where she slept alone, according to the instructions of her relative. It was on one of these expeditions to the forest that the first of the singular incidents with which this girl is connected occurred, the date being about a year after her arrival at the village. The preceding winter had been remarkably severe, the snow drifting to a great depth, and the frost continuing for an unexampled period, and the summer following was as noteworthy for its extreme heat.

On one of the very hottest days in this summer, Helen V left the farmhouse for one of her long rambles in the forest, taking with her, as usual, some bread and meat for lunch. She was seen by some men in the fields making for the old Roman Road, a green causeway which traverses the highest part of the wood, and they were astonished to observe that the girl had taken off her hat, though the heat of the sun was already tropical. As it happened, a labourer, Joseph W. by name, was working in the forest near the Roman Road, and at twelve o'clock his little son, Trevor, brought the man his dinner of bread and cheese. After the meal, the boy, who was about seven years old at the time, left his father at work, and, as he said, went to look for flowers in the wood, and the man, who could hear him shouting with delight at his discoveries, felt no uneasiness. Suddenly, however, he was horrified at hearing the most dreadful screams, evidently the result of great terror, proceeding from the direction in which his son had gone, and he hastily threw down his tools and ran to see what had happened. Tracing his path by the sound, he met the little boy, who was running headlong, and was evidently terribly frightened, and on questioning him the man elicited that after picking a posy of flowers he felt tired, and lay down on the grass and fell asleep. He was suddenly awakened, as he stated, by a peculiar noise, a sort of singing he called it, and on peeping through the branches he saw Helen V playing on the grass with a "strange naked man," who he seemed unable to describe more fully. He said he felt dreadfully frightened and ran away crying for his father. Joseph W. proceeded in the direction indicated by his son, and found Helen V sitting on the grass in the middle of a glade or open space left by charcoal burners. He angrily charged her with frightening his little boy, but she entirely denied the accusation and laughed at the child's story of a "strange man," to which he himself did not attach much credence. Joseph W. came to the conclusion that the boy had woke up with a sudden fright, as children sometimes do, but Trevor persisted in his story, and continued in such evident distress that at last his father took him home, hoping that his mother would be able to soothe him. For many weeks, however, the boy gave his parents much anxiety; he became nervous and strange in his manner, refusing to leave the cottage by himself, and constantly alarming the household by waking in the night with cries of "The man in the wood! father! father!"

In course of time, however, the impression seemed to have worn off, and about three months later he accompanied his father to the home of a gentleman in the neighborhood, for whom Joseph W. occasionally did work. The man was shown into the study, and the little boy was left sitting in the hall, and a few minutes later, while the gentleman was giving W. his instructions, they were both horrified by a piercing shriek and the sound of a fall, and rushing out they found the child lying senseless on the floor, his face contorted with terror. The doctor was immediately summoned, and after some examination he pronounced the child to be suffering form a kind of fit, apparently produced by a sudden shock. The boy was taken to one of the bedrooms, and after sometime recovered consciousness, but only to pass into a condition described by the medical man as one of violent hysteria. The doctor exhibited a strong sedative, and in the course of two hours pronounced him fit to walk home, but in passing through the hall the paroxysms of fright returned and with additional violence. The father perceived that the child was pointing at some object, and heard the old cry, "The man in the wood," and looking in the direction indicated saw a stone head of grotesque appearance, which had been built into the wall above one of the doors. It seems the owner of the house had recently made alterations in his premises, and on digging the foundations for some offices, the men had found a curious head, evidently of the Roman period, which had been placed in the manner described. The head is pronounced by the most experienced archaeologists of the district to be that of a faun or satyr. (Dr. Phillips tells me that he has seen the head in question, and assures me that he has never received such a vivid presentment of intense evil.)

From whatever cause arising, this second shock seemed too severe for the boy Trevor, and at the present date he suffers from a weakness of intellect, which gives but little promise of amending. The matter caused a good deal of sensation at the time, and the girl Helen was closely questioned by Mr. R., but to no purpose, she steadfastly denying that she had frightened or in anyway molested Trevor.

The second event with which this girl's name is connected took place about six years ago, and is of a still more extraordinary character.

At the beginning of the summer of 1882, Helen contracted a friendship of a peculiarly intimate character with Rachel M., the daughter of a prosperous farmer in the neighbourhood. This girl, who was a year younger than Helen, was considered by most people to be the prettier of the two, though Helen's features had to a great extent softened as she became older. The two girls, who were together on every available opportunity, presented a singular contrast, the one with her clear, olive skin and almost Italian appearance, and the other of the proverbial red and white of our rural districts. It must be stated that the payments made to Mr. R. for the maintenance of Helen were known in the village for their excessive liberality, and the impression was general that she would one day inherit a large sum of money from her relative. The parents of Rachel were therefore not averse from their daughter's friendship with the girl, and even encouraged the intimacy, though they now bitterly regret having done so. Helen still retained her extraordinary fondness for the forest, and on several occasions Rachel accompanied her, the two friends setting out early in the morning, and remaining in the wood until dusk. Once or twice after these excursions Mrs. M. thought her daughter's manner rather peculiar; she seemed languid and dreamy, and as it has been expressed, "different from herself," but these peculiarities seem to have been thought too trifling for remark. One evening, however, after Rachel had come home, her mother heard a noise which sounded like suppressed weeping in the girl's room, and on going in found her lying, half undressed, upon the bed, evidently in the greatest distress. As soon as she saw her mother, she exclaimed, "Ah, mother, mother, why did you let me go to the forest with Helen?" Mrs. M. was astonished at so strange a question, and proceeded to make inquiries. Rachel told her a wild story. She said—

Clarke closed the book with a snap, and turned his chair towards the fire. When his friend sat one evening in that very chair, and told his story, Clarke had interrupted him at a point a little subsequent to this, had cut short his words in a paroxysm of horror. "My God!" he had exclaimed, "think, think what you are saying. It is too incredible, too monstrous; such things can never be in this quiet world, where men and women live and die, and struggle, and conquer, or maybe fail, and fall down under sorrow, and grieve and suffer strange fortunes for many a year; but not this, Phillips, not such things as this. There must be some explanation, some way out of the terror. Why, man, if such a case were possible, our earth would be a nightmare."

But Phillips had told his story to the end, concluding:

"Her flight remains a mystery to this day; she vanished in broad sunlight; they saw her walking in a meadow, and a few moments later she was not there."

Clarke tried to conceive the thing again, as he sat by the fire, and again his mind shuddered and shrank back, appalled before the sight of such awful, unspeakable elements enthroned as it were, and triumphant in human flesh. Before him stretched the long dim vista of the green causeway in the forest, as his friend had described it; he saw the swaying leaves and the quivering shadows on the grass, he saw the sunlight and the flowers, and far away, far in the long distance, the two figures moved toward him. One was Rachel, but the other?

Clarke had tried his best to disbelieve it all, but at the end of the account, as he had written it in his book, he had placed the inscription:

Et Diabolus Incarnate Est. Et Homo Factus Est.

III

The City of Resurrections

Herbert! Good God! Is it possible?"

"Yes, my name's Herbert. I think I know your face, too, but I don't remember your name. My memory is very queer."

"Don't you recollect Villiers of Wadham?"

"So it is, so it is. I beg your pardon, Villiers, I didn't think I was begging of an old college friend. Goodnight."

"My dear fellow, this haste is unnecessary. My rooms are close by, but we won't go there just yet. Suppose we walk up Shaftesbury Avenue a little way? But how in heaven's name have you come to this pass, Herbert?"

"It's a long story, Villiers, and a strange one too, but you can hear it if you like."

"Come on, then. Take my arm, you don't seem very strong."

The ill-assorted pair moved slowly up Rupert Street; the one in dirty, evil-looking rags, and the other attired in the regulation uniform of a man about town, trim, glossy, and eminently well-to-do. Villiers had emerged from his restaurant after an excellent dinner of many courses, assisted by an ingratiating little flask of Chianti, and, in that frame of mind which was with him almost chronic, had delayed a moment by the door, peering round in the dimly-lighted street in search of those mysterious incidents and persons with which the streets of London teem in every quarter and every hour. Villiers prided himself as a practised explorer of such obscure mazes and byways of London life, and in this unprofitable pursuit he displayed an assiduity which was worthy of more serious employment. Thus he stood by the lamp-post surveying the passersby with undisguised curiosity, and with that gravity known only to the systematic diner, had just enunciated in his mind the formula: "London has been called the city of encounters; it is more than that, it is the city of Resurrections," when these reflections were suddenly interrupted by a piteous whine at his elbow, and a deplorable appeal for alms. He looked around in some irritation, and with a sudden shock found himself confronted with the embodied proof of his somewhat stilted fancies. There, close beside him, his face altered and disfigured by poverty and disgrace, his body barely covered by greasy ill-fitting rags, stood his old friend Charles Herbert, who had matriculated on the same day as himself, with whom he had been merry and wise for twelve revolving terms. Different occupations and varying interests had interrupted the friendship, and it was six years since Villiers had seen Herbert; and now he looked upon this wreck of a man with grief and dismay, mingled with a certain inquisitiveness as to what dreary chain of circumstances had dragged him down to such a doleful pass. Villiers felt together with compassion all the relish of the amateur in mysteries, and congratulated himself on his leisurely speculations outside the restaurant.

They walked on in silence for sometime, and more than one passerby stared in astonishment at the unaccustomed spectacle of a well-dressed man with an unmistakable beggar hanging on to his arm, and, observing this, Villiers led the way to an obscure street in Soho. Here he repeated his question.

"How on earth has it happened, Herbert? I always understood you would succeed to an excellent position in Dorsetshire. Did your father disinherit you? Surely not?"

"No, Villiers; I came into all the property at my poor father's death; he died a year after I left Oxford. He was a very good father to me, and I mourned his death sincerely enough. But you know what young men are; a few months later I came up to town and went a good deal into society. Of course I had excellent introductions, and I managed to enjoy myself very much in a harmless sort of way. I played a little, certainly, but never for heavy stakes, and the few bets I made on races brought me in money—only a few pounds, you know, but enough to pay for cigars and such petty pleasures. It was in my second season that the tide turned. Of course you have heard of my marriage?"

"No, I never heard anything about it."

"Yes, I married, Villiers. I met a girl, a girl of the most wonderful and most strange beauty, at the house of some people whom I knew. I cannot tell you her age; I never knew it, but, so far as I can guess, I should think she must have been about nineteen when I made her acquaintance. My friends had come to know her at Florence; she told them she was an orphan, the child of an English father and an Italian mother, and she charmed them as she charmed me. The first time I saw her was at an evening party. I was standing by the door talking to a friend, when suddenly above the hum and babble of conversation I heard a voice which seemed to thrill to my heart. She was singing an Italian song. I was introduced to her that evening, and in three months I married Helen. Villiers, that woman, if I can call her woman, corrupted my soul. The night of the wedding I found myself sitting in her bedroom in the hotel, listening to her talk. She was sitting up in bed, and I listened to her as she spoke in her beautiful voice, spoke of things which even now I would not dare whisper in the blackest night, though I stood in the midst of a wilderness. You, Villiers, you may think you know life, and London, and what goes on day and night in this dreadful city; for all I can say you may have heard the talk of the vilest, but I tell you you can have no conception of what I know, not in your most fantastic, hideous dreams can you have imaged forth the faintest shadow of what I have heard—and seen. Yes, seen. I have seen the incredible, such horrors that even I myself sometimes stop in the middle of the street and ask whether it is possible for a man to behold such things and live. In a year, Villiers, I was a ruined man, in body and soul—in body and soul."

"But your property, Herbert? You had land in Dorset."

"I sold it all; the fields and woods, the dear old house—everything."

"And the money?"

"She took it all from me."

"And then left you?"

"Yes; she disappeared one night. I don't know where she went, but I am sure if I saw her again it would kill me. The rest of my story is of no interest; sordid misery, that is all. You may think, Villiers, that I have exaggerated and talked for effect; but I have not told you half. I could tell you certain things which would convince you, but you would never know a happy day again. You would pass the rest of your life, as I pass mine, a haunted man, a man who has seen hell."

Villiers took the unfortunate man to his rooms, and gave him a meal. Herbert could eat little, and scarcely touched the glass of wine set before him. He sat moody and silent by the fire, and seemed relieved when Villiers sent him away with a small present of money.

"By the way, Herbert," said Villiers, as they parted at the door, "what was your wife's name? You said Helen, I think? Helen what?"

"The name she passed under when I met her was Helen Vaughan, but what her real name was I can't say. I don't think she had a name. No, no, not in that sense. Only human beings have names, Villiers; I can't say anymore. Goodbye; yes, I will not fail to call if I see anyway in which you can help me. Goodnight."

The man went out into the bitter night, and Villiers returned to his fireside. There was something about Herbert which shocked him inexpressibly; not his poor rags nor the marks which poverty had set upon his face, but rather an indefinite terror which hung about him like a mist. He had acknowledged that he himself was not devoid of blame; the woman, he had avowed, had corrupted him body and soul, and Villiers felt that this man, once his friend, had been an actor in scenes evil beyond the power of words. His story needed no confirmation: he himself was the embodied proof of it. Villiers mused curiously over the story he had heard, and wondered whether he had heard both the first and the last of it. "No," he thought, "certainly not the last, probably only the beginning. A case like this is like a nest of Chinese boxes; you open one after the other and find a quainter workmanship in every box. Most likely poor Herbert is merely one of the outside boxes; there are stranger ones to follow."

Villiers could not take his mind away from Herbert and his story, which seemed to grow wilder as the night wore on. The fire seemed to burn low, and the chilly air of the morning crept into the room; Villiers got up with a glance over his shoulder, and, shivering slightly, went to bed.

A few days later he saw at his club a gentleman of his acquaintance, named Austin, who was famous for his intimate knowledge of London life, both in its tenebrous and luminous phases. Villiers, still full of his encounter in Soho and its consequences, thought Austin might possibly be able to shed some light on Herbert's history, and so after some casual talk he suddenly put the question:

"Do you happen to know anything of a man named Herbert— Charles Herbert?"

Austin turned round sharply and stared at Villiers with some astonishment.

"Charles Herbert? Weren't you in town three years ago? No; then you have not heard of the Paul Street case? It caused a good deal of sensation at the time."

"What was the case?"

"Well, a gentleman, a man of very good position, was found dead, stark dead, in the area of a certain house in Paul Street, off Tottenham Court Road. Of course the police did not make the discovery; if you happen to be sitting up all night and have a light in your window, the constable will ring the bell, but if you happen to be lying dead in somebody's area, you will be left alone. In this instance, as in many others, the alarm was raised by some kind of vagabond; I don't mean a common tramp, or a public-house loafer, but a gentleman, whose business or pleasure, or both, made him a spectator of the London streets at five o'clock in the morning. This individual was, as he said, 'going home,' it did not appear whence or whither, and had occasion to pass through Paul Street between four and five A.M. Something or other caught his eye at Number 20; he said, absurdly enough, that the house had the most unpleasant physiognomy he had ever observed, but, at any rate, he glanced down the area and was a good deal astonished to see a man lying on the stones, his limbs all huddled together, and his face turned up. Our gentleman thought his face looked peculiarly ghastly, and so set off at a run in search of the nearest policeman. The constable was at first inclined to treat the matter lightly, suspecting common drunkenness; however, he came, and after looking at the man's face, changed his tone, quickly enough. The early bird, who had picked up this fine worm, was sent off for a doctor, and the policeman rang and knocked at the door till a slatternly servant girl came down looking more than half asleep. The constable pointed out the contents of the area to the maid, who screamed loudly enough to wake up the street, but she knew nothing of the man; had never seen him at the house, and so forth. Meanwhile, the original discoverer had come back with a medical man, and the next thing was to get into the area. The gate was open, so the whole quartet stumped down the steps. The doctor hardly needed a moment's examination; he said the poor fellow had been dead for several hours, and it was then the case began to get interesting. The dead man had not been robbed, and in one of his pockets were papers identifying him as—well, as a man of good family and means, a favourite in society, and nobody's enemy, as far as could be known. I don't give his name, Villiers, because it has nothing to do with the story, and because it's no good raking up these affairs about the dead when there are no relations living. The next curious point was that the medical men couldn't agree as to how he met his death. There were some slight bruises on his shoulders, but they were so slight that it looked as if he had been pushed roughly out of the kitchen door, and not thrown over the railings from the street or even dragged down the steps. But there were positively no other marks of violence about him, certainly none that would account for his death; and when they came to the autopsy there wasn't a trace of poison of any kind. Of course the police wanted to know all about the people at Number 20, and here again, so I have heard from private sources, one or two other very curious points came out. It appears that the occupants of the house were a Mr. and Mrs. Charles Herbert; he was said to be a landed proprietor, though it struck most people that Paul Street was not exactly the place to look for country gentry. As for Mrs. Herbert, nobody seemed to know who or what she was, and, between ourselves, I fancy the divers after her history found themselves in rather strange waters. Of course they both denied knowing anything about the deceased, and in default of any evidence against them they were discharged. But some very odd things came out about them. Though it was between five and six in the morning when the dead man was removed, a large crowd had collected, and several of the neighbours ran to see what was going on. They were pretty free with their comments, by all accounts, and from these it appeared that Number 20 was in very bad odour in Paul Street. The detectives tried to trace down these rumours to some solid foundation of fact, but could not get hold of anything. People shook their heads and raised their eyebrows and thought the Herberts rather 'queer,' 'would rather not be seen going into their house,' and so on, but there was nothing tangible. The authorities were morally certain the man met his death in some way or another in the house and was thrown out by the kitchen door, but they couldn't prove it, and the absence of any indications of violence or poisoning left them helpless. An odd case, wasn't it? But curiously enough, there's something more that I haven't told you. I happened to know one of the doctors who was consulted as to the cause of death, and sometime after the inquest I met him, and asked him about it. 'Do you really mean to tell me,' I said, 'that you were baffled by the case, that you actually don't know what the man died of?' 'Pardon me,' he replied, 'I know perfectly well what caused death. Blank died of fright, of sheer, awful terror; I never saw features so hideously contorted in the entire course of my practice, and I have seen the faces of a whole host of dead.' The doctor was usually a cool customer enough, and a certain vehemence in his manner struck me, but I couldn't get anything more out of him. I suppose the Treasury didn't see their way to prosecuting the Herberts for frightening a man to death; at any rate, nothing was done, and the case dropped out of men's minds. Do you happen to know anything of Herbert?"

"Well," replied Villiers, "he was an old college friend of mine."

"You don't say so? Have you ever seen his wife?"

"No, I haven't. I have lost sight of Herbert for many years."

"It's queer, isn't it, parting with a man at the college gate or at Paddington, seeing nothing of him for years, and then finding him pop up his head in such an odd place. But I should like to have seen Mrs. Herbert; people said extraordinary things about her."

"What sort of things?"

"Well, I hardly know how to tell you. Everyone who saw her at the police court said she was at once the most beautiful woman and the most repulsive they had ever set eyes on. I have spoken to a man who saw her, and I assure you he positively shuddered as he tried to describe the woman, but he couldn't tell why. She seems to have been a sort of enigma; and I expect if that one dead man could have told tales, he would have told some uncommonly queer ones. And there you are again in another puzzle; what could a respectable country gentleman like Mr. Blank (we'll call him that if you don't mind) want in such a very queer house as Number 20? It's altogether a very odd case, isn't it?"

"It is indeed, Austin; an extraordinary case. I didn't think, when I asked you about my old friend, I should strike on such strange metal. Well, I must be off; goodday."

Villiers went away, thinking of his own conceit of the Chinese boxes; here was quaint workmanship indeed.

IV

The Discovery in Paul Street

A few months after Villiers' meeting with Herbert, Mr. Clarke was sitting, as usual, by his after-dinner hearth, resolutely guarding his fancies from wandering in the direction of the bureau. For more than a week he had succeeded in keeping away from the "Memoirs," and he cherished hopes of a complete self-reformation; but, in spite of his endeavours, he could not hush the wonder and the strange curiosity that the last case he had written down had excited within him. He had put the case, or rather the outline of it, conjecturally to a scientific friend, who shook his head, and thought Clarke getting queer, and on this particular evening Clarke was making an effort to rationalize the story, when a sudden knock at the door roused him from his meditations.

"Mr. Villiers to see you sir."

"Dear me, Villiers, it is very kind of you to look me up; I have not seen you for many months; I should think nearly a year. Come in, come in. And how are you, Villiers? Want any advice about investments?"

"No, thanks, I fancy everything I have in that way is pretty safe. No, Clarke, I have really come to consult you about a rather curious matter that has been brought under my notice of late. I am afraid you will think it all rather absurd when I tell my tale. I sometimes think so myself, and that's just what I made up my mind to come to you, as I know you're a practical man."

Mr. Villiers was ignorant of the "Memoirs to prove the Existence of the Devil."

"Well, Villiers, I shall be happy to give you my advice, to the best of my ability. What is the nature of the case?"

"It's an extraordinary thing altogether. You know my ways; I always keep my eyes open in the streets, and in my time I have chanced upon some queer customers, and queer cases too, but this, I think, beats all. I was coming out of a restaurant one nasty winter night about three months ago; I had had a capital dinner and a good bottle of Chianti, and I stood for a moment on the pavement, thinking what a mystery there is about London streets and the companies that pass along them. A bottle of red wine encourages these fancies, Clarke, and I dare say

I should have thought a page of small type, but I was cut short by a beggar who had come behind me, and was making the usual appeals. Of course I looked round, and this beggar turned out to be what was left of an old friend of mine, a man named Herbert. I asked him how he had come to such a wretched pass, and he told me. We walked up and down one of those long and dark Soho streets, and there I listened to his story. He said he had married a beautiful girl, some years younger than himself, and, as he put it, she had corrupted him body and soul. He wouldn't go into details; he said he dare not, that what he had seen and heard haunted him by night and day, and when I looked in his face I knew he was speaking the truth. There was something about the man that made me shiver. I don't know why, but it was there. I gave him a little money and sent him away, and I assure you that when he was gone I gasped for breath. His presence seemed to chill one's blood."

"Isn't this all just a little fanciful, Villiers? I suppose the poor fellow had made an imprudent marriage, and, in plain English, gone to the bad."

"Well, listen to this." Villiers told Clarke the story he had heard from Austin.

"You see," he concluded, "there can be but little doubt that this Mr. Blank, whoever he was, died of sheer terror; he saw something so awful, so terrible, that it cut short his life. And what he saw, he most certainly saw in that house, which, somehow or other, had got a bad name in the neighbourhood. I had the curiosity to go and look at the place for myself. It's a saddening kind of street; the houses are old enough to be mean and dreary, but not old enough to be quaint. As far as I could see most of them are let in lodgings, furnished and unfurnished, and almost every door has three bells to it. Here and there the ground floors have been made into shops of the commonest kind; it's a dismal street in every way. I found Number 20 was to let, and I went to the agent's and got the key. Of course I should have heard nothing of the Herberts in that quarter, but I asked the man, fair and square, how long they had left the house and whether there had been other tenants in the meanwhile. He looked at me queerly for a minute, and told me the Herberts had left immediately after the unpleasantness, as he called it, and since then the house had been empty."

Mr. Villiers paused for a moment.

"I have always been rather fond of going over empty houses; there's a sort of fascination about the desolate empty rooms, with the nails sticking in the walls, and the dust thick upon the window-sills. But I didn't enjoy going over Number 20, Paul Street. I had hardly put my foot inside the passage when I noticed a queer, heavy feeling about the air of the house. Of course all empty houses are stuffy, and so forth, but this was something quite different; I can't describe it to you, but it seemed to stop the breath. I went into the front room and the back room, and the kitchens downstairs; they were all dirty and dusty enough, as you would expect, but there was something strange about them all. I couldn't define it to you, I only know I felt queer. It was one of the rooms on the first floor, though, that was the worst. It was a largish room, and once on a time the paper must have been cheerful enough, but when I saw it, paint, paper, and everything were most doleful. But the room was full of horror; I felt my teeth grinding as I put my hand on the door, and when I went in, I thought I should have fallen fainting to the floor. However, I pulled myself together, and stood against the end wall, wondering what on earth there could be about the room to make my limbs tremble, and my heart beat as if I were at the hour of death. In one corner there was a pile of newspapers littered on the floor, and I began looking at them; they were papers of three or four years ago, some of them half torn, and some crumpled as if they had been used for packing. I turned the whole pile over, and amongst them I found a curious drawing; I will show it to you presently. But I couldn't stay in the room; I felt it was overpowering me. I was thankful to come out, safe and sound, into the open air. People stared at me as I walked along the street, and one man said I was drunk. I was staggering about from one side of the pavement to the other, and it was as much as I could do to take the key back to the agent and get home. I was in bed for a week, suffering from what my doctor called nervous shock and exhaustion. One of those days I was reading the evening paper, and happened to notice a paragraph headed: 'Starved to Death.' It was the usual style of thing; a model lodging-house in Marylebone, a door locked for several days, and a dead man in his chair when they broke in. 'The deceased,' said the paragraph, 'was known as Charles Herbert, and is believed to have been once a prosperous country gentleman. His name was familiar to the public three years ago in connection with the mysterious death in Paul Street, Tottenham Court Road, the deceased being the tenant of the house Number 20, in the area of which a gentleman of good position was found dead under circumstances not devoid of suspicion.' A tragic ending, wasn't it? But after all, if what he told me were true, which I am sure it was, the man's life was all a tragedy, and a tragedy of a stranger sort than they put on the boards."

"And that is the story, is it?" said Clarke musingly.

"Yes, that is the story."

"Well, really, Villiers, I scarcely know what to say about it. There are, no doubt, circumstances in the case which seem peculiar, the finding of the dead man in the area of Herbert's house, for instance, and the extraordinary opinion of the physician as to the cause of death; but, after all, it is conceivable that the facts may be explained in a straightforward manner. As to your own sensations, when you went to see the house, I would suggest that they were due to a vivid imagination; you must have been brooding, in a semi-conscious way, over what you had heard. I don't exactly see what more can be said or done in the matter; you evidently think there is a mystery of some kind, but Herbert is dead; where then do you propose to look?"

"I propose to look for the woman; the woman whom he married. She is the mystery."

The two men sat silent by the fireside; Clarke secretly congratulating himself on having successfully kept up the character of advocate of the commonplace, and Villiers wrapped in his gloomy fancies.

"I think I will have a cigarette," he said at last, and put his hand in his pocket to feel for the cigarette-case.

"Ah!" he said, starting slightly, "I forgot I had something to show you. You remember my saying that I had found a rather curious sketch amongst the pile of old newspapers at the house in Paul Street? Here it is."

Villiers drew out a small thin parcel from his pocket. It was covered with brown paper, and secured with string, and the knots were troublesome. In spite of himself Clarke felt inquisitive; he bent forward on his chair as Villiers painfully undid the string, and unfolded the outer covering. Inside was a second wrapping of tissue, and Villiers took it off and handed the small piece of paper to Clarke without a word.

There was dead silence in the room for five minutes or more; the two men sat so still that they could hear the ticking of the tall old-fashioned clock that stood outside in the hall, and in the mind of one of them the slow monotony of sound woke up a far, far memory. He was looking intently at the small pen-and-ink sketch of the woman's head; it had evidently been drawn with great care, and by a true artist, for the woman's soul looked out of the eyes, and the lips were parted with a strange smile. Clarke gazed still at the face; it brought to his memory one summer evening, long ago; he saw again the long lovely valley, the river winding between the hills, the meadows and the cornfields, the dull red sun, and the cold white mist rising from the water. He heard a voice speaking to him across the waves of many years, and saying "Clarke, Mary will see the god Pan!" and then he was standing in the grim room beside the doctor, listening to the heavy ticking of the clock, waiting and watching, watching the figure lying on the green chair beneath the lamplight. Mary rose up, and he looked into her eyes, and his heart grew cold within him.

"Who is this woman?" he said at last. His voice was dry and hoarse.

"That is the woman who Herbert married."

Clarke looked again at the sketch; it was not Mary after all. There certainly was Mary's face, but there was something else, something he had not seen on Mary's features when the white-clad girl entered the laboratory with the doctor, nor at her terrible awakening, nor when she lay grinning on the bed. Whatever it was, the glance that came from those eyes, the smile on the full lips, or the expression of the whole face, Clarke shuddered before it at his inmost soul, and thought, unconsciously, of Dr. Phillip's words, "the most vivid presentment of evil I have ever seen." He turned the paper over mechanically in his hand and glanced at the back.

"Good God! Clarke, what is the matter? You are as white as death."

Villiers had started wildly from his chair, as Clarke fell back with a groan, and let the paper drop from his hands.

"I don't feel very well, Villiers, I am subject to these attacks. Pour me out a little wine; thanks, that will do. I shall feel better in a few minutes."

Villiers picked up the fallen sketch and turned it over as Clarke had done.

"You saw that?" he said. "That's how I identified it as being a portrait of Herbert's wife, or I should say his widow. How do you feel now?"

"Better, thanks, it was only a passing faintness. I don't think I quite catch your meaning. What did you say enabled you to identify the picture?"

"This word—'Helen'—was written on the back. Didn't I tell you her name was Helen? Yes; Helen Vaughan."

Clarke groaned; there could be no shadow of doubt.

"Now, don't you agree with me," said Villiers, "that in the story I have told you tonight, and in the part this woman plays in it, there are some very strange points?"

"Yes, Villiers," Clarke muttered, "it is a strange story indeed; a strange story indeed. You must give me time to think it over; I may be able to help you or I may not. Must you be going now? Well, goodnight, Villiers, goodnight. Come and see me in the course of a week."

V

The Letter of Advice

"Do you know, Austin," said Villiers, as the two friends were pacing sedately along Piccadilly one pleasant morning in May, "do you know I am convinced that what you told me about Paul Street and the Herberts is a mere episode in an extraordinary history? I may as well confess to you that when I asked you about Herbert a few months ago I had just seen him."

"You had seen him? Where?"

"He begged of me in the street one night. He was in the most pitiable plight, but I recognized the man, and I got him to tell me his history, or at least the outline of it. In brief, it amounted to this—he had been ruined by his wife."

"In what manner?"

"He would not tell me; he would only say that she had destroyed him, body and soul. The man is dead now."

"And what has become of his wife?"

"Ah, that's what I should like to know, and I mean to find her sooner or later. I know a man named Clarke, a dry fellow, in fact a man of business, but shrewd enough. You understand my meaning; not shrewd in the mere business sense of the word, but a man who really knows something about men and life. Well, I laid the case before him, and he was evidently impressed. He said it needed consideration, and asked me to come again in the course of a week. A few days later I received this extraordinary letter."

Austin took the envelope, drew out the letter, and read it curiously. It ran as follows:—

My Dear Villiers,

I have thought over the matter on which you consulted me the other night, and my advice to you is this. Throw the portrait into the fire, blot out the story from your mind. Never give it another thought, Villiers, or you will be sorry. You will think, no doubt, that I am in possession of some secret information, and to a certain extent that is the case.

But I only know a little; I am like a traveller who has peered over an abyss, and has drawn back in terror. What I know is strange enough and horrible enough, but beyond my knowledge there are depths and horrors more frightful still, more incredible than any tale told of winter nights about the fire. I have resolved, and nothing shall shake that resolve, to explore no whit farther, and if you value your happiness you will make the same determination.

"Come and see me by all means; but we will talk on more cheerful topics than this."

Austin folded the letter methodically, and returned it to Villiers.

"It is certainly an extraordinary letter," he said, "what does he mean by the portrait?"

"Ah! I forgot to tell you I have been to Paul Street and have made a discovery."

Villiers told his story as he had told it to Clarke, and Austin listened in silence. He seemed puzzled.

"How very curious that you should experience such an unpleasant sensation in that room!" he said at length. "I hardly gather that it was a mere matter of the imagination; a feeling of repulsion, in short."

"No, it was more physical than mental. It was as if I were inhaling at every breath some deadly fume, which seemed to penetrate to every nerve and bone and sinew of my body. I felt racked from head to foot, my eyes began to grow dim; it was like the entrance of death."

"Yes, yes, very strange certainly. You see, your friend confesses that there is some very black story connected with this woman. Did you notice any particular emotion in him when you were telling your tale?"

"Yes, I did. He became very faint, but he assured me that it was a mere passing attack to which he was subject."

"Did you believe him?"

"I did at the time, but I don't now. He heard what I had to say with a good deal of indifference, till I showed him the portrait. It was then that he was seized with the attack of which I spoke. He looked ghastly, I assure you."

"Then he must have seen the woman before. But there might be another explanation; it might have been the name, and not the face, which was familiar to him. What do you think?"

"I couldn't say. To the best of my belief it was after turning the portrait in his hands that he nearly dropped from the chair. The name, you know, was written on the back."

"Quite so. After all, it is impossible to come to any resolution in a case like this. I hate melodrama, and nothing strikes me as more commonplace and tedious than the ordinary ghost story of commerce; but really, Villiers, it looks as if there were something very queer at the bottom of all this."

The two men had, without noticing it, turned up Ashley Street, leading northward from Piccadilly. It was a long street, and rather a gloomy one, but here and there a brighter taste had illuminated the dark houses with flowers, and gay curtains, and a cheerful paint on the doors. Villiers glanced up as Austin stopped speaking, and looked at one of these houses; geraniums, red and white, drooped from every sill, and daffodil-coloured curtains were draped back from each window.

"It looks cheerful, doesn't it?" he said.

"Yes, and the inside is still more cheery. One of the pleasantest houses of the season, so I have heard. I haven't been there myself, but I've met several men who have, and they tell me it's uncommonly jovial."

"Whose house is it?"

"A Mrs. Beaumont's."

"And who is she?"

"I couldn't tell you. I have heard she comes from South America, but after all, who she is is of little consequence. She is a very wealthy woman, there's no doubt of that, and some of the best people have taken her up. I hear she has some wonderful claret, really marvellous wine, which must have cost a fabulous sum. Lord Argentine was telling me about it; he was there last Sunday evening. He assures me he has never tasted such a wine, and Argentine, as you know, is an expert. By the way, that reminds me, she must be an oddish sort of woman, this Mrs. Beaumont. Argentine asked her how old the wine was, and what do you think she said? 'About a thousand years, I believe.' Lord Argentine thought she was chaffing him, you know, but when he laughed she said she was speaking quite seriously and offered to show him the jar. Of course, he couldn't say anything more after that; but it seems rather antiquated for a beverage, doesn't it? Why, here we are at my rooms. Come in, won't you?"

"Thanks, I think I will. I haven't seen the curiosity-shop for a while."

It was a room furnished richly, yet oddly, where every jar and bookcase and table, and every rug and jar and ornament seemed to be a thing apart, preserving each its own individuality.

"Anything fresh lately?" said Villiers after a while.

"No; I think not; you saw those queer jugs, didn't you? I thought so. I don't think I have come across anything for the last few weeks."

Austin glanced around the room from cupboard to cupboard, from shelf to shelf, in search of some new oddity. His eyes fell at last on an odd chest, pleasantly and quaintly carved, which stood in a dark corner of the room.

"Ah," he said, "I was forgetting, I have got something to show you." Austin unlocked the chest, drew out a thick quarto volume, laid it on the table, and resumed the cigar he had put down.

"Did you know Arthur Meyrick the painter, Villiers?"

"A little; I met him two or three times at the house of a friend of mine. What has become of him? I haven't heard his name mentioned for sometime."

"He's dead."

"You don't say so! Quite young, wasn't he?"

"Yes; only thirty when he died."

"What did he die of?"

"I don't know. He was an intimate friend of mine, and a thoroughly good fellow. He used to come here and talk to me for hours, and he was one of the best talkers I have met. He could even talk about painting, and that's more than can be said of most painters. About eighteen months ago he was feeling rather overworked, and partly at my suggestion he went off on a sort of roving expedition, with no very definite end or aim about it. I believe New York was to be his first port, but I never heard from him. Three months ago I got this book, with a very civil letter from an English doctor practising at Buenos Ayres, stating that he had attended the late Mr. Meyrick during his illness, and that the deceased had expressed an earnest wish that the enclosed packet should be sent to me after his death. That was all."

"And haven't you written for further particulars?"

"I have been thinking of doing so. You would advise me to write to the doctor?"

"Certainly. And what about the book?"

"It was sealed up when I got it. I don't think the doctor had seen it."

"It is something very rare? Meyrick was a collector, perhaps?"

"No, I think not, hardly a collector. Now, what do you think of these Ainu jugs?"

"They are peculiar, but I like them. But aren't you going to show me poor Meyrick's legacy?"

"Yes, yes, to be sure. The fact is, it's rather a peculiar sort of thing, and I haven't shown it to anyone. I wouldn't say anything about it if I were you. There it is."

Villiers took the book, and opened it at haphazard.

"It isn't a printed volume, then?" he said.

"No. It is a collection of drawings in black and white by my poor friend Meyrick."

Villiers turned to the first page, it was blank; the second bore a brief inscription, which he read:

Silet per diem universus, nec sine horrore secretus est; lucet nocturnis ignibus, chorus Aegipanum undique personatur: audiuntur et cantus tibiarum, et tinnitus cymbalorum per oram maritimam.

On the third page was a design which made Villiers start and look up at Austin; he was gazing abstractedly out of the window. Villiers turned page after page, absorbed, in spite of himself, in the frightful Walpurgis Night of evil, strange monstrous evil, that the dead artist had set forth in hard black and white. The figures of Fauns and Satyrs and Aegipans danced before his eyes, the darkness of the thicket, the dance on the mountain-top, the scenes by lonely shores, in green vineyards, by rocks and desert places, passed before him: a world before which the human soul seemed to shrink back and shudder. Villiers whirled over the remaining pages; he had seen enough, but the picture on the last leaf caught his eye, as he almost closed the book.

"Austin!"

"Well, what is it?"

"Do you know who that is?"

It was a woman's face, alone on the white page.

"Know who it is? No, of course not."

"I do."

"Who is it?"

"It is Mrs. Herbert."

"Are you sure?"

"I am perfectly sure of it. Poor Meyrick! He is one more chapter in her history."

"But what do you think of the designs?"

"They are frightful. Lock the book up again, Austin. If I were you I would burn it; it must be a terrible companion even though it be in a chest."

"Yes, they are singular drawings. But I wonder what connection there could be between Meyrick and Mrs. Herbert, or what link between her and these designs?"

"Ah, who can say? It is possible that the matter may end here, and we shall never know, but in my own opinion this Helen Vaughan, or Mrs. Herbert, is only the beginning. She will come back to London, Austin; depend on it, she will come back, and we shall hear more about her then. I doubt it will be very pleasant news."

VI

THE SUICIDES

L ord Argentine was a great favourite in London Society. At twenty he had been a poor man, decked with the surname of an illustrious family, but forced to earn a livelihood as best he could, and the most speculative of money-lenders would not have entrusted him with fifty pounds on the chance of his ever changing his name for a title, and his poverty for a great fortune. His father had been near enough to the fountain of good things to secure one of the family livings, but the son, even if he had taken orders, would scarcely have obtained so much as this, and moreover felt no vocation for the ecclesiastical estate. Thus he fronted the world with no better armour than the bachelor's gown and the wits of a younger son's grandson, with which equipment he contrived in some way to make a very tolerable fight of it. At twenty-five Mr. Charles Aubernon saw himself still a man of struggles and of warfare with the world, but out of the seven who stood before him and the high places of his family three only remained. These three, however, were "good lives," but yet not proof against the Zulu assegais and typhoid fever, and so one morning Aubernon woke up and found himself Lord Argentine, a man of thirty who had faced the difficulties of existence, and had conquered. The situation amused him immensely, and he resolved that riches should be as pleasant to him as poverty had always been. Argentine, after some little consideration, came to the conclusion that dining, regarded as a fine art, was perhaps the most amusing pursuit open to fallen humanity, and thus his dinners became famous in London, and an invitation to his table a thing covetously desired. After ten years of lordship and dinners Argentine still declined to be jaded, still persisted in enjoying life, and by a kind of infection had become recognized as the cause of joy in others, in short, as the best of company. His sudden and tragical death therefore caused a wide and deep sensation. People could scarcely believe it, even though the newspaper was before their eyes, and the cry of "Mysterious Death of a Nobleman" came ringing up from the street. But there stood the brief paragraph: "Lord Argentine was found dead this morning by his valet under distressing circumstances. It is stated that there can be no doubt that his lordship committed suicide, though no motive can be assigned for the act. The deceased nobleman was widely known in society, and much liked for his genial manner and sumptuous hospitality. He is succeeded by," etc., etc.

By slow degrees the details came to light, but the case still remained a mystery. The chief witness at the inquest was the deceased's valet, who said that the night before his death Lord Argentine had dined with a lady of good position, whose name was suppressed in the newspaper reports. At about eleven o'clock Lord Argentine had returned, and informed his man that he should not require his services till the next morning. A little later the valet had occasion to cross the hall and was somewhat astonished to see his master quietly letting himself out at the front door. He had taken off his evening clothes, and was dressed in a Norfolk coat and knickerbockers, and wore a low brown hat. The valet had no reason to suppose that Lord Argentine had seen him, and though his master rarely kept late hours, thought little of the occurrence till the next morning, when he knocked at the bedroom door at a quarter to nine as usual. He received no answer, and, after knocking two or three times, entered the room, and saw Lord Argentine's body leaning forward at an angle from the bottom of the bed. He found that his master had tied a cord securely to one of the short bed-posts, and, after making a running noose and slipping it round his neck, the unfortunate man must have resolutely fallen forward, to die by slow strangulation. He was dressed in the light suit in which the valet had seen him go out, and the doctor who was summoned pronounced that life had been extinct for more than four hours. All papers, letters, and so forth seemed in perfect order, and nothing was discovered which pointed in the most remote way to any scandal either great or small. Here the evidence ended; nothing more could be discovered. Several persons had been present at the dinner-party at which Lord Argentine had assisted, and to all these he seemed in his usual genial spirits. The valet, indeed, said he thought his master appeared a little excited when he came home, but confessed that the alteration in his manner was very slight, hardly noticeable, indeed. It seemed hopeless to seek for any clue, and the suggestion that Lord Argentine had been suddenly attacked by acute suicidal mania was generally accepted.

It was otherwise, however, when within three weeks, three more gentlemen, one of them a nobleman, and the two others men of good position and ample means, perished miserably in the almost precisely the same manner. Lord Swanleigh was found one morning in his dressing-room, hanging from a peg affixed to the wall, and Mr. Collier-Stuart and Mr. Herries had chosen to die as Lord Argentine. There was no explanation in either case; a few bald facts; a living man in the evening, and a body with a black swollen face in the morning. The police had been forced to confess themselves powerless to arrest or to explain the sordid murders of Whitechapel; but before the horrible suicides of Piccadilly and Mayfair they were dumbfoundered, for not even the mere ferocity which did duty as an explanation of the crimes of the East End, could be of service in the West. Each of these men who had resolved to die a tortured shameful death was rich, prosperous, and to all appearances in love with the world, and not the acutest research should ferret out any shadow of a lurking motive in either case. There was a horror in the air, and men looked at one another's faces when they met, each wondering whether the other was to be the victim of the fifth nameless tragedy. Journalists sought in vain for their scrapbooks for materials whereof to concoct reminiscent articles; and the morning paper was unfolded in many a house with a feeling of awe; no man knew when or where the next blow would light.

A short while after the last of these terrible events, Austin came to see Mr. Villiers. He was curious to know whether Villiers had succeeded in discovering any fresh traces of Mrs. Herbert, either through Clarke or by other sources, and he asked the question soon after he had sat down.

"No," said Villiers, "I wrote to Clarke, but he remains obdurate, and I have tried other channels, but without any result. I can't find out what became of Helen Vaughan after she left Paul Street, but I think she must have gone abroad. But to tell the truth, Austin, I haven't paid much attention to the matter for the last few weeks; I knew poor Herries intimately, and his terrible death has been a great shock to me, a great shock."

"I can well believe it," answered Austin gravely, "you know Argentine was a friend of mine. If I remember rightly, we were speaking of him that day you came to my rooms."

"Yes; it was in connection with that house in Ashley Street, Mrs. Beaumont's house. You said something about Argentine's dining there."

"Quite so. Of course you know it was there Argentine dined the night before—before his death."

"No, I had not heard that."

"Oh, yes; the name was kept out of the papers to spare Mrs. Beaumont. Argentine was a great favourite of hers, and it is said she was in a terrible state for sometime after."

A curious look came over Villiers' face; he seemed undecided whether to speak or not. Austin began again.

"I never experienced such a feeling of horror as when I read the account of Argentine's death. I didn't understand it at the time, and I don't now. I knew him well, and it completely passes my understanding for what possible cause he—or any of the others for the matter of that—could have resolved in cold blood to die in such an awful manner. You know how men babble away each other's characters in London, you may be sure any buried scandal or hidden skeleton would have been brought to light in such a case as this; but nothing of the sort has taken place. As for the theory of mania, that is very well, of course, for the coroner's jury, but everybody knows that it's all nonsense. Suicidal mania is not small-pox."

Austin relapsed into gloomy silence. Villiers sat silent, also, watching his friend. The expression of indecision still fleeted across his face; he seemed as if weighing his thoughts in the balance, and the considerations he was resolving left him still silent. Austin tried to shake off the remembrance of tragedies as hopeless and perplexed as the labyrinth of Daedalus, and began to talk in an indifferent voice of the more pleasant incidents and adventures of the season.

"That Mrs. Beaumont," he said, "of whom we were speaking, is a great success; she has taken London almost by storm. I met her the other night at Fulham's; she is really a remarkable woman."

"You have met Mrs. Beaumont?"

"Yes; she had quite a court around her. She would be called very handsome, I suppose, and yet there is something about her face which I didn't like. The features are exquisite, but the expression is strange. And all the time I was looking at her, and afterwards, when I was going home, I had a curious feeling that very expression was in some way or another familiar to me."

"You must have seen her in the Row."

"No, I am sure I never set eyes on the woman before; it is that which makes it puzzling. And to the best of my belief I have never seen anyone like her; what I felt was a kind of dim far-off memory, vague but persistent. The only sensation I can compare it to, is that odd feeling one sometimes has in a dream, when fantastic cities and wondrous lands and phantom personages appear familiar and accustomed."

Villiers nodded and glanced aimlessly round the room, possibly in search of something on which to turn the conversation. His eyes fell on an old chest somewhat like that in which the artist's strange legacy lay hid beneath a Gothic scutcheon.

"Have you written to the doctor about poor Meyrick?" he asked.

"Yes; I wrote asking for full particulars as to his illness and death. I don't expect to have an answer for another three weeks or a month. I thought I might as well inquire whether Meyrick knew an Englishwoman named Herbert, and if so, whether the doctor could give me any information about her. But it's very possible that Meyrick fell in with her at New York, or Mexico, or San Francisco; I have no idea as to the extent or direction of his travels."

"Yes, and it's very possible that the woman may have more than one name."

"Exactly. I wish I had thought of asking you to lend me the portrait of her which you possess. I might have enclosed it in my letter to Dr. Matthews."

"So you might; that never occurred to me. We might send it now. Hark! what are those boys calling?"

While the two men had been talking together a confused noise of shouting had been gradually growing louder. The noise rose from the eastward and swelled down Piccadilly, drawing nearer and nearer, a very torrent of sound; surging up streets usually quiet, and making every window a frame for a face, curious or excited. The cries and voices came echoing up the silent street where Villiers lived, growing more distinct as they advanced, and, as Villiers spoke, an answer rang up from the pavement:

"The West End Horrors; Another Awful Suicide; Full Details!"

Austin rushed down the stairs and bought a paper and read out the paragraph to Villiers as the uproar in the street rose and fell. The window was open and the air seemed full of noise and terror.

"Another gentleman has fallen a victim to the terrible epidemic of suicide which for the last month has prevailed in the West End. Mr. Sidney Crashaw, of Stoke House, Fulham, and King's Pomeroy, Devon, was found, after a prolonged search, hanging dead from the branch of a tree in his garden at one o'clock today. The deceased gentleman dined last night at the Carlton Club and seemed in his usual health and spirits. He left the club at about ten o'clock, and was seen walking leisurely up St. James's Street a little later. Subsequent to this his movements cannot be traced. On the discovery of the body medical aid was at once summoned, but life had evidently been long extinct. So far as is known, Mr. Crashaw had no trouble or anxiety of any kind. This painful suicide, it will be remembered, is the fifth of the kind in the last month. The authorities at Scotland Yard are unable to suggest any explanation of these terrible occurrences."

Austin put down the paper in mute horror.

"I shall leave London tomorrow," he said, "it is a city of nightmares. How awful this is, Villiers!"

Mr. Villiers was sitting by the window quietly looking out into the street. He had listened to the newspaper report attentively, and the hint of indecision was no longer on his face.

"Wait a moment, Austin," he replied, "I have made up my mind to mention a little matter that occurred last night. It stated, I think, that Crashaw was last seen alive in St. James's Street shortly after ten?"

"Yes, I think so. I will look again. Yes, you are quite right."

"Quite so. Well, I am in a position to contradict that statement at all events. Crashaw was seen after that; considerably later indeed."

"How do you know?"

"Because I happened to see Crashaw myself at about two o'clock this morning."

"You saw Crashaw? You, Villiers?"

"Yes, I saw him quite distinctly; indeed, there were but a few feet between us."

"Where, in Heaven's name, did you see him?"

"Not far from here. I saw him in Ashley Street. He was just leaving a house."

"Did you notice what house it was?"

"Yes. It was Mrs. Beaumont's."

"Villiers! Think what you are saying; there must be some mistake. How could Crashaw be in Mrs. Beaumont's house at two o'clock in the morning? Surely, surely, you must have been dreaming, Villiers; you were always rather fanciful."

"No; I was wide awake enough. Even if I had been dreaming as you say, what I saw would have roused me effectually."

"What you saw? What did you see? Was there anything strange about Crashaw? But I can't believe it; it is impossible."

"Well, if you like I will tell you what I saw, or if you please, what I think I saw, and you can judge for yourself."

"Very good, Villiers."

The noise and clamour of the street had died away, though now and then the sound of shouting still came from the distance, and the dull, leaden silence seemed like the quiet after an earthquake or a storm. Villiers turned from the window and began speaking.

"I was at a house near Regent's Park last night, and when I came away the fancy took me to walk home instead of taking a hansom. It was a clear pleasant night enough, and after a few minutes I had the streets pretty much to myself. It's a curious thing, Austin, to be alone in London at night, the gas-lamps stretching away in perspective, and the dead silence, and then perhaps the rush and clatter of a hansom on the stones, and the fire starting up under the horse's hoofs. I walked along pretty briskly, for I was feeling a little tired of being out in the night, and as the clocks were striking two I turned down Ashley Street, which, you know, is on my way. It was quieter than ever there, and the lamps were fewer; altogether, it looked as dark and gloomy as a forest in winter. I had done about half the length of the street when I heard a door closed very softly, and naturally I looked up to see who was abroad like myself at such an hour. As it happens, there is a street lamp close to the house in question, and I saw a man standing on the step. He had just shut the door and his face was towards me, and I recognized Crashaw directly. I never knew him to speak to, but I had often seen him, and I am positive that I was not mistaken in my man. I looked into his face for a moment, and then—I will confess the truth—I set off at a good run, and kept it up till I was within my own door."

"Why?"

"Why? Because it made my blood run cold to see that man's face. I could never have supposed that such an infernal medley of passions could have glared out of any human eyes; I almost fainted as I looked. I knew I had looked into the eyes of a lost soul, Austin, the man's outward form remained, but all hell was within it. Furious lust, and hate that was like fire, and the loss of all hope and horror that seemed to shriek aloud to the night, though his teeth were shut; and the utter blackness of despair. I am sure that he did not see me; he saw nothing that you or I can see, but what he saw I hope we never shall. I do not know when he died; I suppose in an hour, or perhaps two, but when I passed down

Ashley Street and heard the closing door, that man no longer belonged to this world; it was a devil's face I looked upon."

There was an interval of silence in the room when Villiers ceased speaking. The light was failing, and all the tumult of an hour ago was quite hushed. Austin had bent his head at the close of the story, and his hand covered his eyes.

"What can it mean?" he said at length.

"Who knows, Austin, who knows? It's a black business, but I think we had better keep it to ourselves, for the present at any rate. I will see if I cannot learn anything about that house through private channels of information, and if I do light upon anything I will let you know."

VII

The Encounter in Soho

Three weeks later Austin received a note from Villiers, asking him to call either that afternoon or the next. He chose the nearer date, and found Villiers sitting as usual by the window, apparently lost in meditation on the drowsy traffic of the street. There was a bamboo table by his side, a fantastic thing, enriched with gilding and queer painted scenes, and on it lay a little pile of papers arranged and docketed as neatly as anything in Mr. Clarke's office.

"Well, Villiers, have you made any discoveries in the last three weeks?"

"I think so; I have here one or two memoranda which struck me as singular, and there is a statement to which I shall call your attention."

"And these documents relate to Mrs. Beaumont? It was really Crashaw whom you saw that night standing on the doorstep of the house in Ashley Street?"

"As to that matter my belief remains unchanged, but neither my inquiries nor their results have any special relation to Crashaw. But my investigations have had a strange issue. I have found out who Mrs. Beaumont is!"

"Who is she? In what way do you mean?"

"I mean that you and I know her better under another name."

"What name is that?"

"Herbert."

"Herbert!" Austin repeated the word, dazed with astonishment.

"Yes, Mrs. Herbert of Paul Street, Helen Vaughan of earlier adventures unknown to me. You had reason to recognize the expression of her face; when you go home look at the face in Meyrick's book of horrors, and you will know the sources of your recollection."

"And you have proof of this?"

"Yes, the best of proof; I have seen Mrs. Beaumont, or shall we say Mrs. Herbert?"

"Where did you see her?"

"Hardly in a place where you would expect to see a lady who lives in Ashley Street, Piccadilly. I saw her entering a house in one of the meanest and most disreputable streets in Soho. In fact, I had made an appointment, though not with her, and she was precise to both time and place."

"All this seems very wonderful, but I cannot call it incredible. You must remember, Villiers, that I have seen this woman, in the ordinary adventure of London society, talking and laughing, and sipping her coffee in a commonplace drawing-room with commonplace people. But you know what you are saying."

"I do; I have not allowed myself to be led by surmises or fancies. It was with no thought of finding Helen Vaughan that I searched for Mrs. Beaumont in the dark waters of the life of London, but such has been the issue."

"You must have been in strange places, Villiers."

"Yes, I have been in very strange places. It would have been useless, you know, to go to Ashley Street, and ask Mrs. Beaumont to give me a short sketch of her previous history. No; assuming, as I had to assume, that her record was not of the cleanest, it would be pretty certain that at some previous time she must have moved in circles not quite so refined as her present ones. If you see mud at the top of a stream, you may be sure that it was once at the bottom. I went to the bottom. I have always been fond of diving into Queer Street for my amusement, and I found my knowledge of that locality and its inhabitants very useful. It is, perhaps, needless to say that my friends had never heard the name of Beaumont, and as I had never seen the lady, and was quite unable to describe her, I had to set to work in an indirect way. The people there know me; I have been able to do some of them a service now and again, so they made no difficulty about giving their information; they were aware I had no communication direct or indirect with Scotland Yard. I had to cast out a good many lines, though, before I got what I wanted, and when I landed the fish I did not for a moment suppose it was my fish. But I listened to what I was told out of a constitutional liking for useless information, and I found myself in possession of a very curious story, though, as I imagined, not the story I was looking for. It was to this effect. Some five or six years ago, a woman named Raymond suddenly made her appearance in the neighbourhood to which I am referring. She was described to me as being quite young, probably not more than seventeen or eighteen, very handsome, and looking as if she came from the country. I should be wrong in saying that she found her level in going to this particular quarter, or associating with these people, for from what I was told, I should think the worst den in London far too good for her. The person from whom I got my information, as you may suppose, no great Puritan, shuddered and grew sick in telling me of the nameless infamies which were laid to her charge. After living there for a year, or perhaps a little more, she disappeared as suddenly as she came, and they saw nothing of her till about the time of the Paul Street case. At first she came to her old haunts only occasionally, then more frequently, and finally took up her abode there as before, and remained for six or eight months. It's of no use my going into details as to the life that woman led; if you want particulars you can look at Meyrick's legacy. Those designs were not drawn from his imagination. She again disappeared, and the people of the place saw nothing of her till a few months ago. My informant told me that she had taken some rooms in a house which he pointed out, and these rooms she was in the habit of visiting two or three times a week and always at ten in the morning. I was led to expect that one of these visits would be paid on a certain day about a week ago, and I accordingly managed to be on the look-out in company with my cicerone at a quarter to ten, and the hour and the lady came with equal punctuality. My friend and I were standing under an archway, a little way back from the street, but she saw us, and gave me a glance that I shall be long in forgetting. That look was quite enough for me; I knew Miss Raymond to be Mrs. Herbert; as for Mrs. Beaumont she had quite gone out of my head. She went into the house, and I watched it till four o'clock, when she came out, and then I followed her. It was a long chase, and I had to be very careful to keep a long way in the background, and yet not lose sight of the woman. She took me down to the Strand, and then to Westminster, and then up St. James's Street, and along Piccadilly. I felt queerish when I saw her turn up Ashley Street; the thought that Mrs. Herbert was Mrs. Beaumont came into my mind, but it seemed too impossible to be true. I waited at the corner, keeping my eye on her all the time, and I took particular care to note the house at which she stopped. It was the house with the gay curtains, the home of flowers, the house out of which Crashaw came the night he hanged himself in his garden. I was just going away with my discovery, when I saw an empty carriage come round and draw up in front of the house, and I came to the conclusion that Mrs. Herbert was going out for a drive, and I was right. There, as it happened, I met a man I know, and we stood talking together a little distance from the carriage-way, to which I had my back. We had not been there for ten minutes when my friend took off his hat, and I glanced round and saw the lady I had been following all day. 'Who is that?' I said, and his answer was 'Mrs. Beaumont; lives in Ashley Street.' Of course there could be no doubt after that. I don't know whether she saw me, but I don't think she did. I went home at once, and, on consideration, I thought that I had a sufficiently good case with which to go to Clarke."

"Why to Clarke?"

"Because I am sure that Clarke is in possession of facts about this woman, facts of which I know nothing."

"Well, what then?"

Mr. Villiers leaned back in his chair and looked reflectively at Austin for a moment before he answered:

"My idea was that Clarke and I should call on Mrs. Beaumont."

"You would never go into such a house as that? No, no, Villiers, you cannot do it. Besides, consider; what result. . ."

"I will tell you soon. But I was going to say that my information does not end here; it has been completed in an extraordinary manner.

"Look at this neat little packet of manuscript; it is paginated, you see, and I have indulged in the civil coquetry of a ribbon of red tape. It has almost a legal air, hasn't it? Run your eye over it, Austin. It is an account of the entertainment Mrs. Beaumont provided for her choicer guests. The man who wrote this escaped with his life, but I do not think he will live many years. The doctors tell him he must have sustained some severe shock to the nerves."

Austin took the manuscript, but never read it. Opening the neat pages at haphazard his eye was caught by a word and a phrase that followed it; and, sick at heart, with white lips and a cold sweat pouring like water from his temples, he flung the paper down.

"Take it away, Villiers, never speak of this again. Are you made of stone, man? Why, the dread and horror of death itself, the thoughts of the man who stands in the keen morning air on the black platform, bound, the bell tolling in his ears, and waits for the harsh rattle of the bolt, are as nothing compared to this. I will not read it; I should never sleep again."

"Very good. I can fancy what you saw. Yes; it is horrible enough; but after all, it is an old story, an old mystery played in our day, and in dim London streets instead of amidst the vineyards and the olive gardens. We know what happened to those who chanced to meet the Great God Pan, and those who are wise know that all symbols are symbols of something, not of nothing. It was, indeed, an exquisite symbol beneath which men long ago veiled their knowledge of the most awful, most secret forces which lie at the heart of all things; forces before which the souls of men must wither and die and blacken, as their bodies blacken under the electric current. Such forces cannot be named, cannot be spoken, cannot be imagined except under a veil and a symbol, a symbol to the most of us appearing a quaint, poetic fancy, to some a foolish tale. But you and I, at all events, have known something of the terror that may dwell in the secret place of life, manifested under human flesh; that which is without form taking to itself a form. Oh, Austin, how can it be? How is it that the very sunlight does not turn to blackness before this thing, the hard earth melt and boil beneath such a burden?"

Villiers was pacing up and down the room, and the beads of sweat stood out on his forehead. Austin sat silent for a while, but Villiers saw him make a sign upon his breast.

"I say again, Villiers, you will surely never enter such a house as that? You would never pass out alive."

"Yes, Austin, I shall go out alive—I, and Clarke with me."

"What do you mean? You cannot, you would not dare. . ."

"Wait a moment. The air was very pleasant and fresh this morning; there was a breeze blowing, even through this dull street, and I thought I would take a walk. Piccadilly stretched before me a clear, bright vista, and the sun flashed on the carriages and on the quivering leaves in the park. It was a joyous morning, and men and women looked at the sky and smiled as they went about their work or their pleasure, and the wind blew as blithely as upon the meadows and the scented gorse. But somehow or other I got out of the bustle and the gaiety, and found myself walking slowly along a quiet, dull street, where there seemed to be no sunshine and no air, and where the few foot-passengers loitered as they walked, and hung indecisively about corners and archways. I walked along, hardly knowing where I was going or what I did there, but feeling impelled, as one sometimes is, to explore still further, with a vague idea of reaching some unknown goal. Thus I forged up the street, noting the small traffic of the milk-shop, and wondering at the incongruous medley of penny pipes, black tobacco, sweets, newspapers, and comic songs which here and there jostled one another in the short compass of a single window. I think it was a cold shudder that suddenly passed through me that first told me that I had found what I wanted. I looked up from the pavement and stopped before a dusty shop, above which the lettering had faded, where the red bricks of two hundred years ago had grimed to black; where the windows had gathered to themselves the dust of winters innumerable. I saw what I required; but I think it was five minutes before I had steadied myself and could walk in and ask for it in a cool voice and with a calm face. I think there must even then have been a tremor in my words, for the old man who came out of the back parlour, and fumbled slowly amongst his goods, looked oddly at me as he tied the parcel. I paid what he asked, and stood leaning by the counter, with a strange reluctance to take up my goods and go. I asked about the business, and learnt that trade was bad and the profits cut down sadly; but then the street was not what it was before traffic had been diverted, but that was done forty years ago, 'just before my father died,' he said. I got away at last, and walked along sharply; it was a dismal street indeed, and I was glad to return to the bustle and the noise. Would you like to see my purchase?"

Austin said nothing, but nodded his head slightly; he still looked white and sick. Villiers pulled out a drawer in the bamboo table, and showed Austin a long coil of cord, hard and new; and at one end was a running noose.

"It is the best hempen cord," said Villiers, "just as it used to be made for the old trade, the man told me. Not an inch of jute from end to end."

Austin set his teeth hard, and stared at Villiers, growing whiter as he looked.

"You would not do it," he murmured at last. "You would not have blood on your hands. My God!" he exclaimed, with sudden vehemence, "you cannot mean this, Villiers, that you will make yourself a hangman?"

"No. I shall offer a choice, and leave Helen Vaughan alone with this cord in a locked room for fifteen minutes. If when we go in it is not done, I shall call the nearest policeman. That is all."

"I must go now. I cannot stay here any longer; I cannot bear this. Goodnight."

"Goodnight, Austin."

The door shut, but in a moment it was open again, and Austin stood, white and ghastly, in the entrance.

"I was forgetting," he said, "that I too have something to tell. I have received a letter from Dr. Harding of Buenos Ayres. He says that he attended Meyrick for three weeks before his death."

"And does he say what carried him off in the prime of life? It was not fever?"

"No, it was not fever. According to the doctor, it was an utter collapse of the whole system, probably caused by some severe shock. But he states that the patient would tell him nothing, and that he was consequently at some disadvantage in treating the case."

"Is there anything more?"

"Yes. Dr. Harding ends his letter by saying: 'I think this is all the information I can give you about your poor friend. He had not been long in Buenos Ayres, and knew scarcely anyone, with the exception of a person who did not bear the best of characters, and has since left—a Mrs. Vaughan.'"

VIII

The Fragments

(Amongst the papers of the well-known physician, Dr. Robert Matheson, of Ashley Street, Piccadilly, who died suddenly, of apoplectic seizure, at the beginning of 1892, a leaf of manuscript paper was found, covered with pencil jottings. These notes were in Latin, much abbreviated, and had evidently been made in great haste. The MS. was only deciphered with difficulty, and some words have up to the present time evaded all the efforts of the expert employed. The date, "XXV Jul. 1888," is written on the right-hand corner of the MS. The following is a translation of Dr. Matheson's manuscript.)

Whether science would benefit by these brief notes if they could be published, I do not know, but rather doubt. But certainly I shall never take the responsibility of publishing or divulging one word of what is here written, not only on account of my oath given freely to those two persons who were present, but also because the details are too abominable. It is probably that, upon mature consideration, and after weighting the good and evil, I shall one day destroy this paper, or at least leave it under seal to my friend D., trusting in his discretion, to use it or to burn it, as he may think fit.

"As was befitting, I did all that my knowledge suggested to make sure that I was suffering under no delusion. At first astounded, I could hardly think, but in a minute's time I was sure that my pulse was steady and regular, and that I was in my real and true senses. I then fixed my eyes quietly on what was before me.

"Though horror and revolting nausea rose up within me, and an odour of corruption choked my breath, I remained firm. I was then privileged or accursed, I dare not say which, to see that which was on the bed, lying there black like ink, transformed before my eyes. The skin, and the flesh, and the muscles, and the bones, and the firm structure of the human body that I had thought to be unchangeable, and permanent as adamant, began to melt and dissolve.

"I know that the body may be separated into its elements by external agencies, but I should have refused to believe what I saw. For here there was some internal force, of which I knew nothing, that caused dissolution and change.

"Here too was all the work by which man had been made repeated before my eyes. I saw the form waver from sex to sex, dividing itself from itself, and then again reunited. Then I saw the body descend to the beasts whence it ascended, and that which was on the heights go down to the depths, even to the abyss of all being. The principle of life, which makes organism, always remained, while the outward form changed.

"The light within the room had turned to blackness, not the darkness of night, in which objects are seen dimly, for I could see clearly and without difficulty. But it was the negation of light; objects were presented to my eyes, if I may say so, without any medium, in such a manner that if there had been a prism in the room I should have seen no colours represented in it.

"I watched, and at last I saw nothing but a substance as jelly. Then the ladder was ascended again. . . (here the MS. is illegible) . . . for one instance I saw a Form, shaped in dimness before me, which I will not farther describe. But the symbol of this form may be seen in ancient sculptures, and in paintings which survived beneath the lava, too foul to be spoken of. . . as a horrible and unspeakable shape, neither man nor beast, was changed into human form, there came finally death.

"I who saw all this, not without great horror and loathing of soul, here write my name, declaring all that I have set on this paper to be true.

ROBERT MATHESON, Med. Dr.

. . . SUCH, RAYMOND, IS THE STORY of what I know and what I have seen. The burden of it was too heavy for me to bear alone, and yet I could tell it to none but you. Villiers, who was with me at the last, knows nothing of that awful secret of the wood, of how what we both saw die, lay upon the smooth, sweet turf amidst the summer flowers, half in sun and half in shadow, and holding the girl Rachel's hand, called and summoned those companions, and shaped in solid form, upon the earth we tread upon, the horror which we can but hint at, which we can only name under a figure. I would not tell Villiers of this, nor of that resemblance, which struck me as with a blow upon my heart, when I saw the portrait, which filled the cup of terror at the end. What this can mean I dare not guess. I know that what I saw perish was not Mary, and yet in the last agony Mary's eyes looked into mine. Whether there can be anyone who can show the last link in this chain of awful mystery, I do not know, but if there be anyone who can do this, you, Raymond, are the man. And if you know the secret, it rests with you to tell it or not, as you please.

I am writing this letter to you immediately on my getting back to town. I have been in the country for the last few days; perhaps you may be able to guess in which part. While the horror and wonder of London was at its height—for "Mrs. Beaumont," as I have told you, was well known in society—I wrote to my friend Dr. Phillips, giving some brief outline, or rather hint, of what happened, and asking him to tell me the name of the village where the events he had related to me occurred. He gave me the name, as he said with the less hesitation, because Rachel's father and mother were dead, and the rest of the family had gone to a relative in the State of Washington six months before. The parents, he said, had undoubtedly died of grief and horror caused by the terrible death of their daughter, and by what had gone before that death. On the evening of the day which I received Phillips' letter I was at Caermaen, and standing beneath the mouldering Roman walls, white with the winters of seventeen hundred years, I looked over the meadow where once had stood the older temple of the "God of the Deeps," and saw a house gleaming in the sunlight. It was the house where Helen had lived. I stayed at Caermaen for several days. The people of the place, I found, knew little and had guessed less. Those whom I spoke to on the matter seemed surprised that an antiquarian (as I professed myself to be) should trouble about a village tragedy, of which they gave a very commonplace version, and, as you may imagine, I told nothing of what I knew. Most of my time was spent in the great wood that rises just above the village and climbs the hillside, and goes down to the river in the valley; such another long lovely valley, Raymond, as that on which we looked one summer night, walking to and fro before your house. For many an hour I strayed through the maze of the forest, turning now to right and now to left, pacing slowly down long alleys of undergrowth, shadowy and chill, even under the midday sun, and halting beneath great oaks; lying on the short turf of a clearing where the faint sweet scent of wild roses came to me on the wind and mixed with the heavy perfume of the elder, whose mingled odour is like the odour of the room of the dead, a vapour of incense and corruption. I stood at the edges of the wood, gazing at all the pomp and procession of the foxgloves towering amidst the bracken and shining red in the broad sunshine, and beyond them into deep thickets of close undergrowth where springs boil up from the rock and nourish the water-weeds, dank and evil. But in all my wanderings I avoided one part of the wood; it was not till yesterday that I climbed to the summit of the hill, and stood upon the ancient Roman road that threads the highest ridge of the wood. Here they had walked, Helen and Rachel, along this quiet causeway, upon the pavement of green turf, shut in on either side by high banks of red earth, and tall hedges of shining beech, and here I followed in their steps, looking out, now and again, through partings in the boughs, and seeing on one side the sweep of the wood stretching far to right and left, and sinking into the broad level, and beyond, the yellow sea, and the land over the sea. On the other side was the valley and the river and hill following hill as wave on wave, and wood and meadow, and cornfield, and white houses gleaming, and a great wall of mountain, and far blue peaks in the north. And so at last I came to the place. The track went up a gentle slope, and widened out into an open space with a wall of thick undergrowth around it, and then, narrowing again, passed on into the distance and the faint blue mist of summer heat. And into this pleasant summer glade Rachel passed a girl, and left it, who shall say what? I did not stay long there.

In a small town near Caermaen there is a museum, containing for the most part Roman remains which have been found in the neighbourhood at various times. On the day after my arrival in Caermaen I walked over to the town in question, and took the opportunity of inspecting the museum. After I had seen most of the sculptured stones, the coffins, rings, coins, and fragments of tessellated pavement which the place contains, I was shown a small square pillar of white stone, which had been recently discovered in the wood of which I have been speaking, and, as I found on inquiry, in that open space where the Roman road broadens out. On one side of the pillar was an inscription, of which I took a note. Some of the letters have been defaced, but I do not think there can be any doubt as to those which I supply. The inscription is as follows:

DEVOMNODENT—I—
FLA—V—IVSSENILISPOSSV—IT—
PROPTERNVP—TIAS—
—QUA—SVIDITSVBVMB—RA—

"To the great god Nodens (the god of the Great Deep or Abyss) Flavius Senilis has erected this pillar on account of the marriage which he saw beneath the shade."

The custodian of the museum informed me that local antiquaries were much puzzled, not by the inscription, or by any difficulty in translating it, but as to the circumstance or rite to which allusion is made.

. . . AND NOW, MY DEAR CLARKE, as to what you tell me about Helen Vaughan, whom you say you saw die under circumstances of the utmost and almost incredible horror. I was interested in your account, but a good deal, nay all, of what you told me I knew already. I can understand the strange likeness you remarked in both the portrait and in the actual face; you have seen Helen's mother. You remember that still summer night so many years ago, when I talked to you of the world beyond the shadows, and of the god Pan. You remember Mary. She was the mother of Helen Vaughan, who was born nine months after that night.

Mary never recovered her reason. She lay, as you saw her, all the while upon her bed, and a few days after the child was born she died. I fancy that just at the last she knew me; I was standing by the bed, and the old look came into her eyes for a second, and then she shuddered and groaned and died. It was an ill work I did that night when you were present; I broke open the door of the house of life, without knowing or caring what might pass forth or enter in. I recollect your telling me at the time, sharply enough, and rightly too, in one sense, that I had ruined the reason of a human being by a foolish experiment, based on an absurd theory. You did well to blame me, but my theory was not all absurdity. What I said Mary would see she saw, but I forgot that no human eyes can look on such a sight with impunity. And I forgot, as I have just said, that when the house of life is thus thrown open, there may enter in that for which we have no name, and human flesh may become the veil of a horror one dare not express. I played with energies which I did not understand, you have seen the ending of it. Helen Vaughan did well to bind the cord about her neck and die, though the death was horrible. The blackened face, the hideous form upon the bed, changing and melting before your eyes from woman to man, from man to beast, and from beast to worse than beast, all the strange horror that you witness, surprises me but little. What you say the doctor whom you sent for saw and shuddered at I noticed long ago; I knew what I had done the moment the child was born, and when it was scarcely five years old I surprised it, not once or twice but several times with a playmate, you may guess of what kind. It was for me a constant, an incarnate horror, and after a few years I felt I could bear it no more, and I sent Helen Vaughan away. You know now what frightened the boy in the wood. The rest of the strange story, and all else that you tell me, as discovered by your friend, I have contrived to learn from time to time, almost to the last chapter. And now Helen is with her companions. . .

THE END

THE INMOST LIGHT

I

One evening in autumn, when the deformities of London were veiled in faint blue mist, and its vistas and far-reaching streets seemed splendid, Mr. Charles Salisbury was slowly pacing down Rupert Street, drawing nearer to his favourite restaurant by slow degrees. His eyes were downcast in study of the pavement, and thus it was that as he passed in at the narrow door a man who had come up from the lower end of the street jostled against him.

"I beg your pardon—wasn't looking where I was going. Why, it's Dyson!"

"Yes, quite so. How are you, Salisbury?"

"Quite well. But where have you been, Dyson? I don't think I can have seen you for the last five years?"

"No; I dare say not. You remember I was getting rather hard up when you came to my place at Charlotte Street?"

"Perfectly. I think I remember your telling me that you owed five weeks' rent, and that you had parted with your watch for a comparatively small sum."

"My dear Salisbury, your memory is admirable. Yes, I was hard up. But the curious thing is that soon after you saw me I became harder up. My financial state was described by a friend as 'stone broke.' I don't approve of slang, mind you, but such was my condition. But suppose we go in; there might be other people who would like to dine—it's a human weakness, Salisbury."

"Certainly; come along. I was wondering as I walked down whether the corner table were taken. It has a velvet back you know."

"I know the spot; it's vacant. Yes, as I was saying, I became even harder up."

"What did you do then?" asked Salisbury, disposing of his hat, and settling down in the corner of the seat, with a glance of fond anticipation at the *menu*.

"What did I do? Why, I sat down and reflected. I had a good classical education, and a positive distaste for business of any kind: that was the capital with which I faced the world. Do you know, I have heard people describe olives as nasty! What lamentable Philistinism! I have often thought, Salisbury, that I could write genuine poetry under the influence of olives and red wine. Let us have Chianti; it may not be very good, but the flasks are simply charming."

"It is pretty good here. We may as well have a big flask."

"Very good. I reflected, then, on my want of prospects, and I determined to embark in literature."

"Really; that was strange. You seem in pretty comfortable circumstances, though."

"Though! What a satire upon a noble profession. I am afraid, Salisbury, you haven't a proper idea of the dignity of an artist. You see me sitting at my desk—or at least you can see me if you care to call—with pen and ink, and simple nothingness before me, and if you come again in a few hours you will (in all probability) find a creation!"

"Yes, quite so. I had an idea that literature was not remunerative."

"You are mistaken; its rewards are great. I may mention, by the way, that shortly after you saw me I succeeded to a small income. An uncle died, and proved unexpectedly generous."

"Ah, I see. That must have been convenient."

"It was pleasant—undeniably pleasant. I have always considered it in the light of an endowment of my researches. I told you I was a man of letters; it would, perhaps, be more correct to describe myself as a man of science."

"Dear me, Dyson, you have really changed very much in the last few years. I had a notion, don't you know, that you were a sort of idler about town, the kind of man one might meet on the north side of Piccadilly everyday from May to July."

"Exactly. I was even then forming myself, though all unconsciously. You know my poor father could not afford to send me to the University. I used to grumble in my ignorance at not having completed my education. That was the folly of youth, Salisbury; my University was Piccadilly. There I began to study the great science which still occupies me."

"What science do you mean?"

"The science of the great city; the physiology of London; literally and metaphysically the greatest subject that the mind of man can conceive. What an admirable *salmi* this is; undoubtedly the final end of the pheasant. Yet I feel sometimes positively overwhelmed with the thought of the vastness and complexity of London. Paris a man may get to understand thoroughly with a reasonable amount of study; but London is always a mystery. In Paris you may say: 'Here live the actresses, here the Bohemians, and the *Ratés*'; but it is different in London. You may point out a street, correctly enough, as the abode of washerwomen; but, in that second floor, a man may be studying Chaldee roots, and in the garret over the way a forgotten artist is dying by inches."

"I see you are Dyson, unchanged and unchangeable," said Salisbury, slowly sipping his Chianti. "I think you are misled by a too fervid imagination; the mystery of London exists only in your fancy. It seems to me a dull place enough. We seldom hear of a really artistic crime in London, whereas I believe Paris abounds in that sort of thing."

"Give me some more wine. Thanks. You are mistaken, my dear fellow, you are really mistaken. London has nothing to be ashamed of in the way of crime. Where we fail is for want of Homers, not Agamemnons. *Carent quia vate sacro*, you know."

"I recall the quotation. But I don't think I quite follow you."

"Well, in plain language, we have no good writers in London who make a speciality of that kind of thing. Our common reporter is a dull dog; every story that he has to tell is spoilt in the telling. His idea of horror and of what excites horror is so lamentably deficient. Nothing will content the fellow but blood, vulgar red blood, and when he can get it he lays it on thick, and considers that he has produced a telling article. It's a poor notion. And, by some curious fatality, it is the most commonplace and brutal murders which always attract the most attention and get written up the most. For instance, I dare say that you never heard of the Harlesden case?"

"No; no, I don't remember anything about it."

"Of course not. And yet the story is a curious one. I will tell you over our coffee. Harlesden, you know, or I expect you don't know, is quite on the out-quarters of London; something curiously different from your fine old crusted suburb like Norwood or Hampstead, different as each of these is from the other. Hampstead, I mean, is where you look for the head of your great China house with his three acres of land and pine-houses, though of late there is the artistic substratum; while Norwood is the home of the prosperous middle-class family who took the house 'because it was near the Palace,' and sickened of the Palace six months afterwards; but Harlesden is a place of no character. It's too new to have any character as yet. There are the rows of red houses and the rows of white houses and the bright green Venetians, and the blistering doorways, and the little backyards they call gardens, and a few feeble shops, and then, just as you think you're going to grasp the physiognomy of the settlement, it all melts away."

"How the dickens is that? The houses don't tumble down before one's eyes, I suppose!"

"Well, no, not exactly that. But Harlesden as an entity disappears. Your street turns into a quiet lane, and your staring houses into elm trees, and the back-gardens into green meadows. You pass instantly from town to country; there is no transition as in a small country town, no soft gradations of wider lawns and orchards, with houses gradually becoming less dense, but a dead stop. I believe the people who live there mostly go into the City. I have seen once or twice a laden bus bound thitherwards. But however that may be, I can't conceive a greater loneliness in a desert at midnight than there is there at mid-day. It is like a city of the dead; the streets are glaring and desolate, and as you pass it suddenly strikes you that this too is part of London. Well, a year or two ago there was a doctor living there; he had set up his brass plate and his red lamp at the very end of one of those shining streets, and from the back of the house, the fields stretched away to the north. I don't know what his reason was in settling down in such an out-of-the-way place, perhaps Dr. Black, as we call him, was a far-seeing man and looked ahead. His relations, so it appeared afterwards, had lost sight of him for many years and didn't even know he was a doctor, much less where he lived. However, there he was settled in Harlesden, with some fragments of a practice, and an uncommonly pretty wife. People used to see them walking out together in the summer evenings soon after they came to Harlesden, and, so far as could be observed, they seemed a very affectionate couple. These walks went on through the autumn, and then ceased, but, of course, as the days grew dark and the weather cold, the lanes near Harlesden might be expected to lose many of their attractions. All through the winter nobody saw anything of Mrs. Black, the doctor used to reply to his patients' inquiries that she was a 'little out of sorts, would be better, no doubt, in the spring.' But the spring came, and the summer, and no Mrs. Black appeared, and at last people began to rumour and talk amongst themselves, and all sorts of queer things were said at 'high teas,' which you may possibly have heard are the only form of entertainment known in such suburbs. Dr. Black began to surprise some very odd looks cast in his direction, and the practice, such as it was, fell off before his eyes. In short, when the neighbours whispered about the matter, they whispered that Mrs. Black was dead, and that the doctor had made away with her. But this wasn't the case; Mrs. Black was seen alive in June. It was a Sunday afternoon, one of those few exquisite days that an English climate offers, and half London had strayed out into the fields, north, south, east, and west to smell the scent of the white May, and to see if the wild roses were yet in blossom in the hedges. I had gone out myself early in the morning, and had had a long ramble, and somehow or other as I was steering homeward I found myself in this very Harlesden we have been talking about. To be exact, I had a glass of beer in the 'General Gordon,' the most flourishing house in the neighbourhood, and as I was wandering rather aimlessly about, I saw an uncommonly tempting gap in a hedgerow, and resolved to explore the meadow beyond. Soft grass is very grateful to the feet after the infernal grit strewn on suburban sidewalks, and after walking about for sometime I thought I should like to sit down on a bank and have a smoke. While I was getting out my pouch, I looked up in the direction of the houses, and as I looked I felt my breath caught back, and my teeth began to chatter, and the stick I had in one hand snapped in two with the grip I gave it. It was as if I had had an electric current down my spine, and yet for some moment of time which seemed long, but which must have been very short, I caught myself wondering what on earth was the matter. Then I knew I what had made my very heart shudder and my bones grind together in an agony. As I glanced up I had looked straight towards the last house in the row before me, and in an upper window of that house I had seen for some short fraction of a second a face. It was the face of a woman, and yet it was not human. You and I, Salisbury, have heard in our time, as we sat in our seats in church in sober English fashion, of a lust that cannot be satiated and of a fire that is unquenchable, but few of us have any notion what these words mean. I hope you never may, for as I saw that face at the window, with the blue sky above me and the warm air playing in gusts about me, I knew I had looked into another world—looked through the window of a commonplace, brand-new house, and seen hell open before me. When the first shock was over, I thought once or twice that I should have fainted; my face streamed with a cold sweat, and my breath came and went in sobs, as if I had been half drowned. I managed to get up at last, and walk round to the street, and there I saw the name 'Dr. Black' on the post by the front gate. As fate or my luck would have it, the door opened and a man came down the steps as I passed by. I had no doubt it was the doctor himself. He was of a type rather common in London; long and thin, with a pasty face and a dull black moustache. He gave me a look as we passed each other on the pavement, and though it was merely the casual glance which one foot-passenger bestows on another, I felt convinced in my mind that here was an ugly customer to deal with. As you may imagine, I went my way a good deal puzzled and horrified too by what I had seen; for I had paid another visit to the 'General Gordon,' and had got together a good deal of the common gossip of the place about the Blacks. I didn't mention the fact that I had seen a woman's face in the window; but I heard that Mrs. Black had been much admired for her beautiful golden hair, and round what had struck me with such a nameless terror, there was a mist of flowing yellow hair, as it were an aureole of glory round the visage of a satyr. The whole thing bothered me in an indescribable manner; and when I got home I tried my best to think of the impression I had received as an illusion, but it was no use. I knew very well I had seen what I have tried to describe to you, and I was morally certain that I had seen Mrs. Black. And then there was the gossip of the place, the suspicion of foul play, which I knew to be false, and my own conviction that there was some deadly mischief or other going on in that bright red house at the corner of Devon Road: how to construct a theory of a reasonable kind out of these two elements. In short, I found myself in a world of mystery; I puzzled my head over it and filled up my leisure moments by gathering together odd threads of speculation, but I never moved a step towards any real solution, and as the summer days went on the matter seemed to grow misty and indistinct, shadowing some vague terror, like a nightmare of last month. I suppose it would before long have faded into the background of my brain—I should not have forgotten it, for such a thing could never be forgotten—but one morning as I was looking over the paper my eye was caught by a heading over some two dozen lines of small type. The words I had seen were simply: 'The Harlesden Case,' and I knew what I was going to read. Mrs. Black was dead. Black had called in another medical man to certify as to cause of death, and something or other had aroused the strange doctor's suspicions and there had been an inquest and *post-mortem*. And the result? That, I will confess, did astonish me considerably; it was the triumph of the unexpected. The two doctors who made the autopsy were obliged to confess that they could not discover the faintest trace of any kind of foul play; their most exquisite tests and reagents failed to detect the presence of poison in the most infinitesimal quantity. Death, they found, had been caused by a somewhat obscure and scientifically interesting form of brain disease. The tissue of the brain and the molecules of the grey

ARTHUR MACHEN

matter had undergone a most extraordinary series of changes; and the younger of the two doctors, who has some reputation, I believe, as a specialist in brain trouble, made some remarks in giving his evidence which struck me deeply at the time, though I did not then grasp their full significance. He said: 'At the commencement of the examination I was astonished to find appearances of a character entirely new to me, notwithstanding my somewhat large experience. I need not specify these appearances at present, it will be sufficient for me to state that as I proceeded in my task I could scarcely believe that the brain before me was that of a human being at all.' There was some surprise at this statement, as you may imagine, and the coroner asked the doctor if he meant that the brain resembled that of an animal. 'No,' he replied, 'I should not put it in that way. Some of the appearances I noticed seemed to point in that direction, but others, and these were the more surprising, indicated a nervous organization of a wholly different character from that either of man or the lower animals.' It was a curious thing to say, but of course the jury brought in a verdict of death from natural causes, and, so far as the public was concerned, the case came to an end. But after I had read what the doctor said I made up my mind that I should like to know a good deal more, and I set to work on what seemed likely to prove an interesting investigation. I had really a good deal of trouble, but I was successful in a measure. Though why—my dear fellow, I had no notion at the time. Are you aware that we have been here nearly four hours? The waiters are staring at us. Let's have the bill and be gone."

The two men went out in silence, and stood a moment in the cool air, watching the hurrying traffic of Coventry Street pass before them to the accompaniment of the ringing bells of hansoms and the cries of the newsboys; the deep far murmur of London surging up ever and again from beneath these louder noises.

"It is a strange case, isn't it?" said Dyson at length. "What do you think of it?"

"My dear fellow. I haven't heard the end, so I will reserve my opinion. When will you give me the sequel?"

"Come to my rooms some evening; say next Thursday. Here's the address. Goodnight; I want to get down to the Strand." Dyson hailed a passing hansom, and Salisbury turned northward to walk home to his lodgings.

II

M r. Salisbury, as may have been gathered from the few remarks which he had found it possible to introduce in the course of the evening, was a young gentleman of a peculiarly solid form of intellect, coy and retiring before the mysterious and the uncommon, with a constitutional dislike of paradox. During the restaurant dinner he had been forced to listen in almost absolute silence to a strange tissue of improbabilities strung together with the ingenuity of a born meddler in plots and mysteries, and it was with a feeling of weariness that he crossed Shaftesbury Avenue, and dived into the recesses of Soho, for his lodgings were in a modest neighbourhood to the north of Oxford Street. As he walked he speculated on the probable fate of Dyson, relying on literature, unbefriended by a thoughtful relative, and could not help concluding that so much subtlety united to a too vivid imagination would in all likelihood have been rewarded with a pair of sandwich-boards or a super's banner. Absorbed in this train of thought, and admiring the perverse dexterity which could transmute the face of a sickly woman and a case of brain disease into the crude elements of romance, Salisbury strayed on through the dimly-lighted streets, not noticing the gusty wind which drove sharply round corners and whirled the stray rubbish of the pavement into the air in eddies, while black clouds gathered over the sickly yellow moon. Even a stray drop or two of rain blown into his face did not rouse him from his meditations, and it was only when with a sudden rush the storm tore down upon the street that he began to consider the expediency of finding some shelter. The rain, driven by the wind, pelted down with the violence of a thunderstorm, dashing up from the stones and hissing through the air, and soon a perfect torrent of water coursed along the kennels and accumulated in pools over the choked-up drains. The few stray passengers who had been loafing rather than walking about the street had scuttered away, like frightened rabbits, to some invisible places of refuge, and though Salisbury whistled loud and long for a hansom, no hansom appeared. He looked about him, as if to discover how far he might be from the haven of Oxford Street, but strolling carelessly along, he had turned out of his way, and found himself in an unknown region, and one to all appearance devoid even of a public-house where shelter could be bought for the modest sum of twopence. The street lamps were

ARTHUR MACHEN

few and at long intervals, and burned behind grimy glasses with the sickly light of oil, and by this wavering glimmer Salisbury could make out the shadowy and vast old houses of which the street was composed. As he passed along, hurrying, and shrinking from the full sweep of the rain, he noticed the innumerable bell-handles, with names that seemed about to vanish of old age graven on brass plates beneath them, and here and there a richly carved penthouse overhung the door, blackening with the grime of fifty years. The storm seemed to grow more and more furious; he was wet through, and a new hat had become a ruin, and still Oxford Street seemed as far off as ever; it was with deep relief that the dripping man caught sight of a dark archway which seemed to promise shelter from the rain if not from the wind. Salisbury took up his position in the driest corner and looked about him; he was standing in a kind of passage contrived under part of a house, and behind him stretched a narrow footway leading between blank walls to regions unknown. He had stood there for sometime, vainly endeavouring to rid himself of some of his superfluous moisture, and listening for the passing wheel of a hansom, when his attention was aroused by a loud noise coming from the direction of the passage behind, and growing louder as it drew nearer. In a couple of minutes he could make out the shrill, raucous voice of a woman, threatening and renouncing and making the very stones echo with her accents, while now and then a man grumbled and expostulated. Though to all appearance devoid of romance, Salisbury had some relish for street rows, and was, indeed, somewhat of an amateur in the more amusing phases of drunkenness; he therefore composed himself to listen and observe with something of the air of a subscriber to grand opera. To his annoyance, however, the tempest seemed suddenly to be composed, and he could hear nothing but the impatient steps of the woman and the slow lurch of the man as they came towards him. Keeping back in the shadow of the wall, he could see the two drawing nearer; the man was evidently drunk, and had much ado to avoid frequent collision with the wall as he tacked across from one side to the other, like some bark beating up against a wind. The woman was looking straight in front of her, with tears streaming from her blazing eyes, but suddenly as they went by the flame blazed up again, and she burst forth into a torrent of abuse, facing round upon her companion.

"You low rascal, you mean, comtemptible cur," she went on, after an incoherent storm of curses, "you think I'm to work and slave for you always, I suppose, while you're after that Green Street girl and drinking every penny you've got? But you're mistaken, Sam—indeed, I'll bear it no longer. Damn you, you dirty thief, I've done with you and your master too, so you can go your own errands, and I only hope they'll get you into trouble."

The woman tore at the bosom of her dress, and taking something out that looked like paper, crumpled it up and flung it away. It fell at Salisbury's feet. She ran out and disappeared in the darkness, while the man lurched slowly into the street, grumbling indistinctly to himself in a perplexed tone of voice. Salisbury looked out after him, and saw him maundering along the pavement, halting now and then and swaying indecisively, and then starting off at some fresh tangent. The sky had cleared, and white fleecy clouds were fleeting across the moon, high in the heaven. The light came and went by turns, as the clouds passed by, and, turning round as the clear, white rays shone into the passage, Salisbury saw the little ball of crumpled paper which the woman had cast down. Oddly curious to know what it might contain, he picked it up and put it in his pocket, and set out afresh on his journey.

III

S alisbury was a man of habit. When he got home, drenched to the skin, his clothes hanging lank about him, and a ghastly dew besmearing his hat, his only thought was of his health, of which he took studious care. So, after changing his clothes and encasing himself in a warm dressing-gown, he proceeded to prepare a sudorific in the shape of hot gin and water, warming the latter over one of those spirit-lamps which mitigate the austerities of the modern hermit's life. By the time this preparation had been exhibited, and Salisbury's disturbed feelings had been soothed by a pipe of tobacco, he was able to get into bed in a happy state of vacancy, without a thought of his adventure in the dark archway, or of the weird fancies with which Dyson had seasoned his dinner. It was the same at breakfast the next morning, for Salisbury made a point of not thinking of anything until that meal was over; but when the cup and saucer were cleared away, and the morning pipe was lit, he remembered the little ball of paper, and began fumbling in the pockets of his wet coat. He did not remember into which pocket he had put it, and as he dived now into one and now into another, he experienced a strange feeling of apprehension lest it should not be there at all, though he could not for the life of him have explained the importance he attached to what was in all probability mere rubbish. But he sighed with relief when his fingers touched the crumpled surface in an inside pocket, and he drew it out gently and laid it on the little desk by his easy chair with as much care as if it had been some rare jewel. Salisbury sat smoking and staring at his find for a few minutes, an odd temptation to throw the thing in the fire and have done with it struggling with as odd a speculation as to its possible contents, and as to the reason why the infuriated woman should have flung a bit of paper from her with such vehemence. As might be expected, it was the latter feeling that conquered in the end, and yet it was with something like repugnance that he at last took the paper and unrolled it, and laid it out before him. It was a piece of common dirty paper, to all appearance torn out of a cheap exercise-book, and in the middle were a few lines written in a queer cramped hand. Salisbury bent his head and stared eagerly at it for a moment, drawing a long breath, and then fell back in his chair gazing blankly before him, till at last with a sudden revulsion he burst into a peal of laughter, so long and loud and uproarious that the landlady's baby in the floor below awoke from sleep and echoed his mirth with hideous yells. But he laughed again and again, and took the paper up to read a second time what seemed such meaningless nonsense.

"Q. has had to go and see his friends in Paris," it began. "Traverse Handel S. 'Once around the grass, and twice around the lass, and thrice around the maple-tree.'"

Salisbury took up the paper and crumpled it as the angry woman had done, and aimed it at the fire. He did not throw it there, however, but tossed it carelessly into the well of the desk, and laughed again. The sheer folly of the thing offended him, and he was ashamed of his own eager speculation, as one who pores over the high-sounding announcements in the agony column of the daily paper, and finds nothing but advertisement and trivality. He walked to the window, and stared out at the languid morning life of his quarter; the maids in slatternly print dresses washing door-steps, the fish-monger and the butcher on their rounds, and the tradesmen standing at the doors of their small shops, drooping for lack of trade and excitement. In the distance a blue haze gave some grandeur to the prospect, but the view as a whole was depressing, and would only have interested a student of the life of London, who finds something rare and choice in its every aspect. Salisbury turned away in disgust, and settled himself in the easy-chair, upholstered in a bright shade of green, and decked with yellow gimp, which was the pride and attraction of the apartments. Here he composed himself to his morning's occupation—the perusal of a novel that dealt with sport and love in a manner that suggested the collaboration of a stud-groom and a ladies' college. In an ordinary way, however, Salisbury would have been carried on by the interest of the story up to lunch-time, but this morning he fidgeted in and out of his chair, took the book up and laid it down again, and swore at last to himself and at himself in mere irritation.

In point of fact the jingle of the paper found in the archway had "got into his head," and do what he would he could not help muttering over and over, "Once around the grass, and twice around the lass, and thrice around the maple-tree." It became a positive pain, like the foolish burden of a music-hall song, everlastingly quoted, and sung at all hours of the day and night, and treasured by the street boys as an unfailing resource for six months together. He went out into the streets, and tried to forget his enemy in the jostling of the crowds and the roar and clatter of the traffic, but presently he would find himself stealing quietly aside, and pacing some deserted byway, vainly puzzling his brains, and trying to fix some meaning to phrases that were meaningless. It was a positive relief when Thursday came, and he remembered that he had made an appointment to go and see Dyson; the flimsy reveries of the self-styled man of letters appeared entertaining when compared with this ceaseless iteration, this maze of thought from which there seemed no possibility of escape. Dyson's abode was in one of the quietest of the quiet streets that lead down from the Strand to the river, and when Salisbury passed from the narrow stairway into his friend's room, he saw that the uncle had been beneficent indeed. The floor glowed and flamed with all the colours of the East; it was, as Dyson pompously remarked, "a sunset in a dream," and the lamplight, the twilight of London streets, was shut out with strangely worked curtains, glittering here and there with threads of gold. In the shelves of an oak *armoire* stood jars and plates of old French china, and the black and white of etchings not to be found in the Haymarket or in Bond Street, stood out against the splendour of a Japanese paper. Salisbury sat down on the settle by the hearth, and sniffed and mingled fumes of incense and tobacco, wondering and dumb before all this splendour after the green rep and the oleographs, the gilt-framed mirror, and the lustres of his own apartment.

"I am glad you have come," said Dyson. "Comfortable little room, isn't it? But you don't look very well, Salisbury. Nothing disagreed with you, has it?"

"No; but I have been a good deal bothered for the last few days. The fact is I had an odd kind of—of—adventure, I suppose I may call it, that night I saw you, and it has worried me a good deal. And the provoking part of it is that it's the merest nonsense—but, however, I will tell you all about it, by and by. You were going to let me have the rest of that odd story you began at the restaurant."

"Yes. But I am afraid, Salisbury, you are incorrigible. You are a slave to what you call matter of fact. You know perfectly well that in your heart you think the oddness in that case is of my making, and that it is all really as plain as the police reports. However, as I have begun, I will go on. But first we will have something to drink, and you may as well light your pipe."

Dyson went up to the oak cupboard, and drew from its depths a rotund bottle and two little glasses, quaintly gilded.

"It's Benedictine," he said. "You'll have some, won't you?"

Salisbury assented, and the two men sat sipping and smoking reflectively for some minutes before Dyson began.

"Let me see," he said at last, "we were at the inquest, weren't we? No, we had done with that. Ah, I remember. I was telling you that on the whole I had been successful in my inquiries, investigation, or whatever you like to call it, into the matter. Wasn't that where I left off?"

"Yes, that was it. To be precise, I think 'though' was the last word you said on the matter."

"Exactly. I have been thinking it all over since the other night, and I have come to the conclusion that that 'though' is a very big 'though' indeed. Not to put too fine a point on it, I have had to confess that what I found out, or thought I found out, amounts in reality to nothing. I am as far away from the heart of the case as ever. However, I may as well tell you what I do know. You may remember my saying that I was impressed a good deal by some remarks of one of the doctors who gave evidence at the inquest. Well, I determined that my first step must be to try if I could get something more definite and intelligible out of that doctor. Somehow or other I managed to get an introduction to the man, and he gave me an appointment to come and see him.

"He turned out to be a pleasant, genial fellow; rather young and not in the least like the typical medical man, and he began the conference by offering me whisky and cigars. I didn't think it worth while to beat about the bush, so I began by saying that part of his evidence at the Harlesden inquest struck me as very peculiar, and I gave him the printed report, with the sentences in question underlined. He just glanced at the slip, and gave me a queer look.

"'It struck you as peculiar, did it?' said he. 'Well, you must remember that the Harlesden case was very peculiar. In fact, I think I may safely say that in some features it was unique—quite unique.'

"'Quite so,' I replied, 'and that's exactly why it interests me, and why I want to know more about it. And I thought that if anybody could give me any information it would be you. What is your opinion of the matter?'

"It was a pretty downright sort of question, and my doctor looked rather taken aback.

"'Well,' he said, 'as I fancy your motive in inquiring into the question must be mere curiosity, I think I may tell you my opinion with tolerable freedom. So, Mr. Dyson, if you want to know my theory, it is this: I believe that Dr. Black killed his wife.'

"'But the verdict,' I answered, 'the verdict was given from your own evidence.'

"'Quite so; the verdict was given in accordance with the evidence of my colleague and myself, and, under the circumstances, I think the jury acted very sensibly. In fact, I don't see what else they could have done. But I stick to my opinion, mind you, and I say this also. I don't wonder at Black's doing what I firmly believe he did. I think he was justified.'

"'Justified! How could that be?' I asked. I was astonished, as you may imagine, at the answer I had got. The doctor wheeled round his chair and looked steadily at me for a moment before he answered.

"'I suppose you are not a man of science yourself? No; then it would be of no use my going into detail. I have always been firmly opposed myself to any partnership between physiology and psychology. I believe that both are bound to suffer. No one recognizes more decidedly than I do the impassable gulf, the fathomless abyss that separates the world of consciousness from the sphere of matter. We know that every change of consciousness is accompanied by a rearrangement of the molecules in the grey matter; and that is all. What the link between them is, or why they occur together, we do not know, and the most authorities believe that we never can know. Yet, I will tell you that as I did my work, the knife in my hand, I felt convinced, in spite of all theories, that what lay before me was not the brain of a dead woman—not the brain of a human being at all. Of course I saw the face; but it was quite placid, devoid of all expression. It must have been a beautiful face, no doubt, but I can honestly say that I would not have looked in that face when there was life behind it for a thousand guineas, no, nor for twice that sum.'"

"'My dear sir,' I said, 'you surprise me extremely. You say that it was not the brain of a human being. What was it, then?'

"'The brain of a devil.' He spoke quite coolly, and never moved a muscle. 'The brain of a devil,' he repeated, 'and I have no doubt that Black found some way of putting an end to it. I don't blame him if he did. Whatever Mrs. Black was, she was not fit to stay in this world. Will you have anything more? No? Goodnight, goodnight.'

"It was a queer sort of opinion to get from a man of science, wasn't it? When he was saying that he would not have looked on that face when alive for a thousand guineas, or two thousand guineas, I was thinking of the face I had seen, but I said nothing. I went again to Harlesden, and passed from one shop to another, making small purchases, and trying to find out whether there was anything about the Blacks which was not already common property, but there was very little to hear. One of the tradesmen to whom I spoke said he had known the dead woman well; she used to buy of him such quantities of grocery as were required for their small household, for they never kept a servant, but had a charwoman in occasionally, and she had not seen Mrs. Black for months before she died. According to this man Mrs. Black was 'a nice lady,' always kind and considerate, and so fond of her husband and he of her, as everyone thought. And yet, to put the doctor's opinion on one side, I knew what I had seen. And then after thinking it over, and putting one thing with another, it seemed to me that the only person likely to give me much assistance would be Black himself, and I made up my mind to find him. Of course he wasn't to be found in Harlesden; he had left, I was told, directly after the funeral. Everything in the house had been sold, and one fine day Black got into the train with a small portmanteau, and went, nobody knew where. It was a chance if he were ever heard of again, and it was by a mere chance that I came across him at last. I was walking one day along Gray's Inn Road, not bound for anywhere in particular, but looking about me, as usual, and holding on to my hat, for it was a gusty day in early March, and the wind was making the treetops in the Inn rock and quiver. I had come up from the Holborn end, and I had almost got to Theobald's Road when I noticed a man walking in front of me, leaning on a stick, and to all appearance very feeble. There was something about his look that made me curious, I don't know why, and I began to walk briskly with the idea of overtaking him, when of a sudden his hat blew off and came bounding along the pavement to my feet. Of course I rescued the hat, and gave it a glance as I went towards its owner. It was a biography in itself; a Piccadilly maker's name in the inside, but t don't think a beggar would have picked it out of the gutter. Then I looked up and saw Dr. Black of Harlesden waiting for me. A queer thing, wasn't it? But, Salisbury, what a change! When I saw Dr. Black come down the steps of his house at Harlesden he was an upright man, walking firmly with well-built limbs; a man, should say, in the prime of his life. And now before me there crouched this wretched creature, bent and feeble, with shrunken cheeks, and hair that was whitening fast, and limbs that trembled and shook together, and misery in his eyes. He thanked me for bringing him his hat, saying, 'I don't think I should ever have got it, I can't run much now. A gusty day, sir, isn't it?' and with this he was turning away, but by little and little I contrived to draw him into the current of conversation, and we walked together eastward. I think the man would have been glad to get rid of

ARTHUR MACHEN

me; but I didn't intend to let him go, and he stopped at last in front of a miserable house in a miserable street. It was, I verily believe, one of the most wretched quarters I have ever seen: houses that must have been sordid and hideous enough when new, that had gathered foulness with every year, and now seemed to lean and totter to their fall. 'I live up there,' said Black, pointing to the tiles, 'not in the front—in the back. I am very quiet there. I won't ask you to come in now, but perhaps some other day—' I caught him up at that, and told him I should be only too glad to come and see him. He gave me an odd sort of glance, as if he were wondering what on earth I or anybody else could care about him, and I left him fumbling with his latch-key. I think you will say I did pretty well when I tell you that within a few weeks I had made myself an intimate friend of Black's. I shall never forget the first time I went to his room; I hope I shall never see such abject, squalid misery again. The foul paper, from which all pattern or trace of a pattern had long vanished, subdued and penetrated with the grime of the evil street, was hanging in mouldering pennons from the wall. Only at the end of the room was it possible to stand upright, and the sight of the wretched bed and the odour of corruption that pervaded the place made me turn faint and sick. Here I found him munching a piece of bread; he seemed surprised to find that I had kept my promise, but he gave me his chair and sat on the bed while we talked. I used to go to see him often, and we had long conversations together, but he never mentioned Harlesden or his wife. I fancy that he supposed me ignorant of the matter, or thought that if I had heard of it, I should never connect the respectable Dr. Black of Harlesden with a poor garreteer in the backwoods of London. He was a strange man, and as we sat together smoking, I often wondered whether he were mad or sane, for I think the wildest dreams of Paracelsus and the Rosicrucians would appear plain and sober fact compared with the theories I have heard him earnestly advance in that grimy den of his. I once ventured to hint something of the sort to him. I suggested that something he had said was in flat contradiction to all science and all experience. 'No,' he answered, 'not all experience, for mine counts for something. I am no dealer in unproved theories; what I say I have proved for myself, and at a terrible cost. There is a region of knowledge which you will never know, which wise men seeing from afar off shun like the plague, as well they may, but into that region I have gone. If you knew, if you could even dream of what may be done, of what one or two men have done in this quiet world of ours, your very soul would shudder and faint within you. What you have heard from me has been but the merest husk and outer covering of true science—that science which means death, and that which is more awful than death, to those who gain it. No, when men say that there are strange things in the world, they little know the awe and the terror that dwell always with them and about them.' There was a sort of fascination about the man that drew me to him, and I was quite sorry to have to leave London for a month or two; I missed his odd talk. A few days after I came back to town I thought I would look him up, but when I gave the two rings at the bell that used to summon him, there was no answer. I rang and rang again, and was just turning to go away, when the door opened and a dirty woman asked me what I wanted. From her look I fancy she took me for a plain-clothes officer after one of her lodgers, but when I inquired if Mr. Black were in, she gave me a stare of another kind. 'There's no Mr. Black lives here,' she said. 'He's gone. He's dead this six weeks. I always thought he was a bit queer in his head, or else had been and got into some trouble or other. He used to go out every morning from ten till one, and one Monday morning we heard him come in, and go into his room and shut the door, and a few minutes after, just as we was a-sitting down to our dinner, there was such a scream that I thought I should have gone right off. And then we heard a stamping, and down he came, raging and cursing most dreadful, swearing he had been robbed of something that was worth millions. And then he just dropped down in the passage, and we thought he was dead. We got him up to his room, and put him on his bed, and I just sat there and waited, while my 'usband he went for the doctor. And there was the winder wide open, and a little tin box he had lying on the floor open and empty, but of course nobody could possible have got in at the winder, and as for him having anything that was worth anything, it's nonsense, for he was often weeks and weeks behind with his rent, and my 'usband he threatened often and often to turn him into the street, for, as he said, we've got a living to myke like other people—and, of course, that's true; but, somehow, I didn't like to do it, though he was an odd kind of a man, and I fancy had been better off. And then the doctor came and looked at him, and said as he couldn't do nothing, and that night he died as I was a-sitting by his bed; and I can tell you that, with one thing and another, we lost money by him, for the few bits of clothes as he had were worth next to nothing when they came to be sold.' I gave the woman half a sovereign for her trouble, and went home thinking of Dr. Black and the epitaph she had made him, and wondering at his strange fancy that he had been robbed. I take it that he had very little to fear on that score, poor fellow; but I suppose that he was really mad, and died in a sudden access of his mania. His landlady said that once or twice when she had had occasion to go into his room (to dun the poor wretch for his rent, most likely), he would keep her at the door for about a minute, and that when she came in she would find him putting away his tin box in the corner by the window; I suppose he had become possessed with the idea of some great treasure, and fancied himself a wealthy man in the midst of all his misery. *Explicit*, my tale is ended, and you see that though I knew Black, I knew nothing of his wife or of the history of her death—That's the Harlesden case, Salisbury, and I think it interests me all the more deeply because there does not seem the shadow of a possibility that I or anyone else will ever know more about it. What do you think of it?"

"Well, Dyson, I must say that I think you have contrived to surround the whole thing with a mystery of your own making. I go for the doctor's solution: Black murdered his wife, being himself in all probability an undeveloped lunatic."

"What? Do you believe, then, that this woman was something too awful, too terrible to be allowed to remain on the earth? You will remember that the doctor said it was the brain of a devil?"

"Yes, yes, but he was speaking, of course, metaphorically. It's really quite a simple matter if you only look at it like that."

"Ah, well, you may be right; but yet I am sure you are not. Well, well, it's not good discussing it anymore. A little more Benedictine? That's right; try some of this tobacco. Didn't you say that you had been bothered by something—something which happened that night we dined together?"

"Yes, I have been worried, Dyson, worried a great deal. I—But it's such a trivial matter—indeed, such an absurdity—that I feel ashamed to trouble you with it."

"Never mind, let's have it, absurd or not."

With many hesitations, and with much inward resentment of the folly of the thing, Salisbury told his tale, and repeated reluctantly the absurd intelligence and the absurder doggerel of the scrap of paper, expecting to hear Dyson burst out into a roar of laughter.

"Isn't it too bad that I should let myself be bothered by such stuff as that?" he asked, when he had stuttered out the jingle of once, and twice, and thrice.

Dyson had listened to it all gravely, even to the end, and meditated for a few minutes in silence.

"Yes," he said at length, "it was a curious chance, your taking shelter in that archway just as those two went by. But I don't know that I should call what was written on the paper nonsense; it is bizarre certainly but I expect it has a meaning for somebody. Just repeat it again, will you, and I will write it down. Perhaps we might find a cipher of some sort, though I hardly think we shall."

Again had the reluctant lips of Salisbury slowly to stammer out the rubbish that he abhorred, while Dyson jotted it down on a slip of paper.

"Look over it, will you?" he said, when it was done; "it may important that I should have every word in its place. Is that all right?"

"Yes; that is an accurate copy. But I don't think you will get much out of it. Depend upon it, it is mere nonsense, a wanton scribble. I must be going now, Dyson. No, no more; that stuff of yours is pretty strong. Goodnight."

"I suppose you would like to hear from me, if I did find out anything?"

"No, not I; I don't want to hear about the thing again. You may regard the discovery, if it is one, as your own."

"Very well. Goodnight."

IV

A good many hours after Salisbury had returned to the company of the green rep chairs, Dyson still sat at his desk, itself a Japanese romance, smoking many pipes, and meditating over his friend's story. The bizarre quality of the inscription which had annoyed Salisbury was to him an attraction, and now and again he took it up and scanned thoughtfully what he had written, especially the quaint jingle at the end. It was a token, a symbol, he decided, and not a cipher, and the woman who had flung it away was in all probability entirely ignorant of its meaning; she was but the agent of the "Sam" she had abused and discarded, and he too was again the agent of someone unknown; possibly of the individual styled Q, who had been forced to visit his French friends. But what to make of "Traverse Handel S." Here was the root and source of the enigma, and not all the tobacco of Virginia seemed likely to suggest any clue here. It seemed almost hopeless, but Dyson regarded himself as the Wellington of mysteries, and went to bed feeling assured that sooner or later he would hit upon the right track. For the next few days he was deeply engaged in his literary labours, labours which were a profound mystery even to the most intimate of his friends, who searched the railway bookstalls in vain for the result of so many hours spent at the Japanese bureau in company with strong tobacco and black tea. On this occasion Dyson confined himself to his room for four days, and it was with genuine relief that he laid down his pen and went out into the streets in quest of relaxation and fresh air. The gas-lamps were being lighted, and the fifth edition of the evening papers was being howled through the streets, and Dyson, feeling that he wanted quiet, turned away from the clamorous Strand, and began to trend away to the north-west. Soon he found himself in streets that echoed to his footsteps, and crossing a broad new thoroughfare, and verging still to the west, Dyson discovered that he had penetrated to the depths of Soho. Here again was life; rare vintages of France and Italy, at prices which seemed contemptibly small, allured the passerby; here were cheeses, vast and rich, here olive oil, and here a grove of Rabelaisian sausages; while in a neighbouring shop the whole Press of Paris appeared to be on sale. In the middle of the roadway a strange miscellany of nations sauntered to and fro, for there cab and hansom rarely ventured; and from window over window the inhabitants looked forth in pleased contemplation of the scene. Dyson made his way slowly along, mingling with the crowd on the cobble-stones, listening to the queer babel of French and German, and Italian and English, glancing now and again at the shop windows with their levelled batteries of bottles, and had almost gained the end of the street, when his attention was arrested by a small shop at the corner, a vivid contrast to its neighbours. It was the typical shop of the poor quarter; a shop entirely English. Here were vended tobacco and sweets, cheap pipes of clay and cherry-wood; penny exercise-books and pen-holders jostled for precedence with comic songs, and story papers with appalling cuts showed that romance claimed its place beside the actualities of the evening paper, the bills of which fluttered at the doorway. Dyson glanced up at the name above the door, and stood by the kennel trembling, for a sharp pang, the pang of one who has made a discovery, had for a moment left him incapable of motion. The name over the shop was Travers. Dyson looked up again, this time at the corner of the wall above the lamppost, and read in white letters on a blue ground the words "Handel Street, W.C." and the legend was repeated in fainter letters just below. He gave a little sigh of satisfaction, and without more ado walked boldly into the shop, and stared full in the face of the fat man who was sitting behind the counter. The fellow rose to his feet, and returned the stare a little curiously, and then began in stereotyped phrase—

"What can I do for you, sir?"

Dyson enjoyed the situation and a dawning perplexity on the man's face. He propped his stick carefully against the counter and leaning over it, said slowly and impressively—

"Once around the grass, and twice around the lass, and thrice around the maple-tree."

Dyson had calculated on his words producing an effect, and he was not disappointed. The vendor of the miscellanies gasped, open-mouthed like a fish, and steadied himself against the counter. When he spoke, after a short interval, it was in a hoarse mutter, tremulous and unsteady.

"Would you mind saying that again, sir? I didn't quite catch it."

"My good man, I shall most certainly do nothing of the kind. You heard what I said perfectly well. You have got a clock in your shop, I see; an admirable time-keeper, I have no doubt. Well, I give you a minute by your own clock."

The man looked about him in a perplexed indecision, and Dyson felt that it was time to be bold.

"Look here, Travers, the time is nearly up. You have heard of Q, I think. Remember, I hold your life in my hands. Now!"

Dyson was shocked at the result of his own audacity. The man shrank and shrivelled in terror, the sweat poured down a face of ashy white, and he held up his hands before him.

"Mr. Davies, Mr. Davies, don't say that—don't for Heaven's sake. I didn't know you at first, I didn't indeed. Good God! Mr. Davies, you wouldn't ruin me? I'll get it in a moment."

"You had better not lose anymore time."

The man slunk piteously out of his own shop, and went into a back parlour. Dyson heard his trembling fingers fumbling with a bunch of keys, and the creak of an opening box. He came back presently with a small package neatly tied up in brown paper in his hands, and still, full of terror, handed it to Dyson.

"I'm glad to be rid of it," he said. "I'll take no more jobs of this sort."

Dyson took the parcel and his stick, and walked out of the shop with a nod, turning round as he passed the door. Travers had sunk into his seat, his face still white with terror, with one hand over his eyes, and Dyson speculated a good deal as he walked rapidly away as to what queer chords those could be on which he had played so roughly. He hailed the first hansom he could see and drove home, and when he had lit his hanging lamp, and laid his parcel on the table, he paused for a moment, wondering on what strange thing the lamplight would soon shine. He locked his door, and cut the strings, and unfolded the paper layer after layer, and came at last to a small wooden box, simply but solidly made. There was no lock, and Dyson had simply to raise the lid, and as he did so he drew a long breath and started back. The lamp seemed to glimmer feebly like a single candle, but the whole room blazed with light—and not with light alone, but with a thousand colours, with all the glories of some painted window; and upon the walls of his room and on the familiar furniture, the glow flamed back and seemed to flow again to its source, the little wooden box. For there upon a bed of soft wool lay the most splendid jewel, a jewel such as Dyson had never dreamed of, and within it shone the blue of far skies, and the green of the sea by the shore, and the red of the ruby, and deep violet rays, and in the middle of all it seemed aflame as if a fountain of fire rose up, and fell, and rose again with sparks like stars for drops. Dyson gave a long deep sigh, and dropped into his chair, and put his hands over his eyes to think. The jewel was like an opal, but from a long experience of the shop-windows he knew there was no such thing as an opal one-quarter or one-eighth of its size. He looked at the stone again, with a feeling that was almost awe, and placed it gently on the table under the lamp, and watched the wonderful flame that shone and sparkled in its centre, and then turned to the box, curious to know whether it might contain other marvels. He lifted the bed of wool on which the opal had reclined, and saw beneath, no more jewels, but a little old pocket-book, worn and shabby with use. Dyson opened it at the first leaf, and dropped the book again appalled. He had read the name of the owner, neatly written in blue ink:

> STEVEN BLACK, M.D.,
> Oranmore,
> Devon Road,
> Harlesden.

It was several minutes before Dyson could bring himself to open the book a second time; he remembered the wretched exile in his garret; and his strange talk, and the memory too of the face he had seen at the window, and of what the specialist had said, surged up in his mind, and as he held his finger on the cover, he shivered, dreading what might be written within. When at last he held it in his hand, and turned the pages, he found that the first two leaves were blank, but the third was covered with clear, minute writing, and Dyson began to read with the light of the opal flaming in his eyes.

V

E ver since I was a young man"—the record began—"I devoted all my leisure and a good deal of time that ought to have been given to other studies to the investigation of curious and obscure branches of knowledge. What are commonly called the pleasures of life had never any attractions for me, and I lived alone in London, avoiding my fellow students, and in my turn avoided by them as a man self-absorbed and unsympathetic. So long as I could gratify my desire of knowledge of a peculiar kind, knowledge of which the very existence is a profound secret to most men, I was intensely happy, and I have often spent whole nights sitting in the darkness of my room, and thinking of the strange world on the brink of which I trod. My professional studies, however, and the necessity of obtaining a degree, for sometime forced my more obscure employment into the background, and soon after I had qualified I met Agnes, who became my wife. We took a new house in this remote suburb, and I began the regular routine of a sober practice, and for some months lived happily enough, sharing in the life about me, and only thinking at odd intervals of that occult science which had once fascinated my whole being. I had learnt enough of the paths I had begun to tread to know that they were beyond all expression difficult and dangerous, that to persevere meant in all probability the wreck of a life, and that they led to regions so terrible, that the mind of man shrinks appalled at the very thought. Moreover, the quiet and the peace I had enjoyed since my marriage had wiled me away to a great extent from places where I knew no peace could dwell. But suddenly—I think indeed it was the work of a single night, as I lay awake on my bed gazing into the darkness—suddenly, I say, the old desire, the former longing, returned, and returned with a force that had been intensified ten times by its absence; and when the day dawned and I looked out of the window, and saw with haggard eyes the sunrise in the east, I knew that my doom had been pronounced; that as I had gone far, so now I must go farther with unfaltering steps. I turned to the bed where my wife was sleeping peacefully, and lay down again, weeping bitter tears, for the sun had set on our happy life and had risen with a dawn of terror to us both. I will not set down here in minute detail what followed; outwardly I went about the day's labour as before, saying nothing to my wife. But she soon saw that I had changed; I spent my spare time in a room which I had fitted up as a laboratory, and often I crept upstairs in the grey dawn of the morning, when the light of many lamps still glowed over London; and each night I had stolen a step nearer to that great abyss which I was to bridge over, the gulf between the world of consciousness and the world of matter. My experiments were many and complicated in their nature, and it was some months before I realised whither they all pointed, and when this was borne in upon me in a moment's time, I felt my face whiten and my heart still within me. But the power to draw back, the power to stand before the doors that now opened wide before me and not to enter in, had long ago been absent; the way was closed, and I could only pass onward. My position was as utterly hopeless as that of the prisoner in an utter dungeon, whose only light is that of the dungeon above him; the doors were shut and escape was impossible. Experiment after experiment gave the same result, and I knew, and shrank even as the thought passed through my mind, that in the work I had to do there must be elements which no laboratory could furnish, which no scales could ever measure. In that work, from which even I doubted to escape with life, life itself must enter; from some human being there must be drawn that essence which men call the soul, and in its place (for in the scheme of the world there is no vacant chamber)—in its place would enter in what the lips can hardly utter, what the mind cannot conceive without a horror more awful than the horror of death itself. And when I knew this, I knew also on whom this fate would fall; I looked into my wife's eyes. Even at that hour, if I had gone out and taken a rope and hanged myself, I might have escaped, and she also, but in no other way. At last I told her all. She shuddered, and wept, and called on her dead mother for help, and asked me if I had no mercy, and I could only sigh. I concealed nothing from her; I told her what she would become, and what would enter in where her life had been; I told her of all the shame and of all the horror. You who will read this when I am dead—if indeed I allow this record to survive—you who have opened the box and have seen what lies there, if you could understand what lies hidden in that opal! For one night my wife consented to what I asked of her, consented with the tears running down her beautiful face, and hot shame flushing red over her neck and breast, consented to undergo this for me. I threw open the window, and we looked together at the sky and the dark earth for the last time; it was a fine star-light night, and there was a pleasant breeze blowing: and I kissed her on her lips, and her tears ran down upon my face. That night she came down to my laboratory, and there, with shutters bolted and barred down, with curtains drawn thick and close, so that the very stars might be shut out from the sight of that room, while the crucible hissed and boiled over the lamp, I did what had to be done, and led out what was no longer a woman. But on the table the opal flamed and sparkled with such light as no eyes of man have ever gazed on, and the rays of the flame that was within it flashed and glittered, and shone even to my heart. My wife had only asked one thing of me; that when there came at last what I had told her, I would kill her. I have kept that promise."

There was nothing more. Dyson let the little pocket-book fall, and turned and looked again at the opal with its flaming inmost light, and then with unutterable irresistible horror surging up in his heart, grasped the jewel, and flung it on the ground, and trampled it beneath his heel. His face was white with terror as he turned away, and for a moment stood sick and trembling, and then with a start he leapt across the room and steadied himself against the door. There was an angry hiss, as of steam escaping under great pressure, and as he gazed, motionless, a volume of heavy yellow smoke was slowly issuing from the very centre of the jewel, and wreathing itself in snakelike coils above it. And then a thin white flame burst forth from the smoke, and shot up into the air and vanished; and on the ground there lay a thing like a cinder, black and crumbling to the touch.

THE END

THE SHINING PYRAMID

I

The Arrow-head Character

H aunted, you said?"

"Yes, haunted. Don't you remember, when I saw you three years ago, you told me about your place in the west with the ancient woods hanging all about it, and the wild, domed hills, and the ragged land? It has always remained a sort of enchanted picture in my mind as I sit at my desk and hear the traffic rattling in the Street in the midst of whirling London. But when did you come up?"

"The fact is, Dyson, I have only just got out of the train. I drove to the station early this morning and caught the 10.45."

"Well, I am very glad you looked in on me. How have you been getting on since we last met? There is no Mrs. Vaughan, I suppose?"

"No," said Vaughan, "I am still a hermit, like yourself. I have done nothing but loaf about."

Vaughn had lit his pipe and sat in the elbow chair, fidgeting and glancing about him in a somewhat dazed and restless manner. Dyson had wheeled round his chair when his visitor entered and sat with one arm fondly reclining on the desk of his bureau, and touching the litter of manuscript.

"And you are still engaged in the old task?" said Vaughan, pointing to the pile of papers and the teeming pigeon-holes.

"Yes, the vain pursuit of literature, as idle as alchemy, and as entrancing. But you have come to town for sometime I suppose; what shall we do tonight?"

"Well, I rather wanted you to try a few days with me down in the west. It would do you a lot of good. I'm sure."

"You are very kind, Vaughan, but London in September is hard to leave. Doré could not have designed anything more wonderful and mystic than Oxford Street as I saw it the other evening; the sunset flaming, the blue haze transmuting the plain street into a road 'far in the spiritual city.'"

"I should like you to come down though. You would enjoy roaming over our hills. Does this racket go on all day and night? It quite bewilders me; I wonder how you can work through it. I am sure you would revel in the great peace of my old home among the woods."

Vaughan lit his pipe again, and looked anxiously at Dyson to see if his inducements had had any effect, but the man of letters shook his head, smiling, and vowed in his heart a firm allegiance to the streets.

"You cannot tempt me," he said.

"Well, you may be right. Perhaps, after all, I was wrong to speak of the peace of the country. There, when a tragedy does occur, it is like a stone thrown into a pond; the circles of disturbance keep on widening, and it seems as if the water would never be still again."

"Have you ever any tragedies where you are?"

"I can hardly say that. But I was a good deal disturbed about a month ago by something that happened; it may or may not have been a tragedy in the usual sense of the word."

"What was the occurrence?"

"Well, the fact is a girl disappeared in a way which seems highly mysterious. Her parents, people of the name of Trevor, are well-to-do farmers, and their eldest daughter Annie was a sort of village beauty; she was really remarkably handsome. One afternoon she thought she would go and see her aunt, a widow who farms her own land, and as the two houses are only about five or six miles apart, she started off, telling her parents she would take the short cut over the hills. She never got to her aunt's, and she never was seen again. That's putting it in a few words."

"What an extraordinary thing! I suppose there are no disused mines, are there, on the hills? I don't think you quite run to anything so formidable as a precipice?"

"No; the path the girl must have taken had no pitfalls of any description; it is just a track over wild, bare hillside, far, even from a byroad. One may walk for miles without meeting a soul, but it is perfectly safe."

"And what do people say about it?"

"Oh, they talk nonsense—among themselves. You have no notion as to how superstitious English cottagers are in out-of-the-way parts like mine. They are as bad as the Irish, every whit, and even more secretive."

"But what do they say?"

"Oh, the poor girl is supposed to have 'gone with the fairies,' or to have been 'taken by the fairies.' Such stuff!" he went on, "one would laugh if it were not for the real tragedy of the case."

Dyson looked somewhat interested.

"Yes," he said, "'fairies' certainly strike a little curiously on the ear in these days. But what do the police say? I presume they do not accept the fairy-tale hypothesis?"

"No; but they seem quite at fault. What I am afraid of is that Annie Trevor must have fallen in with some scoundrels on her way. Castletown is a large seaport, you know, and some of the worst of the foreign sailors occasionally desert their ships and go on the tramp up and down the country. Not many years ago a Spanish sailor named Garcia murdered a whole family for the sake of plunder that was not worth sixpence. They are hardly human, some of these fellows, and I am dreadfully afraid the poor girl must have come to an awful end."

"But no foreign sailor was seen by anyone about the country?"

"No; there is certainly that; and of course country people are quick to notice anyone whose appearance and dress are a little out of the common. Still it seems as if my theory were the only possible explanation."

"There are no data to go upon," said Dyson, thoughtfully. "There was no question of a love affair, or anything of the kind, I suppose?"

"Oh, no, not a hint of such a thing. I am sure if Annie were alive she would have contrived to let her mother know of her safety."

"No doubt, no doubt. Still it is barely possible that she is alive and yet unable to communicate with her friends. But all this must have disturbed you a good deal."

"Yes, it did; I hate a mystery, and especially a mystery which is probably the veil of horror. But frankly, Dyson, I want to make a clean breast of it; I did not come here to tell you all this."

"Of course not," said Dyson, a little surprised at Vaughan's uneasy manner. "You came to have a chat on more cheerful topics."

"No, I did not. What I have been telling you about happened a month ago, but something which seems likely to affect me more personally has taken place within the last few days, and to be quite plain, I came up to town with the idea that you might be able to help me. You recollect that curious case you spoke to me about on our last meeting; something about a spectacle-maker."

"Oh, yes, I remember that. I know I was quite proud of my acumen at the time; even to this day the police have no idea why those peculiar yellow spectacles were wanted. But, Vaughan, you really look quite put out; I hope there is nothing serious?"

"No, I think I have been exaggerating, and I want you to reassure me. But what has happened is very odd."

"And what has happened?"

"I am sure that you will laugh at me, but this is the story. You must know there is a path, a right of way, that goes through my land, and to be precise, close to the wall of the kitchen garden. It is not used by many people; a woodman now and again finds it useful, and five or six children who go to school in the village pass twice a day. Well, a few days ago I was taking a walk about the place before breakfast, and I happened to stop to fill my pipe just by the large doors in the garden wall. The wood, I must tell you, comes to within a few feet of the wall, and the track I spoke of runs right in the shadow of the trees. I thought the shelter from a brisk wind that was blowing rather pleasant, and I stood there smoking with my eyes on the ground. Then something caught my attention. Just under the wall, on the short grass; a number of small flints were arranged in a pattern; something like this": and Mr. Vaughan caught at a pencil and piece of paper, and dotted down a few strokes.

"You see," he went on, "there were, I should think, twelve little stones neatly arranged in lines, and spaced at equal distances, as I have shown it on the paper. They were pointed stones, and the points were very carefully directed one way."

"Yes," said Dyson, without much interest, "no doubt the children you have mentioned had been playing there on their way from school. Children, as you know, are very fond of making such devices with oyster shells or flints or flowers, or with whatever comes in their way."

"So I thought; I just noticed these flints were arranged in a sort of pattern and then went on. But the next morning I was taking the same round, which, as a matter of fact, is habitual with me, and again I saw at the same spot a device in flints. This time it was really a curious pattern; something like the spokes of a wheel, all meeting at a common centre, and this centre formed by a device which looked like a bowl; all, you understand done in flints."

"You are right," said Dyson, "that seems odd enough. Still it is reasonable that your half-a-dozen school children are responsible for these fantasies in stone."

"Well, I thought I would set the matter at rest. The children pass the gate every evening at half-past five, and I walked by at six, and found the device just as I had left it in the morning. The next day I was up and about at a quarter to seven, and I found the whole thing had been changed. There was a pyramid outlined in flints upon the grass. The children I saw going by an hour and a half later, and they ran past the spot without glancing to right or left. In the evening I watched them going home, and this morning when I got to the gate at six o'clock there was a thing like a half moon waiting for me."

"So then the series runs thus: firstly ordered lines, then, the device of the spokes and the bowl, then the pyramid, and finally, this morning, the half moon. That is the order, isn't it?"

"Yes; that is right. But do you know it has made me feel very uneasy? I suppose it seems absurd, but I can't help thinking that some kind of signalling is going on under my nose, and that sort of thing is disquieting."

"But what have you to dread? You have no enemies?"

"No; but I have some very valuable old plate."

"You are thinking of burglars then?" said Dyson, with an accent of considerable interest, "but you must know your neighbours. Are there any suspicious characters about?"

"Not that I am aware of. But you remember what I told you of the sailors."

"Can you trust your servants?"

"Oh, perfectly. The plate is preserved in a strong room; the butler, an old family servant, alone knows where the key is kept. There is nothing wrong there. Still, everybody is aware that I have a lot of old silver, and all country folks are given to gossip. In that way information may have got abroad in very undesirable quarters."

"Yes, but I confess there seems something a little unsatisfactory in the burglar theory. Who is signalling to whom? I cannot see my way to accepting such an explanation. What put the plate into your head in connection with these flints signs, or whatever one may call them?"

"It was the figure of the Bowl," said Vaughan. "I happen to possess a very large and very valuable Charles II punch-bowl. The chasing is really exquisite, and the thing is worth a lot of money. The sign I described to you was exactly the same shape as my punch-bowl."

"A queer coincidence certainly. But the other figures or devices: you have nothing shaped like a pyramid?"

"Ah, you will think that queerer. As it happens, this punch-bowl of mine, together with a set of rare old ladles, is kept in a mahogany chest of a pyramidal shape. The four sides slope upwards, the narrow towards the top."

"I confess all this interests me a good deal," said Dyson. "let us go on then. What about the other figures; how about the Army, as we may call the first sign, and the Crescent or Half moon?"

"Ah, there is no reference that I can make out of these two. Still, you see I have some excuse for curiosity at all events. I should be very vexed to lose any of the old plate; nearly all the pieces have been in the family for generations. And I cannot get it out of my head that some scoundrels mean to rob me, and are communicating with one another every night."

"Frankly," said Dyson, "I can make nothing of it; I am as much in the dark as yourself. Your theory seems certainly the only possible explanation, and yet the difficulties are immense."

He leaned back in his chair, and the two men faced each other, frowning, and perplexed by so bizarre a problem.

"By the way," said Dyson, after a long pause, "what is your geological formation down there?"

Mr. Vaughan looked up, a good deal surprised by the question.

"Old red sandstone and limestone, I believe," he said. "We are just beyond the coal measures, you know."

"But surely there are no flints either in the sandstone or the limestone?"

"No, I never see any flints in the fields. I confess that did strike me as a little curious."

"I should think so! It is very important. By the way, what size were the flints used in making these devices?"

"I happen to have brought one with me; I took it this morning."

"From the Half moon?"

"Exactly. Here it is."

He handed over a small flint, tapering to a point, and about three inches in length.

Dyson's face blazed up with excitement as he took the thing from Vaughan.

"Certainly," he said, after a moment's pause, "you have some curious neighbours in your country. I hardly think they can harbour any designs on your punch-bowl. Do you know this is a flint arrowhead of vast antiquity, and not only that, but an arrow-head of a unique kind? I have seen specimens from all parts of the world, but there are features about this thing that are quite peculiar." He laid down his pipe, and took out a book from a drawer.

"We shall just have time to catch the 5.45 to Castletown," he said.

II

The Eyes on the Wall

M r. Dyson drew in a long breath of the air of the hills and felt all the enchantment of the scene about him. It was very early morning, and he stood on the terrace in the front of the house.

Vaughan's ancestor had built on the lower slope of a great hill, in the shelter of a deep and ancient wood that gathered on three sides about the house, and on the fourth side, the southwest, the land fell gently away and sank to the valley, where a brook wound in and out in mystic esses, and the dark and gleaming alders tracked the stream's course to the eye. On the terrace in the sheltered place no wind blew, and far beyond, the trees were still. Only one sound broke in upon the silence, and Dyson heard the noise of the brook singing far below, the song of clear and shining water rippling over the stones, whispering and murmuring as it sank to dark deep pools.

Across the stream, just below the house, rose a grey stone bridge, vaulted and buttressed, a fragment of the Middle Ages, and then beyond the bridge the hills rose again, vast and rounded like bastions, covered here and there with dark woods and thickets of undergrowth, but the heights were all bare of trees, showing only grey turf and patches of bracken, touched here and there with the gold of fading fronds; Dyson looked to the north and south, and still he saw the wall of the hills, and the ancient woods, and the stream drawn in and out between them; all grey and dim with morning mist beneath a grey sky in a hushed and haunted air.

Mr. Vaughan's voice broke in upon the silence.

"I thought you would be too tired to be about so early," he said. "I see you are admiring the view. It is very pretty, isn't it, though I suppose old Meyrick Vaughan didn't think much about the scenery when he built the house. A queer grey, old place, isn't it?"

"Yes, and how it fits into the surroundings; it seems of a piece with the grey hills and the grey bridge below."

"I am afraid I have brought you down on false pretences, Dyson," said Vaughan, as they began to walk up and down the terrace. "I have been to the place, and there is not a sign of anything this morning."

"Ah, indeed. Well, suppose we go round together."

They walked across the lawn and went by a path through the ilex shrubbery to the back of the house. There Vaughan pointed out the track leading down to the valley and up to the heights above the wood, and presently they stood beneath the garden wall, by the door.

"Here, you see, it was," said Vaughan, pointing to a spot on the turf. "I was standing just where you are now that morning I first saw the flints."

"Yes, quite so. That morning it was the Army, as I call it; then the Bowl, then the Pyramid, and, yesterday, the Half moon. What a queer old stone that is," he went on, pointing to a block of limestone rising out of the turf just beneath the wall. "It looks like a sort of dwarf pillar, but I suppose it is natural."

"Oh, yes, I think so. I imagine it was brought here, though, as we stand on the red sandstone. No doubt it was used as a foundation stone for some older building."

"Very likely," Dyson was peering about him attentively, looking from the ground to the wall, and from the wall to the deep wood that hung almost over the garden and made the place dark even in the morning.

"Look here," said Dyson at length, "it is certainly a case of children this time. Look at that." He was bending down and staring at the dull red surface of the mellowed bricks of the wall.

Vaughan came up and looked hard where Dyson's finger was pointing, and could scarcely distinguish a faint mark in deeper red.

"What is it?" he said. "I can make nothing of it."

"Look a little more closely. Don't you see it is an attempt to draw the human eye?"

"Ah, now I see what you mean. My sight is not very sharp. Yes, so it is, it is meant for an eye, no doubt, as you say. I thought the children learnt drawing at school."

"Well, it is an odd eye enough. Do you notice the peculiar almond shape; almost like the eye of a Chinaman?"

Dyson looked meditatively at the work of the undeveloped artist, and scanned the wall again, going down on his knees in the minuteness of his inquisition.

"I should like very much," he said at length, "to know how a child in this out of the way place could have any idea of the shape of the Mongolian eye. You see the average child has a very distinct impression of the subject; he draws a circle, or something like a circle, and put a dot in the centre. I don't think any child imagines that the eye is really made like that; it's just a convention of infantile art. But this almond-shaped thing puzzles me extremely. Perhaps it may be derived from a gilt Chinaman on a tea-canister in the grocer's shop. Still that's hardly likely."

"But why are you so sure it was done by a child?"

"Why! Look at the height. These old-fashioned bricks are little more than two inches thick; there are twenty courses from the ground to the sketch if we call it so; that gives a height of three and a half feet. Now, just imagine you are going to draw something on this wall. Exactly; your pencil, if you had one, would touch the wall somewhere on the level with your eyes, that is, more than five feet from the ground. It seems, therefore, a very simple deduction to conclude that this eye on the wall was drawn by a child about ten years old."

"Yes, I had not thought of that. Of course one of the children must have done it."

"I suppose so; and yet as I said, there is something singularly unchildlike about those two lines, and the eyeball itself, you see, is almost an oval. To my mind, the thing has an odd, ancient air; and a touch that is not altogether pleasant. I cannot help fancying that if we could see a whole face from the same hand it would not be altogether agreeable. However, that is nonsense, after all, and we are not getting farther in our investigations. It is odd that the flint series has come to such an abrupt end."

The two men walked away towards the house, and as they went in at the porch there was a break in the grey sky, and a gleam of sunshine on the grey hill before them.

All the day Dyson prowled meditatively about the fields and woods surrounding the house. He was thoroughly and completely puzzled by the trivial circumstances he proposed to elucidate, and now he again took the flint arrow-head from his pocket, turning it over and examining it with deep attention. There was something about the thing that was altogether different from the specimens he had seen at the museums and private collections; the shape was of a distinct type, and around the edge there was a line of little punctured dots, apparently a suggestion of ornament. Who, thought Dyson, could possess such things in so remote a place; and who, possessing the flints, could have put them to the fantastic use of designing meaningless figures under Vaughan's garden wall? The rank absurdity of the whole affair offended him unutterably; and as one theory after another rose in his mind only to be rejected, he felt strongly tempted to take the next train back to town. He had seen the silver plate which Vaughan treasured, and had inspected the punch-bowl, the gem of the collection, with close attention; and what he saw and his interview with the butler convinced him that a plot to rob the strong box was out of the limits of enquiry. The chest in which the bowl was kept, a heavy piece of mahogany, evidently dating from the beginning of the century, was certainly strongly suggestive of a pyramid, and Dyson was at first inclined to the inept manoeuvres of the detective, but a little sober thought convinced him of the impossibility of the burglary hypothesis, and he cast wildly about for something more satisfying. He asked Vaughan if there were any gipsies in the neighbourhood, and heard that the Romany had not been seen for years. This dashed him a good deal, as he knew the gipsy habit of leaving queer hieroglyphics on the line of march, and had been much elated when the thought occurred to him. He was facing Vaughan by the old-fashioned hearth when he put the question, and leaned back in his chair in disgust at the destruction of his theory.

"It is odd," said Vaughan, "but the gipsies never trouble us here. Now and then the farmers find traces of fires in the wildest part of the hills, but nobody seems to know who the fire-lighters are."

"Surely that looks like gipsies?"

"No, not in such places as those. Tinkers and gipsies and wanderers of all sorts stick to the roads and don't go very far from the farmhouses."

"Well, I can make nothing of it. I saw the children going by this afternoon, and, as you say, they ran straight on. So we shall have no more eyes on the wall at all events."

"No, I must waylay them one of these days and find out who is the artist."

The next morning when Vaughan strolled in his usual course from the lawn to the back of the house he found Dyson already awaiting him by the garden door, and evidently in a state of high excitement, for he beckoned furiously with his hand, and gesticulated violently.

"What is it?" asked Vaughan. "The flints again?"

"No; but look here, look at the wall. There; don't you see it?"

"There's another of those eyes!"

"Exactly. Drawn, you see, at a little distance from the first, almost on the same level, but slightly lower."

"What on earth is one to make of it? It couldn't have been done by

ARTHUR MACHEN

the children; it wasn't there last night, and they won't pass for another hour. What can it mean?"

"I think the very devil is at the bottom of all this," said Dyson. "Of course, one cannot resist the conclusion that these infernal almond eyes are to be set down to the same agency as the devices in the arrow-heads; and where that conclusion is to lead us is more than I can tell. For my part, I have to put a strong check on my imagination, or it would run wild."

"Vaughan," he said, as they turned away from the wall, "has it struck you that there is one point—a very curious point—in common between the figures done in flints and the eyes drawn on the wall?"

"What is that?" asked Vaughan, on whose face there had fallen a certain shadow of indefinite dread.

"It is this. We know that the signs of the Army, the Bowl, the Pyramid, and the Half moon must have been done at night. Presumably they were meant to be seen at night. Well, precisely the same reasoning applies to those eyes on the wall."

"I do not quite see your point."

"Oh, surely. The nights are dark just now, and have been very cloudy, I know, since I came down. Moreover, those overhanging trees would throw that wall into deep shadow even on a clear night."

"Well?"

"What struck me was this. What very peculiarly sharp eyesight, they, whoever 'they' are, must have to be able to arrange arrow-heads in intricate order in the blackest shadow of the wood, and then draw the eyes on the wall without a trace of bungling, or a false line."

"I have read of persons confined in dungeons for many years who have been able to see quite well in the dark," said Vaughan.

"Yes," said Dyson, "there was the abbé in Monte Cristo. But it is a singular point."

III

The Search for the Bowl

"Who was that old man that touched his hat to you just now?" said Dyson, as they came to the bend of the lane near the house.

"Oh, that was old Trevor. He looks very broken, poor old fellow."

"Who is Trevor?"

"Don't you remember? I told you the story that afternoon I came to your rooms—about a girl named Annie Trevor, who disappeared in the most inexplicable manner about five weeks ago. That was her father."

"Yes, yes, I recollect now. To tell the truth I had forgotten all about it. And nothing has been heard of the girl?"

"Nothing whatever. The police are quite at fault."

"I am afraid I did not pay very much attention to the details you gave me. Which way did the girl go?"

"Her path would take her right across those wild hills above the house: the nearest point in the track must be about two miles from here."

"Is it near that little hamlet I saw yesterday?"

"You mean Croesyceiliog, where the children came from? No; it goes more to the north."

"Ah, I have never been that way."

They went into the house, and Dyson shut himself up in his room, sunk deep in doubtful thought, but yet with the shadow of a suspicion growing within him that for a while haunted his brain, all vague and fantastic, refusing to take definite form. He was sitting by the open window and looking out on the valley and saw, as if in a picture, the intricate winding of the brook, the grey bridge, and the vast hills rising beyond; all still and without a breath of wind to stir the mystic hanging woods, and the evening sunshine glowed warm on the bracken, and down below a faint mist, pure white, began to rise from the stream. Dyson sat by the window as the day darkened and the huge bastioned hills loomed vast and vague, and the woods became dim and more shadowy: and the fancy that had seized him no longer appeared altogether impossible. He passed the rest of the evening in a reverie, hardly hearing what Vaughan said; and when he took his candle in the hall, he paused a moment before bidding his friend goodnight.

"I want a good rest," he said. "I have got some work to do tomorrow."

"Some writing, you mean?"

"No. I am going to look for the Bowl."

"The Bowl! If you mean my punch-bowl, that is safe in the chest."

"I don't mean the punch-bowl. You may take my word for it that your plate has never been threatened. No; I will not bother you with any suppositions. We shall in all probability have something much stronger than suppositions before long. Goodnight, Vaughan."

The next morning Dyson set off after breakfast. He took the path by the garden wall, and noted that there were now eight of the weird almond eyes dimly outlined on the brick.

"Six days more," he said to himself, but as he thought over the theory he had formed, he shrank, in spite of strong conviction, from such a wildly incredible fancy. He struck up through the dense shadows of the wood, and at length came out on the bare hillside, and climbed higher and higher over the slippery turf, keeping well to the north, and following the indications given him by Vaughan. As he went on, he seemed to mount ever higher above the world of human life and customary things; to his right he looked at a fringe of orchard and saw a faint blue smoke rising like a pillar; there was the hamlet from which the children came to school, and there the only sign of life, for the woods embowered and concealed Vaughan's old grey house. As he reached what seemed the summit of the hill, he realized for the first time the desolate loneliness and strangeness of the land; there was nothing but grey sky and grey hill, a high, vast plain that seemed to stretch on forever and ever, and a faint glimpse of a blue-peaked mountain far away and to the north. At length he came to the path, a slight track scarcely noticeable, and from its position and by what Vaughan had told him he knew that it was the way the lost girl, Annie Trevor, must have taken. He followed the path on the bare hill-top, noticing the great limestone rocks that cropped out of the turf, grim and hideous, and of an aspect as forbidding as an idol of the South Seas; and suddenly he halted, astonished, although he had found what he searched for.

Almost without warning the ground shelved suddenly away on all sides, and Dyson looked down into a circular depression, which might well have been a Roman amphitheatre, and the ugly crags of limestone rimmed it round as if with a broken wall. Dyson walked round the hollow, and noted the position of the stones, and then turned on his way home.

"This," he thought to himself, "is more than curious. The Bowl is discovered, but where is the Pyramid?"

"My dear Vaughan," he said, when he got back, "I may tell you that I have found the Bowl, and that that is all I shall tell you for the present. We have six days of absolute inaction before us; there is really nothing to be done."

IV

The Secret of the Pyramid

I have just been round the garden," said Vaughan one morning. "I have been counting those infernal eyes, and I find there are fourteen of them. For heaven's sake, Dyson, tell me what the meaning of it all is."

"I should be very sorry to attempt to do so. I may have guessed this or that, but I always make it a principle to keep my guesses to myself. Besides, it is really not worth while anticipating events; you will remember my telling you that we had six days of inaction before us? Well, this is the sixth day, and the last of idleness. Tonight, I propose we take a stroll."

"A stroll! Is that all the action you mean to take?"

"Well, it may show you some very curious things. To be plain, I want you to start with me at nine o'clock this evening for the hills. We may have to be out all night, so you had better wrap up well, and bring some of that brandy."

"Is it a joke?" asked Vaughan, who was bewildered with strange events and strange surmises.

"No, I don't think there is much joke in it. Unless I am much mistaken we shall find a very serious explanation of the puzzle. You will come with me, I am sure?"

"Very good. Which way do you want to go?"

"By the path you told me of; the path Annie Trevor is supposed to have taken."

Vaughan looked white at the mention of the girl's name.

"I did not think you were on that track," he said. "I thought it was the affair of those devices in flint and of the eyes on the wall that you were engaged on. It's no good saying anymore, but I will go with you."

At a quarter to nine that evening the two men set out, taking the path through the wood, and up the hill-side. It was a dark and heavy night, the sky was thick with clouds, and the valley full of mist, and all the way they seemed to walk in a world of shadow and gloom, hardly speaking, and afraid to break the haunted silence. They came out at last on the steep hill-side, and instead of the oppression of the wood there was the long, dim sweep of the turf, and higher, the fantastic limestone rocks hinted horror through the darkness, and the wind sighed as it passed across the mountain to the sea, and in its passage beat chill about their hearts. They seemed to walk on and on for hours, and the dim outline of the hill still stretched before them, and the haggard rocks still loomed through the darkness, when suddenly Dyson whispered, drawing his breath quickly, and coming close to his companion:

"Here," he said, "we will lie down. I do not think there is anything yet."

"I know the place," said Vaughan, after a moment. "I have often been by in the daytime. The country people are afraid to come here, I believe; it is supposed to be a fairies' castle, or something of the kind. But why on earth have we come here?"

"Speak a little lower," said Dyson. "It might not do us any good if we are overheard."

"Overheard here! There is not a soul within three miles of us."

"Possibly not; indeed, I should say certainly not. But there might be a body somewhat nearer."

"I don't understand you in the least," said Vaughan, whispering to humour Dyson, "but why have we come here?"

"Well, you see this hollow before us is the Bowl. I think we had better not talk even in whispers."

They lay full length upon the turf; the rock between their faces and the Bowl, and now and again, Dyson, slouching his dark, soft hat over his forehead, put out the glint of an eye, and in a moment drew back, not daring to take a prolonged view. Again he laid an ear to the ground and listened, and the hours went by, and the darkness seemed to blacken, and the faint sigh of the wind was the only sound.

Vaughan grew impatient with this heaviness of silence, this watching for indefinite terror; for to him there was no shape or form of apprehension, and he began to think the whole vigil a dreary farce.

"How much longer is this to last?" he whispered to Dyson, and Dyson who had been holding his breath in the agony of attention put his mouth to Vaughan's ear and said:

"Will you listen?" with pauses between each syllable, and in the voice with which the priest pronounces the awful words.

Vaughan caught the ground with his hands, and stretched forward, wondering what he was to hear. At first there was nothing, and then a low and gentle noise came very softly from the Bowl, a faint sound, almost indescribable, but as if one held the tongue against the roof of the mouth and expelled the breath. He listened eagerly and presently the noise grew louder, and became a strident and horrible hissing as if the pit beneath boiled with fervent heat, and Vaughan, unable to remain in suspense any longer, drew his cap half over his face in imitation of Dyson, and looked down to the hollow below.

It did, in truth, stir and seethe like an infernal caldron. The whole of the sides and bottom tossed and writhed with vague and restless forms that passed to and fro without the sound of feet, and gathered thick here and there and seemed to speak to one another in those tones of horrible sibilance, like the hissing of snakes, that he had heard. It was as if the sweet turf and the cleanly earth had suddenly become quickened with some foul writhing growth. Vaughan could not draw back his face, though he felt Dyson's finger touch him, but he peered into the quaking mass and saw faintly that there were things like faces and human limbs, and yet he felt his inmost soul chill with the sure belief that no fellow soul or human thing stirred in all that tossing and hissing host. He looked aghast, choking back sobs of horror, and at length the loathsome forms gathered thickest about some vague object in the middle of the hollow, and the hissing of their speech grew more venomous, and he saw in the uncertain light the abominable limbs, vague and yet too plainly seen, writhe and intertwine, and he thought he heard, very faint, a low human moan striking through the noise of speech that was not of man. At his heart something seemed to whisper ever "the worm of corruption, the worm that dieth not," and grotesquely the image was pictured to his imagination of a piece of putrid offal stirring through and through with bloated and horrible creeping things. The writhing of the dusky limbs continued, they seemed clustered round the dark form in the middle of the hollow, and the sweat dripped and poured off Vaughan's forehead, and fell cold on his hand beneath his face.

Then, it seemed done in an instant, the loathsome mass melted and fell away to the sides of the Bowl, and for a moment Vaughan saw in the middle of the hollow the tossing of human arms.

But a spark gleamed beneath, a fire kindled, and as the voice of a woman cried out loud in a shrill scream of utter anguish and terror, a great pyramid of flame spired up like a bursting of a pent fountain, and threw a blaze of light upon the whole mountain. In that instant Vaughan saw the myriads beneath; the things made in the form of men but stunted like children hideously deformed, the faces with the almond eyes burning with evil and unspeakable lusts; the ghastly yellow of the mass of naked flesh and then as if by magic the place was empty, while the fire roared and crackled, and the flames shone abroad.

"You have seen the Pyramid," said Dyson in his ear, "the Pyramid of fire."

V

The Little People

"Then you recognize the thing?"

"Certainly. It is a brooch that Annie Trevor used to wear on Sundays; I remember the pattern. But where did you find it? You don't mean to say that you have discovered the girl?"

"My dear Vaughan, I wonder you have not guessed where I found the brooch. You have not forgotten last night already?"

"Dyson," said the other, speaking very seriously, "I have been turning it over in my mind this morning while you have been out. I have thought about what I saw, or perhaps I should say about what I thought I saw, and the only conclusion I can come to is this, that the thing won't bear recollection. As men live, I have lived soberly and honestly, in the fear of God, all my days, and all I can do is believe that I suffered from some monstrous delusion, from some phantasmagoria of the bewildered senses. You know we went home together in silence, not a word passed between us as to what I fancied I saw; had we not better agree to keep silence on the subject? When I took my walk in the peaceful morning sunshine, I thought all the earth seemed full of praise, and passing by that wall I noticed there were no more signs recorded, and I blotted out those that remained. The mystery is over, and we can live quietly again. I think some poison has been working for the last few weeks; I have trod on the verge of madness, but I am sane now."

Mr. Vaughan had spoken earnestly, and bent forward in his chair and glanced at Dyson with something of entreaty.

"My dear Vaughan," said the other, after a pause, "what's the use of this? It is much too late to take that tone; we have gone too deep. Besides you know as well as I that there is no delusion in the case; I wish there were with all my heart. No, in justice to myself I must tell you the whole story, so far as I know it."

"Very good," said Vaughan with a sigh, "if you must, you must."

"Then," said Dyson, "we will begin with the end if you please. I found this brooch you have just identified in the place we have called the Bowl. There was a heap of grey ashes, as if a fire had been burning, indeed, the embers were still hot, and this brooch was lying on the ground, just outside the range of the flame. It must have dropped accidentally from the dress of the person who was wearing it. No, don't interrupt me; we can pass now to the beginning, as we have had the end. Let us go back to that day you came to see me in my rooms in London. So far as I can remember, soon after you came in you mentioned, in a somewhat casual manner, that an unfortunate and mysterious incident had occurred in your part of the country; a girl named Annie Trevor had gone to see a relative, and had disappeared. I confess freely that what you said did not greatly interest me; there are so many reasons which may make it extremely convenient for a man and more especially a woman to vanish from the circle of their relations and friends. I suppose, if we were to consult the police, one would find that in London somebody disappears mysteriously every other week, and the officers would, no doubt, shrug their shoulders, and tell you that by the law of averages it could not be otherwise. So I was very culpably careless to your story, and besides, here is another reason for my lack of interest; your tale was inexplicable. You could only suggest a blackguard sailor on the tramp, but I discarded the explanation immediately.

"For many reasons, but chiefly because the occasional criminal, the amateur in brutal crime, is always found out, especially if he selects the country as the scene of his operations. You will remember the case of that Garcia you mentioned; he strolled into a railway station the day after the murder, his trousers covered with blood, and the works of the Dutch clock, his loot, tied in a neat parcel. So rejecting this, your only suggestion, the whole tale became, as I say, inexplicable, and, therefore, profoundly uninteresting. Yes, therefore, it is a perfectly valid conclusion. Do you ever trouble your head about problems which you know to be insoluble? Did you ever bestow much thought on the old puzzle of Achilles and the tortoise? Of course not, because you knew it was a hopeless quest, and so when you told me the story of a country girl who had disappeared I simply placed the whole thing down in the category of the insoluble, and thought no more about the matter. I was mistaken, so it has turned out; but if you remember, you immediately passed on to an affair which interested you more intensely, because personally, I need not go over the very singular narrative of the flint signs, at first I thought it all trivial, probably some children's game, and if not that a hoax of some sort; but your showing me the arrow-head awoke my acute interest. Here, I saw, there was something widely removed from the commonplace, and matter of real curiosity; and as soon as I came here I set to work to find the solution, repeating to myself again and again the signs you had described. First came the sign we have agreed to call the Army; a number of serried lines of flints, all pointing in the same way. Then the lines, like the spokes of a wheel, all converging towards the figure of a Bowl, then the triangle or Pyramid, and last of all the Half moon. I confess that I exhausted conjecture in my efforts to unveil this mystery, and as you will understand it was a duplex or rather triplex problem. For I had not merely to ask myself: what do these figures mean? but also, who can possibly be responsible for the designing of them? And again, who can possibly possess such valuable things, and knowing their value thus throw them down by the wayside? This line of thought led me to suppose that the person or persons in question did not know the value of unique flint arrow-heads, and yet this did not lead me far, for a well-educated man might easily be ignorant on such a subject. Then came the complication of the eye on the wall, and you remember that we could not avoid the conclusion that in the two cases the same agency was at work. The peculiar position of these eyes on the wall made me inquire if there was such a thing as a dwarf anywhere in the neighbourhood, but I found that there was not, and I knew that the children who pass by everyday had nothing to do with the matter. Yet I felt convinced that whoever drew the eyes must be from three and a half to four feet high, since, as I pointed out at the time, anyone who draws on a perpendicular surface chooses by instinct a spot about level with his face. Then again, there was the question of the peculiar shape of the eyes; that marked Mongolian character of which the English countryman could have no conception, and for a final cause of confusion the obvious fact that the designer or designers must be able practically to see in the dark. As you remarked, a man who has been confined for many years in an extremely dark cell or dungeon might acquire that power; but since the days of Edmond Dantés, where would such a prison be found in Europe? A sailor, who had been immured for a considerable period in some horrible Chinese oubliette, seemed the individual I was in search of, and though it looked improbable, it was not absolutely impossible that a sailor or, let us say, a man employed on shipboard, should be a dwarf. But how to account for my imaginary sailor being in possesion of prehistoric arrow-heads? And the possession granted, what was the meaning and object of these mysterious signs of flint, and the almond-shaped eyes? Your theory of a contemplated burglary I saw, nearly from the first, to be quite untenable, and I confess I was utterly at a loss for a working hypothesis. It was a mere accident which put me on the track; we passed poor old Trevor, and your mention of his name and of the disappearance of his daughter, recalled the story which I had forgotten, or which remained unheeded. Here, then, I said to myself, is another problem, uninteresting, it is true, by itself; but what if it prove to be in relation with all these enigmas which torture me? I shut myself in my room, and endeavoured to dismiss all prejudice from my mind, and I went over everything de novo, assuming for theory's sake that the disappearance of Annie Trevor had some connection with the flint signs and the eyes on the wall. This assumption did not lead me very far, and I was on the point of giving the whole problem up in despair, when a possible significance of the Bowl struck me. As you know there is a 'Devil's Punch-bowl' in Surrey, and I saw that the symbol might refer to some feature in the country. Putting the two extremes together, I determined to look for the Bowl near the path which the lost girl had taken, and you know how I found it. I interpreted the sign by what I knew, and read the first, the Army, thus:

'there is to be a gathering or assembly at the Bowl in a fortnight (that is the Half moon) to see the Pyramid, or to build the Pyramid.'

The eyes, drawn one by one, day by day, evidently checked off the days, and I knew that there would be fourteen and no more. Thus far the way seemed pretty plain; I would not trouble myself to inquire as to the nature of the assembly, or as to who was to assemble in the loneliest and most dreaded place among these lonely hills. In Ireland or China or the West of America the question would have been easily answered; a muster of the disaffected, the meeting of a secret society; vigilantes summoned to report: the thing would be simplicity itself; but in this quiet corner of England, inhabited by quiet folk, no such suppositions were possible for a moment. But I knew that I should have an opportunity of seeing and watching the assembly, and I did not care to perplex myself with hopeless research; and in place of reasoning a wild fancy entered into judgment: I remembered what people had said about Annie Trevor's disappearance, that she had been 'taken by the fairies.' I tell you, Vaughan, I am a sane man as you are, my brain is not, I trust, mere vacant space to let to any wild improbability, and I tried my best to thrust the fantasy away. And the hint came of the old name of fairies, 'the little people,' and the very probable belief that they represent a tradition of the prehistoric Turanian inhabitants of the country, who were cave dwellers: and then I realized with a shock that I was looking for a being under four feet in height, accustomed to live in darkness, possessing stone instruments, and familiar with the Mongolian cast of features! I say this, Vaughan, that I should be ashamed to hint at such visionary stuff to you, if it were not for that which you saw with your very eyes last night, and I say that I might doubt the evidence of my senses, if they were not confirmed by yours. But you and I cannot look each other in the face and pretend delusion; as you lay on the turf beside me I felt your flesh shrink and quiver, and I saw your eyes in the light of the flame. And so I tell you without any shame what was in my mind last night as we went through the wood and climbed the hill, and lay hidden beneath the rock.

"There was one thing that should have been most evident that puzzled me to the very last. I told you how I read the sign of the Pyramid; the assembly was to see a pyramid, and the true meaning of the symbol escaped me to the last moment. The old derivation from 'up, fire,' though false, should have set me on the track, but it never occurred to me.

"I think I need say very little more. You know we were quite helpless, even if we had foreseen what was to come. Ah, the particular place where these signs were displayed? Yes, that is a curious question. But this house is, so far as I can judge, in a pretty central situation amongst the hills; and possibly, who can say yes or no, that queer, old limestone pillar by your garden wall was a place of meeting before the Celt set foot in Britain. But there is one thing I must add: I don't regret our inability to rescue the wretched girl. You saw the appearance of those things that gathered thick and writhed in the Bowl; you may be sure that what lay bound in the midst of them was no longer fit for earth."

"So?" said Vaughan.

"So she passed in the Pyramid of Fire," said Dyson, "and they passed again to the underworld, to the places beneath the hills."

THE END

THE HILL OF DREAMS

I

There was a glow in the sky as if great furnace doors were opened.

But all the afternoon his eyes had looked on glamour; he had strayed in fairyland. The holidays were nearly done, and Lucian Taylor had gone out resolved to lose himself, to discover strange hills and prospects that he had never seen before. The air was still, breathless, exhausted after heavy rain, and the clouds looked as if they had been moulded of lead. No breeze blew upon the hill, and down in the well of the valley not a dry leaf stirred, not a bough shook in all the dark January woods.

About a mile from the rectory he had diverged from the main road by an opening that promised mystery and adventure. It was an old neglected lane, little more than a ditch, worn ten feet deep by its winter waters, and shadowed by great untrimmed hedges, densely woven together. On each side were turbid streams, and here and there a torrent of water gushed down the banks, flooding the lane. It was so deep and dark that he could not get a glimpse of the country through which he was passing, but the way went down and down to some unconjectured hollow.

Perhaps he walked two miles between the high walls of the lane before its descent ceased, but he thrilled with the sense of having journeyed very far, all the long way from the known to the unknown. He had come as it were into the bottom of a bowl amongst the hills, and black woods shut out the world. From the road behind him, from the road before him, from the unseen wells beneath the trees, rivulets of waters swelled and streamed down towards the center to the brook that crossed the lane. Amid the dead and wearied silence of the air, beneath leaden and motionless clouds, it was strange to hear such a tumult of gurgling and rushing water, and he stood for a while on the quivering footbridge and watched the rush of dead wood and torn branches and wisps of straw, all hurrying madly past him, to plunge into the heaped spume, the barmy froth that had gathered against a fallen tree.

Then he climbed again, and went up between limestone rocks, higher and higher, till the noise of waters became indistinct, a faint humming of swarming hives in summer. He walked some distance on level ground, till there was a break in the banks and a stile on which he could lean and look out. He found himself, as he had hoped, afar and forlorn; he had strayed into outland and occult territory. From the eminence of the lane, skirting the brow of a hill, he looked down into deep valleys and dingles, and beyond, across the trees, to remoter country, wild bare hills and dark wooded lands meeting the grey still sky. Immediately beneath his feet the ground sloped steep down to the valley, a hillside of close grass patched with dead bracken, and dotted here and there with stunted thorns, and below there were deep oak woods, all still and silent, and lonely as if no one ever passed that way. The grass and bracken and thorns and woods, all were brown and grey beneath the leaden sky, and as Lucian looked he was amazed, as though he were reading a wonderful story, the meaning of which was a little greater than his understanding. Then, like the hero of a fairy-book, he went on and on, catching now and again glimpses of the amazing country into which he had penetrated, and perceiving rather than seeing that as the day waned everything grew more grey and somber. As he advanced he heard the evening sounds of the farms, the low of the cattle, and the barking of the sheepdogs; a faint thin noise from far away. It was growing late, and as the shadows blackened he walked faster, till once more the lane began to descend, there was a sharp turn, and he found himself, with a good deal of relief, and a little disappointment, on familiar ground. He had nearly described a circle, and knew this end of the lane very well; it was not much more than a mile from home. He walked smartly down the hill; the air was all glimmering and indistinct, transmuting trees and hedges into ghostly shapes, and the walls of the White House Farm flickered on the hillside, as if they were moving towards him. Then a change came. First, a little breath of wind brushed with a dry whispering sound through the hedges, the few leaves left on the boughs began to stir, and one or two danced madly, and as the wind freshened and came up from a new quarter, the sapless branches above rattled against one another like bones. The growing breeze seemed to clear the air and lighten it. He was passing the stile where a path led to old Mrs. Gibbon's desolate little cottage, in the middle of the fields, at some distance even from the lane, and he saw the light blue smoke of her chimney rise distinct above the gaunt greengage trees, against a pale band that was broadening along the horizon. As he passed the stile with his head bent, and his eyes on the ground, something white started out from the black shadow of the hedge, and in the strange twilight, now tinged with a flush from the west, a figure seemed to swim past him and disappear. For a moment he wondered who it could be, the light

ARTHUR MACHEN

was so flickering and unsteady, so unlike the real atmosphere of the day, when he recollected it was only Annie Morgan, old Morgan's daughter at the White House. She was three years older than he, and it annoyed him to find that though she was only fifteen, there had been a dreadful increase in her height since the summer holidays. He had got to the bottom of the hill, and, lifting up his eyes, saw the strange changes of the sky. The pale band had broadened into a clear vast space of light, and above, the heavy leaden clouds were breaking apart and driving across the heaven before the wind. He stopped to watch, and looked up at the great mound that jutted out from the hills into mid-valley. It was a natural formation, and always it must have had something of the form of a fort, but its steepness had been increased by Roman art, and there were high banks on the summit which Lucian's father had told him were the *vallum* of the camp, and a deep ditch had been dug to the north to sever it from the hillside. On this summit oaks had grown, queer stunted-looking trees with twisted and contorted trunks, and writhing branches; and these now stood out black against the lighted sky. And then the air changed once more; the flush increased, and a spot like blood appeared in the pond by the gate, and all the clouds were touched with fiery spots and dapples of flame; here and there it looked as if awful furnace doors were being opened.

The wind blew wildly, and it came up through the woods with a noise like a scream, and a great oak by the roadside ground its boughs together with a dismal grating jar. As the red gained in the sky, the earth and all upon it glowed, even the grey winter fields and the bare hillsides crimsoned, the waterpools were cisterns of molten brass, and the very road glittered. He was wonder-struck, almost aghast, before the scarlet magic of the afterglow. The old Roman fort was invested with fire; flames from heaven were smitten about its walls, and above there was a dark floating cloud, like a fume of smoke, and every haggard writhing tree showed as black as midnight against the black of the furnace.

When he got home he heard his mother's voice calling: "Here's Lucian at last. Mary, Master Lucian has come, you can get the tea ready." He told a long tale of his adventures, and felt somewhat mortified when his father seemed perfectly acquainted with the whole course of the lane, and knew the names of the wild woods through which he had passed in awe.

"You must have gone by the Darren, I suppose"—that was all he said. "Yes, I noticed the sunset; we shall have some stormy weather. I don't expect to see many in church tomorrow."

There was buttered toast for tea "because it was holidays." The red curtains were drawn, and a bright fire was burning, and there was the old familiar furniture, a little shabby, but charming from association. It was much pleasanter than the cold and squalid schoolroom; and much better to be reading *Chambers's Journal* than learning Euclid; and better to talk to his father and mother than to be answering such remarks as: "I say, Taylor, I've torn my trousers; how much do you charge for mending?" "Lucy, dear, come quick and sew this button on my shirt."

That night the storm woke him, and he groped with his hands amongst the bedclothes, and sat up, shuddering, not knowing where he was. He had seen himself, in a dream, within the Roman fort, working some dark horror, and the furnace doors were opened and a blast of flame from heaven was smitten upon him.

Lucian went slowly, but not discreditably, up the school, gaining prizes now and again, and falling in love more and more with useless reading and unlikely knowledge. He did his elegiacs and iambics well enough, but he preferred exercising himself in the rhymed Latin of the middle ages. He liked history, but he loved to meditate on a land laid waste, Britain deserted by the legions, the rare pavements riven by frost, Celtic magic still brooding on the wild hills and in the black depths of the forest, the rosy marbles stained with rain, and the walls growing grey. The masters did not encourage these researches; a pure enthusiasm, they felt, should be for cricket and football, the *dilettanti* might even play fives and read Shakespeare without blame, but healthy English boys should have nothing to do with decadent periods. He was once found guilty of recommending Villon to a school-fellow named Barnes. Barnes tried to extract unpleasantness from the text during preparation, and rioted in his place, owing to his incapacity for the language. The matter was a serious one; the headmaster had never heard of Villon, and the culprit gave up the name of his literary admirer without remorse. Hence, sorrow for Lucian, and complete immunity for the miserable illiterate Barnes, who resolved to confine his researches to the Old Testament, a book which the headmaster knew well. As for Lucian, he plodded on, learning his work decently, and sometimes doing very creditable Latin and Greek prose. His school-fellows thought him quite mad, and tolerated him, and indeed were very kind to him in their barbarous manner. He often remembered in after life acts of generosity and good nature done by wretches like Barnes, who had no care for old French nor for curious meters, and such recollections always moved him to emotion. Travelers tell such tales; cast upon cruel shores amongst savage races, they have found no little kindness and warmth of hospitality.

He looked forward to the holidays as joyfully as the rest of them. Barnes and his friend Duscot used to tell him their plans and anticipation; they were going home to brothers and sisters, and to cricket, more cricket, or to football, more football, and in the winter there were parties and jollities of all sorts. In return he would announce his intention of studying the Hebrew language, or perhaps Provençal, with a walk up a bare and desolate mountain by way of open-air amusement, and on a rainy day for choice. Whereupon Barnes would impart to Duscot his confident belief that old Taylor was quite cracked. It was a queer, funny life that of school, and so very unlike anything in *Tom Brown*. He once saw the headmaster patting the head of the bishop's little boy, while he called him "my little man," and smiled hideously. He told the tale grotesquely in the lower fifth room the same day, and earned much applause, but forfeited all liking directly by proposing a voluntary course of scholastic logic. One barbarian threw him to the ground and another jumped on him, but it was done very pleasantly. There were, indeed, some few of a worse class in the school, solemn sycophants, prigs perfected from tender years, who thought life already "serious," and yet, as the headmaster said, were "joyous, manly young fellows." Some of these dressed for dinner at home, and talked of dances when they came back in January. But this virulent sort was comparatively infrequent, and achieved great success in after life. Taking his school days as a whole, he always spoke up for the system, and years afterward he described with enthusiasm the strong beer at a roadside tavern, some way out of the town. But he always maintained that the taste for tobacco, acquired in early life, was the great life, was the great note of the English Public School.

Three years after Lucian's discovery of the narrow lane and the vision of the flaming fort, the August holidays brought him home at a time of great heat. It was one of those memorable years of English weather, when some Provençal spell seems wreathed round the island in the northern sea, and the grasshoppers chirp loudly as the cicadas, the hills smell of rosemary, and white walls of the old farmhouses blaze in the sunlight as if they stood in Arles or Avignon or famed Tarascon by Rhone.

Lucian's father was late at the station, and consequently Lucian bought the *Confessions of an English Opium Eater* which he saw on the bookstall. When his father did drive up, Lucian noticed that the old trap had had a new coat of dark paint, and that the pony looked advanced in years.

"I was afraid that I should be late, Lucian," said his father, "though I made old Polly go like anything. I was just going to tell George to put her into the trap when young Philip Harris came to me in a terrible state. He said his father fell down 'all of a sudden like' in the middle of the field, and they couldn't make him speak, and would I please to come and see him. So I had to go, though I couldn't do anything for the poor fellow. They had sent for Dr. Burrows, and I am afraid he will find it a bad case of sunstroke. The old people say they never remember such a heat before."

The pony jogged steadily along the burning turnpike road, taking revenge for the hurrying on the way to the station. The hedges were white with the limestone dust, and the vapor of heat palpitated over the fields. Lucian showed his *Confessions* to his father, and began to talk of the beautiful bits he had already found. Mr. Taylor knew the book well—had read it many years before. Indeed he was almost as difficult to surprise as that character in Daudet, who had one formula for all the chances of life, and when he saw the drowned Academician dragged out of the river, merely observed *"J'ai vu tout ça."* Mr. Taylor the parson, as his parishioners called him, had read the fine books and loved the hills and woods, and now knew no more of pleasant or sensational surprises. Indeed the living was much depreciated in value, and his own private means were reduced almost to vanishing point, and under such circumstances the great style loses many of its finer savours. He was very fond of Lucian, and cheered by his return, but in the evening he would be a sad man again, with his head resting on one hand, and eyes reproaching sorry fortune.

Nobody called out "Here's your master with Master Lucian; you can get tea ready," when the pony jogged up to the front door. His mother had been dead a year, and a cousin kept house. She was a respectable person called Deacon, of middle age, and ordinary standards; and, consequently, there was cold mutton on the table. There was a cake, but nothing of flour, baked in ovens, would rise at Miss Deacon's evocation. Still, the meal was laid in the beloved "parlor," with the view of hills and valleys and climbing woods from the open window, and the old furniture was still pleasant to see, and the old books in the shelves had many memories. One of the most respected of the armchairs had become weak in the castors and had to be artfully propped up, but Lucian found it very comfortable after the hard forms. When tea was over he went out and strolled in the garden and orchards, and looked over the stile down into the brake, where foxgloves and bracken and broom mingled with the hazel undergrowth, where he knew of secret glades and untracked recesses, deep in the woven green, the cabinets for many years of his lonely meditations. Every path about his home, every field and hedgerow had dear and friendly memories for him; and the odour of the meadowsweet was better than the incense steaming in the sunshine. He loitered, and hung over the stile till the far-off woods began to turn purple, till the white mists were wreathing in the valley.

Day after day, through all that August, morning and evening were wrapped in haze; day after day the earth shimmered in the heat, and the air was strange, unfamiliar. As he wandered in the lanes and sauntered by the cool sweet verge of the woods, he saw and felt that nothing was common or accustomed, for the sunlight transfigured the meadows and changed all the form of the earth. Under the violent Provençal sun, the elms and beeches looked exotic trees, and in the early morning, when the mists were thick, the hills had put on an unearthly shape.

The one adventure of the holidays was the visit to the Roman fort, to that fantastic hill about whose steep bastions and haggard oaks he had seen the flames of sunset writhing nearly three years before. Ever since that Saturday evening in January, the lonely valley had been a desirable place to him; he had watched the green battlements in summer and winter weather, had seen the heaped mounds rising dimly amidst the drifting rain, had marked the violent height swim up from the ice-white mists of summer evenings, had watched the fairy bulwarks glimmer and vanish in hovering April twilight. In the hedge of the lane there was a gate on which he used to lean and look down south to where the hill surged up so suddenly, its summit defined on summer evenings not only by the rounded ramparts but by the ring of dense green foliage that marked the circle of oak trees. Higher up the lane, on the way he had come that Saturday afternoon, one could see the white walls of Morgan's farm on the hillside to the north, and on the south there was the stile with the view of old Mrs. Gibbon's cottage smoke; but down in the hollow, looking over the gate, there was no hint of human work, except those green and antique battlements, on which the oaks stood in circle, guarding the inner wood.

The ring of the fort drew him with stronger fascination during that hot August weather. Standing, or as his headmaster would have said, "mooning" by the gate, and looking into that enclosed and secret valley, it seemed to his fancy as if there were a halo about the hill, an aureole that played like flame around it. One afternoon as he gazed from his station by the gate the sheer sides and the swelling bulwarks were more than ever things of enchantment; the green oak ring stood out against the sky as still and bright as in a picture, and Lucian, in spite of his respect for the law of trespass, slid over the gate. The farmers and their men were busy on the uplands with the harvest, and the adventure was irresistible. At first he stole along by the brook in the shadow of the alders, where the grass and the flowers of wet meadows grew richly; but as he drew nearer to the fort, and its height now rose sheer above him, he left all shelter, and began desperately to mount. There was not a breath of wind; the sunlight shone down on the bare hillside; the loud chirp of the grasshoppers was the only sound. It was a steep ascent and grew steeper as the valley sank away. He turned for a moment, and looked down towards the stream which now seemed to wind remote between the alders; above the valley there were small dark figures moving in the cornfield, and now and again there came the faint echo of a high-pitched voice singing through the air as on a wire. He was wet with heat; the sweat streamed off his face, and he could feel it trickling all over his body. But above him the green bastions rose defiant, and the dark ring of oaks promised coolness. He pressed on, and higher, and at last began to crawl up the *vallum*, on hands and knees, grasping the turf and here and there the roots that had burst through the red earth. And then he lay, panting with deep breaths, on the summit.

Within the fort it was all dusky and cool and hollow; it was as if one stood at the bottom of a great cup. Within, the wall seemed higher than without, and the ring of oaks curved up like a dark green vault. There were nettles growing thick and rank in the foss; they looked different from the common nettles in the lanes, and Lucian, letting his hand touch a leaf by accident, felt the sting burn like fire. Beyond the ditch there was an undergrowth, a dense thicket of trees, stunted and old, crooked and withered by the winds into awkward and ugly forms; beech and oak and hazel and ash and yew twisted and so shortened and deformed that each seemed, like the nettle, of no common kind. He began to fight his way through the ugly growth, stumbling and getting hard knocks from the rebound of twisted boughs. His foot struck once or twice against something harder than wood, and looking down he saw stones white with the leprosy of age, but still showing the work of the axe. And farther, the roots of the stunted trees gripped the foot-high relics of a wall; and a round heap of fallen stones nourished rank, unknown herbs, that smelt poisonous. The earth was black and unctuous, and bubbling under the feet, left no track behind. From it, in the darkest places where the shadow was thickest, swelled the growth of an abominable fungus, making the still air sick with its corrupt odour, and he shuddered as he felt the horrible thing pulped beneath his feet. Then there was a gleam of sunlight, and as he thrust the last boughs apart, he stumbled into the open space in the heart of the camp. It was a lawn of sweet close turf in the center of the matted brake, of clean firm earth from which no shameful growth sprouted, and near the middle of the glade was a stump of a felled yew-tree, left untrimmed by the woodman. Lucian thought it must have been made for a seat; a crooked bough through which a little sap still ran was a support for the back, and he sat down and rested after his toil. It was not really so comfortable a seat as one of the school forms, but the satisfaction was to find anything at all that would serve for a chair. He sat there, still panting after the climb and his struggle through the dank and jungle-like thicket, and he felt as if he were growing hotter and hotter; the sting of the nettle was burning his hand, and the tingling fire seemed to spread all over his body.

Suddenly, he knew that he was alone. Not merely solitary; that he had often been amongst the woods and deep in the lanes; but now it was a wholly different and a very strange sensation. He thought of the valley winding far below him, all its fields by the brook green and peaceful and still, without path or track. Then he had climbed the abrupt surge of the hill, and passing the green and swelling battlements, the ring of oaks, and the matted thicket, had come to the central space. And behind there were, he knew, many desolate fields, wild as common, untrodden, unvisited. He was utterly alone. He still grew hotter as he sat on the stump, and at last lay down at full length on the soft grass, and more at his ease felt the waves of heat pass over his body.

And then he began to dream, to let his fancies stray over half-imagined, delicious things, indulging a virgin mind in its wanderings. The hot air seemed to beat upon him in palpable waves, and the nettle sting tingled and itched intolerably; and he was alone upon the fairy hill, within the great mounds, within the ring of oaks, deep in the heart of the matted thicket. Slowly and timidly he began to untie his boots, fumbling with the laces, and glancing all the while on every side at the ugly misshapen trees that hedged the lawn. Not a branch was straight, not one was free, but all were interlaced and grew one about another; and just above ground, where the cankered stems joined the protuberant roots, there were forms that imitated the human shape, and faces and twining limbs that amazed him. Green mosses were hair, and tresses were stark in grey lichen; a twisted root swelled into a limb; in the hollows of the rotted bark he saw the masks of men. His eyes were fixed and fascinated by the simulacra of the wood, and could not see his hands, and so at last, and suddenly, it seemed, he lay in the sunlight, beautiful with his olive skin, dark haired, dark eyed, the gleaming bodily vision of a strayed faun.

Quick flames now quivered in the substance of his nerves, hints of mysteries, secrets of life passed trembling through his brain, unknown desires stung him. As he gazed across the turf and into the thicket, the sunshine seemed really to become green, and the contrast between the bright glow poured on the lawn and the black shadow of the brake made an odd flickering light, in which all the grotesque postures of stem and root began to stir; the wood was alive. The turf beneath him heaved and sank as with the deep swell of the sea. He fell asleep, and lay still on the grass, in the midst of the thicket.

He found out afterwards that he must have slept for nearly an hour. The shadows had changed when he awoke; his senses came to him with a sudden shock, and he sat up and stared at his bare limbs in stupid amazement. He huddled on his clothes and laced his boots, wondering what folly had beset him. Then, while he stood indecisive, hesitating, his brain a whirl of puzzled thought, his body trembling, his hands shaking; as with electric heat, sudden remembrance possessed him. A flaming blush shone red on his cheeks, and glowed and thrilled through his limbs. As he awoke, a brief and slight breeze had stirred in a nook of the matted boughs, and there was a glinting that might have been the flash of sudden sunlight across shadow, and the branches rustled and murmured for a moment, perhaps at the wind's passage.

He stretched out his hands, and cried to his visitant to return; he entreated the dark eyes that had shone over him, and the scarlet lips that had kissed him. And then panic fear rushed into his heart, and he ran blindly, dashing through the wood. He climbed the *vallum*, and looked out, crouching, lest anybody should see him. Only the shadows were changed, and a breath of cooler air mounted from the brook; the fields were still and peaceful, the black figures moved, far away, amidst the corn, and the faint echo of the high-pitched voices sang thin and distant on the evening wind. Across the stream, in the cleft on the hill, opposite to the fort, the blue wood smoke stole up a spiral pillar from the chimney of old Mrs. Gibbon's cottage. He began to run full tilt down the steep surge of the hill, and never stopped till he was over the gate and in the lane again. As he looked back, down the valley to the south, and saw the violent ascent, the green swelling bulwarks, and the dark ring of oaks; the sunlight seemed to play about the fort with an aureole of flame.

"Where on earth have you been all this time, Lucian?" said his cousin when he got home. "Why, you look quite ill. It is really madness of you to go walking in such weather as this. I wonder you haven't got a sunstroke. And the tea must be nearly cold. I couldn't keep your father waiting, you know."

He muttered something about being rather tired, and sat down to his tea. It was not cold, for the "cozy" had been put over the pot, but it was black and bitter strong, as his cousin expressed it. The draught was unpalatable, but it did him good, and the thought came with great consolation that he had only been asleep and dreaming queer, nightmarish dreams. He shook off all his fancies with resolution, and thought the loneliness of the camp, and the burning sunlight, and possibly the nettle sting, which still tingled most abominably, must have been the only factors in his farrago of impossible recollections. He remembered that when he had felt the sting, he had seized a nettle with thick folds of his handkerchief, and having twisted off a good length, and put it in his pocket to show his father. Mr. Taylor was almost interested when he came in from his evening stroll about the garden and saw the specimen.

"Where did you manage to come across that, Lucian?" he said. "You haven't been to Caermaen, have you?"

"No. I got it in the Roman fort by the common."

"Oh, the twyn. You must have been trespassing then. Do you know what it is?"

"No. I thought it looked different from the common nettles."

"Yes; it's a Roman nettle—*urtica pilulifera*. It's a rare plant. Burrows says it's to be found at Caermaen, but I was never able to come across it. I must add it to the *flora* of the parish."

Mr. Taylor had begun to compile a *flora* accompanied by a *hortus siccus*, but both stayed on high shelves dusty and fragmentary. He put the specimen on his desk, intending to fasten it in the book, but the maid swept it away, dry and withered, in a day or two.

Lucian tossed and cried out in his sleep that night, and the awakening in the morning was, in a measure, a renewal of the awakening in the fort. But the impression was not so strong, and in a plain room it seemed all delirium, a phantasmagoria. He had to go down to Caermaen in the afternoon, for Mrs. Dixon, the vicar's wife, had "commanded" his presence at tea. Mr. Dixon, though fat and short and clean shaven, ruddy of face, was a safe man, with no extreme views on anything. He "deplored" all extreme party convictions, and thought the great needs of our beloved Church were conciliation, moderation, and above all "amolgamation"—so he pronounced the word. Mrs. Dixon was tall, imposing, splendid, well fitted for the Episcopal order, with gifts that would have shone at the palace. There were daughters, who studied German Literature, and thought Miss Frances Ridley Havergal wrote poetry, but Lucian had no fear of them; he dreaded the boys. Everybody said they were such fine, manly fellows, such gentlemanly boys, with such a good manner, sure to get on in the world. Lucian had said "Bother!" in a very violent manner when the gracious invitation was conveyed to him, but there was no getting out of it. Miss Deacon did her best to make him look smart; his ties were all so disgraceful that she had to supply the want with a narrow ribbon of a sky-blue tint; and she brushed him so long and so violently that he quite understood why a horse sometimes bites and sometimes kicks the groom. He set out between two and three in a gloomy frame of mind; he knew too well what spending the afternoon with honest manly boys meant. He found the reality more lurid than his anticipation. The boys were in the field, and the first remark he heard when he got in sight of the group was:

"Hullo, Lucian, how much for the tie?" "Fine tie," another, a stranger, observed. "You bagged it from the kitten, didn't you?"

Then they made up a game of cricket, and he was put in first. He was l.b.w. in his second over, so they all said, and had to field for the rest of the afternoon. Arthur Dixon, who was about his own age, forgetting all the laws of hospitality, told him he was a beastly muff when he missed a catch, rather a difficult catch. He missed several catches, and it seemed as if he were always panting after balls, which, as Edward Dixon said, any fool, even a baby, could have stopped. At last the game broke up, solely from Lucian's lack of skill, as everybody declared. Edward Dixon, who was thirteen, and had a swollen red face and a projecting eye, wanted to fight him for spoiling the game, and the others agreed that he funked the fight in a rather dirty manner. The strange boy, who was called De Carti, and was understood to be faintly related to Lord De Carti of M'Carthytown, said openly that the fellows at his place wouldn't stand such a sneak for five minutes. So the afternoon passed off very pleasantly indeed, till it was time to go into the vicarage for weak tea, homemade cake, and unripe plums. He got away at last. As he went out at the gate, he heard De Carti's final observation:

"We like to dress well at our place. His governor must be beastly poor to let him go about like that. D'ye see his trousers are all ragged at heel? Is old Taylor a gentleman?"

It had been a very gentlemanly afternoon, but there was a certain relief when the vicarage was far behind, and the evening smoke of the little town, once the glorious capital of Siluria, hung haze-like over the ragged roofs and mingled with the river mist. He looked down from the height of the road on the huddled houses, saw the points of light start out suddenly from the cottages on the hillside beyond, and gazed at the long lovely valley fading in the twilight, till the darkness came and all that remained was the somber ridge of the forest. The way was pleasant through the solemn scented lane, with glimpses of dim country, the vague mystery of night overshadowing the woods and meadows. A warm wind blew gusts of odour from the meadowsweet by the brook, now and then bee and beetle span homeward through the air, booming a deep note as from a great organ far away, and from the verge of the wood came the "who-oo, who-oo, who-oo" of the owls, a wild strange sound that mingled with the whirr and rattle of the nightjar, deep in the bracken. The moon swam up through the films of misty cloud, and hung, a golden glorious lantern, in mid-air; and, set in the dusky hedge, the little green fires of the glowworms appeared. He sauntered slowly up the lane, drinking in the religion of the scene, and thinking the country by night as mystic and wonderful as a dimly-lit cathedral. He had quite forgotten the "manly young fellows" and their sports, and only wished as the land began to shimmer and gleam in the moonlight that he knew by some medium of words or colour how to represent the loveliness about his way.

"Had a pleasant evening, Lucian?" said his father when he came in.

"Yes, I had a nice walk home. Oh, in the afternoon we played cricket. I didn't care for it much. There was a boy named De Carti there; he is staying with the Dixons. Mrs. Dixon whispered to me when we were going in to tea, 'He's a second cousin of Lord De Carti's,' and she looked quite grave as if she were in church.'"

The parson grinned grimly and lit his old pipe.

"Baron De Carti's great-grandfather was a Dublin attorney," he remarked. "Which his name was Jeremiah M'Carthy. His prejudiced fellow-citizens called him the Unjust Steward, also the Bloody Attorney, and I believe that 'to hell with M'Carthy' was quite a popular cry about the time of the Union."

Mr. Taylor was a man of very wide and irregular reading and a tenacious memory; he often used to wonder why he had not risen in the Church. He had once told Mr. Dixon a singular and *drolatique* anecdote concerning the bishop's college days, and he never discovered why the prelate did not bow according to his custom when the name of Taylor was called at the next visitation. Some people said the reason was lighted candles, but that was impossible, as the Reverend and Honorable Smallwood Stafford, Lord Beamys's son, who had a cure of souls in the cathedral city, was well known to burn no end of candles, and with him the bishop was on the best of terms. Indeed the bishop often stayed at Coplesey (pronounced "Copsey") Hall, Lord Beamys's place in the west.

Lucian had mentioned the name of De Carti with intention, and had perhaps exaggerated a little Mrs. Dixon's respectful manner. He knew such incidents cheered his father, who could never look at these subjects from a proper point of view, and, as people said, sometimes made the strangest remarks for a clergyman. This irreverent way of treating serious things was one of the great bonds between father and son, but it tended to increase their isolation. People said they would often have liked to asked Mr. Taylor to garden-parties, and tea-parties, and other cheap entertainments, if only he had not been such an *extreme* man and so *queer*. Indeed, a year before, Mr. Taylor had gone to a garden-party at the Castle, Caermaen, and had made such fun of the bishop's recent address on missions to the Portuguese, that the Gervases and Dixons and all who heard him were quite shocked and annoyed. And, as Mrs. Meyrick of Lanyravon observed, his black coat was perfectly *green* with age; so on the whole the Gervases did not like to invite Mr. Taylor again. As for the son, nobody cared to have him; Mrs. Dixon, as she said to her husband, really asked him out of charity.

"I am afraid he seldom gets a real meal at home," she remarked, "so I thought he would enjoy a good wholesome tea for once in a way. But he is such an *unsatisfactory* boy, he would only have one slice of that nice plain cake, and I couldn't get him to take more than two plums. They were really quite ripe too, and boys are usually so fond of fruit."

Thus Lucian was forced to spend his holidays chiefly in his own company, and make the best he could of the ripe peaches on the south wall of the rectory garden. There was a certain corner where the heat of that hot August seemed concentrated, reverberated from one wall to the other, and here he liked to linger of mornings, when the mists were still thick in the valleys, "mooning," meditating, extending his walk from the quince to the medlar and back again, beside the mouldering walls of mellowed brick. He was full of a certain wonder and awe, not unmixed with a swell of strange exultation, and wished more and more to be alone, to think over that wonderful afternoon within the fort. In spite of himself the impression was fading; he could not understand that feeling of mad panic terror that drove him through the thicket and down the steep hillside; yet, he had experienced so clearly the physical shame and reluctance of the flesh; he recollected that for a few seconds after his awakening the sight of his own body had made him shudder and writhe as if it had suffered some profoundest degradation. He saw before him a vision of two forms; a faun with tingling and prickling flesh lay expectant in the sunlight, and there was also the likeness of a miserable shamed boy, standing with trembling body and shaking, unsteady hands. It was all confused, a procession of blurred images, now of rapture and ecstasy, and now of terror and shame, floating in a light that was altogether phantasmal and unreal. He dared not approach the fort again; he lingered in the road to Caermaen that passed behind it, but a mile away, and separated by the wild land and a strip of wood from the towering battlements. Here he was looking over a gate one day, doubtful and wondering, when he heard a heavy step behind him, and glancing round quickly saw it was old Morgan of the White House.

"Good afternoon, Master Lucian," he began. "Mr. Taylor pretty well, I suppose? I be goin' to the house a minute; the men in the fields are wantin' some more cider. Would you come and taste a drop of cider, Master Lucian? It's very good, sir, indeed."

Lucian did not want any cider, but he thought it would please old Morgan if he took some, so he said he should like to taste the cider very much indeed. Morgan was a sturdy, thick-set old man of the ancient stock; a stiff churchman, who breakfasted regularly on fat broth and Caerphilly cheese in the fashion of his ancestors; hot, spiced elder wine was for winter nights, and gin for festal seasons. The farm had always been the freehold of the family, and when Lucian, in the wake of the yeoman, passed through the deep porch by the oaken door, down into the long dark kitchen, he felt as though the seventeenth century still lingered on. One mullioned window, set deep in the sloping wall, gave all the light there was through quarries of thick glass in which there were whorls and circles, so that the lapping rose-branch and the garden and the fields beyond were distorted to the sight. Two heavy beams, oaken but whitewashed, ran across the ceiling; a little glow of fire sparkled in the great fireplace, and a curl of blue smoke fled up the cavern of the chimney. Here was the genuine chimney-corner of our fathers; there were seats on each side of the fireplace where one could sit snug and sheltered on December nights, warm and merry in the blazing light, and listen to the battle of the storm, and hear the flame spit and hiss at the falling snowflakes. At the back of the fire were great blackened tiles with raised initials and a date—I.M., 1684.

"Sit down, Master Lucian, sit down, sir," said Morgan.

"Annie," he called through one of the numerous doors, "here's Master Lucian, the parson, would like a drop of cider. Fetch a jug, will you, directly?"

"Very well, father," came the voice from the dairy and presently the girl entered, wiping the jug she held. In his boyish way Lucian had been a good deal disturbed by Annie Morgan; he could see her on Sundays from his seat in church, and her skin, curiously pale, her lips that seemed as though they were stained with some brilliant pigment, her black hair, and the quivering black eyes, gave him odd fancies which he had hardly shaped to himself. Annie had grown into a woman in three years, and he was still a boy. She came into the kitchen, curtsying and smiling.

"Goodday, Master Lucian, and how is Mr. Taylor, sir?"

"Pretty well, thank you. I hope you are well."

"Nicely, sir, thank you. How nice your voice do sound in church, Master

Lucian, to be sure. I was telling father about it last Sunday."

LUCIAN GRINNED AND FELT UNCOMFORTABLE, and the girl set down the jug on the round table and brought a glass from the dresser. She bent close over him as she poured out the green oily cider, fragrant of the orchard; her hand touched his shoulder for a moment, and she said, "I beg your pardon, sir," very prettily. He looked up eagerly at her face; the black eyes, a little oval in shape, were shining, and the lips smiled. Annie wore a plain dress of some black stuff, open at the throat; her skin was beautiful. For a moment the ghost of a fancy hovered unsubstantial in his mind; and then Annie curtsied as she handed him the cider, and replied to his thanks with, "And welcome kindly, sir."

The drink was really good; not thin, nor sweet, but round and full and generous, with a fine yellow flame twinkling through the green when one held it up to the light. It was like a stray sunbeam hovering on the grass in a deep orchard, and he swallowed the glassful with relish, and had some more, warmly commending it. Mr. Morgan was touched.

"I see you do know a good thing, sir," he said. "Is, indeed, now, it's good stuff, though it's my own makin'. My old grandfather he planted the trees in the time of the wars, and he was a very good judge of an apple in his day and generation. And a famous grafter he was, to be sure. You will never see no swelling in the trees he grafted at all whatever. Now there's James Morris, Penyrhaul, he's a famous grafter, too, and yet them Redstreaks he grafted for me five year ago, they be all swollen-like below the graft already. Would you like to taste a Blemmin pippin, now, Master Lucian? there be a few left in the loft, I believe."

Lucian said he should like an apple very much, and the farmer went out by another door, and Annie stayed in the kitchen talking. She said Mrs. Trevor, her married sister, was coming to them soon to spend a few days.

"She's got such a beautiful baby," said Annie, "and he's quite sensible-like already, though he's only nine months old. Mary would like to see you, sir, if you would be so kind as to step in; that is, if it's not troubling you at all, Master Lucian. I suppose you must be getting a fine scholar now, sir?"

"I am doing pretty well, thank you," said the boy. "I was first in my form last term."

"Fancy! To think of that! D'you hear, father, what a scholar Master Lucian be getting?"

"He be a rare grammarian, I'm sure," said the farmer. "You do take after your father, sir; I always do say that nobody have got such a good deliverance in the pulpit."

Lucian did not find the Blenheim Orange as good as the cider, but he ate it with all the appearance of relish, and put another, with thanks, in his pocket. He thanked the farmer again when he got up to go; and Annie curtsied and smiled, and wished him goodday, and welcome, kindly.

Lucian heard her saying to her father as he went out what a nice-mannered young gentleman he was getting, to be sure; and he went on his way, thinking that Annie was really very pretty, and speculating as to whether he would have the courage to kiss her, if they met in a dark lane. He was quite sure she would only laugh, and say, "Oh, Master Lucian!"

For many months he had occasional fits of recollection, both cold and hot; but the bridge of time, gradually lengthening, made those dreadful and delicious images grow more and more indistinct, till at last they all passed into that wonderland which a youth looks back upon in amazement, not knowing why this used to be a symbol of terror or that of joy. At the end of each term he would come home and find his father a little more despondent, and harder to cheer even for a moment; and the wall paper and the furniture grew more and more dingy and shabby. The two cats, loved and ancient beasts, that he remembered when he was quite a little boy, before he went to school, died miserably, one after the other. Old Polly, the pony, at last fell down in the stable from the weakness of old age, and had to be killed there; the battered old trap ran no longer along the well-remembered lanes. There was long meadow grass on the lawn, and the trained fruit trees on the wall had got quite out of hand. At last, when Lucian was seventeen, his father was obliged to take him from school; he could no longer afford the fees. This was the sorry ending of many hopes, and dreams of a double-first, a fellowship, distinction and glory that the poor parson had long entertained for his son, and the two moped together, in the shabby room, one on each side of the sulky fire, thinking of dead days and finished plans, and seeing a grey future in the years that advanced towards them. At one time there seemed some chance of a distant relative coming forward to Lucian's assistance; and indeed it was quite settled that he should go up to London with certain definite aims. Mr. Taylor told the good news to his acquaintances—his coat was too green now for any pretence of friendship; and Lucian himself spoke of his plans to Burrows the doctor and Mr. Dixon, and one or two others. Then the whole scheme fell through, and the parson and his son suffered much sympathy. People, of course, had to say they were sorry, but in reality the news was received with high spirits, with the joy with which one sees a stone, as it rolls down a steep place, give yet another bounding leap towards the pool beneath. Mrs. Dixon heard the pleasant tidings from Mrs. Colley, who came in to talk about the Mothers' Meeting and the Band of Hope. Mrs. Dixon was nursing little Æthelwig, or some such name, at the time, and made many affecting observations on the general righteousness with which the world was governed. Indeed, poor Lucian's disappointment seemed distinctly to increase her faith in the Divine Order, as if it had been some example in Butler's *Analogy*.

"Aren't Mr. Taylor's views very *extreme?*" she said to her husband the same evening.

"I am afraid they are," he replied. "I was quite *grieved* at the last Diocesan Conference at the way in which he spoke. The dear old bishop had given an address on Auricular Confession; he was *forced* to do so, you know, after what had happened, and I must say that I never felt prouder of our beloved Church."

Mr. Dixon told all the Homeric story of the conference, reciting the achievements of the champions, "deploring" this and applauding that. It seemed that Mr. Taylor had had the audacity to quote authorities which the bishop could not very well repudiate, though they were directly opposed to the "safe" Episcopal pronouncement.

Mrs. Dixon of course was grieved; it was "sad" to think of a clergyman behaving so shamefully.

"But you know, dear," she proceeded, "I have been thinking about that unfortunate Taylor boy and his disappointments, and after what you've just told me, I am sure it's some kind of judgment on them both. Has Mr. Taylor forgotten the vows he took at his ordination? But don't you think, dear, I am right, and that he has been punished: 'The sins of the fathers'?"

Somehow or other Lucian divined the atmosphere of threatenings and judgments, and shrank more and more from the small society of the countryside. For his part, when he was not "mooning" in the beloved fields and woods of happy memory, he shut himself up with books, reading whatever could be found on the shelves, and amassing a store of incongruous and obsolete knowledge. Long did he linger with the men of the seventeenth century; delaying in the gay sunlit streets with Pepys, and listening to the charmed sound of the Restoration Revel; roaming by peaceful streams with Izaak Walton, and the great Catholic divines; enchanted with the portrait of Herbert the loving ascetic; awed by the mystic breath of Crashaw. Then the cavalier poets sang their gallant songs; and Herrick made Dean Prior magic ground by the holy incantation of a verse. And in the old proverbs and homely sayings of the time he found the good and beautiful English life, a time full of grace and dignity and rich merriment. He dived deeper and deeper into his books; he had taken all obsolescence to be his province; in his disgust at the stupid usual questions, "Will it pay?" "What good is it?" and so forth, he would only read what was uncouth and useless. The strange pomp and symbolism of the Cabala, with its hint of more terrible things; the Rosicrucian mysteries of Fludd, the enigmas of Vaughan, dreams of alchemists—all these were his delight. Such were his companions, with the hills and hanging woods, the brooks and lonely waterpools; books, the thoughts of books, the stirrings of imagination, all fused into one phantasy by the magic of the outland country. He held himself aloof from the walls of the fort; he was content to see the heaped mounds, the violent height with faerie bulwarks, from the gate in the lane, and to leave all within the ring of oaks in the mystery of his boyhood's vision. He professed to laugh at himself and at his fancies of that hot August afternoon, when sleep came to him within the thicket, but in his heart of hearts there was something that never faded—something that glowed like the red glint of a gypsy's fire seen from afar across the hills and mists of the night, and known to be burning in a wild land. Sometimes, when he was sunken in his books, the flame of delight shot up, and showed him a whole province and continent of his nature, all shining and aglow; and in the midst of the exultation and triumph he would draw back, a little afraid. He had become ascetic in his studious and melancholy isolation, and the vision of such ecstasies frightened him. He began to write a little; at first very tentatively and feebly, and then with more confidence. He showed some of his verses to his father, who told him with a sigh that he had once hoped to write—in the old days at Oxford, he added.

"They are very nicely done," said the parson; "but I'm afraid you won't find anybody to print them, my boy."

So he pottered on; reading everything, imitating what struck his fancy, attempting the effect of the classic meters in English verse, trying his hand at a masque, a Restoration comedy, forming impossible plans for books which rarely got beyond half a dozen lines on a sheet of paper; beset with splendid fancies which refused to abide before the pen. But the vain joy of conception was not altogether vain, for it gave him some armor about his heart.

The months went by, monotonous, and sometimes blotted with despair. He wrote and planned and filled the waste-paper basket with hopeless efforts. Now and then he sent verses or prose articles to magazines, in pathetic ignorance of the trade. He felt the immense difficulty of the career of literature without clearly understanding it; the battle was happily in a mist, so that the host of the enemy, terribly arrayed, was to some extent hidden. Yet there was enough of difficulty to appall; from following the intricate course of little nameless brooks, from hushed twilight woods, from the vision of the mountains, and the breath of the great wind, passing from deep to deep, he would come home filled with thoughts and emotions, mystic fancies which he yearned to translate into the written word. And the result of the effort seemed always to be bathos! Wooden sentences, a portentous stilted style, obscurity, and awkwardness clogged the pen; it seemed impossible to win the great secret of language; the stars glittered only in the darkness, and vanished away in clearer light. The periods of despair were often long and heavy, the victories very few and trifling; night after night he sat writing after his father had knocked out his last pipe, filling a page with difficulty in an hour, and usually forced to thrust the stuff away in despair, and go unhappily to bed, conscious that after all his labour he had done nothing. And these were moments when the accustomed vision of the land alarmed him, and the wild domed hills and darkling woods seemed symbols of some terrible secret in the inner life of that stranger—himself. Sometimes when he was deep in his books and papers, sometimes on a lonely walk, sometimes amidst the tiresome chatter of Caermaen "society," he would thrill with a sudden sense of awful hidden things, and there ran that quivering flame through his nerves that brought back the recollection of the matted thicket, and that earlier appearance of the bare black boughs enwrapped with flames. Indeed, though he avoided the solitary lane, and the sight of the sheer height, with its ring of oaks and moulded mounds, the image of it grew more intense as the symbol of certain hints and suggestions. The exultant and insurgent flesh seemed to have its temple and castle within those olden walls, and he longed with all his heart to escape, to set himself free in the wilderness of London, and to be secure amidst the murmur of modern streets.

II

Lucian was growing really anxious about his manuscript. He had gained enough experience at twenty-three to know that editors and publishers must not be hurried; but his book had been lying at Messrs. Beit's office for more than three months. For six weeks he had not dared to expect an answer, but afterwards life had become agonizing. Every morning, at post-time, the poor wretch nearly choked with anxiety to know whether his sentence had arrived, and the rest of the day was racked with alternate pangs of hope and despair. Now and then he was almost assured of success; conning over these painful and eager pages in memory, he found parts that were admirable, while again, his inexperience reproached him, and he feared he had written a raw and awkward book, wholly unfit for print. Then he would compare what he remembered of it with notable magazine articles and books praised by reviewers, and fancy that after all there might be good points in the thing; he could not help liking the first chapter for instance. Perhaps the letter might come tomorrow. So it went on; week after week of sick torture made more exquisite by such gleams of hope; it was as if he were stretched in anguish on the rack, and the pain relaxed and kind words spoken now and again by the tormentors, and then once more the grinding pang and burning agony. At last he could bear suspense no longer, and he wrote to Messrs. Beit, inquiring in a humble manner whether the manuscript had arrived in safety. The firm replied in a very polite letter, expressing regret that their reader had been suffering from a cold in the head, and had therefore been unable to send in his report. A final decision was promised in a week's time, and the letter ended with apologies for the delay and a hope that he had suffered no inconvenience. Of course the "final decision" did not come at the end of the week, but the book was returned at the end of three weeks, with a circular thanking the author for his kindness in submitting the manuscript, and regretting that the firm did not see their way to producing it. He felt relieved; the operation that he had dreaded and deprecated for so long was at last over, and he would no longer grow sick of mornings when the letters were brought in. He took his parcel to the sunny corner of the garden, where the old wooden seat stood sheltered from the biting March winds. Messrs. Beit had put in with the circular one of their short lists, a neat booklet, headed: *Messrs. Beit & Co.'s Recent Publications*.

He settled himself comfortably on the seat, lit his pipe, and began to read: "*A Bad Un to Beat:* a Novel of Sporting Life, by the Honorable Mrs. Scudamore Runnymede, author of *Yoicks, With the Mudshire Pack, The Sportleigh Stables*, etc., etc., 3 vols. At all Libraries." The *Press*, it seemed, pronounced this to be "a charming book. Mrs. Runnymede has wit and humor enough to furnish forth half-a-dozen ordinary sporting novels." "Told with the sparkle and vivacity of a past-mistress in the art of novel writing," said the *Review*; while Miranda, of *Smart Society*, positively bubbled with enthusiasm. "You must forgive me, Aminta," wrote this young person, "if I have not sent the description I promised of Madame Lulu's new creations and others of that ilk. I must a tale unfold; Tom came in yesterday and began to rave about the Honorable Mrs. Scudamore Runnymede's last novel, *A Bad Un to Beat*. He says all the Smart Set are talking of it, and it seems the police have to regulate the crowd at Mudie's. You know I read everything Mrs. Runnymede writes, so I set out Miggs directly to beg, borrow or steal a copy, and I confess I burnt the midnight oil before I laid it down. Now, mind you get it, you will find it so awfully *chic*." Nearly all the novelists on Messrs. Beit's list were ladies, their works all ran to three volumes, and all of them pleased the *Press*, the *Review*, and Miranda of *Smart Society*. One of these books, *Millicent's Marriage*, by Sarah Pocklington Sanders, was pronounced fit to lie on the school-room table, on the drawing-room bookshelf, or beneath the pillow of the most gently nurtured of our daughters. "This," the reviewer went on, "is high praise, especially in these days when we are deafened by the loud-voiced clamor of self-styled 'artists.' We would warn the young men who prate so persistently of style and literature, construction and prose harmonies, that we believe the English reading public will have none of them. Harmless amusement, a gentle flow of domestic interest, a faithful reproduction of the open and manly life of the hunting field, pictures of innocent and healthy English girlhood such as Miss Sanders here affords us; these are the topics that will always find a welcome in our homes, which remain bolted and barred against the abandoned artist and the scrofulous stylist."

He turned over the pages of the little book and chuckled in high relish; he discovered an honest enthusiasm, a determination to strike a blow for the good and true that refreshed and exhilarated. A beaming face, spectacled and whiskered probably, an expansive waistcoat, and a tender heart, seemed to shine through the words which Messrs.

Beit had quoted; and the alliteration of the final sentence; that was good too; there was style for you if you wanted it. The champion of the blushing cheek and the gushing eye showed that he too could handle the weapons of the enemy if he cared to trouble himself with such things. Lucian leant back and roared with indecent laughter till the tabby tom-cat who had succeeded to the poor dead beasts looked up reproachfully from his sunny corner, with a face like the reviewer's, innocent and round and whiskered. At last he turned to his parcel and drew out some half-dozen sheets of manuscript, and began to read in a rather desponding spirit; it was pretty obvious, he thought, that the stuff was poor and beneath the standard of publication. The book had taken a year and a half in the making; it was a pious attempt to translate into English prose the form and mystery of the domed hills, the magic of occult valleys, the sound of the red swollen brook swirling through leafless woods. Day-dreams and toil at nights had gone into the eager pages, he had laboured hard to do his very best, writing and rewriting, weighing his cadences, beginning over and over again, grudging no patience, no trouble if only it might be pretty good; good enough to print and sell to a reading public which had become critical. He glanced through the manuscript in his hand, and to his astonishment, he could not help thinking that in its measure it was decent work. After three months his prose seemed fresh and strange as if it had been wrought by another man, and in spite of himself he found charming things, and impressions that were not commonplace. He knew how weak it all was compared with his own conceptions; he had seen an enchanted city, awful, glorious, with flame smitten about its battlements, like the cities of the Sangraal, and he had moulded his copy in such poor clay as came to his hand; yet, in spite of the gulf that yawned between the idea and the work, he knew as he read that the thing accomplished was very far from a failure. He put back the leaves carefully, and glanced again at Messrs. Beit's list. It had escaped his notice that *A Bad Un to Beat* was in its third three-volume edition. It was a great thing, at all events, to know in what direction to aim, if he wished to succeed. If he worked hard, he thought, he might some day win the approval of the coy and retiring Miranda of *Smart Society*; that modest maiden might in his praise interrupt her task of disinterested advertisement, her philanthropic counsels to "go to Jumper's, and mind you ask for Mr. C. Jumper, who will show you the lovely blue paper with the yellow spots at ten shillings the piece." He put down the pamphlet, and laughed again at the books and the reviewers: so that he might not weep. This then was English fiction, this was English criticism, and farce, after all, was but an ill-played tragedy.

The rejected manuscript was hidden away, and his father quoted Horace's maxim as to the benefit of keeping literary works for sometime "in the wood." There was nothing to grumble at, though Lucian was inclined to think the duration of the reader's catarrh a little exaggerated. But this was a trifle; he did not arrogate to himself the position of a small commercial traveler, who expects prompt civility as a matter of course, and not at all as a favor. He simply forgot his old book, and resolved that he would make a better one if he could. With the hot fit of resolution, the determination not to be snuffed out by one refusal upon him, he began to beat about in his mind for some new scheme. At first it seemed that he had hit upon a promising subject; he began to plot out chapters and scribble hints for the curious story that had entered his mind, arranging his circumstances and noting the effects to be produced with all the enthusiasm of the artist. But after the first breath the aspect of the work changed; page after page was tossed aside as hopeless, the beautiful sentences he had dreamed of refused to be written, and his puppets remained stiff and wooden, devoid of life or motion. Then all the old despairs came back, the agonies of the artificer who strives and perseveres in vain; the scheme that seemed of amorous fire turned to cold hard ice in his hands. He let the pen drop from his fingers, and wondered how he could have ever dreamed of writing books. Again, the thought occurred that he might do something if he could only get away, and join the sad procession in the murmuring London streets, far from the shadow of those awful hills. But it was quite impossible; the relative who had once promised assistance was appealed to, and wrote expressing his regret that Lucian had turned out a "loafer," wasting his time in scribbling, instead of trying to earn his living. Lucian felt rather hurt at this letter, but the parson only grinned grimly as usual. He was thinking of how he signed a check many years before, in the days of his prosperity, and the check was payable to this didactic relative, then in but a poor way, and of a thankful turn of mind.

The old rejected manuscript had almost passed out of his recollection. It was recalled oddly enough. He was looking over the *Reader*, and enjoying the admirable literary criticisms, some three months after the return of his book, when his eye was attracted by a quoted passage in one of the notices. The thought and style both wakened memory, the cadences were familiar and beloved. He read through the review from the beginning; it was a very favorable one, and pronounced the volume an immense advance on Mr. Ritson's previous work. "Here, undoubtedly, the author has discovered a vein of pure metal," the reviewer added, "and we predict that he will go far." Lucian had not yet reached his father's stage, he was unable to grin in the manner of that irreverent parson. The passage selected for high praise was taken almost word for word from the manuscript now resting in his room, the work that had not reached the high standard of Messrs. Beit & Co., who, curiously enough, were the publishers of the book reviewed in the *Reader*. He had a few shillings in his possession, and wrote at once to a bookseller in London for a copy of *The Chorus in Green*, as the author had oddly named the book. He wrote on June 21st and thought he might fairly expect to receive the interesting volume by the 24th; but the postman, true to his tradition, brought nothing for him, and in the afternoon he resolved to walk down to Caermaen, in case it might have come by a second post; or it might have been mislaid at the office; they forgot parcels sometimes, especially when the bag was heavy and the weather hot. This 24th was a sultry and oppressive day; a grey veil of cloud obscured the sky, and a vaporous mist hung heavily over the land, and fumed up from the valleys. But at five o'clock, when he started, the clouds began to break, and the sunlight suddenly streamed down through the misty air, making ways and channels of rich glory, and bright islands in the gloom. It was a pleasant and shining evening when, passing by devious back streets to avoid the barbarians (as he very rudely called the respectable inhabitants of the town), he reached the post-office; which was also the general shop.

"Yes, Mr. Taylor, there is something for you, sir," said the man. "William the postman forgot to take it up this morning," and he handed over the packet. Lucian took it under his arm and went slowly through the ragged winding lanes till he came into the country. He got over the first stile on the road, and sitting down in the shelter of a hedge, cut the strings and opened the parcel. *The Chorus in Green* was got up in what reviewers call a dainty manner: a bronze-green cloth, well-cut gold lettering, wide margins and black "old-face" type, all witnessed to the good taste of Messrs. Beit & Co. He cut the pages hastily and began to read. He soon found that he had wronged Mr. Ritson—that old literary hand had by no means stolen his book wholesale, as he had expected. There were about two hundred pages in the pretty little volume, and of these about ninety were Lucian's, dovetailed into a rather different scheme with skill that was nothing short of exquisite. And Mr. Ritson's own work was often very good; spoilt here and there for some tastes by the "cataloguing" method, a somewhat materialistic way of taking an inventory of the holy country things; but, for that very reason, contrasting to a great advantage with Lucian's hints and dreams and note of haunting. And here and there Mr. Ritson had made little alterations in the style of the passages he had conveyed, and most of these alterations were amendments, as Lucian was obliged to confess, though he would have liked to argue one or two points with his collabourator and corrector. He lit his pipe and leant back comfortably in the hedge, thinking things over, weighing very coolly his experience of humanity, his contact with the "society" of the countryside, the affair of the *The Chorus in Green*, and even some little incidents that had struck him as he was walking through the streets of Caermaen that evening. At the post-office, when he was inquiring for his parcel, he had heard two old women grumbling in the street; it seemed, so far as he could make out, that both had been disappointed in much the same way. One was a Roman Catholic, hardened, and beyond the reach of conversion; she had been advised to ask alms of the priests, "who are always creeping and crawling about." The other old sinner was a Dissenter, and, "Mr. Dixon has quite enough to do to relieve good Church people." Mrs. Dixon, assisted by Henrietta, was, it seemed, the lady high almoner, who dispensed these charities. As she said to Mrs. Colley, they would end by keeping all the beggars in the county, and they really couldn't afford it. A large family was an expensive thing, and the girls *must* have new frocks. "Mr. Dixon is always telling me and the girls that we must not *demoralize* the people by indiscriminate charity." Lucian had heard of these sage counsels, and through it them as he listened to the bitter complaints of the gaunt, hungry old women. In the back street by which he passed out of the town he saw a large "healthy" boy kicking a sick cat; the poor creature had just strength enough to crawl under an outhouse door; probably to die in torments. He did not find much satisfaction in thrashing the boy, but he did it with hearty good will. Further on, at the corner where the turnpike used to be, was a big notice, announcing a meeting at the school-room in aid of the missions to the Portuguese. "Under the Patronage of the Lord Bishop of the Diocese," was the imposing headline; the Reverend Merivale Dixon, vicar of Caermaen, was to be in the chair, supported by Stanley Gervase, Esq., J.P., and by many of the clergy and gentry of the neighborhood. Senhor Diabo, "formerly a Romanist priest, now an evangelist in Lisbon," would address the meeting. "Funds are urgently needed to carry on this good work," concluded the notice. So he lay well back in the shade of the hedge, and thought whether some sort of an article could not be made by vindicating the terrible Yahoos; one might point out that they were in many respects a simple and unsophisticated race, whose faults were the result of their enslaved position, while such virtues as they had were all their own. They might be compared, he thought, much to their advantage, with more complex civilizations. There was no hint of anything like the Beit system of publishing in existence amongst them; the great Yahoo nation would surely never feed and encourage a scabby Houyhnhnm, expelled for his foulness from the horse-community, and the witty dean, in all his minuteness, had said nothing of "safe" Yahoos. On reflection, however, he did not feel quite secure of this part of his defense; he remembered that the leading brutes had favorites, who were employed in certain simple domestic offices about their masters, and it seemed doubtful whether the contemplated vindication would not break down on this point. He smiled queerly to himself as he thought of these comparisons, but his heart burned with a dull fury. Throwing back his unhappy memory, he recalled all the contempt and scorn he had suffered; as a boy he had heard the masters murmuring their disdain of him and of his desire to learn other than ordinary school work. As a young man he had suffered the insolence of these wretched people about him; their cackling laughter at his poverty jarred and grated in his ears; he saw the acrid grin of some miserable idiot woman, some creature beneath the swine in intelligence and manners, merciless, as he went by with his eyes on the dust, in his ragged clothes. He and his father seemed to pass down an avenue of jeers and contempt, and contempt from such animals as these! This putrid filth, moulded into human shape, made only to fawn on the rich and beslaver them, thinking no foulness too foul if it were done in honor of those in power and authority; and no refined cruelty of contempt too cruel if it were contempt of the poor and humble and oppressed; it was to this obscene and ghastly throng that he was something to be pointed at. And these men and women spoke of sacred things, and knelt before the awful altar of God, before the altar of tremendous fire, surrounded as they professed by Angels and Archangels and all the Company of Heaven; and in their very church they had one aisle for the rich and another for the poor. And the species was not peculiar to Caermaen; the rich business men in London and the successful brother author were probably amusing themselves at the expense of the poor struggling creature they had injured and wounded; just as the "healthy" boy had burst into a great laugh when the miserable sick cat cried out in bitter agony, and trailed its limbs slowly, as it crept away to die. Lucian looked into his own life and his own will; he saw that in spite of his follies, and his want of success, he had not been consciously malignant, he had never deliberately aided in oppression, or looked on it with enjoyment and approval, and he felt that when he lay dead beneath the earth, eaten by swarming worms, he would be in a purer company than now, when he lived amongst human creatures. And he was to call this loathsome beast, all sting and filth, brother! "I had rather call the devils my brothers," he said in his heart, "I would fare better in hell." Blood was in his eyes, and as he looked up the sky seemed of blood, and the earth burned with fire.

The sun was sinking low on the mountain when he set out on the way again. Burrows, the doctor, coming home in his trap, met him a little lower on the road, and gave him a friendly goodnight.

"A long way round on this road, isn't it?" said the doctor. "As you have come so far, why don't you try the short cut across the fields? You will find it easily enough; second stile on the left hand, and then go straight ahead."

He thanked Dr. Burrows and said he would try the short cut, and Burrows span on homeward. He was a gruff and honest bachelor, and often felt very sorry for the lad, and wished he could help him. As he drove on, it suddenly occurred to him that Lucian had an awful look on his face, and he was sorry he had not asked him to jump in, and to come to supper. A hearty slice of beef, with strong ale, whisky and soda afterwards, a good pipe, and certain Rabelaisian tales which the doctor had treasured for many years, would have done the poor fellow a lot of good, he was certain. He half turned round on his seat, and looked to see if Lucian were still in sight, but he had passed the corner, and the doctor drove on, shivering a little; the mists were beginning to rise from the wet banks of the river.

Lucian trailed slowly along the road, keeping a look out for the stile the doctor had mentioned. It would be a little of an adventure, he thought, to find his way by an unknown track; he knew the direction in which his home lay, and he imagined he would not have much difficulty in crossing from one stile to another. The path led him up a steep bare field, and when he was at the top, the town and the valley winding up to the north stretched before him. The river was stilled at the flood, and the yellow water, reflecting the sunset, glowed in its deep pools like dull brass. These burning pools, the level meadows fringed with shuddering reeds, the long dark sweep of the forest on the hill, were all clear and distinct, yet the light seemed to have clothed them with a new garment, even as voices from the streets of Caermaen sounded strangely, mounting up thin with the smoke. There beneath him lay the huddled cluster of Caermaen, the ragged and uneven roofs that marked the winding and sordid streets, here and there a pointed gable rising above its meaner fellows; beyond he recognized the piled mounds that marked the circle of the amphitheatre, and the dark edge of trees that grew where the Roman wall whitened and waxed old beneath the frosts and rains of eighteen hundred years. Thin and strange, mingled together, the voices came up to him on the hill; it was as if an outland race inhabited the ruined city and talked in a strange language of strange and terrible things. The sun had slid down the sky, and hung quivering over the huge dark dome of the mountain like a burnt sacrifice, and then suddenly vanished. In the afterglow the clouds began to writhe and turn scarlet, and shone so strangely reflected in the pools of the snake-like river, that one would have said the still waters stirred, the fleeting and changing of the clouds seeming to quicken the stream, as if it bubbled and sent up gouts of blood. But already about the town the darkness was forming; fast, fast the shadows crept upon it from the forest, and from all sides banks and wreaths of curling mist were gathering, as if a ghostly leaguer were being built up against the city, and the strange race who lived in its streets. Suddenly there burst out from the stillness the clear and piercing music of the *réveillé*, calling, recalling, iterated, reiterated, and ending with one long high fierce shrill note with which the steep hills rang. Perhaps a boy in the school band was practicing on his bugle, but for Lucian it was magic. For him it was the note of the Roman trumpet, *tuba mirum spargens sonum*, filling all the hollow valley with its command, reverberated in dark places in the far forest, and resonant in the old graveyards without the walls. In his imagination he saw the earthen gates of the tombs broken open, and the serried legion swarming to the eagles. Century by century they passed by; they rose, dripping, from the river bed, they rose from the level, their armor shone in the quiet orchard, they gathered in ranks and companies from the cemetery, and as the trumpet sounded, the hill fort above the town gave up its dead. By hundreds and thousands the ghostly battle surged about the standard, behind the quaking mist, ready to march against the mouldering walls they had built so many years before.

He turned sharply; it was growing very dark, and he was afraid of missing his way. At first the path led him by the verge of a wood; there was a noise of rustling and murmuring from the trees as if they were taking evil counsel together. A high hedge shut out the sight of the darkening valley, and he stumbled on mechanically, without taking much note of the turnings of the track, and when he came out from the wood shadow to the open country, he stood for a moment quite bewildered and uncertain. A dark wild twilight country lay before him, confused dim shapes of trees near at hand, and a hollow below his feet, and the further hills and woods were dimmer, and all the air was very still. Suddenly the darkness about him glowed; a furnace fire had shot up on the mountain, and for a moment the little world of the woodside and the steep hill shone in a pale light, and he thought he saw his path beaten out in the turf before him. The great flame sank down to a red glint of fire, and it led him on down the ragged slope, his feet striking against ridges of ground, and falling from beneath him at a sudden dip. The bramble bushes shot out long prickly vines, amongst which he was entangled, and lower he was held back by wet bubbling earth. He had descended into a dark and shady valley, beset and tapestried with gloomy thickets; the weird wood noises were the only sounds, strange, unutterable mutterings, dismal, inarticulate. He pushed on in what he hoped was the right direction, stumbling from stile to gate, peering through mist and shadow, and still vainly seeking for any known landmark. Presently another sound broke upon the grim air, the murmur of water poured over stones, gurgling against the old misshapen roots of trees, and running clear in a deep channel. He passed into the chill breath of the brook, and almost fancied he heard two voices speaking in its murmur; there seemed a ceaseless utterance of words, an endless argument. With a mood of horror pressing on him, he listened to the noise of waters, and the wild fancy seized him that he was not deceived, that two unknown beings stood together there in the darkness and tried the balances of his life, and spoke his doom. The hour in the matted thicket rushed over the great bridge of years to his thought; he had sinned against the earth, and the earth trembled and shook for vengeance. He stayed still for a moment, quivering with fear, and at last went on blindly, no longer caring for the path, if only he might escape from the toils of that dismal shuddering hollow. As he plunged through the hedges the bristling thorns tore his face and hands; he fell amongst stinging-nettles and was pricked as he beat out his way amidst the gorse. He raced headlong, his head over his shoulder, through a windy wood, bare of undergrowth; there lay about the ground mouldering stumps, the relics of trees that had thundered to their fall, crashing and tearing to earth, long ago; and from these remains there flowed out a pale thin radiance, filling the spaces of the sounding wood with a dream of light. He had lost all count of the track; he felt he had fled for hours, climbing and descending, and yet not advancing; it was as if he stood still and the shadows of the land went by, in a vision. But at last a hedge, high and straggling, rose before him, and as he broke through it, his feet slipped, and he fell headlong down a steep bank into a lane. He lay still, half-stunned, for a moment, and then rising unsteadily, he looked desperately into the darkness before him, uncertain and bewildered. In front it was black as a midnight cellar, and he turned about, and saw a glint in the distance, as if a candle were flickering in a farm-house window. He began to walk with trembling feet towards the light, when suddenly something pale started out from the shadows before him, and seemed to swim and float down the air. He was going down hill, and he hastened onwards, and he could see the bars of a stile framed dimly against the sky, and the figure still advanced with that gliding motion. Then, as the road declined to the valley, the landmark he had been seeking appeared. To his right there surged up in the darkness the darker summit of the Roman fort, and the streaming fire of the great full moon glowed through the bars of the wizard oaks, and made a halo shine about the hill. He was now quite close to the white appearance, and saw that it was only a woman walking swiftly down the lane; the floating movement was an effect due to the somber air and the moon's glamour. At the gate, where he had spent so many hours gazing at the fort, they walked foot to foot, and he saw it was Annie Morgan.

"Good evening, Master Lucian," said the girl, "it's very dark, sir, indeed."

"Good evening, Annie," he answered, calling her by her name for the first time, and he saw that she smiled with pleasure. "You are out late, aren't you?"

"Yes, sir; but I've been taking a bit of supper to old Mrs. Gibbon.

She's been very poorly the last few days, and there's nobody to do anything for her."

Then there were really people who helped one another; kindness and pity were not mere myths, fictions of "society," as useful as Doe and Roe, and as non-existent. The thought struck Lucian with a shock; the evening's passion and delirium, the wild walk and physical fatigue had almost shattered him in body and mind. He was "degenerate," *decadent*, and the rough rains and blustering winds of life, which a stronger man would have laughed at and enjoyed, were to him "hail-storms and fire-showers." After all, Messrs. Beit, the publishers, were only sharp men of business, and these terrible Dixons and Gervases and Colleys merely the ordinary limited clergy and gentry of a quiet country town; sturdier sense would have dismissed Dixon as an old humbug, Stanley Gervase, Esquire, J.P., as a "bit of a bounder," and the ladies as "rather a shoddy lot." But he was walking slowly now in painful silence, his heavy, lagging feet striking against the loose stones. He was not thinking of the girl beside him; only something seemed to swell and grow and swell within his heart; it was all the torture of his days, weary hopes and weary disappointment, scorn rankling and throbbing, and the thought "I had rather call the devils my brothers and live with them in hell." He choked and gasped for breath, and felt involuntary muscles working in his face, and the impulses of a madman stirring him; he himself was in truth the realization of the vision of Caermaen that night, a city with mouldering walls beset by the ghostly legion. Life and the world and the laws of the sunlight had passed away, and the resurrection and kingdom of the dead began. The Celt assailed him, becoming from the weird wood he called the world, and his far-off ancestors, the "little people," crept out of their caves, muttering charms and incantations in hissing inhuman speech; he was beleaguered by desires that had slept in his race for ages.

"I am afraid you are very tired, Master Lucian. Would you like me to give you my hand over this rough bit?"

He had stumbled against a great round stone and had nearly fallen. The woman's hand sought his in the darkness; as he felt the touch of the soft warm flesh he moaned, and a pang shot through his arm to his heart. He looked up and found he had only walked a few paces since Annie had spoken; he had thought they had wandered for hours together. The moon was just mounting above the oaks, and the halo round the dark hill brightened. He stopped short, and keeping his hold of Annie's hand, looked into her face. A hazy glory of moonlight shone around them and lit up their eyes. He had not greatly altered since his boyhood; his face was pale olive in colour, thin and oval; marks of pain had gathered about the eyes, and his black hair was already stricken with grey. But the eager, curious gaze still remained, and what he saw before him lit up his sadness with a new fire. She stopped too, and did not offer to draw away, but looked back with all her heart. They were alike in many ways; her skin was also of that olive colour, but her face was sweet as a beautiful summer night, and her black eyes showed no dimness, and the smile on the scarlet lips was like a flame when it brightens a dark and lonely land.

"You are sorely tired, Master Lucian, let us sit down here by the gate."

It was Lucian who spoke next: "My dear, my dear." And their lips were together again, and their arms locked together, each holding the other fast. And then the poor lad let his head sink down on his sweetheart's breast, and burst into a passion of weeping. The tears streamed down his face, and he shook with sobbing, in the happiest moment that he had ever lived. The woman bent over him and tried to comfort him, but his tears were his consolation and his triumph. Annie was whispering to him, her hand laid on his heart; she was whispering beautiful, wonderful words, that soothed him as a song. He did not know what they meant.

"Annie, dear, dear Annie, what are you saying to me? I have never heard such beautiful words. Tell me, Annie, what do they mean?"

She laughed, and said it was only nonsense that the nurses sang to the children.

"No, no, you are not to call me Master Lucian anymore," he said, when they parted, "you must call me Lucian; and I, I worship you, my dear Annie."

He fell down before her, embracing her knees, and adored, and she allowed him, and confirmed his worship. He followed slowly after her, passing the path which led to her home with a longing glance. Nobody saw any difference in Lucian when he reached the rectory. He came in with his usual dreamy indifference, and told how he had lost his way by trying the short cut. He said he had met Dr. Burrows on the road, and that he had recommended the path by the fields. Then, as dully as if he had been reading some story out of a newspaper, he gave his father the outlines of the Beit case, producing the pretty little book called *The Chorus in Green*. The parson listened in amazement.

"You mean to tell me that *you* wrote this book?" he said. He was quite roused.

"No; not all of it. Look; that bit is mine, and that; and the beginning of this chapter. Nearly the whole of the third chapter is by me."

He closed the book without interest, and indeed he felt astonished at his father's excitement. The incident seemed to him unimportant.

"And you say that eighty or ninety pages of this book are yours, and these scoundrels have stolen your work?"

"Well, I suppose they have. I'll fetch the manuscript, if you would like to look at it."

The manuscript was duly produced, wrapped in brown paper, with Messrs.

Beit's address label on it, and the post-office dated stamps.

"And the other book has been out a month." The parson, forgetting the sacerdotal office, and his good habit of grinning, swore at Messrs. Beit and Mr. Ritson, calling them damned thieves, and then began to read the manuscript, and to compare it with the printed book.

"Why, it's splendid work. My poor fellow," he said after a while, "I had no notion you could write so well. I used to think of such things in the old days at Oxford; 'old Bill,' the tutor, used to praise my essays, but I never wrote anything like this. And this infernal ruffian of a Ritson has taken all your best things and mixed them up with his own rot to make it go down. Of course you'll expose the gang?"

Lucian was mildly amused; he couldn't enter into his father's feelings at all. He sat smoking in one of the old easy chairs, taking the rare relish of a hot grog with his pipe, and gazing out of his dreamy eyes at the violent old parson. He was pleased that his father liked his book, because he knew him to be a deep and sober scholar and a cool judge of good letters; but he laughed to himself when he saw the magic of print. The parson had expressed no wish to read the manuscript when it came back in disgrace; he had merely grinned, said something about boomerangs, and quoted Horace with relish. Whereas now, before the book in its neat case, lettered with another man's name, his approbation of the writing and his disapproval of the "scoundrels," as he called them, were loudly expressed, and, though a good smoker, he blew and puffed vehemently at his pipe.

"You'll expose the rascals, of course, won't you?" he said again.

"Oh no, I think not. It really doesn't matter much, does it? After all, there are some very weak things in the book; doesn't it strike you as 'young?' I have been thinking of another plan, but I haven't done much with it lately. But I believe I've got hold of a really good idea this time, and if I can manage to see the heart of it I hope to turn out a manuscript worth stealing. But it's so hard to get at the core of an idea—the heart, as I call it," he went on after a pause. "It's like having a box you can't open, though you know there's something wonderful inside. But I do believe I've a fine thing in my hands, and I mean to try my best to work it."

Lucian talked with enthusiasm now, but his father, on his side, could not share these ardors. It was his part to be astonished at excitement over a book that was not even begun, the mere ghost of a book flitting elusive in the world of unborn masterpieces and failures. He had loved good letters, but he shared unconsciously in the general belief that literary attempt is always pitiful, though he did not subscribe to the other half of the popular faith—that literary success is a matter of very little importance. He thought well of books, but only of printed books; in manuscripts he put no faith, and the *paulo-post-futurum* tense he could not in any manner conjugate. He returned once more to the topic of palpable interest.

"But about this dirty trick these fellows have played on you. You won't sit quietly and bear it, surely? It's only a question of writing to the papers."

"They wouldn't put the letter in. And if they did, I should only get laughed at. Sometime ago a man wrote to the *Reader*, complaining of his play being stolen. He said that he had sent a little one-act comedy to Burleigh, the great dramatist, asking for his advice. Burleigh gave his advice and took the idea for his own very successful play. So the man said, and I daresay it was true enough. But the victim got nothing by his complaint. 'A pretty state of things,' everybody said. 'Here's a Mr. Tomson, that no one has ever heard of, bothers Burleigh with his rubbish, and then accuses him of petty larceny. Is it likely that a man of Burleigh's position, a playwright who can make his five thousand a year easily, would borrow from an unknown Tomson?' I should think it very likely, indeed," Lucian went on, chuckling, "but that was their verdict. No; I don't think I'll write to the papers."

"Well, well, my boy, I suppose you know your own business best. I think you are mistaken, but you must do as you like."

"It's all so unimportant," said Lucian, and he really thought so. He had sweeter things to dream of, and desired no communion of feeling with that madman who had left Caermaen some few hours before. He felt he had made a fool of himself, he was ashamed to think of the fatuity of which he had been guilty, such boiling hatred was not only wicked, but absurd. A man could do no good who put himself into a position of such violent antagonism against his fellow-creatures; so Lucian rebuked his heart, saying that he was old enough to know better. But he remembered that he had sweeter things to dream of; there was a secret ecstasy that he treasured and locked tight away, as a joy too exquisite even for thought till he was quite alone; and then there was that scheme for a new book that he had laid down hopelessly sometime ago; it seemed to have arisen into life again within the last hour; he understood that he had started on a false tack, he had taken the wrong aspect of his idea. Of course the thing couldn't be written in that way; it was like trying to read a page turned upside down; and he saw those characters he had vainly sought suddenly disambushed, and a splendid inevitable sequence of events unrolled before him.

It was a true resurrection; the dry plot he had constructed revealed itself as a living thing, stirring and mysterious, and warm as life itself. The parson was smoking stolidly to all appearance, but in reality he was full of amazement at his own son, and now and again he slipped sly furtive glances towards the tranquil young man in the arm-chair by the empty hearth. In the first place, Mr. Taylor was genuinely impressed by what he had read of Lucian's work; he had so long been accustomed to look upon all effort as futile that success amazed him. In the abstract, of course, he was prepared to admit that some people did write well and got published and made money, just as other persons successfully backed an outsider at heavy odds; but it had seemed as improbable that Lucian should show even the beginnings of achievement in one direction as in the other. Then the boy evidently cared so little about it; he did not appear to be proud of being worth robbing, nor was he angry with the robbers.

He sat back luxuriously in the disreputable old chair, drawing long slow wreaths of smoke, tasting his whisky from time to time, evidently well at ease with himself. The father saw him smile, and it suddenly dawned upon him that his son was very handsome; he had such kind gentle eyes and a kind mouth, and his pale cheeks were flushed like a girl's. Mr. Taylor felt moved. What a harmless young fellow Lucian had been; no doubt a little queer and different from others, but wholly inoffensive and patient under disappointment. And Miss Deacon, her contribution to the evening's discussion had been characteristic; she had remarked, firstly, that writing was a very unsettling occupation, and secondly, that it was extremely foolish to entrust one's property to people of whom one knew nothing. Father and son had smiled together at these observations, which were probably true enough. Mr. Taylor at last left Lucian along; he shook hands with a good deal of respect, and said, almost deferentially:

"You mustn't work too hard, old fellow. I wouldn't stay up too late, if I were you, after that long walk. You must have gone miles out of your way."

"I'm not tired now, though. I feel as if I could write my new book on the spot"; and the young man laughed a gay sweet laugh that struck the father as a new note in his son's life.

He sat still a moment after his father had left the room. He cherished his chief treasure of thought in its secret place; he would not enjoy it yet. He drew up a chair to the table at which he wrote or tried to write, and began taking pens and paper from the drawer. There was a great pile of ruled paper there; all of it used, on one side, and signifying many hours of desperate scribbling, of heart-searching and rack of his brain; an array of poor, eager lines written by a waning fire with waning hope; all useless and abandoned. He took up the sheets cheerfully, and began in delicious idleness to look over these fruitless efforts. A page caught his attention; he remembered how he wrote it while a November storm was dashing against the panes; and there was another, with a queer blot in one corner; he had got up from his chair and looked out, and all the earth was white fairyland, and the snowflakes whirled round and round in the wind. Then he saw the chapter begun of a night in March: a great gale blew that night and rooted up one of the ancient yews in the churchyard. He had heard the trees shrieking in the woods, and the long wail of the wind, and across the heaven a white moon fled awfully before the streaming clouds. And all these poor abandoned pages now seemed sweet, and past unhappiness was transmuted into happiness, and the nights of toil were holy. He turned over half a dozen leaves and began to sketch out the outlines of the new book on the unused pages; running out a skeleton plan on one page, and dotting fancies, suggestions, hints on others. He wrote rapidly, overjoyed to find that loving phrases grew under his pen; a particular scene he had imagined filled him with desire; he gave his hand free course, and saw the written work glowing; and action and all the heat of existence quickened and beat on the wet page. Happy fancies took shape in happier words, and when at last he leant back in his chair he felt the stir and rush of the story as if it had been some portion of his own life. He read over what he had done with a renewed pleasure in the nimble and flowing workmanship, and as he put the little pile of manuscript tenderly in the drawer he paused to enjoy the anticipation of tomorrow's labour.

And then—but the rest of the night was given to tender and delicious things, and when he went up to bed a scarlet dawn was streaming from the east.

III

For days Lucian lay in a swoon of pleasure, smiling when he was addressed, sauntering happily in the sunlight, hugging recollection warm to his heart. Annie had told him that she was going on a visit to her married sister, and said, with a caress, that he must be patient. He protested against her absence, but she fondled him, whispering her charms in his ear till he gave in and then they said goodbye, Lucian adoring on his knees. The parting was as strange as the meeting, and that night when he laid his work aside, and let himself sink deep into the joys of memory, all the encounter seemed as wonderful and impossible as magic.

"And you really don't mean to do anything about those rascals?" said his father.

"Rascals? Which rascals? Oh, you mean Beit. I had forgotten all about it.

No; I don't think I shall trouble. They're not worth powder and shot."

And he returned to his dream, pacing slowly from the medlar to the quince and back again. It seemed trivial to be interrupted by such questions; he had not even time to think of the book he had recommenced so eagerly, much less of this labour of long ago. He recollected without interest that it cost him many pains, that it was pretty good here and there, and that it had been stolen, and it seemed that there was nothing more to be said on the matter. He wished to think of the darkness in the lane, of the kind voice that spoke to him, of the kind hand that sought his own, as he stumbled on the rough way. So far, it was wonderful. Since he had left school and lost the company of the worthy barbarians who had befriended him there, he had almost lost the sense of kinship with humanity; he had come to dread the human form as men dread the hood of the cobra. To Lucian a man or a woman meant something that stung, that spoke words that rankled, and poisoned his life with scorn. At first such malignity shocked him: he would ponder over words and glances and wonder if he were not mistaken, and he still sought now and then for sympathy. The poor boy had romantic ideas about women; he believed they were merciful and pitiful, very kind to the unlucky and helpless. Men perhaps had to be different; after all, the duty of a man was to get on in the world, or, in plain language, to make money, to be successful; to cheat rather than to be cheated, but always to be successful; and he could understand that one who fell below this high standard must expect to be severely judged by his fellows. For example, there was young Bennett, Miss Spurry's nephew. Lucian had met him once or twice when he was spending his holidays with Miss Spurry, and the two young fellows compared literary notes together. Bennett showed some beautiful things he had written, over which Lucian had grown both sad and enthusiastic. It was such exquisite magic verse, and so much better than anything he ever hoped to write, that there was a touch of anguish in his congratulations. But when Bennett, after many vain prayers to his aunt, threw up a safe position in the bank, and betook himself to a London garret, Lucian was not surprised at the general verdict.

Mr. Dixon, as a clergyman, viewed the question from a high standpoint and found it all deplorable, but the general opinion was that Bennett was a hopeless young lunatic. Old Mr. Gervase went purple when his name was mentioned, and the young Dixons sneered very merrily over the adventure.

"I always thought he was a beastly young ass," said Edward Dixon, "but I didn't think he'd chuck away his chances like that. Said he couldn't stand a bank! I hope he'll be able to stand bread and water. That's all those littery fellows get, I believe, except Tennyson and Mark Twain and those sort of people."

Lucian of course sympathized with the unfortunate Bennett, but such judgments were after all only natural. The young man might have stayed in the bank and succeeded to his aunt's thousand a year, and everybody would have called him a very nice young fellow—"clever, too." But he had deliberately chosen, as Edward Dixon had said, to chuck his chances away for the sake of literature; piety and a sense of the main chance had alike pointed the way to a delicate course of wheedling, to a little harmless practicing on Miss Spurry's infirmities, to frequent compliances of a soothing nature, and the "young ass" had been blind to the direction of one and the other. It seemed almost right that the vicar should moralize, that Edward Dixon should sneer, and that Mr. Gervase should grow purple with contempt. Men, Lucian thought, were like judges, who may pity the criminal in their hearts, but are forced to vindicate the outraged majesty of the law by a severe sentence. He felt the same considerations applied to his own case; he knew that his father should have had more money, that his clothes should be newer and of a better cut, that he should have gone to the university and made good friends. If such had been his fortune he could have looked his fellow-men proudly in the face, upright and unashamed. Having put on the whole armor of a first-rate West End tailor, with money in his purse, having taken anxious thought for the morrow, and having some useful friends and good prospects; in such a case he might have held his head high in a gentlemanly and Christian community. As it was he had usually avoided the reproachful glance of his fellows, feeling that he deserved their condemnation. But he had cherished for a long time his romantic sentimentalities about women; literary conventions borrowed from the minor poets and pseudo-medievalists, or so he thought afterwards. But, fresh from school, wearied a little with the perpetual society of barbarian though worthy boys, he had in his soul a charming image of womanhood, before which he worshipped with mingled passion and devotion. It was a nude figure, perhaps, but the shining arms were to be wound about the neck of a vanquished knight; there was rest for the head of a wounded lover; the hands were stretched forth to do works of pity, and the smiling lips were to murmur not love alone, but consolation in defeat. Here was the refuge for a broken heart; here the scorn of men would but make tenderness increase; here was all pity and all charity with loving-kindness. It was a delightful picture, conceived in the "come rest on this bosom," and "a ministering angel thou" manner, with touches of allurement that made devotion all the sweeter. He soon found that he had idealized a little; in the affair of young Bennett, while the men were contemptuous the women were virulent. He had been rather fond of Agatha Gervase, and she, so other ladies said, had "set her cap" at him. Now, when he rebelled, and lost the goodwill of his aunt, dear Miss Spurry, Agatha insulted him with all conceivable rapidity. "After all, Mr. Bennett," she said, "you will be nothing better than a beggar; now, will you? You mustn't think me cruel, but I can't help speaking the truth. *Write books!*" Her expression filled up the incomplete sentence; she waggled with indignant emotion. These passages came to Lucian's ears, and indeed the Gervases boasted of "how well poor Agatha had behaved."

"Never mind, Gathy," old Gervase had observed. "If the impudent young puppy comes here again, we'll see what Thomas can do with the horse-whip."

"Poor dear child," Mrs. Gervase added in telling the tale, "and she was so fond of him too. But of course it couldn't go on after his shameful behavior."

But Lucian was troubled; he sought vainly for the ideal womanly, the tender note of "come rest on this bosom." Ministering angels, he felt convinced, do not rub red pepper and sulfuric acid into the wounds of suffering mortals.

Then there was the case of Mr. Vaughan, a squire in the neighborhood, at whose board all the aristocracy of Caermaen had feasted for years. Mr. Vaughan had a first-rate cook, and his cellar was rare, and he was never so happy as when he shared his good things with his friends. His mother kept his house, and they delighted all the girls with frequent dances, while the men sighed over the amazing champagne. Investments proved disastrous, and Mr. Vaughan had to sell the grey manor-house by the river. He and his mother took a little modern stucco villa in Caermaen, wishing to be near their dear friends. But the men were "very sorry; rough on you, Vaughan. Always thought those Patagonians were risky, but you wouldn't hear of it. Hope we shall see you before very long; you and Mrs. Vaughan must come to tea some day after Christmas."

"Of course we are all very sorry for them," said Henrietta Dixon. "No, we haven't called on Mrs. Vaughan yet. They have no regular servant, you know; only a woman in the morning. I hear old mother Vaughan, as Edward will call her, does nearly everything. And their house is absurdly small; it's little more than a cottage. One really can't call it a gentleman's house."

Then Mr. Vaughan, his heart in the dust, went to the Gervases and tried to borrow five pounds of Mr. Gervase. He had to be ordered out of the house, and, as Edith Gervase said, it was all very painful; "he went out in such a funny way," she added, "just like the dog when he's had a whipping. Of course it's sad, even if it is all his own fault, as everybody says, but he looked so ridiculous as he was going down the steps that I couldn't help laughing." Mr. Vaughan heard the ringing, youthful laughter as he crossed the lawn.

Young girls like Henrietta Dixon and Edith Gervase naturally viewed the Vaughans' comical position with all the high spirits of their age, but the elder ladies could not look at matters in this frivolous light.

"Hush, dear, hush," said Mrs. Gervase, "it's all too shocking to be a laughing matter. Don't you agree with me, Mrs. Dixon? The sinful extravagance that went on at Pentre always *frightened* me. You remember that ball they gave last year? Mr. Gervase assured me that the champagne must have cost *at least* a hundred and fifty shillings the dozen."

"It's dreadful, isn't it," said Mrs. Dixon, "when one thinks of how many poor people there are who would be thankful for a crust of bread?"

"Yes, Mrs. Dixon," Agatha joined in, "and you know how absurdly the Vaughans spoilt the cottagers. Oh, it was really wicked; one would think Mr. Vaughan wished to make them above their station. Edith and I went for a walk one day nearly as far as Pentre, and we begged a glass of water of old Mrs. Jones who lives in that pretty cottage near the brook. She began praising the Vaughans in the most fulsome manner, and showed us some flannel things they had given her at Christmas. I assure you, my dear Mrs. Dixon, the flannel was the very best quality; no lady could wish for better. It couldn't have cost less than half-a-crown a yard."

"I know, my dear, I know. Mr. Dixon always said it couldn't last. How often I have heard him say that the Vaughans were pauperizing all the common people about Pentre, and putting everyone else in a most unpleasant position. Even from a worldly point of view it was very poor taste on their part. So different from the *true* charity that Paul speaks of."

"I only wish they had given away nothing worse than flannel," said Miss Colley, a young lady of very strict views. "But I assure you there was a perfect orgy, I can call it nothing else, every Christmas. Great joints of prime beef, and barrels of strong beer, and snuff and tobacco distributed wholesale; as if the poor wanted to be encouraged in their disgusting habits. It was really impossible to go through the village for weeks after; the whole place was poisoned with the fumes of horrid tobacco pipes."

"Well, we see how that sort of thing ends," said Mrs. Dixon, summing up judicially. "We had intended to call, but I really think it would be impossible after what Mrs. Gervase has told us. The idea of Mr. Vaughan trying to sponge on poor Mr. Gervase in that shabby way! I think meanness of that kind is so hateful."

It was the practical side of all this that astonished Lucian. He saw that in reality there was no high-flown quixotism in a woman's nature; the smooth arms, made he had thought for caressing, seemed muscular; the hands meant for the doing of works of pity in his system, appeared dexterous in the giving of "stingers," as Barnes might say, and the smiling lips could sneer with great ease. Nor was he more fortunate in his personal experiences. As has been told, Mrs. Dixon spoke of him in connection with "judgments," and the younger ladies did not exactly cultivate his acquaintance. Theoretically they "adored" books and thought poetry "too sweet," but in practice they preferred talking about mares and fox-terriers and their neighbors.

They were nice girls enough, very like other young ladies in other country towns, content with the teaching of their parents, reading the Bible every morning in their bedrooms, and sitting every Sunday in church amongst the well-dressed "sheep" on the right hand. It was not their fault if they failed to satisfy the ideal of an enthusiastic dreamy boy, and indeed, they would have thought his feigned woman immodest, absurdly sentimental, a fright ("never wears stays, my dear") and *horrid*.

At first he was a good deal grieved at the loss of that charming tender woman, the work of his brain. When the Miss Dixons went haughtily by with a scornful waggle, when the Miss Gervases passed in the wagonette laughing as the mud splashed him, the poor fellow would look up with a face of grief that must have been very comic; "like a dying duck," as Edith Gervase said. Edith was really very pretty, and he would have liked to talk to her, even about fox-terriers, if she would have listened. One afternoon at the Dixons' he really forced himself upon her, and with all the obtuseness of an enthusiastic boy tried to discuss the *Lotus Eaters* of Tennyson. It was too absurd. Captain Kempton was making signals to Edith all the time, and Lieutenant Gatwick had gone off in disgust, and he had promised to bring her a puppy "by Vick out of Wasp." At last the poor girl could bear it no longer:

"Yes, it's very sweet," she said at last. "When did you say you were going to London, Mr. Taylor?"

It was about the time that his disappointment became known to everybody, and the shot told. He gave her a piteous look and slunk off, "just like the dog when he's had a whipping," to use Edith's own expression. Two or three lessons of this description produced their due effect; and when he saw a male Dixon or Gervase approaching him he bit his lip and summoned up his courage. But when he descried a "ministering angel" he made haste and hid behind a hedge or took to the woods. In course of time the desire to escape became an instinct, to be followed as a matter of course; in the same way he avoided the adders on the mountain. His old ideals were almost if not quite forgotten; he knew that the female of the *bête humaine*, like the adder, would in all probability sting, and he therefore shrank from its trail, but without any feeling of special resentment. The one had a poisoned tongue as the other had a poisoned fang, and it was well to leave them both alone. Then had come that sudden fury of rage against all humanity, as he went out of Caermaen carrying the book that had been stolen from him by the enterprising Beit. He shuddered as he though of how nearly he had approached the verge of madness, when his eyes filled with blood and the earth seemed to burn with fire. He remembered how he had looked up to the horizon and the sky was blotched with scarlet; and the earth was deep red, with red woods and red fields. There was something of horror in the memory, and in the vision of that wild night walk through dim country, when every shadow seemed a symbol of some terrible impending doom. The murmur of the brook, the wind shrilling through the wood, the pale light flowing from the mouldered trunks, and the picture of his own figure fleeing and fleeting through the shades; all these seemed unhappy things that told a story in fatal hieroglyphics. And then the life and laws of the sunlight had passed away, and the resurrection and kingdom of the dead began. Though his limbs were weary, he had felt his muscles grow strong as steel; a woman, one of the hated race, was beside him in the darkness, and the wild beast woke within him, ravening for blood and brutal lust; all the raging desires of the dim race from which he came assailed his heart. The ghosts issued out from the weird wood and from the caves in the hills, besieging him, as he had imagined the spiritual legion besieging Caermaen, beckoning him to a hideous battle and a victory that he had never imagined in his wildest dreams. And then out of the darkness the kind voice spoke again, and the kind hand was stretched out to draw him up from the pit. It was sweet to think of that which he had found at last; the boy's picture incarnate, all the passion and compassion of his longing, all the pity and love and consolation. She, that beautiful passionate woman offering up her beauty in sacrifice to him, she was worthy indeed of his worship. He remembered how his tears had fallen upon her breast, and how tenderly she had soothed him, whispering those wonderful unknown words that sang to his heart. And she had made herself defenseless before him, caressing and fondling the body that had been so despised. He exulted in the happy thought that he had knelt down on the ground before her, and had embraced her knees and worshipped. The woman's body had become his religion; he lay awake at night looking into the darkness with hungry eyes; wishing for a miracle, that the appearance of the so-desired form might be shaped before him. And when he was alone in quiet places in the wood, he fell down again on his knees, and even on his face, stretching out vain hands in the air, as if they would feel her flesh. His father noticed in those days that the inner pocket of his coat was stuffed with papers; he would see Lucian walking up and down in a secret shady place at the bottom of the orchard, reading from his sheaf of manuscript, replacing the leaves, and again drawing them out. He would walk a few quick steps, and pause as if enraptured, gazing in the air as if he looked through the shadows of the world into some sphere of glory, feigned by his thought. Mr. Taylor was almost alarmed at the sight; he concluded of course that Lucian was writing a book. In the first place, there seemed something immodest in seeing the operation performed under one's eyes; it was as if the "make-up" of a beautiful actress were done on the stage, in full audience; as if one saw the rounded calves fixed in position, the fleshings drawn on, the voluptuous outlines of the figure produced by means purely mechanical, blushes mantling from the paint-pot, and the golden tresses well secured by the wigmaker. Books, Mr. Taylor thought, should swim into one's ken mysteriously; they should appear all printed and bound, without apparent genesis; just as children are suddenly told that they have a little sister, found by mamma in the garden. But Lucian was not only engaged in composition; he was plainly rapturous, enthusiastic; Mr. Taylor saw him throw up his hands, and bow his head with strange gesture. The parson began to fear that his son was like some of those mad Frenchmen of whom he had read, young fellows who had a sort of fury of literature, and gave their whole lives to it, spending days over a page, and years over a book, pursuing art as Englishmen pursue money, building up a romance as if it were a business. Now Mr. Taylor held firmly by the "walking-stick" theory; he believed that a man of letters should have a real profession, some solid employment in life. "Get something to do," he would have liked to say, "and then you can write as much as you please. Look at Scott, look at Dickens and Trollope." And then there was the social point of view; it might be right, or it might be wrong, but there could be no doubt that the literary man, as such, was not thought much of in English society. Mr. Taylor knew his Thackeray, and he remembered that old Major Pendennis, society personified, did not exactly boast of his nephew's occupation. Even Warrington was rather ashamed to own his connection with journalism, and Pendennis himself laughed openly at his novel-writing as an agreeable way of making money, a useful appendage to the cultivation of dukes, his true business in life. This was the plain English view, and Mr. Taylor was no doubt right enough in thinking it good, practical common sense. Therefore when he saw Lucian loitering and sauntering, musing amorously over his manuscript, exhibiting manifest signs of that fine fury which Britons have ever found absurd, he felt grieved at heart, and more than ever sorry that he had not been able to send the boy to Oxford.

"B.N.C. would have knocked all this nonsense out of him," he thought. "He would have taken a double First like my poor father and made something of a figure in the world. However, it can't be helped." The poor man sighed, and lit his pipe, and walked in another part of the garden.

But he was mistaken in his diagnosis of the symptoms. The book that Lucian had begun lay unheeded in the drawer; it was a secret work that he was engaged on, and the manuscripts that he took out of that inner pocket never left him day or night. He slept with them next to his heart, and he would kiss them when he was quite alone, and pay them such devotion as he would have paid to her whom they symbolized. He wrote on these leaves a wonderful ritual of praise and devotion; it was the liturgy of his religion. Again and again he copied and recopied this madness of a lover; dallying all days over the choice of a word, searching for more exquisite phrases. No common words, no such phrases as he might use in a tale would suffice; the sentences of worship must stir and be quickened, they must glow and burn, and be decked out as with rare work of jewelry. Every part of that holy and beautiful body must be adored; he sought for terms of extravagant praise, he bent his soul and mind low before her, licking the dust under her feet, abased and yet rejoicing as a Templar before the image of Baphomet. He exulted more especially in the knowledge that there was nothing of the conventional or common in his ecstasy; he was not the fervent, adoring lover of Tennyson's poems, who loves with passion and yet with a proud respect, with the love always of a gentleman for a lady. Annie was not a lady; the Morgans had farmed their land for hundreds of years; they were what Miss Gervase and Miss Colley and the rest of them called common people. Tennyson's noble gentleman thought of their ladies with something of reticence; they imagined them dressed in flowing and courtly robes, walking with slow dignity; they dreamed of them as always stately, the future mistresses of their houses, mothers of their heirs. Such lovers bowed, but not too low, remembering their own honor, before those who were to be equal companions and friends as well as wives. It was not such conceptions as these that he embodied in the amazing emblems of his ritual; he was not, he told himself, a young officer, "something in the city," or a rising barrister engaged to a Miss Dixon or a Miss Gervase. He had not thought of looking out for a nice little house in a good residential suburb where they would have pleasant society; there were to be no consultations about wall-papers, or jocose whispers from friends as to the necessity of having a room that would do for a nursery. No glad young thing had leant on his arm while they chose the suite in white enamel, and china for "our bedroom," the modest salesman doing his best to spare their blushes. When Edith Gervase married she would get mamma to look out for two really good servants, "as we must begin quietly," and mamma would make sure that the drains and everything were right. Then her "girl friends" would come on a certain solemn day to see all her "lovely things." "Two dozen of everything!" "Look, Ethel, did you ever see such ducky frills?" "And that insertion, isn't it quite too sweet?" "My dear Edith, you *are* a lucky girl." "All the underlinen specially made by Madame Lulu!" "What delicious things!" "I hope he knows what a prize he is winning." "Oh! do look at those lovely ribbon-bows!" "You darling, how happy you must be." "Real Valenciennes!" Then a whisper in the lady's ear, and her reply, "Oh, *don't*, Nelly!" So they would chirp over their treasures, as in Rabelais they chirped over their cups; and everything would be done in due order till the wedding-day, when mamma, who had strained her sinews and the commandments to bring the match about, would weep and look indignantly at the unhappy bridegroom. "I *hope* you'll be kind to her, Robert." Then in a rapid whisper to the bride: "Mind, you *insist* on Wyman's flushing the drains when you come back; servants are so careless and dirty too. Don't let him go about by himself in Paris. Men are so *queer*, one never knows. You *have* got the pills?" And aloud, after these *secreta*, "God bless you, my dear; goodbye! *cluck, cluck*, goodbye!"

There were stranger things written in the manuscript pages that Lucian cherished, sentences that burnt and glowed like "coals of fire which hath a most vehement flame." There were phrases that stung and tingled as he wrote them, and sonorous words poured out in ecstasy and rapture, as in some of the old litanies. He hugged the thought that a great part of what he had invented was in the true sense of the word occult: page after page might have been read aloud to the uninitiated without betraying the inner meaning. He dreamed night and day over these symbols, he copied and recopied the manuscript nine times before he wrote it out fairly in a little book which he made himself of a skin of creamy vellum. In his mania for acquirements that should be entirely useless he had gained some skill in illumination, or limning as he preferred to call it, always choosing the obscurer word as the obscurer arts. First he set himself to the severe practice of the text; he spent many hours and days of toil in struggling to fashion the serried columns of black letter, writing and rewriting till he could shape the massive character with firm true hand. He cut his quills with the patience of a monk in the scriptorium, shaving and altering the nib, lightening and increasing the pressure and flexibility of the points, till the pen satisfied him, and gave a stroke both broad and even. Then he made experiments in inks, searching for some medium that would rival the glossy black letter of the old manuscripts; and not till he could produce a fair page of text did he turn to the more entrancing labour of the capitals and borders and ornaments. He mused long over the Lombardic letters, as glorious in their way as a cathedral, and trained his hand to execute the bold and flowing lines; and then there was the art of the border, blossoming in fretted splendor all about the page. His cousin, Miss Deacon, called it all a great waste of time, and his father thought he would have done much better in trying to improve his ordinary handwriting, which was both ugly and illegible. Indeed, there seemed but a poor demand for the limner's art. He sent some specimens of his skill to an "artistic firm" in London; a verse of the "Maud," curiously emblazoned, and a Latin hymn with the notes pricked on a red stave. The firm wrote civilly, telling him that his work, though good, was not what they wanted, and enclosing an illuminated text. "We have great demand for this sort of thing," they concluded, "and if you care to attempt something in this style we should be pleased to look at it." The said text was "Thou, God, seest me." The letter was of a degraded form, bearing much the same relation to the true character as a "churchwarden gothic" building does to Canterbury Cathedral; the colours were varied. The initial was pale gold, the *h* pink, the *o* black, the *u* blue, and the first letter was somehow connected with a bird's nest containing the young of the pigeon, who were waited on by the female bird.

"What a pretty text," said Miss Deacon. "I should like to nail it up in my room. Why don't you try to do something like that, Lucian? You might make something by it."

"I sent them these," said Lucian, "but they don't like them much."

"My dear boy! I should think not! Like them! What were you thinking of to draw those queer stiff flowers all round the border? Roses? They don't look like roses at all events. Where do you get such ideas from?"

"But the design is appropriate; look at the words."

"My dear Lucian, I can't read the words; it's such a queer old-fashioned writing. Look how plain that text is; one can see what it's about. And this other one; I can't make it out at all."

"It's a Latin hymn."

"A Latin hymn? Is it a Protestant hymn? I may be old-fashioned, but *Hymns Ancient and Modern* is quite good enough for me. This is the music, I suppose? But, my dear boy, there are only four lines, and who ever heard of notes shaped like that: you have made some square and some diamond-shape? Why didn't you look in your poor mother's old music? It's in the ottoman in the drawing-room. I could have shown you how to make the notes; there are crotchets, you know, and quavers."

Miss Deacon laid down the illuminated *Urbs Beata* in despair; she felt convinced that her cousin was "next door to an idiot."

And he went out into the garden and raged behind a hedge. He broke two flower-pots and hit an apple-tree very hard with his stick, and then, feeling more calm, wondered what was the use in trying to do anything. He would not have put the thought into words, but in his heart he was aggrieved that his cousin liked the pigeons and the text, and did not like his emblematical roses and the Latin hymn. He knew he had taken great pains over the work, and that it was well done, and being still a young man he expected praise. He found that in this hard world there was a lack of appreciation; a critical spirit seemed abroad. If he could have been scientifically observed as he writhed and smarted under the strictures of "the old fool," as he rudely called his cousin, the spectacle would have been extremely diverting. Little boys sometimes enjoy a very similar entertainment; either with their tiny fingers or with mamma's nail scissors they gradually deprive a fly of its wings and legs. The odd gyrations and queer thin buzzings of the creature as it spins comically round and round never fail to provide a fund of harmless amusement. Lucian, indeed, fancied himself a very ill-used individual; but he should have tried to imitate the nervous organization of the flies, which, as mamma says, "can't really feel."

But now, as he prepared the vellum leaves, he remembered his art with joy; he had not laboured to do beautiful work in vain. He read over his manuscript once more, and thought of the designing of the pages. He made sketches on furtive sheets of paper, and hunted up books in his father's library for suggestions. There were books about architecture, and medieval iron work, and brasses which contributed hints for adornment; and not content with mere pictures he sought in the woods and hedges, scanning the strange forms of trees, and the poisonous growth of great water-plants, and the parasite twining of honeysuckle and briony. In one of these rambles he discovered a red earth which he made into a pigment, and he found in the unctuous juice of a certain fern an ingredient which he thought made his black ink still more glossy. His book was written all in symbols, and in the same spirit of symbolism he decorated it, causing wonderful foliage to creep about the text, and showing the blossom of certain mystical flowers, with emblems of strange creatures, caught and bound in rose thickets. All was dedicated to love and a lover's madness, and there were songs in it which haunted him with their lilt and refrain. When the book was finished it replaced the loose leaves as his constant companion by day and night. Three times a day he repeated his ritual to himself, seeking out the loneliest places in the woods, or going up to his room; and from the fixed intentness and rapture of his gaze, the father thought him still severely employed in the questionable process of composition. At night he contrived to wake for his strange courtship; and he had a peculiar ceremony when he got up in the dark and lit his candle. From a steep and wild hillside, not far from the house, he had cut from time to time five large boughs of spiked and prickly gorse. He had brought them into the house, one by one, and had hidden them in the big box that stood beside his bed. Often he woke up weeping and murmuring to himself the words of one of his songs, and then when he had lit the candle, he would draw out the gorse-boughs, and place them on the floor, and taking off his nightgown, gently lay himself down on the bed of thorns and spines. Lying on his face, with the candle and the book before him, he would softly and tenderly repeat the praises of his dear, dear Annie, and as he turned over page after page, and saw the raised gold of the majuscules glow and flame in the candle-light, he pressed the thorns into his flesh. At such moments he tasted in all its acute savour the joy of physical pain; and after two or three experiences of such delights he altered his book, making a curious sign in vermilion on the margin of the passages where he was to inflict on himself this sweet torture. Never did he fail to wake at the appointed hour, a strong effort of will broke through all the heaviness of sleep, and he would rise up, joyful though weeping, and reverently set his thorny bed upon the floor, offering his pain with his praise. When he had whispered the last word, and had risen from the ground, his body would be all freckled with drops of blood; he used to view the marks with pride. Here and there a spine would be left deep in the flesh, and he would pull these out roughly, tearing through the skin. On some nights when he had pressed with more fervor on the thorns his thighs would stream with blood, red beads standing out on the flesh, and trickling down to his feet. He had some difficulty in washing away the bloodstains so as not to leave any traces to attract the attention of the servant; and after a time he returned no more to his bed when his duty had been accomplished. For a coverlet he had a dark rug, a good deal worn, and in this he would wrap his naked bleeding body, and lie down on the hard floor, well content to add an aching rest to the account of his pleasures. He was covered with scars, and those that healed during the day were torn open afresh at night; the pale olive skin was red with the angry marks of blood, and the graceful form of the young man appeared like the body of a tortured martyr. He grew thinner and thinner everyday, for he ate but little; the skin was stretched on the bones of his face, and the black eyes burnt in dark purple hollows. His relations noticed that he was not looking well.

"Now, Lucian, it's perfect madness of you to go on like this," said Miss Deacon, one morning at breakfast. "Look how your hand shakes; some people would say that you have been taking brandy. And all that you want is a little medicine, and yet you won't be advised. You know it's not my fault; I have asked you to try Dr. Jelly's Cooling Powders again and again."

He remembered the forcible exhibition of the powders when he was a boy, and felt thankful that those days were over. He only grinned at his cousin and swallowed a great cup of strong tea to steady his nerves, which were shaky enough. Mrs. Dixon saw him one day in Caermaen; it was very hot, and he had been walking rather fast. The scars on his body burnt and tingled, and he tottered as he raised his hat to the vicar's wife. She decided without further investigation that he must have been drinking in public-houses.

"It seems a mercy that poor Mrs. Taylor was taken," she said to her husband. "She has certainly been spared a great deal. That wretched young man passed me this afternoon; he was quite intoxicated."

"How very said," said Mr. Dixon. "A little port, my dear?"

"Thank you, Merivale, I will have another glass of sherry. Dr. Burrows is always scolding me and saying I *must* take something to keep up my energy, and this sherry is so weak."

The Dixons were not teetotalers. They regretted it deeply, and blamed the doctor, who "insisted on some stimulant." However, there was some consolation in trying to convert the parish to total abstinence, or, as they curiously called it, temperance. Old women were warned of the sin of taking a glass of beer for supper; aged labourers were urged to try Cork-ho, the new temperance drink; an uncouth beverage, styled coffee, was dispensed at the reading-room. Mr. Dixon preached an eloquent "temperance" sermon, soon after the above conversation, taking as his text: *Beware of the leaven of the Pharisees*. In his discourse he showed that fermented liquor and leaven had much in common, that beer was at the present day "put away" during Passover by the strict Jews; and in a moving peroration he urged his dear brethren, "and more especially those amongst us who are poor in this world's goods," to beware indeed of that evil leaven which was sapping the manhood of our nation. Mrs. Dixon cried after church:

"Oh, Merivale, what a beautiful sermon! How earnest you were. I hope it will do good."

Mr. Dixon swallowed his port with great decorum, but his wife fuddled herself every evening with cheap sherry. She was quite unaware of the fact, and sometimes wondered in a dim way why she always had to scold the children after dinner. And so strange things sometimes happened in the nursery, and now and then the children looked queerly at one another after a red-faced woman had gone out, panting.

Lucian knew nothing of his accuser's trials, but he was not long in hearing of his own intoxication. The next time he went down to Caermaen he was hailed by the doctor.

"Been drinking again today?"

"No," said Lucian in a puzzled voice. "What do you mean?"

"Oh, well, if you haven't, that's all right, as you'll be able to take a drop with me. Come along in?"

Over the whisky and pipes Lucian heard of the evil rumors affecting his character.

"Mrs. Dixon assured me you were staggering from one side of the street to the other. You quite frightened her, she said. Then she asked me if I recommended her to take one or two ounces of spirit at bedtime for the palpitation; and of course I told her two would be better. I have my living to make here, you know. And upon my word, I think she wants it; she's always gurgling inside like a waterworks. I wonder how old Dixon can stand it."

"I like 'ounces of spirit,'" said Lucian. "That's taking it medicinally, I suppose. I've often heard of ladies who have to 'take it medicinally'; and that's how it's done?"

"That's it. 'Dr. Burrows won't *listen* to me': 'I tell him how I dislike the taste of spirits, but he says they are absolutely *necessary* for my constitution': 'my medical man *insists* on something at bedtime'; that's the style."

Lucian laughed gently; all these people had become indifferent to him; he could no longer feel savage indignation at their little hypocrisies and malignancies. Their voices uttering calumny, and morality, and futility had become like the thin shrill angry note of a gnat on a summer evening; he had his own thoughts and his own life, and he passed on without heeding.

"You come down to Caermaen pretty often, don't you?" said the doctor.

"I've seen you two or three times in the last fortnight."

"Yes, I enjoy the walk."

"Well, look me up whenever you like, you know. I am often in just at this time, and a chat with a human being isn't bad, now and then. It's a change for me; I'm often afraid I shall lose my patients."

The doctor had the weakness of these terrible puns, dragged headlong into the conversation. He sometimes exhibited them before Mrs. Gervase, who would smile in a faint and dignified manner, and say:

"Ah, I see. Very amusing indeed. We had an old coachmen once who was very clever, I believe, at that sort of thing, but Mr. Gervase was obliged to send him away, the laughter of the other domestics was so very boisterous."

Lucian laughed, not boisterously, but good-humouredly, at the doctor's joke. He liked Burrows, feeling that he was a man and not an automatic gabbling machine.

"You look a little pulled down," said the doctor, when Lucian rose to go. "No, you don't want my medicine. Plenty of beef and beer will do you more good than drugs. I daresay it's the hot weather that has thinned you a bit. Oh, you'll be all right again in a month."

As Lucian strolled out of the town on his way home, he passed a small crowd of urchins assembled at the corner of an orchard. They were enjoying themselves immensely. The "healthy" boy, the same whom he had seen some weeks ago operating on a cat, seemed to have recognized his selfishness in keeping his amusements to himself. He had found a poor lost puppy, a little creature with bright pitiful eyes, almost human in their fond, friendly gaze. It was not a well-bred little dog; it was certainly not that famous puppy "by Vick out of Wasp"; it had rough hair and a foolish long tail which it wagged beseechingly, at once deprecating severity and asking kindness. The poor animal had evidently been used to gentle treatment; it would look up in a boy's face, and give a leap, fawning on him, and then bark in a small doubtful voice, and cower a moment on the ground, astonished perhaps at the strangeness, the bustle and animation. The boys were beside themselves with eagerness; there was quite a babble of voices, arguing, discussing, suggesting. Each one had a plan of his own which he brought before the leader, a stout and sturdy youth.

"Drown him! What be you thinkin' of, mun?" he was saying. "'Tain't no sport at all. You shut your mouth, gwaes. Be you goin' to ask your mother for the boiling-water? Is, Bob Williams, I do know all that: but where be you a-going to get the fire from? Be quiet, mun, can't you? Thomas Trevor, be this dog yourn or mine? Now, look you, if you don't all of you shut your bloody mouths, I'll take the dog 'ome and keep him. There now!"

He was a born leader of men. A singular depression and lowness of spirit showed itself on the boys' faces. They recognized that the threat might very possibly be executed, and their countenances were at once composed to humble attention. The puppy was still cowering on the ground in the midst of them: one or two tried to relieve the tension of their feelings by kicking him in the belly with their hobnail boots. It cried out with the pain and writhed a little, but the poor little beast did not attempt to bite or even snarl. It looked up with those beseeching friendly eyes at its persecutors, and fawned on them again, and tried to wag its tail and be merry, pretending to play with a straw on the road, hoping perhaps to win a little favor in that way.

The leader saw the moment for his master-stroke. He slowly drew a piece of rope from his pocket.

"What do you say to that, mun? Now, Thomas Trevor! We'll hang him over that there bough. Will that suit you, Bobby Williams?"

There was a great shriek of approval and delight. All was again bustle and animation. "I'll tie it round his neck?" "Get out, mun, you don't know how it be done." "Is, I do, Charley." "Now, let me, gwaes, now do let me." "You be sure he won't bite?" "He bain't mad, be he?" "Suppose we were to tie up his mouth first?"

The puppy still fawned and curried favor, and wagged that sorry tail, and lay down crouching on one side on the ground, sad and sorry in his heart, but still with a little gleam of hope; for now and again he tried to play, and put up his face, praying with those fond, friendly eyes. And then at last his gambols and poor efforts for mercy ceased, and he lifted up his wretched voice in one long dismal whine of despair. But he licked the hand of the boy that tied the noose.

He was slowly and gently swung into the air as Lucian went by unheeded; he struggled, and his legs twisted and writhed. The "healthy" boy pulled the rope, and his friends danced and shouted with glee. As Lucian turned the corner, the poor dangling body was swinging to and fro, the puppy was dying, but he still kicked a little.

Lucian went on his way hastily, and shuddering with disgust. The young of the human creature were really too horrible; they defiled the earth, and made existence unpleasant, as the pulpy growth of a noxious and obscene fungus spoils an agreeable walk. The sight of those malignant little animals with mouths that uttered cruelty and filthy, with hands dexterous in torture, and feet swift to run all evil errands, had given him a shock and broken up the world of strange thoughts in which he had been dwelling. Yet it was no good being angry with them: it was their nature to be very loathsome. Only he wished they would go about their hideous amusements in their own back gardens where nobody could see them at work; it was too bad that he should be interrupted and offended in a quiet country road. He tried to put the incident out of his mind, as if the whole thing had been a disagreeable story, and the visions amongst which he wished to move were beginning to return, when he was again rudely disturbed. A little girl, a pretty child of eight or nine, was coming along the lane to meet him. She was crying bitterly and looking to left and right, and calling out some word all the time.

"Jack, Jack, Jack! Little Jackie! Jack!"

Then she burst into tears afresh, and peered into the hedge, and tried to peep through a gate into a field.

"Jackie, Jackie, Jackie!"

She came up to Lucian, sobbing as if her heart would break, and dropped him an old-fashioned curtsy.

"Oh, please sir, have you seen my little Jackie?"

"What do you mean?" said Lucian. "What is it you've lost?"

"A little dog, please sir. A little terrier dog with white hair. Father gave me him a month ago, and said I might keep him. Someone did leave the garden gate open this afternoon, and he must 'a got away, sir, and I was so fond of him sir, he was so playful and loving, and I be afraid he be lost."

She began to call again, without waiting for an answer.

"Jack, Jack, Jack!"

"I'm afraid some boys have got your little dog," said Lucian. "They've killed him. You'd better go back home."

He went on, walking as fast as he could in his endeavor to get beyond the noise of the child's crying. It distressed him, and he wished to think of other things. He stamped his foot angrily on the ground as he recalled the annoyances of the afternoon, and longed for some hermitage on the mountains, far above the stench and the sound of humanity.

A little farther, and he came to Croeswen, where the road branched off to right and left. There was a triangular plot of grass between the two roads; there the cross had once stood, "the goodly and famous roode" of the old local chronicle. The words echoed in Lucian's ears as he went by on the right hand. "There were five steps that did go up to the first pace, and seven steps to the second pace, all of clene hewn ashler. And all above it was most curiously and gloriously wrought with thorowgh carved work; in the highest place was the Holy Roode with Christ upon the Cross having Marie on the one syde and John on the other. And below were six splendent and glisteringe archaungels that bore up the roode, and beneath them in their stories were the most fair and noble images of the twelve Apostles and of divers other Saints and Martirs. And in the lowest storie there was a marvelous imagerie of divers Beasts, such as oxen and horses and swine, and little dogs and peacocks, all done in the finest and most curious wise, so that they all seemed as they were caught in a Wood of Thorns, the which is their torment of this life. And here once in the year was a marvelous solemn service, when the parson of Caermaen came out with the singers and all the people, singing the psalm *Benedicite omnia opera* as they passed along the road in their procession. And when they stood at the roode the priest did there his service, making certain prayers for the beasts, and then he went up to the first pace and preached a sermon to the people, shewing them that as our lord Jhu dyed upon the Tree of his deare mercy for us, so we too owe mercy to the beasts his Creatures, for that they are all his poor lieges and silly servants. And that like as the Holy Aungells do their suit to him on high, and the Blessed xii Apostles and the Martirs, and all the Blissful Saints served him aforetime on earth and now praise him in heaven, so also do the beasts serve him, though they be in torment of life and below men. For their spirit goeth downward, as Holy Writ teacheth us."

It was a quaint old record, a curious relic of what the modern inhabitants of Caermaen called the Dark Ages. A few of the stones that had formed the base of the cross still remained in position, grey with age, blotched with black lichen and green moss. The remainder of the famous rood had been used to mend the roads, to build pigsties and domestic offices; it had turned Protestant, in fact. Indeed, if it had remained, the parson of Caermaen would have had no time for the service; the coffee-stall, the Portuguese Missions, the Society for the Conversion of the Jews, and important social duties took up all his leisure. Besides, he thought the whole ceremony unscriptural.

Lucian passed on his way, wondering at the strange contrasts of the Middle Ages. How was it that people who could devise so beautiful a service believed in witchcraft, demoniacal possession and obsession, in the incubus and succubus, and in the Sabbath and in many other horrible absurdities? It seemed astonishing that anybody could even pretend to credit such monstrous tales, but there could be no doubt that the dread of old women who rode on broomsticks and liked black cats was once a very genuine terror.

A cold wind blew up from the river at sunset, and the scars on his body began to burn and tingle. The pain recalled his ritual to him, and he began to recite it as he walked along. He had cut a branch of thorn from the hedge and placed it next to his skin, pressing the spikes into the flesh with his hand till the warm blood ran down. He felt it was an exquisite and sweet observance for her sake; and then he thought of the secret golden palace he was building for her, the rare and wonderful city rising in his imagination. As the solemn night began to close about the earth, and the last glimmer of the sun faded from the hills, he gave himself anew to the woman, his body and his mind, all that he was, and all that he had.

IV

I n the course of the week Lucian again visited Caermaen. He wished to view the amphitheatre more precisely, to note the exact position of the ancient walls, to gaze up the valley from certain points within the town, to imprint minutely and clearly on his mind the surge of the hills about the city, and the dark tapestry of the hanging woods. And he lingered in the museum where the relics of the Roman occupation had been stored; he was interested in the fragments of tessellated floors, in the glowing gold of drinking cups, the curious beads of fused and coloured glass, the carved amber-work, the scent-flagons that still retained the memory of unctuous odours, the necklaces, brooches, hair-pins of gold and silver, and other intimate objects which had once belonged to Roman ladies. One of the glass flagons, buried in damp earth for many hundred years, had gathered in its dark grave all the splendors of the light, and now shone like an opal with a moonlight glamour and gleams of gold and pale sunset green, and imperial purple. Then there were the wine jars of red earthenware, the memorial stones from graves, and the heads of broken gods, with fragments of occult things used in the secret rites of Mithras. Lucian read on the labels where all these objects were found: in the churchyard, beneath the turf of the meadow, and in the old cemetery near the forest; and whenever it was possible he would make his way to the spot of discovery, and imagine the long darkness that had hidden gold and stone and amber. All these investigations were necessary for the scheme he had in view, so he became for sometime quite a familiar figure in the dusty deserted streets and in the meadows by the river. His continual visits to Caermaen were a tortuous puzzle to the inhabitants, who flew to their windows at the sound of a step on the uneven pavements. They were at a loss in their conjectures; his motive for coming down three times a week must of course be bad, but it seemed undiscoverable. And Lucian on his side was at first a good deal put out by occasional encounters with members of the Gervase or Dixon or Colley tribes; he had often to stop and exchange a few conventional expressions, and such meetings, casual as they were, annoyed and distracted him. He was no longer infuriated or wounded by sneers of contempt or by the cackling laughter of the young people when they passed him on the road (his hat was a shocking one and his untidiness terrible), but such incidents were unpleasant just as the smell of a drain was unpleasant, and threw the strange mechanism of his thoughts out of fear for the time. Then he had been disgusted by the affair of the boys and the little dog; the loathsomeness of it had quite broken up his fancies. He had read books of modern occultism, and remembered some of the experiments described. The adept, it was alleged, could transfer the sense of consciousness from his brain to the foot or hand, he could annihilate the world around him and pass into another sphere. Lucian wondered whether he could not perform some such operation for his own benefit. Human beings were constantly annoying him and getting in his way, was it not possible to annihilate the race, or at all events to reduce them to wholly insignificant forms? A certain process suggested itself to his mind, a work partly mental and partly physical, and after two or three experiments he found to his astonishment and delight that it was successful. Here, he thought, he had discovered one of the secrets of true magic; this was the key to the symbolic transmutations of the Eastern tales. The adept could, in truth, change those who were obnoxious to him into harmless and unimportant shapes, not as in the letter of the old stories, by transforming the enemy, but by transforming himself. The magician puts men below him by going up higher, as one looks down on a mountain city from a loftier crag. The stones on the road and such petty obstacles do not trouble the wise man on the great journey, and so Lucian, when obliged to stop and converse with his fellow-creatures, to listen to their poor pretences and inanities, was no more inconvenienced than when he had to climb an awkward stile in the course of a walk. As for the more unpleasant manifestations of humanity; after all they no longer concerned him. Men intent on the great purpose did not suffer the current of their thoughts to be broken by the buzzing of a fly caught in a spider's web, so why should he be perturbed by the misery of a puppy in the hands of village boys? The fly, no doubt, endured its tortures; lying helpless and bound in those slimy bands, it cried out in its thin voice when the claws of the horrible monster fastened on it; but its dying agonies had never vexed the reverie of a lover. Lucian saw no reason why the boys should offend him more than the spider, or why he should pity the dog more than he pitied the fly. The talk of the men and women might be wearisome and inept and often malignant; but he could not imagine an alchemist at the moment of success, a general in the hour of victory, or a financier with a gigantic scheme of swindling well on the market being annoyed by the buzz of insects. The spider is, no doubt, a very terrible brute with a hideous mouth and hairy tiger-like claws when seen through the microscope; but Lucian had taken away the microscope from his eyes. He could now walk the streets of Caermaen confident and secure, without any dread of interruption, for at a moment's notice the transformation could be effected. Once Dr. Burrows caught him and made him promise to attend a bazaar that was to be held in aid of the Hungarian Protestants; Lucian assented the more willingly as he wished to pay a visit to certain curious mounds on a hill a little way out of the town, and he calculated on slinking off from the bazaar early in the afternoon. Lord Beamys was visiting Sir Vivian Ponsonby, a local magnate, and had kindly promised to drive over and declare the bazaar open. It was a solemn moment when the carriage drew up and the great man alighted. He was rather an evil-looking old nobleman, but the clergy and gentry, their wives and sons and daughters welcomed him with great and unctuous joy. Conversations were broken off in mid-sentence, slow people gaped, not realizing why their friends had so suddenly left them, the Meyricks came up hot and perspiring in fear lest they should be too late, Miss Colley, a yellow virgin of austere regard, smiled largely, Mrs. Dixon beckoned wildly with her parasol to the "girls" who were idly strolling in a distant part of the field, and the archdeacon ran at full speed. The air grew dark with bows, and resonant with the genial laugh of the archdeacon, the cackle of the younger ladies, and the shrill parrot-like voices of the matrons; those smiled who had never smiled before, and on some maiden faces there hovered that look of adoring ecstasy with which the old maidens graced their angels. Then, when all the due rites had been performed, the company turned and began to walk towards the booths of their small Vanity Fair. Lord Beamys led the way with Mrs. Gervase, Mrs. Dixon followed with Sir Vivian Ponsonby, and the multitudes that followed cried, saying, "What a dear old man!"—"Isn't it *kind* of him to come all this way?"—"What a sweet expression, isn't it?"—"I think he's an old love"—"One of the good old sort"—"Real English nobleman"—"Oh most correct, I assure you; if a girl gets into trouble, notice to quit at once"—"Always stands by the Church"—"Twenty livings in his gift"—"Voted for the Public Worship Regulation Act"—"Ten thousand acres strictly preserved." The old lord was leering pleasantly and muttering to himself: "Some fine gals here. Like the looks of that filly with the pink hat. Ought to see more of her. She'd give Lotty points."

The pomp swept slowly across the grass: the archdeacon had got hold of Mr. Dixon, and they were discussing the misdeeds of some clergyman in the rural deanery.

"I can scarce credit it," said Mr. Dixon.

"Oh, I assure you, there can be no doubt. We have witnesses. There can be no question that there was a procession at Llanfihangel on the Sunday before Easter; the choir and minister went round the church, carrying palm branches in their hands."

"Very shocking."

"It has distressed the bishop. Martin is a hard-working man enough, and all that, but those sort of things can't be tolerated. The bishop told me that he had set his face against processions."

"Quite right: the bishop is perfectly right. Processions are unscriptural."

"It's the thin end of the wedge, you know, Dixon."

"Exactly. I have always resisted anything of the kind here."

"Right. *Principiis obsta*, you know. Martin is so *imprudent*. There's a *way* of doing things."

THE "SCRIPTURAL" PROCESSION LED BY Lord Beamys broke up when the stalls were reached, and gathered round the nobleman as he declared the bazaar open.

Lucian was sitting on a garden-seat, a little distance off, looking dreamily before him. And all that he saw was a swarm of flies clustering and buzzing about a lump of tainted meat that lay on the grass. The spectacle in no way interrupted the harmony of his thoughts, and soon after the opening of the bazaar he went quietly away, walking across the fields in the direction of the ancient mounds he desired to inspect.

All these journeys of his to Caermaen and its neighborhood had a peculiar object; he was gradually leveling to the dust the squalid kraals of modern times, and rebuilding the splendid and golden city of Siluria. All this mystic town was for the delight of his sweetheart and himself; for her the wonderful villas, the shady courts, the magic of tessellated pavements, and the hangings of rich stuffs with their intricate and glowing patterns. Lucian wandered all day through the shining streets, taking shelter sometimes in the gardens beneath the dense and gloomy ilex trees, and listening to the plash and trickle of the fountains. Sometimes he would look out of a window and watch the crowd and colour of the market-place, and now and again a ship came up the river bringing exquisite silks and the merchandise of unknown lands in the

Far East. He had made a curious and accurate map of the town he proposed to inhabit, in which every villa was set down and named. He drew his lines to scale with the gravity of a surveyor, and studied the plan till he was able to find his way from house to house on the darkest summer night. On the southern slopes about the town there were vineyards, always under a glowing sun, and sometimes he ventured to the furthest ridge of the forest, where the wild people still lingered, that he might catch the golden gleam of the city far away, as the light quivered and scintillated on the glittering tiles. And there were gardens outside the city gates where strange and brilliant flowers grew, filling the hot air with their odour, and scenting the breeze that blew along the streets. The dull modern life was far away, and people who saw him at this period wondered what was amiss; the abstraction of his glance was obvious, even to eyes not over-sharp. But men and women had lost all their power of annoyance and vexation; they could no longer even interrupt his thought for a moment. He could listen to Mr. Dixon with apparent attention, while he was in reality enraptured by the entreating music of the double flute, played by a girl in the garden of Avallaunius, for that was the name he had taken. Mr. Dixon was innocently discoursing archeology, giving a brief *résumé* of the view expressed by Mr. Wyndham at the last meeting of the antiquarian society.

"There can be no doubt that the temple of Diana stood there in pagan times," he concluded, and Lucian assented to the opinion, and asked a few questions which seemed pertinent enough. But all the time the flute notes were sounding in his ears, and the ilex threw a purple shadow on the white pavement before his villa. A boy came forward from the garden; he had been walking amongst the vines and plucking the ripe grapes, and the juice had trickled down over his breast. Standing beside the girl, unashamed in the sunlight, he began to sing one of Sappho's love songs. His voice was as full and rich as a woman's, but purged of all emotion; he was an instrument of music in the flesh. Lucian looked at him steadily; the white perfect body shone against the roses and the blue of the sky, clear and gleaming as marble in the glare of the sun. The words he sang burned and flamed with passion, and he was as unconscious of their meaning as the twin pipes of the flute. And the girl was smiling. The vicar shook hands and went on, well pleased with his remarks on the temple of Diana, and also with Lucian's polite interest.

"He is by no means wanting in intelligence," he said to his family. "A little curious in manner, perhaps, but not stupid."

"Oh, papa," said Henrietta, "don't you think he is rather silly? He can't talk about anything—anything interesting, I mean. And he pretends to know a lot about books, but I heard him say the other day he had never read *The Prince of the House of David* or *Ben-Hur*. Fancy!"

The vicar had not interrupted Lucian. The sun still beat upon the roses, and a little breeze bore the scent of them to his nostrils together with the smell of grapes and vine-leaves. He had become curious in sensation, and as he leant back upon the cushions covered with glistening yellow silk, he was trying to analyze a strange ingredient in the perfume of the air. He had penetrated far beyond the crude distinctions of modern times, beyond the rough: "there's a smell of roses," "there must be sweetbriar somewhere." Modern perceptions of odour were, he knew, far below those of the savage in delicacy. The degraded black fellow of Australia could distinguish odours in a way that made the consumer of "damper" stare in amazement, but the savage's sensations were all strictly utilitarian. To Lucian as he sat in the cool porch, his feet on the marble, the air came laden with scents as subtly and wonderfully interwoven and contrasted as the harmonica of a great master. The stained marble of the pavement gave a cool reminiscence of the Italian mountain, the blood-red roses palpitating in the sunlight sent out an odour mystical as passion itself, and there was the hint of inebriation in the perfume of the trellised vines. Besides these, the girl's desire and the unripe innocence of the boy were as distinct as benzoin and myrrh, both delicious and exquisite, and exhaled as freely as the scent of the roses. But there was another element that puzzled him, an aromatic suggestion of the forest. He understood it at last; it was the vapor of the great red pines that grew beyond the garden; their spicy needles were burning in the sun, and the smell was as fragrant as the fume of incense blown from far. The soft entreaty of the flute and the swelling rapture of the boy's voice beat on the air together, and Lucian wondered whether there were in the nature of things any true distinction between the impressions of sound and scent and colour. The violent blue of the sky, the song, and the odours seemed rather varied symbols of one mystery than distinct entities. He could almost imagine that the boy's innocence was indeed a perfume, and that the palpitating roses had become a sonorous chant.

In the curious silence which followed the last notes, when the boy and girl had passed under the purple ilex shadow, he fell into a reverie. The fancy that sensations are symbols and not realities hovered in his mind, and led him to speculate as to whether they could not actually be transmuted one into another. It was possible, he thought, that a whole continent of knowledge had been undiscovered; the energies of men having been expended in unimportant and foolish directions. Modern ingenuity had been employed on such trifles as locomotive engines, electric cables, and cantilever bridges; on elabourate devices for bringing uninteresting people nearer together; the ancients had been almost as foolish, because they had mistaken the symbol for the thing signified. It was not the material banquet which really mattered, but the thought of it; it was almost as futile to eat and take emetics and eat again as to invent telephones and high-pressure boilers. As for some other ancient methods of enjoying life, one might as well set oneself to improve calico printing at once.

"Only in the garden of Avallaunius," said Lucian to himself, "is the true and exquisite science to be found."

He could imagine a man who was able to live in one sense while he pleased; to whom, for example, every impression of touch, taste, hearing, or seeing should be translated into odour; who at the desired kiss should be ravished with the scent of dark violets, to whom music should be the perfume of a rose-garden at dawn.

When, now and again, he voluntarily resumed the experience of common life, it was that he might return with greater delight to the garden in the city of refuge. In the actual world the talk was of Nonconformists, the lodger franchise, and the Stock Exchange; people were constantly reading newspapers, drinking Australian Burgundy, and doing other things equally absurd. They either looked shocked when the fine art of pleasure was mentioned, or confused it with going to musical comedies, drinking bad whisky, and keeping late hours in disreputable and vulgar company. He found to his amusement that the profligate were by many degrees duller than the pious, but that the most tedious of all were the persons who preached promiscuity, and called their system of "pigging" the "New Morality."

He went back to the city lovingly, because it was built and adorned for his love. As the metaphysicians insist on the consciousness of the ego as the implied basis of all thought, so he knew that it was she in whom he had found himself, and through whom and for whom all the true life existed. He felt that Annie had taught him the rare magic which had created the garden of Avallaunius. It was for her that he sought strange secrets and tried to penetrate the mysteries of sensation, for he could only give her wonderful thoughts and a wonderful life, and a poor body stained with the scars of his worship.

It was with this object, that of making the offering of himself a worthy one, that he continually searched for new and exquisite experiences. He made lovers come before him and confess their secrets; he pried into the inmost mysteries of innocence and shame, noting how passion and reluctance strive together for the mastery. In the amphitheatre he sometimes witnessed strange entertainments in which such tales as *Daphnis and Chloe* and *The Golden Ass* were performed before him. These shows were always given at nighttime; a circle of torch-bearers surrounded the stage in the center, and above, all the tiers of seats were dark. He would look up at the soft blue of the summer sky, and at the vast dim mountain hovering like a cloud in the west, and then at the scene illumined by a flaring light, and contrasted with violent shadows. The subdued mutter of conversation in a strange language rising from bench after bench, swift hissing whispers of explanation, now and then a shout or a cry as the interest deepened, the restless tossing of the people as the end drew near, an arm lifted, a cloak thrown back, the sudden blaze of a torch lighting up purple or white or the gleam of gold in the black serried ranks; these were impressions that seemed always amazing. And above, the dusky light of the stars, around, the sweet-scented meadows, and the twinkle of lamps from the still city, the cry of the sentries about the walls, the wash of the tide filling the river, and the salt savour of the sea. With such a scenic ornament he saw the tale of Apuleius represented, heard the names of Fotis and Byrrhaena and Lucius proclaimed, and the deep intonation of such sentences as *Ecce Veneris hortator et armiger Liber advenit ultro*. The tale went on through all its marvelous adventures, and Lucian left the amphitheatre and walked beside the river where he could hear indistinctly the noise of voices and the singing Latin, and note how the rumor of the stage mingled with the murmur of the shuddering reeds and the cool lapping of the tide. Then came the farewell of the cantor, the thunder of applause, the crash of cymbals, the calling of the flutes, and the surge of the wind in the great dark wood.

At other times it was his chief pleasure to spend a whole day in a vineyard planted on the steep slope beyond the bridge. A grey stone seat had been placed beneath a shady laurel, and here he often sat without motion or gesture for many hours. Below him the tawny river swept round the town in a half circle; he could see the swirl of the yellow water, its eddies and miniature whirlpools, as the tide poured up from the south. And beyond the river the strong circuit of the walls, and within, the city glittered like a charming piece of mosaic. He freed himself from the obtuse modern view of towns as places where human beings live and make money and rejoice or suffer, for from the standpoint of the moment such facts were wholly impertinent. He knew perfectly well that for his present purpose the tawny sheen and shimmer of the tide was the only fact of importance about the river, and so he regarded the city as a curious work in jewelry. Its radiant marble porticoes, the white walls of the villas, a dome of burning copper, the flash and scintillation of tiled roofs, the quiet red of brickwork, dark groves of ilex, and cypress, and laurel, glowing rose-gardens, and here and there the silver of a fountain, seemed arranged and contrasted with a wonderful art, and the town appeared a delicious ornament, every cube of colour owing its place to the thought and inspiration of the artificer. Lucian, as he gazed from his arbour amongst the trellised vines, lost none of the subtle pleasures of the sight; noting every *nuance* of colour, he let his eyes dwell for a moment on the scarlet flash of poppies, and then on a glazed roof which in the glance of the sun seemed to spout white fire. A square of vines was like some rare green stone; the grapes were massed so richly amongst the vivid leaves, that even from far off there was a sense of irregular flecks and stains of purple running through the green. The laurel garths were like cool jade; the gardens, where red, yellow, blue and white gleamed together in a mist of heat, had the radiance of opal; the river was a band of dull gold. On every side, as if to enhance the preciousness of the city, the woods hung dark on the hills; above, the sky was violet, specked with minute feathery clouds, white as snowflakes. It reminded him of a beautiful bowl in his villa; the ground was of that same brilliant blue, and the artist had fused into the work, when it was hot, particles of pure white glass.

For Lucian this was a spectacle that enchanted many hours; leaning on one hand, he would gaze at the city glowing in the sunlight till the purple shadows grew down the slopes and the long melodious trumpet sounded for the evening watch. Then, as he strolled beneath the trellises, he would see all the radiant facets glimmering out, and the city faded into haze, a white wall shining here and there, and the gardens veiled in a dim glow of colour. On such an evening he would go home with the sense that he had truly lived a day, having received for many hours the most acute impressions of beautiful colour.

ARTHUR MACHEN

Often he spent the night in the cool court of his villa, lying amidst soft cushions heaped upon the marble bench. A lamp stood on the table at his elbow, its light making the water in the cistern twinkle. There was no sound in the court except the soft continual plashing of the fountain. Throughout these still hours he would meditate, and he became more than ever convinced that man could, if he pleased, become lord of his own sensations. This, surely, was the true meaning concealed under the beautiful symbolism of alchemy. Some years before he had read many of the wonderful alchemical books of the later Middle Ages, and had suspected that something other than the turning of lead into gold was intended. This impression was deepened when he looked into *Lumen de Lumine* by Vaughan, the brother of the Silurist, and he had long puzzled himself in the endeavor to find a reasonable interpretation of the hermetic mystery, and of the red powder, "glistening and glorious in the sun." And the solution shone out at last, bright and amazing, as he lay quiet in the court of Avallaunius. He knew that he himself had solved the riddle, that he held in his hand the powder of projection, the philosopher's stone transmuting all it touched to fine gold; the gold of exquisite impressions. He understood now something of the alchemical symbolism; the crucible and the furnace, the "Green Dragon," and the "Son Blessed of the Fire" had, he saw, a peculiar meaning. He understood, too, why the uninitiated were warned of the terror and danger through which they must pass; and the vehemence with which the adepts disclaimed all desire for material riches no longer struck him as singular. The wise man does not endure the torture of the furnace in order that he may be able to compete with operators in pork and company promoters; neither a steam yacht, nor a grouse-moor, nor three liveried footmen would add at all to his gratifications. Again Lucian said to himself:

"Only in the court of Avallaunius is the true science of the exquisite to be found."

He saw the true gold into which the beggarly matter of existence may be transmuted by spagyric art; a succession of delicious moments, all the rare flavors of life concentrated, purged of their lees, and preserved in a beautiful vessel. The moonlight fell green on the fountain and on the curious pavements, and in the long sweet silence of the night he lay still and felt that thought itself was an acute pleasure, to be expressed perhaps in terms of odour or colour by the true artist.

And he gave himself other and even stranger gratifications. Outside the city walls, between the baths and the amphitheatre, was a tavern, a place where wonderful people met to drink wonderful wine. There he saw priests of Mithras and Isis and of more occult rites from the East, men who wore robes of bright colours, and grotesque ornaments, symbolizing secret things. They spoke amongst themselves in a rich jargon of coloured words, full of hidden meanings and the sense of matters unintelligible to the uninitiated, alluding to what was concealed beneath roses, and calling each other by strange names. And there were actors who gave the shows in the amphitheatre, officers of the legion who had served in wild places, singers, and dancing girls, and heroes of strange adventure.

The walls of the tavern were covered with pictures painted in violent hues; blues and reds and greens jarring against one another and lighting up the gloom of the place. The stone benches were always crowded, the sunlight came in through the door in a long bright beam, casting a dancing shadow of vine leaves on the further wall. There a painter had made a joyous figure of the young Bacchus driving the leopards before him with his ivy-staff, and the quivering shadow seemed a part of the picture. The room was cool and dark and cavernous, but the scent and heat of the summer gushed in through the open door. There was ever a full sound, with noise and vehemence, there, and the rolling music of the Latin tongue never ceased.

"The wine of the siege, the wine that we saved," cried one.

"Look for the jar marked *Faunus*; you will be glad."

"Bring me the wine of the Owl's Face."

"Let us have the wine of Saturn's Bridge."

The boys who served brought the wine in dull red jars that struck a charming note against their white robes. They poured out the violet and purple and golden wine with calm sweet faces as if they were assisting in the mysteries, without any sign that they heard the strange words that flashed from side to side. The cups were all of glass; some were of deep green, of the colour of the sea near the land, flawed and specked with the bubbles of the furnace. Others were of brilliant scarlet, streaked with irregular bands of white, and having the appearance of white globules in the moulded stem. There were cups of dark glowing blue, deeper and more shining than the blue of the sky, and running through the substance of the glass were veins of rich gamboge yellow, twining from the brim to the foot. Some cups were of a troubled and clotted red, with alternating blotches of dark and light, some were variegated with white and yellow stains, some wore a film of rainbow colours, some glittered, shot with gold threads through the clear crystal, some were as if sapphires hung suspended in running water, some sparkled with the glint of stars, some were black and golden like tortoiseshell.

A strange feature was the constant and fluttering motion of hands and arms. Gesture made a constant commentary on speech; white fingers, whiter arms, and sleeves of all colours, hovered restlessly, appeared and disappeared with an effect of threads crossing and re-crossing on the loom. And the odour of the place was both curious and memorable; something of the damp cold breath of the cave meeting the hot blast of summer, the strangely mingled aromas of rare wines as they fell plashing and ringing into the cups, the drugged vapor of the East that the priests of Mithras and Isis bore from their steaming temples; these were always strong and dominant. And the women were scented, sometimes with unctuous and overpowering perfumes, and to the artist the experiences of those present were hinted in subtle and delicate *nuances* of odour.

They drank their wine and caressed all day in the tavern. The women threw their round white arms about their lover's necks, they intoxicated them with the scent of their hair, the priests muttered their fantastic jargon of Theurgy. And through the sonorous clash of voices there always seemed the ring of the cry:

"Look for the jar marked *Faunus*; you will be glad."

Outside, the vine tendrils shook on the white walls glaring in the sunshine; the breeze swept up from the yellow river, pungent with the salt sea savour.

These tavern scenes were often the subject of Lucian's meditation as he sat amongst the cushions on the marble seat. The rich sound of the voices impressed him above all things, and he saw that words have a far higher reason than the utilitarian office of imparting a man's thought. The common notion that language and linked words are important only as a means of expression he found a little ridiculous; as if electricity were to be studied solely with the view of "wiring" to people, and all its other properties left unexplored, neglected. Language, he understood, was chiefly important for the beauty of its sounds, by its possession of words resonant, glorious to the ear, by its capacity, when exquisitely arranged, of suggesting wonderful and indefinable impressions, perhaps more ravishing and farther removed from the domain of strict thought than the impressions excited by music itself. Here lay hidden the secret of the sensuous art of literature; it was the secret of suggestion, the art of causing delicious sensation by the use of words. In a way, therefore, literature was independent of thought; the mere English listener, if he had an ear attuned, could recognize the beauty of a splendid Latin phrase.

Here was the explanation of the magic of *Lycidas*. From the standpoint of the formal understanding it was an affected lament over some wholly uninteresting and unimportant Mr. King; it was full of nonsense about "shepherds" and "flocks" and "muses" and such stale stock of poetry; the introduction of St. Peter on a stage thronged with nymphs and river gods was blasphemous, absurd, and, in the worst taste; there were touches of greasy Puritanism, the twang of the conventicle was only too apparent. And *Lycidas* was probably the most perfect piece of pure literature in existence; because every word and phrase and line were sonorous, ringing and echoing with music.

"Literature," he re-enunciated in his mind, "is the sensuous art of causing exquisite impressions by means of words."

And yet there was something more; besides the logical thought, which was often a hindrance, a troublesome though inseparable accident, besides the sensation, always a pleasure and a delight, besides these there were the indefinable inexpressible images which all fine literature summons to the mind. As the chemist in his experiments is sometimes astonished to find unknown, unexpected elements in the crucible or the receiver, as the world of material things is considered by some a thin veil of the immaterial universe, so he who reads wonderful prose or verse is conscious of suggestions that cannot be put into words, which do not rise from the logical sense, which are rather parallel to than connected with the sensuous delight. The world so disclosed is rather the world of dreams, rather the world in which children sometimes live, instantly appearing, and instantly vanishing away, a world beyond all expression or analysis, neither of the intellect nor of the senses. He called these fancies of his "Meditations of a Tavern," and was amused to think that a theory of letters should have risen from the eloquent noise that rang all day about the violet and golden wine.

"Let us seek for more exquisite things," said Lucian to himself. He could almost imagine the magic transmutation of the senses accomplished, the strong sunlight was an odour in his nostrils; it poured down on the white marble and the palpitating roses like a flood. The sky was a glorious blue, making the heart joyous, and the eyes could rest in the dark green leaves and purple shadow of the ilex. The earth seemed to burn and leap beneath the sun, he fancied he could see the vine tendrils stir and quiver in the heat, and the faint fume of the scorching pine needles was blown across the gleaming garden to the seat beneath the porch. Wine was before him in a cup of carved amber; a wine of the colour of a dark rose, with a glint as of a star or of a jet of flame deep beneath the brim; and the cup was twined about with a delicate wreath of ivy. He was often loath to turn away from the still contemplation of such things, from the mere joy of the violent sun, and the responsive earth. He loved his garden and the view of the tessellated city from the vineyard on the hill, the strange clamor of the tavern, and white Fotis appearing on the torch-lit stage. And there were shops in the town in which he delighted, the shops of the perfume makers, and jewelers, and dealers in curious ware. He loved to see all things made for ladies' use, to touch the gossamer silks that were to touch their bodies, to finger the beads of amber and the gold chains which would stir above their hearts, to handle the carved hairpins and brooches, to smell odours which were already dedicated to love.

But though these were sweet and delicious gratifications, he knew that there were more exquisite things of which he might be a spectator. He had seen the folly of regarding fine literature from the standpoint of the logical intellect, and he now began to question the wisdom of looking at life as if it were a moral representation. Literature, he knew, could not exist without some meaning, and considerations of right and wrong were to a certain extent inseparable from the conception of life, but to insist on ethics as the chief interest of the human pageant was surely absurd. One might as well read *Lycidas* for the sake of its denunciation of "our corrupted Clergy," or Homer for "manners and customs." An artist entranced by a beautiful landscape did not greatly concern himself with the geological formation of the hills, nor did the lover of a wild sea inquire as to the chemical analysis of the water. Lucian saw a coloured and complex life displayed before him, and he sat enraptured at the spectacle, not concerned to know whether actions were good or bad, but content if they were curious.

In this spirit he made a singular study of corruption. Beneath his feet, as he sat in the garden porch, was a block of marble through which there ran a scarlet stain. It began with a faint line, thin as a hair, and grew as it advanced, sending out offshoots to right and left, and broadening to a pool of brilliant red. There were strange lives into which he looked that were like the block of marble; women with grave sweet faces told him the astounding tale of their adventures, and how, they said, they had met the faun when they were little children. They told him how they had played and watched by the vines and the fountains, and dallied with the nymphs, and gazed at images reflected in the water pools, till the authentic face appeared from the wood. He heard others tell how they had loved the satyrs for many years before they knew their race; and there were strange stories of those who had longed to speak but knew not the word of the enigma, and searched in all strange paths and ways before they found it.

He heard the history of the woman who fell in love with her slave-boy, and tempted him for three years in vain. He heard the tale from the woman's full red lips, and watched her face, full of the ineffable sadness of lust, as she described her curious stratagems in mellow phrases. She was drinking a sweet yellow wine from a gold cup as she spoke, and the odour in her hair and the aroma of the precious wine seemed to mingle with the soft strange words that flowed like an unguent from a carven jar. She told how she bought the boy in the market of an Asian city, and had him carried to her house in the grove of fig-trees. "Then," she went on, "he was led into my presence as I sat between the columns of my court. A blue veil was spread above to shut out the heat of the sun, and rather twilight than light shone on the painted walls, and the wonderful colours of the pavement, and the images of Love and the Mother of Love. The men who brought the boy gave him over to my girls, who undressed him before me, one drawing gently away his robe, another stroking his brown and flowing hair, another praising the whiteness of his limbs, and another caressing him, and speaking loving words in his ear. But the boy looked sullenly at them all, striking away their hands, and pouting with his lovely and splendid lips, and I saw a blush, like the rosy veil of dawn, reddening his body and his cheeks. Then I made them bathe him, and anoint him with scented oils from head to foot, till his limbs shone and glistened with the gentle and mellow glow of an ivory statue. Then I said: 'You are bashful, because you shine alone amongst us all; see, we too will be your fellows.' The girls began first of all, fondling and kissing one another, and doing for each other the offices of waiting-maids. They drew out the pins and loosened the bands of their hair, and I never knew before that they were so lovely. The soft and shining tresses flowed down, rippling like sea-waves; some had hair golden and radiant as this wine in my cup, the faces of others appeared amidst the blackness of ebony; there were locks that seemed

ARTHUR MACHEN

of burnished and scintillating copper, some glowed with hair of tawny splendor, and others were crowned with the brightness of the sardonyx. Then, laughing, and without the appearance of shame, they unfastened the brooches and bands which sustained their robes, and so allowed silk and linen to flow swiftly to the stained floor, so that one would have said there was a sudden apparition of the fairest nymphs. With many festive and jocose words they began to incite each other to mirth, praising the beauties that shone on every side, and calling the boy by a girl's name, they invited him to be their playmate. But he refused, shaking his head, and still standing dumb-founded and abashed, as if he saw a forbidden and terrible spectacle. Then I ordered the women to undo my hair and my clothes, making them caress me with the tenderness of the fondest lover, but without avail, for the foolish boy still scowled and pouted out his lips, stained with an imperial and glorious scarlet."

She poured out more of the topaz-coloured wine in her cup, and Lucian saw it glitter as it rose to the brim and mirrored the gleam of the lamps. The tale went on, recounting a hundred strange devices. The woman told how she had tempted the boy by idleness and ease, giving him long hours of sleep, and allowing him to recline all day on soft cushions, that swelled about him, enclosing his body. She tried the experiment of curious odours: causing him to smell always about him the oil of roses, and burning in his presence rare gums from the East. He was allured by soft dresses, being clothed in silks that caressed the skin with the sense of a fondling touch. Three times a day they spread before him a delicious banquet, full of savour and odour and colour; three times a day they endeavored to intoxicate him with delicate wine.

"And so," the lady continued, "I spared nothing to catch him in the glistening nets of love; taking only sour and contemptuous glances in return. And at last in an incredible shape I won the victory, and then, having gained a green crown, fighting in agony against his green and crude immaturity, I devoted him to the theatre, where he amused the people by the splendor of his death."

On another evening he heard the history of the man who dwelt alone, refusing all allurements, and was at last discovered to be the lover of a black statue. And there were tales of strange cruelties, of men taken by mountain robbers, and curiously maimed and disfigured, so that when they escaped and returned to the town, they were thought to be monsters and killed at their own doors. Lucian left no dark or secret nook of life unvisited; he sat down, as he said, at the banquet, resolved to taste all the savours, and to leave no flagon unvisited.

His relations grew seriously alarmed about him at this period. While he heard with some inner ear the suave and eloquent phrases of singular tales, and watched the lamp-light in amber and purple wine, his father saw a lean pale boy, with black eyes that burnt in hollows, and sad and sunken cheeks.

"You ought to try and eat more, Lucian," said the parson; "and why don't you have some beer?"

He was looking feebly at the roast mutton and sipping a little water; but he would not have eaten or drunk with more relish if the choicest meat and drink had been before him.

His bones seemed, as Miss Deacon said, to be growing through his skin; he had all the appearance of an ascetic whose body has been reduced to misery by long and grievous penance. People who chanced to see him could not help saying to one another: "How ill and wretched that Lucian Taylor looks!" They were of course quite unaware of the joy and luxury in which his real life was spent, and some of them began to pity him, and to speak to him kindly.

It was too late for that. The friendly words had as much lost their meaning as the words of contempt. Edward Dixon hailed him cheerfully in the street one day:

"Come in to my den, won't you, old fellow?" he said. "You won't see the pater. I've managed to bag a bottle of his old port. I know you smoke like a furnace, and I've got some ripping cigars. You will come, won't you! I can tell you the pater's booze is first rate."

He gently declined and went on. Kindness and unkindness, pity and contempt had become for him mere phrases; he could not have distinguished one from the other. Hebrew and Chinese, Hungarian and Pushtu would be pretty much alike to an agricultural labourer; if he cared to listen he might detect some general differences in sound, but all four tongues would be equally devoid of significance.

To Lucian, entranced in the garden of Avallaunius, it seemed very strange that he had once been so ignorant of all the exquisite meanings of life. Now, beneath the violet sky, looking through the brilliant trellis of the vines, he saw the picture; before, he had gazed in sad astonishment at the squalid rag which was wrapped about it.

V

A nd he was at last in the city of the unending murmuring streets, a part of the stirring shadow, of the amber-lighted gloom.

It seemed a long time since he had knelt before his sweetheart in the lane, the moon-fire streaming upon them from the dark circle of the fort, the air and the light and his soul full of haunting, the touch of the unimaginable thrilling his heart; and now he sat in a terrible "bed-sitting-room" in a western suburb, confronted by a heap and litter of papers on the desk of a battered old bureau.

He had put his breakfast-tray out on the landing, and was thinking of the morning's work, and of some very dubious pages that he had blackened the night before. But when he had lit his disreputable briar, he remembered there was an unopened letter waiting for him on the table; he had recognized the vague, staggering script of Miss Deacon, his cousin. There was not much news; his father was "just the same as usual," there had been a good deal of rain, the farmers expected to make a lot of cider, and so forth. But at the close of the letter Miss Deacon became useful for reproof and admonition.

"I was at Caermaen on Tuesday," she said, "and called on the Gervases and the Dixons. Mr. Gervase smiled when I told him you were a literary man, living in London, and said he was afraid you wouldn't find it a very practical career. Mrs. Gervase was very proud of Henry's success; he passed fifth for some examination, and will begin with nearly four hundred a year. I don't wonder the Gervases are delighted. Then I went to the Dixons, and had tea. Mrs. Dixon wanted to know if you had published anything yet, and I said I thought not. She showed me a book everybody is talking about, called the *Dog and the Doctor*. She says it's selling by thousands, and that one can't take up a paper without seeing the author's name. She told me to tell you that you ought to try to write something like it. Then Mr. Dixon came in from the study, and your name was mentioned again. He said he was afraid you had made rather a mistake in trying to take up literature as if it were a profession, and seemed to think that a place in a house of business would be more *suitable* and more practical. He pointed out that you had not had the advantages of a university training, and said that you would find men who had made good friends, and had the *tone* of the university, would be before you at every step. He said Edward was doing very well at Oxford.

He writes to them that he knows several noblemen, and that young Philip Bullingham (son of Sir John Bullingham) is his most intimate friend; of course this is *very* satisfactory for the Dixons. I am afraid, my dear Lucian, you have rather overrated your powers. Wouldn't it be better, even now, to look out for some *real work* to do, instead of wasting your time over those silly old books? I know quite well how the Gervases and the Dixons feel; they think idleness so injurious for a young man, and likely to lead to *bad habits*. You know, my dear Lucian, I am only writing like this because of my affection for you, so I am sure, my dear boy, you won't be offended."

Lucian pigeon-holed the letter solemnly in the receptacle lettered "Barbarians." He felt that he ought to ask himself some serious questions: "Why haven't I passed fifth? why isn't Philip (son of Sir John) my most intimate friend? why am I an idler, liable to fall into bad habits?" but he was eager to get to his work, a curious and intricate piece of analysis. So the battered bureau, the litter of papers, and the thick fume of his pipe, engulfed him and absorbed him for the rest of the morning. Outside were the dim October mists, the dreary and languid life of a side street, and beyond, on the main road, the hum and jangle of the gliding trains. But he heard none of the uneasy noises of the quarter, not even the shriek of the garden gates nor the yelp of the butcher on his round, for delight in his great task made him unconscious of the world outside.

He had come by curious paths to this calm hermitage between Shepherd's Bush and Acton Vale. The golden weeks of the summer passed on in their enchanted procession, and Annie had not returned, neither had she written. Lucian, on his side, sat apart, wondering why his longing for her were not sharper. As he though of his raptures he would smile faintly to himself, and wonder whether he had not lost the world and Annie with it. In the garden of Avallaunius his sense of external things had grown dim and indistinct; the actual, material life seemed everyday to become a show, a fleeting of shadows across a great white light. At last the news came that Annie Morgan had been married from her sister's house to a young farmer, to whom, it appeared, she had been long engaged, and Lucian was ashamed to find himself only conscious of amusement, mingled with gratitude. She had been the key that opened the shut palace, and he was now secure on the throne of ivory and gold. A few days after he had heard the news he repeated the adventure of his boyhood; for the second time he scaled the steep hillside, and penetrated the matted brake. He expected violent disillusion, but his feeling was rather astonishment at the activity of boyish imagination. There was no terror nor amazement now in the green bulwarks, and the stunted undergrowth did not seem in anyway extraordinary. Yet he did not laugh at the memory of his sensations, he was not angry at the cheat. Certainly it had been all illusion, all the heats and chills of boyhood, its thoughts of terror were without significance. But he recognized that the illusions of the child only differed from those of the man in that they were more picturesque; belief in fairies and belief in the Stock Exchange as bestowers of happiness were equally vain, but the latter form of faith was ugly as well as inept. It was better, he knew, and wiser, to wish for a fairy coach than to cherish longings for a well-appointed brougham and liveried servants.

He turned his back on the green walls and the dark oaks without any feeling of regret or resentment. After a little while he began to think of his adventures with pleasure; the ladder by which he had mounted had disappeared, but he was safe on the height. By the chance fancy of a beautiful girl he had been redeemed from a world of misery and torture, the world of external things into which he had come a stranger, by which he had been tormented. He looked back at a kind of vision of himself seen as he was a year before, a pitiable creature burning and twisting on the hot coals of the pit, crying lamentably to the laughing bystanders for but one drop of cold water wherewith to cool his tongue. He confessed to himself, with some contempt, that he had been a social being, depending for his happiness on the goodwill of others; he had tried hard to write, chiefly, it was true, from love of the art, but a little from a social motive. He had imagined that a written book and the praise of responsible journals would ensure him the respect of the county people. It was a quaint idea, and he saw the lamentable fallacies naked; in the first place, a painstaking artist in words was not respected by the respectable; secondly, books should not be written with the object of gaining the goodwill of the landed and commercial interests; thirdly and chiefly, no man should in anyway depend on another.

From this utter darkness, from danger of madness, the ever dear and sweet Annie had rescued him. Very beautifully and fitly, as Lucian thought, she had done her work without any desire to benefit him, she had simply willed to gratify her own passion, and in doing this had handed to him the priceless secret. And he, on his side, had reversed the process; merely to make himself a splendid offering for the acceptance of his sweetheart, he had cast aside the vain world, and had found the truth, which now remained with him, precious and enduring.

And since the news of the marriage he found that his worship of her had by no means vanished; rather in his heart was the eternal treasure of a happy love, untarnished and spotless; it would be like a mirror of gold without alloy, bright and lustrous forever. For Lucian, it was no defect in the woman that she was desirous and faithless; he had not conceived an affection for certain moral or intellectual accidents, but for the very woman. Guided by the self-evident axiom that humanity is to be judged by literature, and not literature by humanity, he detected the analogy between *Lycidas* and Annie. Only the dullard would object to the nauseous cant of the one, or to the indiscretions of the other. A sober critic might say that the man who could generalize Herbert and Laud, Donne and Herrick, Sanderson and Juxon, Hammond and Lancelot Andrewes into "our corrupted Clergy" must be either an imbecile or a scoundrel, or probably both. The judgment would be perfectly true, but as a criticism of *Lycidas* it would be a piece of folly. In the case of the woman one could imagine the attitude of the conventional lover; of the chevalier who, with his tongue in his cheek, "reverences and respects" all women, and coming home early in the morning writes a leading article on St. English Girl. Lucian, on the other hand, felt profoundly grateful to the delicious Annie, because she had at precisely the right moment voluntarily removed her image from his way. He confessed to himself that, latterly, he had a little dreaded her return as an interruption; he had shivered at the thought that their relations would become what was so terribly called an "intrigue" or "affair." There would be all the threadbare and common stratagems, the vulgarity of secret assignations, and an atmosphere suggesting the period of Mr. Thomas Moore and Lord Byron and "segars." Lucian had been afraid of all this; he had feared lest love itself should destroy love.

He considered that now, freed from the torment of the body, leaving untasted the green water that makes thirst more burning, he was perfectly initiated in the true knowledge of the splendid and glorious love. There seemed to him a monstrous paradox in the assertion that there could be no true love without a corporal presence of the beloved; even the popular sayings of "Absence makes the heart grow fonder," and "familiarity breeds contempt," witnessed to the contrary. He thought, sighing, and with compassion, of the manner in which men are continually led astray by the cheat of the senses. In order that

ARTHUR MACHEN

the unborn might still be added to the born, nature had inspired men with the wild delusion that the bodily companionship of the lover and the beloved was desirable above all things, and so, by the false show of pleasure, the human race was chained to vanity, and doomed to an eternal thirst for the non-existent.

Again and again he gave thanks for his own escape; he had been set free from a life of vice and sin and folly, from all the dangers and illusions that are most dreaded by the wise. He laughed as he remembered what would be the common view of the situation. An ordinary lover would suffer all the sting of sorrow and contempt; there would be grief for a lost mistress, and rage at her faithlessness, and hate in the heart; one foolish passion driving on another, and driving the man to ruin. For what would be commonly called the real woman he now cared nothing; if he had heard that she had died in her farm in Utter Gwent, he would have experienced only a passing sorrow, such as he might feel at the death of anyone he had once known. But he did not think of the young farmer's wife as the real Annie; he did not think of the frost-bitten leaves in winter as the real rose. Indeed, the life of many reminded him of the flowers; perhaps more especially of those flowers which to all appearance are for many years but dull and dusty clumps of green, and suddenly, in one night, burst into the flame of blossom, and fill all the misty lawns with odour; till the morning. It was in that night that the flower lived, not through the long unprofitable years; and, in like manner, many human lives, he thought, were born in the evening and dead before the coming of day. But he had preserved the precious flower in all its glory, not suffering it to wither in the hard light, but keeping it in a secret place, where it could never be destroyed. Truly now, and for the first time, he possessed Annie, as a man possesses the gold which he has dug from the rock and purged of its baseness.

He was musing over these things when a piece of news, very strange and unexpected, arrived at the rectory. A distant, almost a mythical relative, known from childhood as "Cousin Edward in the Isle of Wight," had died, and by some strange freak had left Lucian two thousand pounds. It was a pleasure to give his father five hundred pounds, and the rector on his side forgot for a couple of days to lean his head on his hand. From the rest of the capital, which was well invested, Lucian found he would derive something between sixty and seventy pounds a year, and his old desires for literature and a refuge in the murmuring streets returned to him. He longed to be free from the incantations that surrounded him in the country, to work and live in a new atmosphere; and so, with many good wishes from his father, he came to the retreat in the waste places of London.

He was in high spirits when he found the square, clean room, horribly furnished, in the by-street that branched from the main road, and advanced in an unlovely sweep to the mud pits and the desolation that was neither town nor country. On every side monotonous grey streets, each house the replica of its neighbor, to the east an unexplored wilderness, north and west and south the brickfields and market-gardens, everywhere the ruins of the country, the tracks where sweet lanes had been, gangrened stumps of trees, the relics of hedges, here and there an oak stripped of its bark, white and haggard and leprous, like a corpse. And the air seemed always grey, and the smoke from the brickfields was grey.

At first he scarcely realized the quarter into which chance had led him. His only thought was of the great adventure of letters in which he proposed to engage, and his first glance round his "bed-sitting-room" showed him that there was no piece of furniture suitable for his purpose. The table, like the rest of the suite, was of bird's-eye maple; but the maker seemed to have penetrated the druidic secret of the rocking-stone, the thing was in a state of unstable equilibrium perpetually. For some days he wandered through the streets, inspecting the second-hand furniture shops, and at last, in a forlorn byway, found an old Japanese bureau, dishonored and forlorn, standing amongst rusty bedsteads, sorry china, and all the refuse of homes dead and desolate. The bureau pleased him in spite of its grime and grease and dirt. Inlaid mother-of-pearl, the gleam of lacquer dragons in red gold, and hints of curious design shone through the film of neglect and ill-usage, and when the woman of the shop showed him the drawers and well and pigeon-holes, he saw that it would be an apt instrument for his studies.

The bureau was carried to his room and replaced the "bird's-eye" table under the gas-jet. As Lucian arranged what papers he had accumulated: the sketches of hopeless experiments, shreds and tatters of stories begun but never completed, outlines of plots, two or three notebooks scribbled through and through with impressions of the abandoned hills, he felt a thrill of exaltation at the prospect of work to be accomplished, of a new world all open before him.

He set out on the adventure with a fury of enthusiasm; his last thought at night when all the maze of streets was empty and silent was of the problem, and his dreams ran on phrases, and when he awoke in the morning he was eager to get back to his desk. He immersed himself in a minute, almost a microscopic analysis of fine literature. It was no longer enough, as in the old days, to feel the charm and incantation of a line or a word; he wished to penetrate the secret, to understand something of the wonderful suggestion, all apart from the sense, that seemed to him the *differentia* of literature, as distinguished from the long follies of "character-drawing," "psychological analysis," and all the stuff that went to make the three-volume novel of commerce.

He found himself curiously strengthened by the change from the hills to the streets. There could be no doubt, he thought, that living a lonely life, interested only in himself and his own thoughts, he had become in a measure inhuman. The form of external things, black depths in woods, pools in lonely places, those still valleys curtained by hills on every side, sounding always with the ripple of their brooks, had become to him an influence like that of a drug, giving a certain peculiar colour and outline to his thoughts. And from early boyhood there had been another strange flavor in his life, the dream of the old Roman world, those curious impressions that he had gathered from the white walls of Caermaen, and from the looming bastions of the fort. It was in reality the subconscious fancies of many years that had rebuilt the golden city, and had shown him the vine-trellis and the marbles and the sunlight in the garden of Avallaunius. And the rapture of love had made it all so vivid and warm with life, that even now, when he let his pen drop, the rich noise of the tavern and the chant of the theatre sounded above the murmur of the streets. Looking back, it was as much a part of his life as his schooldays, and the tessellated pavements were as real as the square of faded carpet beneath his feet.

But he felt that he had escaped. He could now survey those splendid and lovely visions from without, as if he read of opium dreams, and he no longer dreaded a weird suggestion that had once beset him, that his very soul was being moulded into the hills, and passing into the black mirror of still waterpools. He had taken refuge in the streets, in the harbor of a modern suburb, from the vague, dreaded magic that had charmed his life. Whenever he felt inclined to listen to the old wood-whisper or to the singing of the fauns he bent more earnestly to his work, turning a deaf ear to the incantations.

In the curious labour of the bureau he found refreshment that was continually renewed. He experienced again, and with a far more violent impulse, the enthusiasm that had attended the writing of his book a year or two before, and so, perhaps, passed from one drug to another. It was, indeed, with something of rapture that he imagined the great procession of years all to be devoted to the intimate analysis of words, to the construction of the sentence, as if it were a piece of jewelry or mosaic.

Sometimes, in the pauses of the work, he would pace up and down his cell, looking out of the window now and again and gazing for an instant into the melancholy street. As the year advanced the days grew more and more misty, and he found himself the inhabitant of a little island wreathed about with the waves of a white and solemn sea. In the afternoon the fog would grow denser, shutting out not only sight but sound; the shriek of the garden gates, the jangling of the tram-bell echoed as if from a far way. Then there were days of heavy incessant rain; he could see a grey drifting sky and the drops plashing in the street, and the houses all dripping and saddened with wet.

He cured himself of one great aversion. He was no longer nauseated at the sight of a story begun and left unfinished. Formerly, even when an idea rose in his mind bright and wonderful, he had always approached the paper with a feeling of sickness and dislike, remembering all the hopeless beginnings he had made. But now he understood that to begin a romance was almost a separate and special art, a thing apart from the story, to be practiced with sedulous care. Whenever an opening scene occurred to him he noted it roughly in a book, and he devoted many long winter evenings to the elabouration of these beginnings. Sometimes the first impression would yield only a paragraph or a sentence, and once or twice but a splendid and sonorous word, which seemed to Lucian all dim and rich with unsurmised adventure. But often he was able to write three or four vivid pages, studying above all things the hint and significance of the words and actions, striving to work into the lines the atmosphere of expectation and promise, and the murmur of wonderful events to come.

In this one department of his task the labour seemed almost endless. He would finish a few pages and then rewrite them, using the same incident and nearly the same words, but altering that indefinite something which is scarcely so much style as manner, or atmosphere. He was astonished at the enormous change that was thus effected, and often, though he himself had done the work, he could scarcely describe in words how it was done. But it was clear that in this art of manner, or suggestion, lay all the chief secrets of literature, that by it all the great miracles were performed. Clearly it was not style, for style in itself was untranslatable, but it was that high theurgic magic that made the English *Don Quixote*, roughly traduced by some Jervas, perhaps the best of all English books. And it was the same element that made the journey of Roderick Random to London, so ostensibly a narrative of coarse jokes and common experiences and burlesque manners, told in no very choice diction, essentially a wonderful vision of the eighteenth century, carrying to one's very nostrils the aroma of the Great North Road, iron-bound under black frost, darkened beneath shuddering woods, haunted by highwaymen, with an adventure waiting beyond every turn, and great old echoing inns in the midst of lonely winter lands.

It was this magic that Lucian sought for his opening chapters; he tried to find that quality that gives to words something beyond their sound and beyond their meaning, that in the first lines of a book should whisper things unintelligible but all significant. Often he worked for many hours without success, and the grim wet dawn once found him still searching for hieroglyphic sentences, for words mystical, symbolic. On the shelves, in the upper part of his bureau, he had placed the books which, however various as to matter, seemed to have a part in this curious quality of suggestion, and in that sphere which might almost be called supernatural. To these books he often had recourse, when further effort appeared altogether hopeless, and certain pages in Coleridge and Edgar Allan Poe had the power of holding him in a trance of delight, subject to emotions and impressions which he knew to transcend altogether the realm of the formal understanding. Such lines as:

> *Bottomless vales and boundless floods,*
> *And chasms, and caves, and Titan woods,*
> *With forms that no man can discover*
> *For the dews that drip all over;*

had for Lucian more than the potency of a drug, lulling him into a splendid waking-sleep, every word being a supreme incantation. And it was not only his mind that was charmed by such passages, for he felt at the same time a strange and delicious bodily languor that held him motionless, without the desire or power to stir from his seat. And there were certain phrases in *Kubla Khan* that had such a magic that he would sometimes wake up, as it were, to the consciousness that he had been lying on the bed or sitting in the chair by the bureau, repeating a single line over and over again for two or three hours. Yet he knew perfectly well that he had not been really asleep; a little effort recalled a constant impression of the wall-paper, with its pink flowers on a buff ground, and of the muslin-curtained window, letting in the grey winter light. He had been some seven months in London when this odd experience first occurred to him. The day opened dreary and cold and clear, with a gusty and restless wind whirling round the corner of the street, and lifting the dead leaves and scraps of paper that littered the roadway into eddying mounting circles, as if a storm of black rain were to come. Lucian had sat late the night before, and rose in the morning feeling weary and listless and heavy-headed. While he dressed, his legs dragged him as with weights, and he staggered and nearly fell in bending down to the mat outside for his tea-tray. He lit the spirit lamp on the hearth with shaking, unsteady hands, and could scarcely pour out the tea when it was ready. A delicate cup of tea was one of his few luxuries; he was fond of the strange flavor of the green leaf, and this morning he drank the straw-coloured liquid eagerly, hoping it would disperse the cloud of languor. He tried his best to coerce himself into the sense of vigor and enjoyment with which he usually began the day, walking briskly up and down and arranging his papers in order. But he could not free himself from depression; even as he opened the dear bureau a wave of melancholy came upon him, and he began to ask himself whether he were not pursuing a vain dream, searching for treasures that had no existence. He drew out his cousin's letter and read it again, sadly enough. After all there was a good deal of truth in what she said; he had "overrated" his powers, he had no friends, no real education. He began to count up the months since he had come to London; he had received his two thousand pounds in March, and in May he had said goodbye to the woods and to the dear and friendly paths. May, June, July, August, September, October, November, and half of December had gone by; and what had he to show? Nothing but the experiment, the attempt, futile scribblings which had no end nor shining purpose. There was nothing in his desk that he could produce as evidence of his capacity, no fragment even of accomplishment. It was a thought of intense bitterness, but it seemed as if the barbarians were in the right—a place in a house of business would have been more suitable. He leaned his head on his desk overwhelmed with the severity of his own judgment. He tried to comfort himself again by the thought of all the hours of happy enthusiasm he had spent amongst his papers, working for a great idea with infinite patience. He recalled to mind something that he had always tried to keep in the background of his hopes, the foundation-stone of his life, which he had hidden out of sight. Deep in his heart was the hope that he might one day write a valiant book; he scarcely dared to entertain the aspiration, he felt his incapacity too deeply, but yet this longing was the foundation of all his painful and patient effort. This he had proposed in secret to himself, that if he laboured without ceasing, without tiring, he might produce something which would at all events be art, which would stand wholly apart from the objects shaped like books, printed with printers' ink, and called by the name of books that he had read. Giotto, he knew, was a painter, and the man who imitated walnut-wood on the deal doors opposite was a painter, and he had wished to be a very humble pupil in the class of the former. It was better, he thought, to fail in attempting exquisite things than to succeed in the department of the utterly contemptible; he had vowed he would be the dunce of Cervantes's school rather than top-boy in the academy of *A Bad Un to Beat* and *Millicent's Marriage*. And with this purpose he had devoted himself to labourious and joyous years, so that however mean his capacity, the pains should not be wanting. He tried now to rouse himself from a growing misery by the recollection of this high aim, but it all seemed hopeless vanity. He looked out into the grey street, and it stood a symbol of his life, chill and dreary and grey and vexed with a horrible wind. There were the dull inhabitants of the quarter going about their common business; a man was crying "mackerel" in a doleful voice, slowly passing up the street, and staring into the white-curtained "parlors," searching for the face of a purchaser behind the India-rubber plants, stuffed birds, and piles of gaudy gilt books that adorned the windows. One of the blistered doors over the way banged, and a woman came scurrying out on some errand, and the garden gate shrieked two melancholy notes as she opened it and let it swing back after her. The little patches called gardens were mostly untilled, uncared for, squares of slimy moss, dotted with clumps of coarse ugly grass, but here and there were the blackened and rotting remains of sunflowers and marigolds. And beyond, he knew, stretched the labyrinth of streets more or less squalid, but all grey and dull, and behind were the mud pits and the steaming heaps of yellowish bricks, and to the north was a great wide cold waste, treeless, desolate, swept by bitter wind. It was all like his own life, he said again to himself, a maze of unprofitable dreariness and desolation, and his mind grew as black and hopeless as the winter sky. The morning went thus dismally till twelve o'clock, and he put on his hat and great-coat. He always went out for an hour everyday between twelve and one; the exercise was a necessity, and the landlady made his bed in the interval. The wind blew the smoke from the chimneys into his face as he shut the door, and with the acrid smoke came the prevailing odour of the street, a blend of cabbage-water and burnt bones and the faint sickly vapor from the brickfields. Lucian walked mechanically for the hour, going eastward, along the main road. The wind pierced him, and the dust was blinding, and the dreariness of the street increased his misery. The row of common shops, full of common things, the blatant public-houses, the Independent chapel, a horrible stucco parody of a Greek temple with a façade of hideous columns that was a nightmare, villas like smug Pharisees, shops again, a church in cheap Gothic, an old garden blasted and riven by the builder, these were the pictures of the way. When he got home again he flung himself on the bed, and lay there stupidly till sheer hunger roused him. He ate a hunch of bread and drank some water, and began to pace up and down the room, wondering whether there were no escape from despair. Writing seemed quite impossible, and hardly knowing what he did he opened his bureau and took out a book from the shelves. As his eyes fell on the page the air grew dark and heavy as night, and the wind wailed suddenly, loudly, terribly.

"By woman wailing for her Demon lover." The words were on his lips when he raised his eyes again. A broad band of pale clear light was shining into the room, and when he looked out of the window he saw the road all brightened by glittering pools of water, and as the last drops of the rain-storm starred these mirrors the sun sank into the wrack. Lucian gazed about him, perplexed, till his eyes fell on the clock above his empty hearth. He had been sitting, motionless, for nearly two hours without any sense of the passage of time, and without ceasing he had murmured those words as he dreamed an endless wonderful story. He experienced somewhat the sensations of Coleridge himself; strange, amazing, ineffable things seemed to have been presented to him, not in the form of the idea, but actually and materially, but he was less fortunate than Coleridge in that he could not, even vaguely, image to himself what he had seen. Yet when he searched his mind he knew that the consciousness of the room in which he sat had never left him; he had seen the thick darkness gather, and had heard the whirl of rain hissing through the air. Windows had been shut down with a crash, he had noted the pattering footsteps of people running to shelter, the landlady's voice crying to someone to look at the rain coming in under the door. It was like peering into some old bituminous picture, one could see at last that the mere blackness resolved itself into the likeness of trees and rocks and travelers. And against this background of his room, and the storm, and the noises of the street, his vision stood out illuminated, he felt he had descended to the very depths, into the caverns that are hollowed beneath the soul. He tried vainly to record the history of his impressions; the symbols remained in his memory, but the meaning was all conjecture.

The next morning, when he awoke, he could scarcely understand or realize the bitter depression of the preceding day. He found it had all vanished away and had been succeeded by an intense exaltation. Afterwards, when at rare intervals he experienced the same strange possession of the consciousness, he found this to be the invariable result, the hour of vision was always succeeded by a feeling of delight, by sensations of brightened and intensified powers. On that bright December day after the storm he rose joyously, and set about the labour of the bureau with the assurance of success, almost with the hope of formidable difficulties to be overcome. He had long busied himself with those curious researches which Poe had indicated in the *Philosophy of Composition*, and many hours had been spent in analyzing the singular effects which may be produced by the sound and resonance of words. But he had been struck by the thought that in the finest literature there were more subtle tones than the loud and insistent music of "never more," and he endeavored to find the secret of those pages and sentences which spoke, less directly, and less obviously, to the soul rather than to the ear, being filled with a certain grave melody and the sensation of singing voices. It was admirable, no doubt, to write phrases that showed at a glance their designed rhythm, and rang with sonorous words, but he dreamed of a prose in which the music should be less explicit, of names rather than notes. He was astonished that morning at his own fortune and facility; he succeeded in covering a page of ruled paper wholly to his satisfaction, and the sentences, when he read them out, appeared to suggest a weird elusive chanting, exquisite but almost imperceptible, like the echo of the plainsong reverberated from the vault of a monastic church.

He thought that such happy mornings well repaid him for the anguish of depression which he sometimes had to suffer, and for the strange experience of "possession" recurring at rare intervals, and usually after many weeks of severe diet. His income, he found, amounted to sixty-five pounds a year, and he lived for weeks at a time on fifteen shillings a week. During these austere periods his only food was bread, at the rate of a loaf a day; but he drank huge draughts of green tea, and smoked a black tobacco, which seemed to him a more potent mother of thought than any drug from the scented East. "I hope you go to some nice place for dinner," wrote his cousin; "there used to be some excellent eating-houses in London where one could get a good cut from the joint, *with plenty of gravy*, and a boiled potato, for a shilling. Aunt Mary writes that you should try Mr. Jones's in Water Street, Islington, whose father came from near Caermaen, and was always most comfortable in her day. I daresay the walk there would do you good. It is such a pity you smoke that horrid tobacco. I had a letter from Mrs. Dolly (Jane Diggs, who married your cousin John Dolly) the other day, and she said they would have been delighted to take you for only twenty-five shillings a week for the sake of the family if you had not been a smoker. She told me to ask you if you had ever seen a horse or a dog smoking tobacco. They are such nice, comfortable people, and the children would have been company for you. Johnnie, who used to be such a dear little fellow, has just gone into an office in the City, and seems to have excellent prospects. How I wish, my dear Lucian, that you could do something in the same way. Don't forget Mr. Jones's in Water Street, and you might mention your name to him."

Lucian never troubled Mr. Jones; but these letters of his cousin's always refreshed him by the force of contrast. He tried to imagine himself a part of the Dolly family, going dutifully every morning to the City on the bus, and returning in the evening for high tea. He could conceive the fine odour of hot roast beef hanging about the decorous house on Sunday afternoons, papa asleep in the dining-room, mamma lying down, and the children quite good and happy with their "Sundays books." In the evening, after supper, one read the *Quiver* till bedtime. Such pictures as these were to Lucian a comfort and a help, a remedy against despair. Often when he felt overwhelmed by the difficulty of the work he had undertaken, he thought of the alternative career, and was strengthened.

He returned again and again to that desire of a prose which should sound faintly, not so much with an audible music, but with the memory and echo of it. In the night, when the last tram had gone jangling by, and he had looked out and seen the street all wrapped about in heavy folds of the mist, he conducted some of his most delicate experiments. In that white and solitary midnight of the suburban street he experienced the curious sense of being on a tower, remote and apart and high above all the troubles of the earth. The gas lamp, which was nearly opposite, shone in a pale halo of light, and the houses themselves were merely indistinct marks and shadows amidst that palpable whiteness, shutting out the world and its noises. The knowledge of the swarming life that was so still, though it surrounded him, made the silence seem deeper than that of the mountains before the dawn; it was as if he alone stirred and looked out amidst a host sleeping at his feet. The fog came in by the open window in freezing puffs, and as Lucian watched he noticed that it shook and wavered like the sea, tossing up wreaths and drifts across the pale halo of the lamp, and, these vanishing, others succeeded. It was as if the mist passed by from the river to the north, as if it still passed by in the silence.

He would shut his window gently, and sit down in his lighted room with all the consciousness of the white advancing shroud upon him. It was then that he found himself in the mood for curious labours, and able to handle with some touch of confidence the more exquisite instruments of the craft. He sought for that magic by which all the glory and glamour of mystic chivalry were made to shine through the burlesque and gross adventures of Don Quixote, by which Hawthorne had lit his infernal Sabbath fires, and fashioned a burning aureole about the village tragedy of the *Scarlet Letter*. In Hawthorne the story and the suggestion, though quite distinct and of different worlds, were rather parallel than opposed to one another; but Cervantes had done a stranger thing. One read of Don Quixote, beaten, dirty, and ridiculous, mistaking windmills for giants, sheep for an army; but the impression was of the enchanted forest, of Avalon, of the San Graal, "far in the spiritual city." And Rabelais showed him, beneath the letter, the Tourainian sun shining on the hot rock above Chinon, on the maze of narrow, climbing streets, on the high-pitched, gabled roofs, on the grey-blue *tourelles*, pricking upward from the fantastic labyrinth of walls. He heard the sound of sonorous plain-song from the monastic choir, of gross exuberant gaiety from the rich vineyards; he listened to the eternal mystic mirth of those that halted in the purple shadow of the *sorbier* by the white, steep road.

The gracious and ornate *châteaux* on the Loire and the Vienne rose fair and shining to confront the incredible secrets of vast, dim, far-lifted Gothic naves, that seemed ready to take the great deep, and float away from the mist and dust of earthly streets to anchor in the haven of the clear city that hath foundations. The rank tale of the *garderobe*, of the farm-kitchen, mingled with the reasoned, endless legend of the schools, with luminous Platonic argument; the old pomp of the Middle Ages put on the robe of a fresh life. There was a smell of wine and of incense, of June meadows and of ancient books, and through it all he hearkened, intent, to the exultation of chiming bells ringing for a new feast in a new land. He would cover pages with the analysis of these marvels, tracking the suggestion concealed beneath the words, and yet glowing like the golden threads in a robe of samite, or like that device of the old binders by which a vivid picture appeared on the shut edges of a book. He tried to imitate this art, to summon even the faint shadow of the great effect, rewriting a page of Hawthorne, experimenting and changing an epithet here and there, noting how sometimes the alteration of a trifling word would plunge a whole scene into darkness, as if one of those blood-red fires had instantly been extinguished. Sometimes, for severe practice, he attempted to construct short tales in the manner of this or that master. He sighed over these desperate attempts, over the clattering pieces of mechanism which would not even simulate life; but he urged himself to an infinite perseverance. Through the white hours he worked on amidst the heap and litter of papers; books and manuscripts overflowed from the bureau to the floor; and if he looked out he saw the mist still pass by, still passing from the river to the north.

It was not till the winter was well advanced that he began at all to explore the region in which he lived. Soon after his arrival in the grey street he had taken one or two vague walks, hardly noticing where he went or what he saw; but for all the summer he had shut himself in his room, beholding nothing but the form and colour of words. For his morning walk he almost invariably chose the one direction, going along the Uxbridge Road towards Notting Hill, and returning by the same monotonous thoroughfare. Now, however, when the new year was beginning its dull days, he began to diverge occasionally to right and left, sometimes eating his luncheon in odd corners, in the bulging parlors of eighteenth-century taverns, that still fronted the surging sea of modern streets, or perhaps in brand new "publics" on the broken borders of the brickfields, smelling of the clay from which they had swollen. He found waste by-places behind railway embankments where he could smoke his pipe sheltered from the wind; sometimes there was a wooden fence by an old pear-orchard where he sat and gazed at the wet desolation of the market-gardens, munching a few currant biscuits by way of dinner. As he went farther afield a sense of immensity slowly grew upon him; it was as if, from the little island of his room, that one friendly place, he pushed out into the grey unknown, into a city that for him was uninhabited as the desert.

He came back to his cell after these purposeless wanderings always with a sense of relief, with the thought of taking refuge from grey. As he lit the gas and opened the desk of his bureau and saw the pile of papers awaiting him, it was as if he had passed from the black skies and the stinging wind and the dull maze of the suburb into all the warmth and sunlight and violent colour of the south.

VI

It was in this winter after his coming to the grey street that Lucian first experienced the pains of desolation. He had all his life known the delights of solitude, and had acquired that habit of mind which makes a man find rich company on the bare hillside and leads him into the heart of the wood to meditate by the dark waterpools. But now in the blank interval when he was forced to shut up his desk, the sense of loneliness overwhelmed him and filled him with unutterable melancholy. On such days he carried about with him an unceasing gnawing torment in his breast; the anguish of the empty page awaiting him in his bureau, and the knowledge that it was worse than useless to attempt the work. He had fallen into the habit of always using this phrase "the work" to denote the adventure of literature; it had grown in his mind to all the austere and grave significance of "the great work" on the lips of the alchemists; it included every trifling and labourious page and the vague magnificent fancies that sometimes hovered below him. All else had become mere by-play, unimportant, trivial; the work was the end, and the means and the food of his life—it raised him up in the morning to renew the struggle, it was the symbol which charmed him as he lay down at night. All through the hours of toil at the bureau he was enchanted, and when he went out and explored the unknown coasts, the one thought allured him, and was the coloured glass between his eyes and the world. Then as he drew nearer home his steps would quicken, and the more weary and grey the walk, the more he rejoiced as he thought of his hermitage and of the curious difficulties that awaited him there. But when, suddenly and without warning, the faculty disappeared, when his mind seemed a hopeless waste from which nothing could arise, then he became subject to a misery so piteous that the barbarians themselves would have been sorry for him. He had known some foretaste of these bitter and inexpressible griefs in the old country days, but then he had immediately taken refuge in the hills, he had rushed to the dark woods as to an anodyne, letting his heart drink in all the wonder and magic of the wild land. Now in these days of January, in the suburban street, there was no such refuge.

He had been working steadily for some weeks, well enough satisfied on the whole with the daily progress, glad to awake in the morning, and to read over what he had written on the night before. The new year opened with faint and heavy weather and a breathless silence in the air, but in a few days the great frost set in. Soon the streets began to suggest the appearance of a beleaguered city, the silence that had preceded the frost deepened, and the mist hung over the earth like a dense white smoke. Night after night the cold increased, and people seemed unwilling to go abroad, till even the main thoroughfares were empty and deserted, as if the inhabitants were lying close in hiding. It was at this dismal time that Lucian found himself reduced to impotence. There was a sudden break in his thought, and when he wrote on valiantly, hoping against hope, he only grew more aghast on the discovery of the imbecilities he had committed to paper. He ground his teeth together and persevered, sick at heart, feeling as if all the world were fallen from under his feet, driving his pen on mechanically, till he was overwhelmed. He saw the stuff he had done without veil or possible concealment, a lamentable and wretched sheaf of verbiage, worse, it seemed, than the efforts of his boyhood. He was not longer tautological, he avoided tautology with the infernal art of a leader-writer, filling his wind bags and mincing words as if he had been a trained journalist on the staff of the *Daily Post*. There seemed all the matter of an insufferable tragedy in these thoughts; that his patient and enduring toil was in vain, that practice went for nothing, and that he had wasted the labour of Milton to accomplish the tenth-rate. Unhappily he could not "give in"; the longing, the fury for the work burnt within him like a burning fire; he lifted up his eyes in despair.

It was then, while he knew that no one could help him, that he languished for help, and then, though he was aware that no comfort was possible, he fervently wished to be comforted. The only friend he had was his father, and he knew that his father would not even understand his distress. For him, always, the printed book was the beginning and end of literature; the agony of the maker, his despair and sickness, were as accursed as the pains of labour. He was ready to read and admire the work of the great Smith, but he did not wish to hear of the period when the great Smith had writhed and twisted like a scotched worm, only hoping to be put out of his misery, to go mad or die, to escape somehow from the bitter pains. And Lucian knew no one else. Now and then he read in the paper the fame of the great *littérateurs*; the Gypsies were entertaining the Prince of Wales, the Jolly Beggars were dining with the Lord Mayor, the Old Mumpers were mingling amicably and gorgeously with the leading members of the Stock Exchange. He was so unfortunate as to know none of these gentlemen, but it hardly seemed likely that they could have done much for him in any case. Indeed, in his heart, he was certain that help and comfort from without were in the nature of things utterly impossible, his ruin and grief were within, and only his own assistance could avail. He tried to reassure himself, to believe that his torments were a proof of his vocation, that the facility of the novelist who stood six years deep in contracts to produce romances was a thing wholly undesirable, but all the while he longed for but a drop of that inexhaustible fluency which he professed to despise.

He drove himself out from that dreary contemplation of the white paper and the idle pen. He went into the frozen and deserted streets, hoping that he might pluck the burning coal from his heart, but the fire was not quenched. As he walked furiously along the grim iron roads he fancied that those persons who passed him cheerfully on their way to friends and friendly hearths shrank from him into the mists as they went by. Lucian imagined that the fire of his torment and anguish must in some way glow visibly about him; he moved, perhaps, in a nimbus that proclaimed the blackness and the flames within. He knew, of course, that in misery he had grown delirious, that the well-coated, smooth-hatted personages who loomed out of the fog upon him were in reality shuddering only with cold, but in spite of common sense he still conceived that he saw on their faces an evident horror and disgust, and something of the repugnance that one feels at the sight of a venomous snake, half-killed, trailing its bleeding vileness out of sight. By design Lucian tried to make for remote and desolate places, and yet when he had succeeded in touching on the open country, and knew that the icy shadow hovering through the mist was a field, he longed for some sound and murmur of life, and turned again to roads where pale lamps were glimmering, and the dancing flame of firelight shone across the frozen shrubs. And the sight of these homely fires, the thought of affection and consolation waiting by them, stung him the more sharply perhaps because of the contrast with his own chills and weariness and helpless sickness, and chiefly because he knew that he had long closed an everlasting door between his heart and such felicities. If those within had come out and had called him by his name to enter and be comforted, it would have been quite unavailing, since between them and him there was a great gulf fixed. Perhaps for the first time he realized that he had lost the art of humanity forever. He had thought when he closed his ears to the wood whisper and changed the fauns' singing for the murmur of the streets, the black pools for the shadows and amber light of London, that he had put off the old life, and had turned his soul to healthy activities, but the truth was that he had merely exchanged one drug for another. He could not be human, and he wondered whether there were some drop of the fairy blood in his body that made him foreign and a stranger in the world.

He did not surrender to desolation without repeated struggles. He strove to allure himself to his desk by the promise of some easy task; he would not attempt invention, but he had memoranda and rough jottings of ideas in his note-books, and he would merely amplify the suggestions ready to his hand. But it was hopeless, again and again it was hopeless. As he read over his notes, trusting that he would find some hint that might light up the dead fires, and kindle again that pure flame of enthusiasm, he found how desperately his fortune had fallen. He could see no light, no colour in the lines he had scribbled with eager trembling fingers; he remembered how splendid all these things had been when he wrote them down, but now they were meaningless, faded into grey. The few words he had dashed on to the paper, enraptured at the thought of the happy hours they promised, had become mere jargon, and when he understood the idea it seemed foolish, dull, unoriginal. He discovered something at last that appeared to have a grain of promise, and determined to do his best to put it into shape, but the first paragraph appalled him; it might have been written by an unintelligent schoolboy. He tore the paper in pieces, and shut and locked his desk, heavy despair sinking like lead into his heart. For the rest of that day he lay motionless on the bed, smoking pipe after pipe in the hope of stupefying himself with tobacco fumes. The air in the room became blue and thick with smoke; it was bitterly cold, and he wrapped himself up in his great-coat and drew the counterpane over him. The night came on and the window darkened, and at last he fell asleep.

He renewed the effort at intervals, only to plunge deeper into misery. He felt the approaches of madness, and knew that his only hope was to walk till he was physically exhausted, so that he might come home almost fainting with fatigue, but ready to fall asleep the moment he got into bed. He passed the mornings in a kind of torpor, endeavoring to avoid thought, to occupy his mind with the pattern of the paper, with the advertisements at the end of a book, with the curious greyness of the light that glimmered through the mist into his room, with the muffled voices that rumbled now and then from the street. He tried to make out the design that had once coloured the faded carpet on the floor, and wondered about the dead artist in Japan, the adorner of his bureau. He speculated as to what his thoughts had been as he inserted the rainbow mother-of-pearl and made that great flight of shining birds, dipping their wings as they rose from the reeds, or how he had conceived the lacquer dragons in red gold, and the fantastic houses in the garden of peach-trees. But sooner or later the oppression of his grief returned, the loud shriek and clang of the garden-gate, the warning bell of some passing bicyclist steering through the fog, the noise of his pipe falling to the floor, would suddenly awaken him to the sense of misery. He knew that it was time to go out; he could not bear to sit still and suffer. Sometimes he cut a slice of bread and put it in his pocket, sometimes he trusted to the chance of finding a public-house, where he could have a sandwich and a glass of beer. He turned always from the main streets and lost himself in the intricate suburban byways, willing to be engulfed in the infinite whiteness of the mist.

The roads had stiffened into iron ridges, the fences and trees were glittering with frost crystals, everything was of strange and altered aspect. Lucian walked on and on through the maze, now in a circle of shadowy villas, awful as the buried streets of Herculaneum, now in lanes dipping onto open country, that led him past great elm-trees whose white boughs were all still, and past the bitter lonely fields where the mist seemed to fade away into grey darkness. As he wandered along these unfamiliar and ghastly paths he became the more convinced of his utter remoteness from all humanity, he allowed that grotesque suggestion of there being something visibly amiss in his outward appearance to grow upon him, and often he looked with a horrible expectation into the faces of those who passed by, afraid lest his own senses gave him false intelligence, and that he had really assumed some frightful and revolting shape. It was curious that, partly by his own fault, and largely, no doubt, through the operation of mere coincidence, he was once or twice strongly confirmed in this fantastic delusion. He came one day into a lonely and unfrequented byway, a country lane falling into ruin, but still fringed with elms that had formed an avenue leading to the old manor-house. It was now the road of communication between two far outlying suburbs, and on these winter nights lay as black, dreary, and desolate as a mountain track. Soon after the frost began, a gentleman had been set upon in this lane as he picked his way between the corner where the bus had set him down, and his home where the fire was blazing, and his wife watched the clock. He was stumbling uncertainly through the gloom, growing a little nervous because the walk seemed so long, and peering anxiously for the lamp at the end of his street, when the two footpads rushed at him out of the fog. One caught him from behind, the other struck him with a heavy bludgeon, and as he lay senseless they robbed him of his watch and money, and vanished across the fields. The next morning all the suburb rang with the story; the unfortunate merchant had been grievously hurt, and wives watched their husbands go out in the morning with sickening apprehension, not knowing what might happen at night. Lucian of course was ignorant of all these rumors, and struck into the gloomy by-road without caring where he was or whither the way would lead him.

He had been driven out that day as with whips, another hopeless attempt to return to the work had agonised him, and existence seemed an intolerable pain. As he entered the deeper gloom, where the fog hung heavily, he began, half consciously, to gesticulate; he felt convulsed with torment and shame, and it was a sorry relief to clench his nails into his palm and strike the air as he stumbled heavily along, bruising his feet against the frozen ruts and ridges. His impotence was hideous, he said to himself, and he cursed himself and his life, breaking out into a loud oath, and stamping on the ground. Suddenly he was shocked at a scream of terror, it seemed in his very ear, and looking up he saw for a moment a woman gazing at him out of the mist, her features distorted and stiff with fear. A momentary convulsion twitched her arms into the ugly mimicry of a beckoning gesture, and she turned and ran for dear life, howling like a beast.

Lucian stood still in the road while the woman's cries grew faint and died away. His heart was chilled within him as the significance of this strange incident became clear. He remembered nothing of his violent gestures; he had not known at the time that he had sworn out loud, or that he was grinding his teeth with impotent rage. He only thought of that ringing scream, of the horrible fear on the white face that had looked upon him, of the woman's headlong flight from his presence. He stood trembling and shuddering, and in a little while he was feeling his face, searching for some loathsome mark, for the stigmata of evil branding his forehead. He staggered homewards like a drunken man, and when he came into the Uxbridge Road some children saw him and called after him as he swayed and caught at the lamp-post. When he got to his room he sat down at first in the dark. He did not dare to light the gas. Everything in the room was indistinct, but he shut his eyes as he passed the dressing-table, and sat in a corner, his face turned to the wall. And when at last he gathered courage and the flame leapt hissing from the jet, he crept piteously towards the glass, and ducked his head, crouching miserably, and struggling with his terrors before he could look at his own image.

To the best of his power he tried to deliver himself from these more grotesque fantasies; he assured himself that there was nothing terrific in his countenance but sadness, that his face was like the face of other men. Yet he could not forget that reflection he had seen in the woman's eyes, how the surest mirrors had shown him a horrible dread, her soul itself quailing and shuddering at an awful sight. Her scream rang and rang in his ears; she had fled away from him as if he offered some fate darker than death.

He looked again and again into the glass, tortured by a hideous uncertainty. His senses told him there was nothing amiss, yet he had had a proof, and yet, as he peered most earnestly, there was, it seemed, something strange and not altogether usual in the expression of the eyes. Perhaps it might be the unsteady flare of the gas, or perhaps a flaw in the cheap looking-glass, that gave some slight distortion to the image. He walked briskly up and down the room and tried to gaze steadily, indifferently, into his own face. He would not allow himself to be misguided by a word. When he had pronounced himself incapable of humanity, he had only meant that he could not enjoy the simple things of common life. A man was not necessarily monstrous, merely because he did not appreciate high tea, a quiet chat about the neighbors, and a happy noisy evening with the children. But with what message, then, did he appear charged that the woman's mouth grew so stark? Her hands had jerked up as if they had been pulled with frantic wires; she seemed for the instant like a horrible puppet. Her scream was a thing from the nocturnal Sabbath.

He lit a candle and held it close up to the glass so that his own face glared white at him, and the reflection of the room became an indistinct darkness. He saw nothing but the candle flame and his own shining eyes, and surely they were not as the eyes of common men. As he put down the light, a sudden suggestion entered his mind, and he drew a quick breath, amazed at the thought. He hardly knew whether to rejoice or to shudder. For the thought he conceived was this: that he had mistaken all the circumstances of the adventure, and had perhaps repulsed a sister who would have welcomed him to the Sabbath.

He lay awake all night, turning from one dreary and frightful thought to the other, scarcely dozing for a few hours when the dawn came. He tried for a moment to argue with himself when he got up; knowing that his true life was locked up in the bureau, he made a desperate attempt to drive the phantoms and hideous shapes from his mind. He was assured that his salvation was in the work, and he drew the key from his pocket, and made as if he would have opened the desk. But the nausea, the remembrances of repeated and utter failure, were too powerful. For many days he hung about the Manor Lane, half dreading, half desiring another meeting, and he swore he would not again mistake the cry of rapture, nor repulse the arms extended in a frenzy of delight. In those days he dreamed of some dark place where they might celebrate and make the marriage of the Sabbath, with such rites as he had dared to imagine.

It was perhaps only the shock of a letter from his father that rescued him from these evident approaches to madness. Mr. Taylor wrote how they had missed him at Christmas, how the farmers had inquired after him, of the homely familiar things that recalled his boyhood, his mother's voice, the friendly fireside, and the good old fashions that had nurtured him. He remembered that he had once been a boy, loving the cake and puddings and the radiant holly, and all the seventeenth-century mirth that lingered on in the ancient farmhouses. And there came to him the more holy memory of Mass on Christmas morning. How sweet the dark and frosty earth had smelt as he walked beside his mother down the winding lane, and from the stile near the church they had seen the world glimmering to the dawn, and the wandering lanthorns advancing across the fields. Then he had come into the church and seen it shining with candles and holly, and his father in pure vestments of white linen sang the longing music of the liturgy at the altar, and the people answered him, till the sun rose with the grave notes of the Paternoster, and a red beam stole through the chancel window.

The worst horror left him as he recalled the memory of these dear and holy things. He cast away the frightful fancy that the scream he had heard was a shriek of joy, that the arms, rigidly jerked out, invited him to an embrace. Indeed, the thought that he had longed for such an obscene illusion, that he had gloated over the recollection of that stark mouth, filled him with disgust. He resolved that his senses were deceived, that he had neither seen nor heard, but had for a moment externalized his own slumbering and morbid dreams. It was perhaps necessary that he should be wretched, that his efforts should be discouraged, but he would not yield utterly to madness.

Yet when he went abroad with such good resolutions, it was hard to resist an influence that seemed to come from without and within. He did not know it, but people were everywhere talking of the great frost, of the fog that lay heavy on London, making the streets dark and terrible, of strange birds that came fluttering about the windows in the silent squares. The Thames rolled out duskily, bearing down the jarring ice-blocks, and as one looked on the black water from the bridges it was like a river in a northern tale. To Lucian it all seemed mythical, of the same substance as his own fantastic thoughts. He rarely saw a newspaper, and did not follow from day to day the systematic readings of the thermometer, the reports of ice-fairs, of coaches driven across the river at Hampton, of the skating on the fens; and hence the iron roads, the beleaguered silence and the heavy folds of mist appeared as amazing as a picture, significant, appalling. He could not look out and see a common suburban street foggy and dull, nor think of the inhabitants as at work or sitting cheerfully eating nuts about their fires; he saw a vision of a grey road vanishing, of dim houses all empty and deserted, and the silence seemed eternal. And when he went out and passed through street after street, all void, by the vague shapes of houses that appeared for a moment and were then instantly swallowed up, it seemed to him as if he had strayed into a city that had suffered some inconceivable doom, that he alone wandered where myriads had once dwelt. It was a town as great as Babylon, terrible as Rome, marvelous as Lost Atlantis, set in the midst of a white wilderness surrounded by waste places. It was impossible to escape from it; if he skulked between hedges, and crept away beyond the frozen pools, presently the serried stony lines confronted him like an army, and far and far they swept away into the night, as some fabled wall that guards an empire in the vast dim east. Or in that distorting medium of the mist, changing all things, he imagined that he trod an infinite desolate plain, abandoned from ages, but circled and encircled with dolmen and menhir that loomed out at him, gigantic, terrible. All London was one grey temple of an awful rite, ring within ring of wizard stones circled about some central place, every circle was an initiation, every initiation eternal loss. Or perhaps he was astray forever in a land of grey rocks. He had seen the light of home, the flicker of the fire on the walls; close at hand, it seemed, was the open door, and he had heard dear voices calling to him across the gloom, but he had just missed the path. The lamps vanished, the voices sounded thin and died away, and yet he knew that those within were waiting, that they could not bear to close the door, but waited, calling his name, while he had missed the way, and wandered in the pathless desert of the grey rocks. Fantastic, hideous, they beset him wherever he turned, piled up into strange shapes, pricked with sharp peaks, assuming the appearance of goblin towers, swelling into a vague dome like a fairy rath, huge and terrible. And as one dream faded into another, so these last fancies were perhaps the most tormenting and persistent; the rocky avenues became the camp and fortalice of some half-human, malignant race who swarmed in hiding, ready to bear him away into the heart of their horrible hills. It was awful to think that all his goings were surrounded, that in the darkness he was watched and surveyed, that every step but led him deeper and deeper into the labyrinth.

When, of an evening, he was secure in his room, the blind drawn down and the gas flaring, he made vigorous efforts toward sanity. It was not of his free will that he allowed terror to overmaster him, and he desired nothing better than a placid and harmless life, full of work and clear thinking. He knew that he deluded himself with imagination, that he had been walking through London suburbs and not through Pandemonium, and that if he could but unlock his bureau all those ugly forms would be resolved into the mist. But it was hard to say if he consoled himself effectually with such reflections, for the return to common sense meant also the return to the sharp pangs of defeat. It recalled him to the bitter theme of his own inefficiency, to the thought that he only desired one thing of life, and that this was denied him. He was willing to endure the austerities of a monk in a severe cloister, to suffer cold, to be hungry, to be lonely and friendless, to forbear all the consolation of friendly speech, and to be glad of all these things, if only he might be allowed to illuminate the manuscript in quietness. It seemed a hideous insufferable cruelty, that he should so fervently desire that which he could never gain.

He was led back to the old conclusion; he had lost the sense of humanity, he was wretched because he was an alien and a stranger amongst citizens. It seemed probable that the enthusiasm of literature, as he understood it, the fervent desire for the fine art, had in it something of the inhuman, and dissevered the enthusiast from his fellow-creatures. It was possible that the barbarian suspected as much, that by some slow process of rumination he had arrived at his fixed and inveterate impression, by no means a clear reasoned conviction; the average Philistine, if pressed for the reasons of his dislike, would either become inarticulate, exclamating "faugh" and "pah" like an old-fashioned Scots Magazine, or else he would give some imaginary and absurd reason, alleging that all "littery men" were poor, that composers never cut their hair, that painters were rarely public-school men, that sculptors couldn't ride straight to hounds to save their lives, but clearly these imbecilities were mere afterthoughts; the average man hated the artist from a deep instinctive dread of all that was strange, uncanny, alien to his nature; he gibbered, uttered his harsh, semi-bestial "faugh," and dismissed Keats to his gallipots from much the same motives as usually impelled the black savages to dismiss the white man on an even longer journey.

Lucian was not especially interested in this hatred of the barbarian for the maker, except from this point, that it confirmed him in his belief that the love of art dissociated the man from the race. One touch of art made the whole world alien, but surely miseries of the civilized man cast amongst savages were not so much caused by dread of their ferocity as by the terror of his own thoughts; he would perhaps in his last despair leave his retreat and go forth to perish at their hands, so that he might at least die in company, and hear the sound of speech before death. And Lucian felt most keenly that in his case there was a double curse; he was as isolated as Keats, and as inarticulate as his reviewers. The consolation of the work had failed him, and he was suspended in the void between two worlds.

It was no doubt the composite effect of his failures, his loneliness of soul, and solitude of life, that had made him invest those common streets with such grim and persistent terrors. He had perhaps yielded to a temptation without knowing that he had been tempted, and, in the manner of De Quincey, had chosen the subtle in exchange for the more tangible pains. Unconsciously, but still of free will, he had preferred the splendor and the gloom of a malignant vision before his corporal pains, before the hard reality of his own impotence. It was better to dwell in vague melancholy, to stray in the forsaken streets of a city doomed from ages, to wander amidst forlorn and desperate rocks than to awake to a gnawing and ignoble torment, to confess that a house of business would have been more suitable and more practical, that he had promised what he could never perform. Even as he struggled to beat back the phantasmagoria of the mist, and resolved that he would no longer make all the streets a stage of apparitions, he hardly realized what he had done, or that the ghosts he had called might depart and return again.

He continued his long walks, always with the object of producing a physical weariness and exhaustion that would enable him to sleep of nights. But even when he saw the foggy and deserted avenues in their proper shape, and allowed his eyes to catch the pale glimmer of the lamps, and the dancing flame of the firelight, he could not rid himself of the impression that he stood afar off, that between those hearths and himself there was a great gulf fixed. As he paced down the footpath he could often see plainly across the frozen shrubs into the homely and cheerful rooms. Sometimes, late in the evening, he caught a passing glimpse of the family at tea, father, mother, and children laughing and talking together, well pleased with each other's company. Sometimes a wife or a child was standing by the garden gate peering anxiously through the fog, and the sight of it all, all the little details, the hideous but comfortable armchairs turned ready to the fire, maroon-red curtains being drawn close to shut out the ugly night, the sudden blaze and illumination as the fire was poked up so that it might be cheerful for father; these trivial and common things were acutely significant. They brought back to him the image of a dead boy—himself. They recalled the shabby old "parlor" in the country, with its shabby old furniture and fading carpet, and renewed a whole atmosphere of affection and homely comfort. His mother would walk to the end of the drive and look out for him when he was late (wandering then about the dark woodlands); on winter evenings she would make the fire blaze, and have his slippers warming by the hearth, and there was probably buttered toast "as a treat." He dwelt on all these insignificant petty circumstances, on the genial glow and light after the muddy winter lanes, on the relish of the buttered toast and the smell of the hot tea, on the two old cats curled fast asleep before the fender, and made them instruments of exquisite pain and regret. Each of these strange houses that he passed was identified in his mind with his own vanished home; all was prepared and ready as in the old days, but he was shut out, judged and condemned to wander in the frozen mist, with weary feet, anguished and forlorn, and they that would pass from within to help him could not, neither could he pass to them. Again, for the hundredth time, he came back to the sentence:

he could not gain the art of letters and he had lost the art of humanity. He saw the vanity of all his thoughts; he was an ascetic caring nothing for warmth and cheerfulness and the small comforts of life, and yet he allowed his mind to dwell on such things. If one of those passersby, who walked briskly, eager for home, should have pitied him by some miracle and asked him to come in, it would have been worse than useless, yet he longed for pleasures that he could not have enjoyed. It was as if he were come to a place of torment, where they who could not drink longed for water, where they who could feel no warmth shuddered in the eternal cold. He was oppressed by the grim conceit that he himself still slept within the matted thicket, imprisoned by the green bastions of the Roman fort. He had never come out, but a changeling had gone down the hill, and now stirred about the earth.

Beset by such ingenious terrors, it was not wonderful that outward events and common incidents should abet his fancies. He had succeeded one day in escaping from the mesh of the streets, and fell on a rough and narrow lane that stole into a little valley. For the moment he was in a somewhat happier mood; the afternoon sun glowed through the rolling mist, and the air grew clearer. He saw quiet and peaceful fields, and a wood descending in a gentle slope from an old farmstead of warm red brick. The farmer was driving the slow cattle home from the hill, and his loud halloo to his dog came across the land a cheerful mellow note. From another side a cart was approaching the clustered barns, hesitating, pausing while the great horses rested, and then starting again into lazy motion. In the well of the valley a wandering line of bushes showed where a brook crept in and out amongst the meadows, and, as Lucian stood, lingering, on the bridge, a soft and idle breath ruffled through the boughs of a great elm. He felt soothed, as by calm music, and wondered whether it would not be better for him to live in some such quiet place, within reach of the streets and yet remote from them. It seemed a refuge for still thoughts; he could imagine himself sitting at rest beneath the black yew tree in the farm garden, at the close of a summer day. He had almost determined that he would knock at the door and ask if they would take him as a lodger, when he saw a child running towards him down the lane. It was a little girl, with bright curls tossing about her head, and, as she came on, the sunlight glowed upon her, illuminating her brick-red frock and the yellow king-cups in her hat. She had run with her eyes on the ground, chirping and laughing to herself, and did not see Lucian till she was quite near him. She started and glanced into his eyes for a moment, and began to cry; he stretched out his hand, and she ran from him screaming, frightened no doubt by what was to her a sudden and strange apparition. He turned back towards London, and the mist folded him in its thick darkness, for on that evening it was tinged with black.

It was only by the intensest strain of resolution that he did not yield utterly to the poisonous anodyne which was always at hand. It had been a difficult struggle to escape from the mesh of the hills, from the music of the fauns, and even now he was drawn by the memory of these old allurements. But he felt that here, in his loneliness, he was in greater danger, and beset by a blacker magic. Horrible fancies rushed wantonly into his mind; he was not only ready to believe that something in his soul sent a shudder through all that was simple and innocent, but he came trembling home one Saturday night, believing, or half-believing, that he was in communion with evil. He had passed through the clamorous and blatant crowd of the "high street," where, as one climbed the hill, the shops seemed all aflame, and the black night air glowed with the flaring gas-jets and the naphtha-lamps, hissing and wavering before the February wind. Voices, raucous, clamant, abominable, were belched out of the blazing public-houses as the doors swung to and fro, and above these doors were hideous brassy lamps, very slowly swinging in a violent blast of air, so that they might have been infernal thuribles, censing the people. Some man was calling his wares in one long continuous shriek that never stopped or paused, and, as a respond, a deeper, louder voice roared to him from across the road. An Italian whirled the handle of his piano-organ in a fury, and a ring of imps danced mad figures around him, danced and flung up their legs till the rags dropped from some of them, and they still danced on. A flare of naphtha, burning with a rushing noise, threw a light on one point of the circle, and Lucian watched a lank girl of fifteen as she came round and round to the flash. She was quite drunk, and had kicked her petticoats away, and the crowd howled laughter and applause at her. Her black hair poured down and leapt on her scarlet bodice; she sprang and leapt round the ring, laughing in Bacchic frenzy, and led the orgy to triumph. People were crossing to and fro, jostling against each other, swarming about certain shops and stalls in a dense dark mass that quivered and sent out feelers as if it were one writhing organism. A little farther a group of young men, arm in arm, were marching down the roadway chanting some music-hall verse in full chorus, so that it sounded like plainsong. An impossible hubbub, a hum of voices angry as swarming bees, the squeals of five or six girls who ran in and out, and dived up dark passages and darted back into the crowd; all these mingled together till his ears quivered. A young fellow was playing the concertina, and he touched the keys with such slow fingers that the tune wailed solemn into a dirge; but there was nothing so strange as the burst of sound that swelled out when the public-house doors were opened.

He walked amongst these people, looked at their faces, and looked at the children amongst them. He had come out thinking that he would see the English working class, "the best-behaved and the best-tempered crowd in the world," enjoying the simple pleasure of the Saturday night's shopping. Mother bought the joint for Sunday's dinner, and perhaps a pair of boots for father; father had an honest glass of beer, and the children were given bags of sweets, and then all these worthy people went decently home to their well-earned rest. De Quincey had enjoyed the sight in his day, and had studied the rise and fall of onions and potatoes. Lucian, indeed, had desired to take these simple emotions as an opiate, to forget the fine fret and fantastic trouble of his own existence in plain things and the palpable joy of rest after labour. He was only afraid lest he should be too sharply reproached by the sight of these men who fought bravely year after year against starvation, who knew nothing of intricate and imagined grief, but only the weariness of relentless labour, of the long battle for their wives and children. It would be pathetic, he thought, to see them content with so little, brightened by the expectation of a day's rest and a good dinner, forced, even then, to reckon every penny, and to make their children laugh with halfpence. Either he would be ashamed before so much content, or else he would be again touched by the sense of his inhumanity which could take no interest in the common things of life. But still he went to be at least taken out of himself, to be forced to look at another side of the world, so that he might perhaps forget a little while his own sorrows.

He was fascinated by what he saw and heard. He wondered whether De Quincey also had seen the same spectacle, and had concealed his impressions out of reverence for the average reader. Here there were no simple joys of honest toilers, but wonderful orgies, that drew out his heart to horrible music. At first the violence of sound and sight had overwhelmed him; the lights flaring in the night wind, the array of naphtha lamps, the black shadows, the roar of voices. The dance about the piano-organ had been the first sign of an inner meaning, and the face of the dark girl as she came round and round to the flame had been amazing in its utter furious abandon. And what songs they were singing all around him, and what terrible words rang out, only to excite peals of laughter. In the public-houses the workmen's wives, the wives of small tradesmen, decently dressed in black, were drinking their faces to a flaming red, and urging their husbands to drink more. Beautiful young women, flushed and laughing, put their arms round the men's necks and kissed them, and then held up the glass to their lips. In the dark corners, at the openings of side streets, the children were talking together, instructing each other, whispering what they had seen; a boy of fifteen was plying a girl of twelve with whisky, and presently they crept away. Lucian passed them as they turned to go, and both looked at him. The boy laughed, and the girl smiled quietly. It was above all in the faces around him that he saw the most astounding things, the Bacchic fury unveiled and unashamed. To his eyes it seemed as if these revelers recognized him as a fellow, and smiled up in his face, aware that he was in the secret. Every instinct of religion, of civilization even, was swept away; they gazed at one another and at him, absolved of all scruples, children of the earth and nothing more. Now and then a couple detached themselves from the swarm, and went away into the darkness, answering the jeers and laughter of their friends as they vanished.

On the edge of the pavement, not far from where he was standing, Lucian noticed a tall and lovely young woman who seemed to be alone. She was in the full light of a naphtha flame, and her bronze hair and flushed cheeks shone illuminate as she viewed the orgy. She had dark brown eyes, and a strange look as of an old picture in her face; and her eyes brightened with an urgent gleam. He saw the revelers nudging each other and glancing at her, and two or three young men went up and asked her to come for a walk. She shook her head and said "No thank you" again and again, and seemed as if she were looking for somebody in the crowd.

"I'm expecting a friend," she said at last to a man who proposed a drink and a walk afterwards; and Lucian wondered what kind of friend would ultimately appear. Suddenly she turned to him as he was about to pass on, and said in a low voice:

"I'll go for a walk with you if you like; you just go on, and I'll follow in a minute."

For a moment he looked steadily at her. He saw that the first glance has misled him; her face was not flushed with drink as he had supposed, but it was radiant with the most exquisite colour, a red flame glowed and died on her cheek, and seemed to palpitate as she spoke. The head was set on the neck nobly, as in a statue, and about the ears the bronze hair strayed into little curls. She was smiling and waiting for his answer.

He muttered something about being very sorry, and fled down the hill out of the orgy, from the noise of roaring voices and the glitter of the great lamps very slowly swinging in the blast of wind. He knew that he had touched the brink of utter desolation; there was death in the woman's face, and she had indeed summoned him to the Sabbath. Somehow he had been able to refuse on the instant, but if he had delayed he knew he would have abandoned himself to her, body and soul. He locked himself in his room and lay trembling on the bed, wondering if some subtle sympathy had shown the woman her perfect companion. He looked in the glass, not expecting now to see certain visible and outward signs, but searching for the meaning of that strange glance that lit up his eyes. He had grown even thinner than before in the last few months, and his cheeks were wasted with hunger and sorrow, but there were still about his features the suggestion of a curious classic grace, and the look as of a faun who has strayed from the vineyards and olive gardens. He had broken away, but now he felt the mesh of her net about him, a desire for her that was a madness, as if she held every nerve in his body and drew him to her, to her mystic world, to the rosebush where every flower was a flame.

He dreamed all night of the perilous things he had refused, and it was loss to awake in the morning, pain to return to the world. The frost had broken and the fog had rolled away, and the grey street was filled with a clear grey light. Again he looked out on the long dull sweep of the monotonous houses, hidden for the past weeks by a curtain of mist. Heavy rain had fallen in the night, and the garden rails were still dripping, the roofs still dark with wet, all down the line the dingy white blinds were drawn in the upper windows. Not a soul walked the street; everyone was asleep after the exertions of the night before; even on the main road it was only at intervals that some straggler paddled by. Presently a woman in a brown ulster shuffled off on some errand, then a man in shirt-sleeves poked out his head, holding the door half-open, and stared up at a window opposite. After a few minutes he slunk in again, and three loafers came slouching down the street, eager for mischief or beastliness of some sort. They chose a house that seemed rather smarter than the rest, and, irritated by the neat curtains, the little grass plot with its dwarf shrub, one of the ruffians drew out a piece of chalk and wrote some words on the front door. His friends kept watch for him, and the adventure achieved, all three bolted, bellowing yahoo laughter. Then a bell began, tang, tang, tang, and here and there children appeared on their way to Sunday-school, and the chapel "teachers" went by with verjuice eyes and lips, scowling at the little boy who cried "Piper, piper!" On the main road many respectable people, the men shining and ill-fitted, the women hideously bedizened, passed in the direction of the Independent nightmare, the stuccoed thing with Doric columns, but on the whole life was stagnant. Presently Lucian smelt the horrid fumes of roast beef and cabbage; the early risers were preparing the one-o'clock meal, but many lay in bed and put off dinner till three, with the effect of prolonging the cabbage atmosphere into the late afternoon. A drizzly rain began as the people were coming out of church, and the mothers of little boys in velvet and little girls in foolishness of every kind were impelled to slap their offspring, and to threaten them with father. Then the torpor of beef and beer and cabbage settled down on the street; in some houses they snorted and read the Parish Magazine, in some they snored and read the murders and collected filth of the week; but the only movement of the afternoon was a second procession of children, now bloated and distended with food, again answering the summons of tang, tang, tang. On the main road the trams, laden with impossible people, went humming to and fro, and young men who wore bright blue ties cheerfully haw-hawed and smoked penny cigars. They annoyed the shiny and respectable and verjuice-lipped, not by the frightful stench of the cigars, but because they were cheerful on Sunday. By and by the children, having heard about Moses in the Bulrushes and Daniel in the Lion's Den, came straggling home in an evil humor. And all the day it was as if on a grey sheet grey shadows flickered, passing by.

And in the rose-garden every flower was a flame! He thought in symbols, using the Persian imagery of a dusky court, surrounded by white cloisters, gilded by gates of bronze. The stars came out, the sky glowed a darker violet, but the cloistered wall, the fantastic trellises in stone, shone whiter. It was like a hedge of may-blossom, like a lily within a cup of lapis-lazuli, like sea-foam tossed on the heaving sea at dawn. Always those white cloisters trembled with the lute music, always the garden sang with the clear fountain, rising and falling in the mysterious dusk. And there was a singing voice stealing through the white lattices and the bronze gates, a soft voice chanting of the Lover and the Beloved, of the Vineyard, of the Gate and the Way. Oh! the language was unknown; but the music of the refrain returned again and again, swelling and trembling through the white nets of the latticed cloisters. And every rose in the dusky air was a flame.

He had seen the life which he expressed by these symbols offered to him, and he had refused it; and he was alone in the grey street, with its lamps just twinkling through the dreary twilight, the blast of a ribald chorus sounding from the main road, a doggerel hymn whining from some parlor, to the accompaniment of the harmonium. He wondered why he had turned away from that woman who knew all secrets, in whose eyes were all the mysteries. He opened the desk of his bureau, and was confronted by the heap and litter of papers, lying in confusion as he had left them. He knew that there was the motive of his refusal; he had been unwilling to abandon all hope of the work. The glory and the torment of his ambition glowed upon him as he looked at the manuscript; it seemed so pitiful that such a single desire should be thwarted. He was aware that if he chose to sit down now before the desk he could, in a manner, write easily enough—he could produce a tale which would be formally well constructed and certain of favorable reception. And it would not be the utterly commonplace, entirely hopeless favorite of the circulating library; it would stand in those ranks where the real thing is skillfully counterfeited, amongst the books which give the reader his orgy of emotions, and yet contrive to be superior, and "art," in his opinion. Lucian had often observed this species of triumph, and had noted the acclamation that never failed the clever sham. *Romola*, for example, had made the great host of the serious, the portentous, shout for joy, while the real book, *The Cloister and the Hearth*, was a comparative failure.

He knew that he could write a *Romola*; but he thought the art of counterfeiting half-crowns less detestable than this shabby trick of imitating literature. He had refused definitely to enter the atelier of the gentleman who pleased his clients by ingeniously simulating the grain of walnut; and though he had seen the old oaken ambry kicked out contemptuously into the farmyard, serving perhaps the necessities of hens or pigs, he would not apprentice himself to the masters of veneer. He paced up and down the room, glancing now and again at his papers, and wondering if there were not hope for him. A great thing he could never do, but he had longed to do a true thing, to imagine sincere and genuine pages.

He was stirred again to this fury for the work by the event of the evening before, by all that had passed through his mind since the melancholy dawn. The lurid picture of that fiery street, the flaming shops and flaming glances, all its wonders and horrors, lit by the naphtha flares and by the burning souls, had possessed him; and the noises, the shriek and the whisper, the jangling rattle of the piano-organ, the long-continued scream of the butcher as he dabbled in the blood, the lewd litany of the singers, these seemed to be resolved into an infernal overture, loud with the expectation of lust and death. And how the spectacle was set in the cloud of dark night, a phantom play acted on that fiery stage, beneath those hideous brassy lamps, very slowly swinging in a violent blast. As all the medley of outrageous sights and sounds now fused themselves within his brain into one clear impression, it seemed that he had indeed witnessed and acted in a drama, that all the scene had been prepared and vested for him, and that the choric songs he had heard were but preludes to a greater act. For in that woman was the consummation and catastrophe of it all, and the whole stage waited for their meeting. He fancied that after this the voices and the lights died away, that the crowd sank swiftly into the darkness, and that the street was at once denuded of the great lamps and of all its awful scenic apparatus.

Again, he thought, the same mystery would be represented before him; suddenly on some dark and gloomy night, as he wandered lonely on a deserted road, the wind hurrying before him, suddenly a turn would bring him again upon the fiery stage, and the antique drama would be re-enacted. He would be drawn to the same place, to find that woman still standing there; again he would watch the rose radiant and palpitating upon her cheek, the argent gleam in her brown eyes, the bronze curls gilding the white splendor of her neck. And for the second time she would freely offer herself. He could hear the wail of the singers swelling to a shriek, and see the dusky dancers whirling round in a faster frenzy, and the naphtha flares tinged with red, as the woman and he went away into the dark, into the cloistered court where every flower was a flame, whence he would never come out.

His only escape was in the desk; he might find salvation if he could again hide his heart in the heap and litter of papers, and again be rapt by the cadence of a phrase. He threw open his window and looked out on the dim world and the glimmering amber lights. He resolved that he would rise early in the morning, and seek once more for his true life in the work.

But there was a strange thing. There was a little bottle on the mantelpiece, a bottle of dark blue glass, and he trembled and shuddered before it, as if it were a fetish.

VII

I t was very dark in the room. He seemed by slow degrees to awake from a long and heavy torpor, from an utter forgetfulness, and as he raised his eyes he could scarcely discern the pale whiteness of the paper on the desk before him. He remembered something of a gloomy winter afternoon, of driving rain, of gusty wind: he had fallen asleep over his work, no doubt, and the night had come down.

He lay back in his chair, wondering whether it were late; his eyes were half closed, and he did not make the effort and rouse himself. He could hear the stormy noise of the wind, and the sound reminded him of the half-forgotten days. He thought of his boyhood, and the old rectory, and the great elms that surrounded it. There was something pleasant in the consciousness that he was still half dreaming; he knew he could wake up whenever he pleased, but for the moment he amused himself by the pretence that he was a little boy again, tired with his rambles and the keen air of the hills. He remembered how he would sometimes wake up in the dark at midnight, and listen sleepily for a moment to the rush of the wind straining and crying amongst the trees, and hear it beat upon the walls, and then he would fall to dreams again, happy in his warm, snug bed.

The wind grew louder, and the windows rattled. He half opened his eyes and shut them again, determined to cherish that sensation of long ago. He felt tired and heavy with sleep; he imagined that he was exhausted by some effort; he had, perhaps, been writing furiously without rest. He could not recollect at the instant what the work had been; it would be delightful to read the pages when he had made up his mind to bestir himself.

Surely that was the noise of boughs, swaying and grinding in the wind. He remembered one night at home when such a sound had roused him suddenly from a deep sweet sleep. There was a rushing and beating as of wings upon the air, and a heavy dreary noise, like thunder far away upon the mountain. He had got out of bed and looked from behind the blind to see what was abroad. He remembered the strange sight he had seen, and he pretended it would be just the same if he cared to look out now. There were clouds flying awfully from before the moon, and a pale light that made the familiar land look strange and terrible. The blast of wind came with a great shriek, and the trees tossed and bowed and quivered; the wood was scourged and horrible, and the night air was ghastly with a confused tumult, and voices as of a host. A huge black cloud rolled across the heaven from the west and covered up the moon, and there came a torrent of bitter hissing rain.

It was all a vivid picture to him as he sat in his chair, unwilling to wake. Even as he let his mind stray back to that night of the past years, the rain beat sharply on the window-panes, and though there were no trees in the grey suburban street, he heard distinctly the crash of boughs. He wandered vaguely from thought to thought, groping indistinctly amongst memories, like a man trying to cross from door to door in a darkened unfamiliar room. But, no doubt, if he were to look out, by some magic the whole scene would be displayed before him. He would not see the curve of monotonous two-storied houses, with here and there a white blind, a patch of light, and shadows appearing and vanishing, not the rain plashing in the muddy road, not the amber of the gas-lamp opposite, but the wild moonlight poured on the dearly loved country; far away the dim circle of the hills and woods, and beneath him the tossing trees about the lawn, and the wood heaving under the fury of the wind.

He smiled to himself, amidst his lazy meditations, to think how real it seemed, and yet it was all far away, the scenery of an old play long ended and forgotten. It was strange that after all these years of trouble and work and change he should be in any sense the same person as that little boy peeping out, half frightened, from the rectory window. It was as if looking in the glass one should see a stranger, and yet know that the image was a true reflection.

The memory of the old home recalled his father and mother to him, and he wondered whether his mother would come if he were to cry out suddenly. One night, on just such a night as this, when a great storm blew from the mountain, a tree had fallen with a crash and a bough had struck the roof, and he awoke in a fright, calling for his mother. She had come and had comforted him, soothing him to sleep, and now he shut his eyes, seeing her face shining in the uncertain flickering candle light, as she bent over his bed. He could not think she had died; the memory was but a part of the evil dreams that had come afterwards.

He said to himself that he had fallen asleep and dreamed sorrow and agony, and he wished to forget all the things of trouble. He would return to happy days, to the beloved land, to the dear and friendly paths across the fields. There was the paper, white before him, and when he chose to stir, he would have the pleasure of reading his work. He could not quite recollect what he had been about, but he was somehow conscious that the had been successful and had brought some long labour to a worthy ending. Presently he would light the gas, and enjoy the satisfaction that only the work could give him, but for the time he preferred to linger in the darkness, and to think of himself as straying from stile to stile through the scented meadows, and listening to the bright brook that sang to the alders.

It was winter now, for he heard the rain and the wind, and the swaying of the trees, but in those old days how sweet the summer had been. The great hawthorn bush in blossom, like a white cloud upon the earth, had appeared to him in twilight, he had lingered in the enclosed valley to hear the nightingale, a voice swelling out from the rich gloom, from the trees that grew around the well. The scent of the meadowsweet was blown to him across the bridge of years, and with it came the dream and the hope and the longing, and the afterglow red in the sky, and the marvel of the earth. There was a quiet walk that he knew so well; one went up from a little green byroad, following an unnamed brooklet scarce a foot wide, but yet wandering like a river, gurgling over its pebbles, with its dwarf bushes shading the pouring water. One went through the meadow grass, and came to the larch wood that grew from hill to hill across the stream, and shone a brilliant tender green, and sent vague sweet spires to the flushing sky. Through the wood the path wound, turning and dipping, and beneath, the brown fallen needles of last year were soft and thick, and the resinous cones gave out their odour as the warm night advanced, and the shadows darkened. It was quite still; but he stayed, and the faint song of the brooklet sounded like the echo of a river beyond the mountains. How strange it was to look into the wood, to see the tall straight stems rising, pillar-like, and then the dusk, uncertain, and then the blackness. So he came out from the larch wood, from the green cloud and the vague shadow, into the dearest of all hollows, shut in on one side by the larches and before him by high violent walls of turf, like the slopes of a fort, with a clear line dark against the twilight sky, and a weird thorn bush that grew large, mysterious, on the summit, beneath the gleam of the evening star.

And he retraced his wanderings in those deep old lanes that began from the common road and went away towards the unknown, climbing steep hills, and piercing the woods of shadows, and dipping down into valleys that seemed virgin, unexplored, secret for the foot of man. He entered such a lane not knowing where it might bring him, hoping he had found the way to fairyland, to the woods beyond the world, to that vague territory that haunts all the dreams of a boy. He could not tell where he might be, for the high banks rose steep, and the great hedges made a green vault above. Marvelous ferns grew rich and thick in the dark red earth, fastening their roots about the roots of hazel and beech and maple, clustering like the carven capitals of a cathedral pillar. Down, like a dark shaft, the lane dipped to the well of the hills, and came amongst the limestone rocks. He climbed the bank at last, and looked out into a country that seemed for a moment the land he sought, a mysterious realm with unfamiliar hills and valleys and fair plains all golden, and white houses radiant in the sunset light.

And he thought of the steep hillsides where the bracken was like a wood, and of bare places where the west wind sang over the golden gorse, of still circles in mid-lake, of the poisonous yew-tree in the middle of the wood, shedding its crimson cups on the dank earth. How he lingered by certain black waterpools hedged on every side by drooping wych-elms and black-stemmed alders, watching the faint waves widening to the banks as a leaf or a twig dropped from the trees.

And the whole air and wonder of the ancient forest came back to him. He had found his way to the river valley, to the long lovely hollow between the hills, and went up and up beneath the leaves in the warm hush of midsummer, glancing back now and again through the green alleys, to the river winding in mystic esses beneath, passing hidden glens receiving the streams that rushed down the hillside, ice-cold from the rock, passing the immemorial tumulus, the graves where the legionaries waited for the trumpet, the grey farmhouses sending the blue wreaths of wood smoke into the still air. He went higher and higher, till at last he entered the long passage of the Roman road, and from this, the ridge and summit of the wood, he saw the waves of green swell and dip and sink towards the marshy level and the gleaming yellow sea. He looked on the surging forest, and thought of the strange deserted city mouldering into a petty village on its verge, of its encircling walls melting into the turf, of vestiges of an older temple which the earth had buried utterly.

It was winter now, for he heard the wail of the wind, and a sudden gust drove the rain against the panes, but he thought of the bee's song in the clover, of the foxgloves in full blossom, of the wild roses, delicate, enchanting, swaying on a long stem above the hedge. He had been in strange places, he had known sorrow and desolation, and had grown grey and weary in the work of letters, but he lived again in the sweetness, in the clear bright air of early morning, when the sky was blue in June, and the mist rolled like a white sea in the valley. He laughed when he recollected that he had sometimes fancied himself unhappy in those days; in those days when he could be glad because the sun shone, because the wind blew fresh on the mountain. On those bright days he had been glad, looking at the fleeting and passing of the clouds upon the hills, and had gone up higher to the broad dome of the mountain, feeling that joy went up before him.

He remembered how, a boy, he had dreamed of love, of an adorable and ineffable mystery which transcended all longing and desire. The time had come when all the wonder of the earth seemed to prefigure this alone, when he found the symbol of the Beloved in hill and wood and stream, and every flower and every dark pool discoursed a pure ecstasy. It was the longing for longing, the love of love, that had come to him when he awoke one morning just before the dawn, and for the first time felt the sharp thrill of passion.

He tried in vain to express to himself the exquisite joys of innocent desire. Even now, after troubled years, in spite of some dark cloud that overshadowed the background of his thought, the sweetness of the boy's imagined pleasure came like a perfume into his reverie. It was no love of a woman but the desire of womanhood, the Eros of the unknown, that made the heart tremble. He hardly dreamed that such a love could ever be satisfied, that the thirst of beauty could be slaked. He shrank from all contact of actuality, not venturing so much as to imagine the inner place and sanctuary of the mysteries. It was enough for him to adore in the outer court, to know that within, in the sweet gloom, were the vision and the rapture, the altar and the sacrifice.

He remembered, dimly, the passage of many heavy years since that time of hope and passion, but, perhaps, the vague shadow would pass away, and he could renew the boy's thoughts, the unformed fancies that were part of the bright day, of the wild roses in the hedgerow. All other things should be laid aside, he would let them trouble him no more after this winter night. He saw now that from the first he had allowed his imagination to bewilder him, to create a fantastic world in which he suffered, moulding innocent forms into terror and dismay. Vividly, he saw again the black circle of oaks, growing in a haggard ring upon the bastions of the Roman fort. The noise of the storm without grew louder, and he thought how the wind had come up the valley with the sound of a scream, how a great tree had ground its boughs together, shuddering before the violent blast. Clear and distinct, as if he were standing now in the lane, he saw the steep slopes surging from the valley, and the black crown of the oaks set against the flaming sky, against a blaze and glow of light as if great furnace doors were opened. He saw the fire, as it were, smitten about the bastions, about the heaped mounds that guarded the fort, and the crooked evil boughs seemed to writhe in the blast of flame that beat from heaven. Strangely with the sight of the burning fort mingled the impression of a dim white shape floating up the dusk of the lane towards him, and he saw across the valley of years a girl's face, a momentary apparition that shone and vanished away.

Then there was a memory of another day, of violent summer, of white farmhouse walls blazing in the sun, and a far call from the reapers in the cornfields. He had climbed the steep slope and penetrated the matted thicket and lay in the heat, alone on the soft short grass that grew within the fort. There was a cloud of madness, and confusion of broken dreams that had no meaning or clue but only an indefinable horror and defilement. He had fallen asleep as he gazed at the knotted fantastic boughs of the stunted brake about him, and when he woke he was ashamed, and fled away fearing that "they" would pursue him. He did not know who "they" were, but it seemed as if a woman's face watched him from between the matted boughs, and that she summoned to her side awful companions who had never grown old through all the ages.

He looked up, it seemed, at a smiling face that bent over him, as he sat in the cool dark kitchen of the old farmhouse, and wondered why the sweetness of those red lips and the kindness of the eyes mingled with the nightmare in the fort, with the horrible Sabbath he had imagined as he lay sleeping on the hot soft turf. He had allowed these disturbed fancies, all this mad wreck of terror and shame that he had gathered in his mind, to trouble him for too long a time; presently he would light up the room, and leave all the old darkness of his life behind him, and from henceforth he would walk in the day.

He could still distinguish, though very vaguely, the pile of papers beside him, and he remembered, now, that he had finished a long task that afternoon, before he fell asleep. He could not trouble himself to recollect the exact nature of the work, but he was sure that he had done well; in a few minutes, perhaps, he would strike a match, and read the title, and amuse himself with his own forgetfulness. But the sight of the papers lying there in order made him think of his beginnings, of those first unhappy efforts which were so impossible and so hopeless. He saw himself bending over the table in the old familiar room, desperately scribbling, and then laying down his pen dismayed at the sad results on the page. It was late at night, his father had been long in bed, and the house was still. The fire was almost out, with only a dim glow here and there amongst the cinders, and the room was growing chilly. He rose at last from his work and looked out on a dim earth and a dark and cloudy sky.

Night after night he had laboured on, persevering in his effort, even through the cold sickness of despair, when every line was doomed as it was made. Now, with the consciousness that he knew at least the conditions of literature, and that many years of thought and practice had given him some sense of language, he found these early struggles both pathetic and astonishing. He could not understand how he had persevered so stubbornly, how he had had the heart to begin a fresh page when so many folios of blotted, painful effort lay torn, derided, impossible in their utter failure. It seemed to him that it must have been a miracle or an infernal possession, a species of madness, that had driven him on, everyday disappointed, and everyday hopeful.

And yet there was a joyous side to the illusion. In these dry days that he lived in, when he had bought, by a long experience and by countless hours of misery, a knowledge of his limitations, of the vast gulf that yawned between the conception and the work, it was pleasant to think of a time when all things were possible, when the most splendid design seemed an affair of a few weeks. Now he had come to a frank acknowledgment; so far as he was concerned, he judged every book wholly impossible till the last line of it was written, and he had learnt patience, the art of sighing and putting the fine scheme away in the pigeon-hole of what could never be. But to think of those days! Then one could plot out a book that should be more curious than Rabelais, and jot down the outlines of a romance to surpass Cervantes, and design renaissance tragedies and volumes of *contes*, and comedies of the Restoration; everything was to be done, and the masterpiece was always the rainbow cup, a little way before him.

He touched the manuscript on the desk, and the feeling of the pages seemed to restore all the papers that had been torn so long ago. It was the atmosphere of the silent room that returned, the light of the shaded candle falling on the abandoned leaves. This had been painfully excogitated while the snowstorm whirled about the lawn and filled the lanes, this was of the summer night, this of the harvest moon rising like a fire from the tithebarn on the hill. How well he remembered those half-dozen pages of which he had once been so proud; he had thought out the sentences one evening, while he leaned on the foot-bridge and watched the brook swim across the road. Every word smelt of the meadowsweet that grew thick upon the banks; now, as he recalled the cadence and the phrase that had seemed so charming, he saw again the ferns beneath the vaulted roots of the beech, and the green light of the glowworm in the hedge.

And in the west the mountains swelled to a great dome, and on the dome was a mound, the memorial of some forgotten race, that grew dark and large against the red sky, when the sun set. He had lingered below it in the solitude, amongst the winds, at evening, far away from home; and oh, the labour and the vain efforts to make the form of it and the awe of it in prose, to write the hush of the vast hill, and the sadness of the world below sinking into the night, and the mystery, the suggestion of the rounded hillock, huge against the magic sky.

He had tried to sing in words the music that the brook sang, and the sound of the October wind rustling through the brown bracken on the hill. How many pages he had covered in the effort to show a white winter world, a sun without warmth in a grey-blue sky, all the fields, all the land white and shining, and one high summit where the dark pines towered, still in the still afternoon, in the pale violet air.

To win the secret of words, to make a phrase that would murmur of summer and the bee, to summon the wind into a sentence, to conjure the odour of the night into the surge and fall and harmony of a line; this was the tale of the long evenings, of the candle flame white upon the paper and the eager pen.

He remembered that in some fantastic book he had seen a bar or two of music, and, beneath, the inscription that here was the musical expression of Westminster Abbey. His boyish effort seemed hardly less ambitious, and he no longer believed that language could present the melody and the awe and the loveliness of the earth. He had long known that he, at all events, would have to be content with a far approach, with a few broken notes that might suggest, perhaps, the magistral everlasting song of the hill and the streams.

But in those far days the impossible was but a part of wonderland that lay before him, of the world beyond the wood and the mountain.

ARTHUR MACHEN

All was to be conquered, all was to be achieved; he had but to make the journey and he would find the golden world and the golden word, and hear those songs that the sirens sang. He touched the manuscript; whatever it was, it was the result of painful labour and disappointment, not of the old flush of hope, but it came of weary days, of correction and re-correction. It might be good in its measure; but afterwards he would write no more for a time. He would go back again to the happy world of masterpieces, to the dreams of great and perfect books, written in an ecstasy.

Like a dark cloud from the sea came the memory of the attempt he had made, of the poor piteous history that had once embittered his life. He sighed and said alas, thinking of his folly, of the hours when he was shaken with futile, miserable rage. Some silly person in London had made his manuscript more saleable and had sold it without rendering an account of the profits, and for that he had been ready to curse humanity. Black, horrible, as the memory of a stormy day, the rage of his heart returned to his mind, and he covered his eyes, endeavoring to darken the picture of terror and hate that shone before him. He tried to drive it all out of his thought, it vexed him to remember these foolish trifles; the trick of a publisher, the small pomposities and malignancies of the country folk, the cruelty of a village boy, had inflamed him almost to the pitch of madness. His heart had burnt with fury, and when he looked up the sky was blotched, and scarlet as if it rained blood.

Indeed he had almost believed that blood had rained upon him, and cold blood from a sacrifice in heaven; his face was wet and chill and dripping, and he had passed his hand across his forehead and looked at it. A red cloud had seemed to swell over the hill, and grow great, and come near to him; he was but an ace removed from raging madness.

It had almost come to that; the drift and the breath of the scarlet cloud had well-nigh touched him. It was strange that he had been so deeply troubled by such little things, and strange how after all the years he could still recall the anguish and rage and hate that shook his soul as with a spiritual tempest.

The memory of all that evening was wild and troubled; he resolved that it should vex him no more, that now, for the last time, he would let himself be tormented by the past. In a few minutes he would rise to a new life, and forget all the storms that had gone over him.

Curiously, every detail was distinct and clear in his brain. The figure of the doctor driving home, and the sound of the few words he had spoken came to him in the darkness, through the noise of the storm and the pattering of the rain. Then he stood upon the ridge of the hill and saw the smoke drifting up from the ragged roofs of Caermaen, in the evening calm; he listened to the voices mounting thin and clear, in a weird tone, as if some outland folk were speaking in an unknown tongue of awful things.

He saw the gathering darkness, the mystery of twilight changing the huddled squalid village into an unearthly city, into some dreadful Atlantis, inhabited by a ruined race. The mist falling fast, the gloom that seemed to issue from the black depths of the forest, to advance palpably towards the walls, were shaped before him; and beneath, the river wound, snake-like, about the town, swimming to the flood and glowing in its still pools like molten brass. And as the water mirrored the afterglow and sent ripples and gouts of blood against the shuddering reeds, there came suddenly the piercing trumpet-call, the loud reiterated summons that rose and fell, that called and recalled, echoing through all the valley, crying to the dead as the last note rang. It summoned the legion from the river and the graves and the battlefield, the host floated up from the sea, the centuries swarmed about the eagles, the array was set for the last great battle, behind the leaguer of the mist.

He could imagine himself still wandering through the dim unknown, terrible country, gazing affrighted at the hills and woods that seemed to have put on an unearthly shape, stumbling amongst the briars that caught his feet. He lost his way in a wild country, and the red light that blazed up from the furnace on the mountains only showed him a mysterious land, in which he strayed aghast, with the sense of doom weighing upon him. The dry mutter of the trees, the sound of an unseen brook, made him afraid as if the earth spoke of his sin, and presently he was fleeing through a desolate shadowy wood, where a pale light flowed from the mouldering stumps, a dream of light that shed a ghostly radiance.

And then again the dark summit of the Roman fort, the black sheer height rising above the valley, and the moonfire streaming around the ring of oaks, glowing about the green bastions that guarded the thicket and the inner place.

The room in which he sat appeared the vision, the trouble of the wind and rain without was but illusion, the noise of the waves in the seashell. Passion and tears and adoration and the glories of the summer night returned, and the calm sweet face of the woman appeared, and he thrilled at the soft touch of her hand on his flesh.

She shone as if she had floated down into the lane from the moon that swam between films of cloud above the black circle of the oaks. She led him away from all terror and despair and hate, and gave herself to him with rapture, showing him love, kissing his tears away, pillowing his cheek upon her breast.

His lips dwelt on her lips, his mouth upon the breath of her mouth, her arms were strained about him, and oh! she charmed him with her voice, with sweet kind words, as she offered her sacrifice. How her scented hair fell down, and floated over his eyes, and there was a marvelous fire called the moon, and her lips were aflame, and her eyes shone like a light on the hills.

All beautiful womanhood had come to him in the lane. Love had touched him in the dusk and had flown away, but he had seen the splendor and the glory, and his eyes had seen the enchanted light.

Ave Atque Vale

The old words sounded in his ears like the ending of a chant, and he heard the music's close. Once only in his weary hapless life, once the world had passed away, and he had known her, the dear, dear Annie, the symbol of all mystic womanhood.

The heaviness of languor still oppressed him, holding him back amongst these old memories, so that he could not stir from his place. Oddly, there seemed something unaccustomed about the darkness of the room, as if the shadows he had summoned had changed the aspect of the walls. He was conscious that on this night he was not altogether himself; fatigue, and the weariness of sleep, and the waking vision had perplexed him. He remembered how once or twice when he was a little boy startled by an uneasy dream, and had stared with a frightened gaze into nothingness, not knowing where he was, all trembling, and breathing quick, till he touched the rail of his bed, and the familiar outlines of the looking-glass and the chiffonier began to glimmer out of the gloom. So now he touched the pile of manuscript and the desk at which he had worked so many hours, and felt reassured, though he smiled at himself, and he felt the old childish dread, the longing to cry out for someone to bring a candle, and show him that he really was in his own room. He glanced up for an instant, expecting to see perhaps the glitter of the brass gas jet that was fixed on the wall, just beside his bureau, but it was too dark, and he could not rouse himself and make the effort that would drive the cloud and the muttering thoughts away.

He leant back again, picturing the wet street without, the rain driving like fountain spray about the gas lamp, the shrilling of the wind on those waste places to the north. It was strange how in the brick and stucco desert where no trees were, he all the time imagined the noise of tossing boughs, the grinding of the boughs together. There was a great storm and tumult in this wilderness of London, and for the sound of the rain and the wind he could not hear the hum and jangle of the trams, and the jar and shriek of the garden gates as they opened and shut. But he could imagine his street, the rain-swept desolate curve of it, as it turned northward, and beyond the empty suburban roads, the twinkling villa windows, the ruined field, the broken lane, and then yet another suburb rising, a solitary gas-lamp glimmering at a corner, and the plane tree lashing its boughs, and driving great showers against the glass.

It was wonderful to think of. For when these remote roads were ended one dipped down the hill into the open country, into the dim world beyond the glint of friendly fires. Tonight, how waste they were, these wet roads, edged with the red-brick houses, with shrubs whipped by the wind against one another, against the paling and the wall. There the wind swayed the great elms scattered on the sidewalk, the remnants of the old stately fields, and beneath each tree was a pool of wet, and a torment of raindrops fell with every gust. And one passed through the red avenues, perhaps by a little settlement of flickering shops, and passed the last sentinel wavering lamp, and the road became a ragged lane, and the storm screamed from hedge to hedge across the open fields. And then, beyond, one touched again upon a still remoter avant-garde of London, an island amidst the darkness, surrounded by its pale of twinkling, starry lights.

He remembered his wanderings amongst these outposts of the town, and thought how desolate all their ways must be tonight. They were solitary in wet and wind, and only at long intervals someone pattered and hurried along them, bending his eyes down to escape the drift of rain. Within the villas, behind the close-drawn curtains, they drew about the fire, and wondered at the violence of the storm, listening for each great gust as it gathered far away, and rocked the trees, and at last rushed with a huge shock against their walls as if it were the coming of the sea. He thought of himself walking, as he had often walked, from lamp to lamp on such a night, treasuring his lonely thoughts, and weighing the hard task awaiting him in his room. Often in the evening, after a long day's labour, he had thrown down his pen in utter listlessness, feeling that he could struggle no more with ideas and words, and he had gone out into driving rain and darkness, seeking the word of the enigma as he tramped on and on beneath these outer battlements of London.

Or on some grey afternoon in March or November he had sickened of the dull monotony and the stagnant life that he saw from his window, and had taken his design with him to the lonely places, halting now and again by a gate, and pausing in the shelter of a hedge through which the austere wind shivered, while, perhaps, he dreamed of Sicily, or of sunlight on the Provençal olives. Often as he strayed solitary from street to field, and passed the Syrian fig tree imprisoned in Britain, nailed to an ungenial wall, the solution of the puzzle became evident, and he laughed and hurried home eager to make the page speak, to note the song he had heard on his way.

Sometimes he had spent many hours treading this edge and brim of London, now lost amidst the dun fields, watching the bushes shaken by the wind, and now looking down from a height whence he could see the dim waves of the town, and a barbaric water tower rising from a hill, and the snuff-coloured cloud of smoke that seemed blown up from the streets into the sky.

There were certain ways and places that he had cherished; he loved a great old common that stood on high ground, curtained about with ancient spacious houses of red brick, and their cedarn gardens. And there was on the road that led to this common a space of ragged uneven ground with a pool and a twisted oak, and here he had often stayed in autumn and looked across the mist and the valley at the great theatre of the sunset, where a red cloud like a charging knight shone and conquered a purple dragon shape, and golden lances glittered in a field of faerie green.

Or sometimes, when the unending prospect of trim, monotonous, modern streets had wearied him, he had found an immense refreshment in the discovery of a forgotten hamlet, left in a hollow, while all new London pressed and surged on every side, threatening the rest of the red roofs with its vulgar growth. These little peaceful houses, huddled together beneath the shelter of trees, with their bulging leaded windows and uneven roofs, somehow brought back to him the sense of the country, and soothed him with the thought of the old farmhouses, white or grey, the homes of quiet lives, harbors where, perhaps, no tormenting thoughts ever broke in.

For he had instinctively determined that there was neither rest nor health in all the arid waste of streets about him. It seemed as if in those dull rows of dwellings, in the prim new villas, red and white and staring, there must be a leaven working which transformed all to base vulgarity. Beneath the dull sad slates, behind the blistered doors, love turned to squalid intrigue, mirth to drunken clamor, and the mystery of life became a common thing; religion was sought for in the greasy piety and flatulent oratory of the Independent chapel, the stuccoed nightmare of the Doric columns. Nothing fine, nothing rare, nothing exquisite, it seemed, could exist in the weltering suburban sea, in the habitations which had risen from the stench and slime of the brickfields. It was as if the sickening fumes that steamed from the burning bricks had been sublimed into the shape of houses, and those who lived in these grey places could also claim kinship with the putrid mud.

Hence he had delighted in the few remains of the past that he could find still surviving on the suburb's edge, in the grave old houses that stood apart from the road, in the mouldering taverns of the eighteenth century, in the huddled hamlets that had preserved only the glow and the sunlight of all the years that had passed over them. It appeared to him that vulgarity and greasiness and squalor had come with a flood, that not only the good but also the evil in man's heart had been made common and ugly, that a sordid scum was mingled with all the springs, of death as of life. It would be alike futile to search amongst these mean two-storied houses for a splendid sinner as for a splendid saint; the very vices of these people smelt of cabbage water and a pothouse vomit.

And so he had often fled away from the serried maze that encircled him, seeking for the old and worn and significant as an antiquary looks for the fragments of the Roman temple amidst the modern shops. In some way the gusts of wind and the beating rain of the night reminded him of an old house that had often attracted him with a strange indefinable curiosity. He had found it on a grim grey day in March, when he had gone out under a leaden-moulded sky, cowering from a dry freezing wind that brought with it the gloom and the doom of far unhappy Siberian plains. More than ever that day the suburb had oppressed him; insignificant, detestable, repulsive to body and mind, it was the only hell that a vulgar age could conceive or make, an inferno created not by Dante but by the jerry-builder. He had gone out to the north, and when he lifted up his eyes again he found that he had chanced to turn up by one of the little lanes that still strayed across the broken fields. He had never chosen this path before because the lane at its outlet was so wholly degraded and offensive, littered with rusty tins and broken crockery, and hedged in with a paling fashioned out of scraps of wire, rotting timber, and bending worn-out rails. But on this day, by happy chance, he had fled from the high road by the first opening that offered, and he no longer groped his way amongst obscene refuse, sickened by the bloated bodies of dead dogs, and fetid odours from unclean decay, but the malpassage had become a peaceful winding lane, with warm shelter beneath its banks from the dismal wind. For a mile he had walked quietly, and then a turn in the road showed him a little glen or hollow, watered by such a tiny rushing brooklet as his own woods knew, and beyond, alas, the glaring foreguard of a "new neighborhood"; raw red villas, semi-detached, and then a row of lamentable shops.

But as he was about to turn back, in the hope of finding some other outlet, his attention was charmed by a small house that stood back a little from the road on his right hand. There had been a white gate, but the paint had long faded to grey and black, and the wood crumbled under the touch, and only moss marked out the lines of the drive. The iron railing round the lawn had fallen, and the poor flower-beds were choked with grass and a faded growth of weeds. But here and there a rosebush lingered amidst suckers that had sprung grossly from the root, and on each side of the hall door were box trees, untrimmed, ragged, but still green. The slate roof was all stained and livid, blotched with the drippings of a great elm that stood at one corner of the neglected lawn, and marks of damp and decay were thick on the uneven walls, which had been washed yellow many years before. There was a porch of trellis work before the door, and Lucian had seen it rock in the wind, swaying as if every gust must drive it down. There were two windows on the ground floor, one on each side of the door, and two above, with a blind space where a central window had been blocked up.

This poor and desolate house had fascinated him. Ancient and poor and fallen, disfigured by the slate roof and the yellow wash that had replaced the old mellow dipping tiles and the warm red walls, and disfigured again by spots and patches of decay; it seemed as if its happy days were forever ended. To Lucian it appealed with a sense of doom and horror; the black streaks that crept upon the walls, and the green drift upon the roof, appeared not so much the work of foul weather and dripping boughs, as the outward signs of evil working and creeping in the lives of those within.

The stage seemed to him decked for doom, painted with the symbols of tragedy; and he wondered as he looked whether anyone were so unhappy as to live there still. There were torn blinds in the windows, but he had asked himself who could be so brave as to sit in that room, darkened by the dreary box, and listen of winter nights to the rain upon the window, and the moaning of wind amongst the tossing boughs that beat against the roof.

He could not imagine that any chamber in such a house was habitable. Here the dead had lain, through the white blind the thin light had filtered on the rigid mouth, and still the floor must be wet with tears and still that great rocking elm echoed the groaning and the sobs of those who watched. No doubt, the damp was rising, and the odour of the earth filled the house, and made such as entered draw back, foreseeing the hour of death.

Often the thought of this strange old house had haunted him; he had imagined the empty rooms where a heavy paper peeled from the walls and hung in dark strips; and he could not believe that a light ever shone from those windows that stared black and glittering on the neglected lawn. But tonight the wet and the storm seemed curiously to bring the image of the place before him, and as the wind sounded he thought how unhappy those must be, if any there were, who sat in the musty chambers by a flickering light, and listened to the elm-tree moaning and beating and weeping on the walls.

And tonight was Saturday night; and there was about that phrase something that muttered of the condemned cell, of the agony of a doomed man. Ghastly to his eyes was the conception of anyone sitting in that room to the right of the door behind the larger box tree, where the wall was cracked above the window and smeared with a black stain in an ugly shape.

He knew how foolish it had been in the first place to trouble his mind with such conceits of a dreary cottage on the outskirts of London. And it was more foolish now to meditate these things, fantasies, feigned forms, the issue of a sad mood and a bleak day of spring. For soon, in a few moments, he was to rise to a new life. He was but reckoning up the account of his past, and when the light came he was to think no more of sorrow and heaviness, of real or imagined terrors. He had stayed

ARTHUR MACHEN

too long in London, and he would once more taste the breath of the hills, and see the river winding in the long lovely valley; ah! he would go home.

Something like a thrill, the thrill of fear, passed over him as he remembered that there was no home. It was in the winter, a year and a half after his arrival in town, that he had suffered the loss of his father. He lay for many days prostrate, overwhelmed with sorrow and with the thought that now indeed he was utterly alone in the world. Miss Deacon was to live with another cousin in Yorkshire; the old home was at last ended and done. He felt sorry that he had not written more frequently to his father: there were things in his cousin's letters that had made his heart sore. "Your poor father was always looking for your letters," she wrote, "they used to cheer him so much. He nearly broke down when you sent him that money last Christmas; he got it into his head that you were starving yourself to send it him. He was hoping so much that you would have come down this Christmas, and kept asking me about the plum-puddings months ago."

It was not only his father that had died, but with him the last strong link was broken, and the past life, the days of his boyhood, grew faint as a dream. With his father his mother died again, and the long years died, the time of his innocence, the memory of affection. He was sorry that his letters had gone home so rarely; it hurt him to imagine his father looking out when the post came in the morning, and forced to be sad because there was nothing. But he had never thought that his father valued the few lines that he wrote, and indeed it was often difficult to know what to say. It would have been useless to write of those agonizing nights when the pen seemed an awkward and outlandish instrument, when every effort ended in shameful defeat, or of the happier hours when at last wonder appeared and the line glowed, crowned and exalted. To poor Mr. Taylor such tales would have seemed but trivial histories of some Oriental game, like an odd story from a land where men have time for the infinitely little, and can seriously make a science of arranging blossoms in a jar, and discuss perfumes instead of politics. It would have been useless to write to the rectory of his only interest, and so he wrote seldom.

And then he had been sorry because he could never write again and never see his home. He had wondered whether he would have gone down to the old place at Christmas, if his father had lived. It was curious how common things evoked the bitterest griefs, but his father's anxiety that the plum-pudding should be good, and ready for him, had brought the tears into his eyes. He could hear him saying in a nervous voice that attempted to be cheerful: "I suppose you will be thinking of the Christmas puddings soon, Jane; you remember how fond Lucian used to be of plum-pudding. I hope we shall see him this December." No doubt poor Miss Deacon paled with rage at the suggestion that she should make Christmas pudding in July; and returned a sharp answer; but it was pathetic. The wind wailed, and the rain dashed and beat again and again upon the window. He imagined that all his thoughts of home, of the old rectory amongst the elms, had conjured into his mind the sound of the storm upon the trees, for, tonight, very clearly he heard the creaking of the boughs, the noise of boughs moaning and beating and weeping on the walls, and even a pattering of wet, on wet earth, as if there were a shrub near the window that shook off the raindrops, before the gust.

That thrill, as it were a shudder of fear, passed over him again, and he knew not what had made him afraid. There were some dark shadow on his mind that saddened him; it seemed as if a vague memory of terrible days hung like a cloud over his thought, but it was all indefinite, perhaps the last grim and ragged edge of the melancholy wrack that had swelled over his life and the bygone years. He shivered and tried to rouse himself and drive away the sense of dread and shame that seemed so real and so awful, and yet he could not grasp it. But the torpor of sleep, the burden of the work that he had ended a few hours before, still weighed down his limb and bound his thoughts. He could scarcely believe that he had been busy at his desk a little while ago, and that just before the winter day closed it and the rain began to fall he had laid down the pen with a sigh of relief, and had slept in his chair. It was rather as if he had slumbered deeply through a long and weary night, as if an awful vision of flame and darkness and the worm that dieth not had come to him sleeping. But he would dwell no more on the darkness; he went back to the early days in London when he had said farewell to the hills and to the waterpools, and had set to work in this little room in the dingy street.

How he had toiled and laboured at the desk before him! He had put away the old wild hopes of the masterpiece conceived and executed in a fury of inspiration, wrought out in one white heat of creative joy; it was enough if by dint of long perseverance and singleness of desire he could at last, in pain and agony and despair, after failure and disappointment and effort constantly renewed, fashion something of which he need not be ashamed. He had put himself to school again, and had, with what patience he could command, ground his teeth into the rudiments, resolved that at last he would test out the heart of the mystery. They were good nights to remember, these; he was glad to think of the little ugly room, with its silly wall-paper and its "bird's-eye" furniture, lighted up, while he sat at the bureau and wrote on into the cold stillness of the London morning, when the flickering lamplight and the daystar shone together. It was an interminable labour, and he had always known it to be as hopeless as alchemy. The gold, the great and glowing masterpiece, would never shine amongst the dead ashes and smoking efforts of the crucible, but in the course of the life, in the interval between the failures, he might possibly discover curious things.

These were the good nights that he could look back on without any fear or shame, when he had been happy and content on a diet of bread and tea and tobacco, and could hear of some imbecility passing into its hundredth thousand, and laugh cheerfully—if only that last page had been imagined aright, if the phrases noted in the still hours rang out their music when he read them in the morning. He remembered the drolleries and fantasies that the worthy Miss Deacon used to write to him, and how he had grinned at her words of reproof, admonition, and advice. She had once instigated Dolly *fils* to pay him a visit, and that young prop of respectability had talked about the extraordinary running of Bolter at the Scurragh meeting in Ireland; and then, glancing at Lucian's books, had inquired whether any of them had "warm bits." He had been kind though patronizing, and seemed to have moved freely in the most brilliant society of Stoke Newington. He had not been able to give any information as to the present condition of Edgar Allan Poe's old school. It appeared eventually that his report at home had not been a very favorable one, for no invitation to high tea had followed, as Miss Deacon had hoped. The Dollys knew many nice people, who were well off, and Lucian's cousin, as she afterwards said, had done *her* best to introduce him to the *beau monde* of those northern suburbs.

But after the visit of the young Dolly, with what joy he had returned to the treasures which he had concealed from profane eyes. He had looked out and seen his visitor on board the tram at the street corner, and he laughed out loud, and locked his door. There had been moments when he was lonely, and wished to hear again the sound of friendly speech, but, after such an irruption of suburban futility, it was a keen delight, to feel that he was secure on his tower, that he could absorb himself in his wonderful task as safe and silent as if he were in mid-desert.

But there was one period that he dared not revive; he could not bear to think of those weeks of desolation and terror in the winter after his coming to London. His mind was sluggish, and he could not quite remember how many years had passed since that dismal experience; it sounded all an old story, but yet it was still vivid, a flaming scroll of terror from which he turned his eyes away. One awful scene glowed into his memory, and he could not shut out the sight of an orgy, of dusky figures whirling in a ring, of lurid naphtha flares blazing in the darkness, of great glittering lamps, like infernal thuribles, very slowly swaying in a violent blast of air. And there was something else, something which he could not remember, but it filled him with terror, but it slunk in the dark places of his soul, as a wild beast crouches in the depths of a cave.

Again, and without reason, he began to image to himself that old mouldering house in the field. With what a loud incessant noise the wind must be clamoring about on this fearful night, how the great elm swayed and cried in the storm, and the rain dashed and pattered on the windows, and dripped on the sodden earth from the shaking shrubs beside the door. He moved uneasily on his chair, and struggled to put the picture out of his thoughts; but in spite of himself he saw the stained uneven walls, that ugly blot of mildew above the window, and perhaps a feeble gleam of light filtered through the blind, and someone, unhappy above all and forever lost, sat within the dismal room. Or rather, every window was black, without a glimmer of hope, and he who was shut in thick darkness heard the wind and the rain, and the noise of the elm-tree moaning and beating and weeping on the walls.

For all his effort the impression would not leave him, and as he sat before his desk looking into the vague darkness he could almost see that chamber which he had so often imagined; the low whitewashed ceiling held up by a heavy beam, the smears of smoke and long usage, the cracks and fissures of the plaster. Old furniture, shabby, deplorable, battered, stood about the room; there was a horsehair sofa worn and tottering, and a dismal paper, patterned in a livid red, blackened and mouldered near the floor, and peeled off and hung in strips from the dank walls. And there was that odour of decay, of the rank soil steaming, of rotting wood, a vapor that choked the breath and made the heart full of fear and heaviness.

ARTHUR MACHEN

Lucian again shivered with a thrill of dread; he was afraid that he had overworked himself and that he was suffering from the first symptoms of grave illness. His mind dwelt on confused and terrible recollections, and with a mad ingenuity gave form and substance to phantoms; and even now he drew a long breath, almost imagining that the air in his room was heavy and noisome, that it entered his nostrils with some taint of the crypt. And his body was still languid, and though he made a half motion to rise he could not find enough energy for the effort, and he sank again into the chair. At all events, he would think no more of that sad house in the field; he would return to those long struggles with letters, to the happy nights when he had gained victories.

He remembered something of his escape from the desolation and the worse than desolation that had obsessed him during that first winter in London. He had gone free one bleak morning in February, and after those dreary terrible weeks the desk and the heap and litter of papers had once more engulfed and absorbed him. And in the succeeding summer, of a night when he lay awake and listened to the birds, shining images came wantonly to him. For an hour, while the dawn brightened, he had felt the presence of an age, the resurrection of the life that the green fields had hidden, and his heart stirred for joy when he knew that he held and possessed all the loveliness that had so long mouldered. He could scarcely fall asleep for eager and leaping thoughts, and as soon as his breakfast was over he went out and bought paper and pens of a certain celestial stationer in Notting Hill. The street was not changed as he passed to and fro on his errand. The rattling wagons jostled by at intervals, a rare hansom came spinning down from London, there sounded the same hum and jangle of the gliding trams. The languid life of the pavement was unaltered; a few people, un-classed, without salience or possible description, lounged and walked from east to west, and from west to east, or slowly dropped into the byways to wander in the black waste to the north, or perhaps go astray in the systems that stretched towards the river. He glanced down these by-roads as he passed, and was astonished, as always, at their mysterious and desert aspect. Some were utterly empty; lines of neat, appalling residences, trim and garnished as if for occupation, edging the white glaring road; and not a soul was abroad, and not a sound broke their stillness. It was a picture of the desolation of midnight lighted up, but empty and waste as the most profound and solemn hours before the day. Other of these by-roads, of older settlement, were furnished with more important houses, standing far back from the pavement, each in a little wood of greenery, and thus one might look down as through a forest vista, and see a way smooth and guarded with low walls and yet untrodden, and all a leafy silence. Here and there in some of these echoing roads a figure seemed lazily advancing in the distance, hesitating and delaying, as if lost in the labyrinth. It was difficult to say which were the more dismal, these deserted streets that wandered away to right and left, or the great main thoroughfare with its narcotic and shadowy life. For the latter appeared vast, interminable, grey, and those who traveled by it were scarcely real, the bodies of the living, but rather the uncertain and misty shapes that come and go across the desert in an Eastern tale, when men look up from the sand and see a caravan pass them, all in silence, without a cry or a greeting. So they passed and repassed each other on those pavements, appearing and vanishing, each intent on his own secret, and wrapped in obscurity. One might have sworn that not a man saw his neighbor who met him or jostled him, that here everyone was a phantom for the other, though the lines of their paths crossed and recrossed, and their eyes stared like the eyes of live men. When two went by together, they mumbled and cast distrustful glances behind them as though afraid all the world was an enemy, and the pattering of feet was like the noise of a shower of rain. Curious appearances and simulations of life gathered at points in the road, for at intervals the villas ended and shops began in a dismal row, and looked so hopeless that one wondered who could buy. There were women fluttering uneasily about the greengrocers, and shabby things in rusty black touched and retouched the red lumps that an unshaven butcher offered, and already in the corner public there was a confused noise, with a tossing of voices that rose and fell like a Jewish chant, with the senseless stir of marionettes jerked into an imitation of gaiety. Then, in crossing a side street that seemed like grey mid-winter in stone, he trespassed from one world to another, for an old decayed house amidst its garden held the opposite corner. The laurels had grown into black skeletons, patched with green drift, the ilex gloomed over the porch, the deodar had blighted the flower-beds. Dark ivies swarmed over an elm-tree, and a brown clustering fungus sprang in gross masses on the lawn, showing where the roots of dead trees mouldered. The blue verandah, the blue balcony over the door, had faded to grey, and the stucco was blotched with ugly marks of weather, and a dank smell of decay, that vapor of black rotten earth in old town gardens, hung heavy about the gates. And then a row of musty villas had pushed out in shops

ARTHUR MACHEN

to the pavement, and the things in faded black buzzed and stirred about the limp cabbages, and the red lumps of meat.

It was the same terrible street, whose pavements he had trodden so often, where sunshine seemed but a gaudy light, where the fume of burning bricks always drifted. On black winter nights he had seen the sparse lights glimmering through the rain and drawing close together, as the dreary road vanished in long perspective. Perhaps this was its most appropriate moment, when nothing of its smug villas and skeleton shops remained but the bright patches of their windows, when the old house amongst its mouldering shrubs was but a dark cloud, and the streets to the north and south seemed like starry wastes, beyond them the blackness of infinity. Always in the daylight it had been to him abhorred and abominable, and its grey houses and purlieus had been fungus-like sproutings, an efflorescence of horrible decay.

But on that bright morning neither the dreadful street nor those who moved about it appalled him. He returned joyously to his den, and reverently laid out the paper on his desk. The world about him was but a grey shadow hovering on a shining wall; its noises were faint as the rustling of trees in a distant wood. The lovely and exquisite forms of those who served the Amber Venus were his distinct, clear, and manifest visions, and for one amongst them who came to him in a fire of bronze hair his heart stirred with the adoration of love. She it was who stood forth from all the rest and fell down prostrate before the radiant form in amber, drawing out her pins in curious gold, her glowing brooches of enamel, and pouring from a silver box all her treasures of jewels and precious stones, chrysoberyl and sardonyx, opal and diamond, topaz and pearl. And then she stripped from her body her precious robes and stood before the goddess in the glowing mist of her hair, praying that to her who had given all and came naked to the shrine, love might be given, and the grace of Venus. And when at last, after strange adventures, her prayer was granted, then when the sweet light came from the sea, and her lover turned at dawn to that bronze glory, he saw beside him a little statuette of amber. And in the shrine, far in Britain where the black rains stained the marble, they found the splendid and sumptuous statue of the Golden Venus, the last fine robe of silk that the lady had dedicated falling from her fingers, and the jewels lying at her feet. And her face was like the lady's face when the sun had brightened it on that day of her devotion.

The bronze mist glimmered before Lucian's eyes; he felt as though the soft floating hair touched his forehead and his lips and his hands. The fume of burning bricks, the reek of cabbage water, never reached his nostrils that were filled with the perfume of rare unguents, with the breath of the violet sea in Italy. His pleasure was an inebriation, an ecstasy of joy that destroyed all the vile Hottentot kraals and mud avenues as with one white lightning flash, and through the hours of that day he sat enthralled, not contriving a story with patient art, but rapt into another time, and entranced by the urgent gleam in the lady's eyes.

The little tale of *The Amber Statuette* had at last issued from a humble office in the spring after his father's death. The author was utterly unknown; the author's Murray was a wholesale stationer and printer in process of development, so that Lucian was astonished when the book became a moderate success. The reviewers had been sadly irritated, and even now he recollected with cheerfulness an article in an influential daily paper, an article pleasantly headed: "Where are the disinfectants?"

And then—but all the months afterwards seemed doubtful, there were only broken revelations of the labourious hours renewed, and the white nights when he had seen the moonlight fade and the gaslight grow wan at the approach of dawn.

He listened. Surely that was the sound of rain falling on sodden ground, the heavy sound of great swollen drops driven down from wet leaves by the gust of wind, and then again the strain of boughs sang above the tumult of the air; there was a doleful noise as if the storm shook the masts of a ship. He had only to get up and look out of the window and he would see the treeless empty street, and the rain starring the puddles under the gas-lamp, but he would wait a little while.

He tried to think why, in spite of all his resolutions, a dark horror seemed to brood more and more over all his mind. How often he had sat and worked on just such nights as this, contented if the words were in accord though the wind might wail, though the air were black with rain. Even about the little book that he had made there seemed some taint, some shuddering memory that came to him across the gulf of forgetfulness. Somehow the remembrance of the offering to Venus, of the phrases that he had so lovingly invented, brought back again the dusky figures that danced in the orgy, beneath the brassy glittering lamps; and again the naphtha flares showed the way to the sad house in the fields, and the red glare lit up the mildewed walls and the black hopeless windows. He gasped for breath, he seemed to inhale a heavy

ARTHUR MACHEN

air that reeked of decay and rottenness, and the odour of the clay was in his nostrils.

That unknown cloud that had darkened his thoughts grew blacker and engulfed him, despair was heavy upon him, his heart fainted with a horrible dread. In a moment, it seemed, a veil would be drawn away and certain awful things would appear.

He strove to rise from his chair, to cry out, but he could not. Deep, deep the darkness closed upon him, and the storm sounded far away. The Roman fort surged up, terrific, and he saw the writhing boughs in a ring, and behind them a glow and heat of fire. There were hideous shapes that swarmed in the thicket of the oaks; they called and beckoned to him, and rose into the air, into the flame that was smitten from heaven about the walls. And amongst them was the form of the beloved, but jets of flame issued from her breasts, and beside her was a horrible old woman, naked; and they, too, summoned him to mount the hill.

He heard Dr. Burrows whispering of the strange things that had been found in old Mrs. Gibbon's cottage, obscene figures, and unknown contrivances. She was a witch, he said, and the mistress of witches.

He fought against the nightmare, against the illusion that bewildered him. All his life, he thought, had been an evil dream, and for the common world he had fashioned an unreal red garment, that burned in his eyes. Truth and the dream were so mingled that now he could not divide one from the other. He had let Annie drink his soul beneath the hill, on the night when the moonfire shone, but he had not surely seen her exalted in the flame, the Queen of the Sabbath. Dimly he remembered Dr. Burrows coming to see him in London, but had he not imagined all the rest?

Again he found himself in the dusky lane, and Annie floated down to him from the moon above the hill. His head sank upon her breast again, but, alas, it was aflame. And he looked down, and he saw that his own flesh was aflame, and he knew that the fire could never be quenched.

There was a heavy weight upon his head, his feet were nailed to the floor, and his arms bound tight beside him. He seemed to himself to rage and struggle with the strength of a madman; but his hand only stirred and quivered a little as it lay upon the desk.

Again he was astray in the mist; wandering through the waste avenues of a city that had been ruined from ages. It had been splendid as Rome, terrible as Babylon, and forever the darkness had covered it, and it lay desolate forever in the accursed plain. And far and far the grey passages stretched into the night, into the icy fields, into the place of eternal gloom.

Ring within ring the awful temple closed around him; unending circles of vast stones, circle within circle, and every circle less throughout all ages. In the center was the sanctuary of the infernal rite, and he was borne thither as in the eddies of a whirlpool, to consummate his ruin, to celebrate the wedding of the Sabbath. He flung up his arms and beat the air, resisting with all his strength, with muscles that could throw down mountains; and this time his little finger stirred for an instant, and his foot twitched upon the floor.

Then suddenly a flaring street shone before him. There was darkness round about him, but it flamed with hissing jets of light and naphtha fires, and great glittering lamps swayed very slowly in a violent blast of air. A horrible music, and the exultation of discordant voices, swelled in his ears, and he saw an uncertain tossing crowd of dusky figures that circled and leapt before him. There was a noise like the chant of the lost, and then there appeared in the midst of the orgy, beneath a red flame, the figure of a woman. Her bronze hair and flushed cheeks were illuminate, and an argent light shone from her eyes, and with a smile that froze his heart her lips opened to speak to him. The tossing crowd faded away, falling into a gulf of darkness, and then she drew out from her hair pins of curious gold, and glowing brooches in enamel, and poured out jewels before him from a silver box, and then she stripped from her body her precious robes, and stood in the glowing mist of her hair, and held out her arms to him. But he raised his eyes and saw the mould and decay gaining on the walls of a dismal room, and a gloomy paper was dropping to the rotting floor. A vapor of the grave entered his nostrils, and he cried out with a loud scream; but there was only an indistinct guttural murmur in his throat.

And presently the woman fled away from him, and he pursued her. She fled away before him through midnight country, and he followed after her, chasing her from thicket to thicket, from valley to valley. And at last he captured her and won her with horrible caresses, and they went up to celebrate and make the marriage of the Sabbath. They were within the matted thicket, and they writhed in the flames, insatiable, forever. They were tortured, and tortured one another, in the sight of thousands who gathered thick about them; and their desire rose up like a black smoke.

Without, the storm swelled to the roaring of an awful sea, the wind grew to a shrill long scream, the elm-tree was riven and split with the crash of a thunderclap. To Lucian the tumult and the shock came as a gentle murmur, as if a brake stirred before a sudden breeze in summer. And then a vast silence overwhelmed him.

A few minutes later there was a shuffling of feet in the passage, and the door was softly opened. A woman came in, holding a light, and she peered curiously at the figure sitting quite still in the chair before the desk. The woman was half dressed, and she had let her splendid bronze hair flow down, her cheeks were flushed, and as she advanced into the shabby room, the lamp she carried cast quaking shadows on the mouldering paper, patched with marks of rising damp, and hanging in strips from the wet, dripping wall. The blind had not been drawn, but no light or glimmer of light filtered through the window, for a great straggling box tree that beat the rain upon the panes shut out even the night. The woman came softly, and as she bent down over Lucian an argent gleam shone from her brown eyes, and the little curls upon her neck were like golden work upon marble. She put her hand to his heart, and looked up, and beckoned to someone who was waiting by the door.

"Come in, Joe," she said. "It's just as I thought it would be: 'Death by misadventure'"; and she held up a little empty bottle of dark blue glass that was standing on the desk. "He would take it, and I always knew he would take a drop too much one of these days."

"What's all those papers that he's got there?"

"Didn't I tell you? It was crool to see him. He got it into 'is 'ead he could write a book; he's been at it for the last six months. Look 'ere."

She spread the neat pile of manuscript broadcast over the desk, and took a sheet at haphazard. It was all covered with illegible hopeless scribblings; only here and there it was possible to recognize a word.

"Why, nobody could read it, if they wanted to."

"It's all like that. He thought it was beautiful. I used to 'ear him jabbering to himself about it, dreadful nonsense it was he used to talk. I did my best to tongue him out of it, but it wasn't any good."

"He must have been a bit dotty. He's left you everything."

"Yes."

"You'll have to see about the funeral."

"There'll be the inquest and all that first."

"You've got evidence to show he took the stuff."

"Yes, to be sure I have. The doctor told him he would be certain to do for himself, and he was found two or three times quite silly in the streets. They had to drag him away from a house in Halden Road. He was carrying on dreadful, shaking at the gaite, and calling out it was 'is 'ome and they wouldn't let him in. I heard Dr. Manning myself tell 'im in this very room that he'd kill 'imself one of these days. Joe! Aren't you ashamed of yourself. I declare you're quite rude, and it's almost Sunday too. Bring the light over here, can't you?"

The man took up the blazing paraffin lamp, and set it on the desk, beside the scattered heap of that terrible manuscript. The flaring light shone through the dead eyes into the dying brain, and there was a glow within, as if great furnace doors were opened.

THE END

THE WHITE PEOPLE

Prologue

S orcery and sanctity," said Ambrose, "these are the only realities. Each is an ecstasy, a withdrawal from the common life."

Cotgrave listened, interested. He had been brought by a friend to this mouldering house in a northern suburb, through an old garden to the room where Ambrose the recluse dozed and dreamed over his books.

"Yes," he went on, "magic is justified of her children. There are many, I think, who eat dry crusts and drink water, with a joy infinitely sharper than anything within the experience of the 'practical' epicure."

"You are speaking of the saints?"

"Yes, and of the sinners, too. I think you are falling into the very general error of confining the spiritual world to the supremely good; but the supremely wicked, necessarily, have their portion in it. The merely carnal, sensual man can no more be a great sinner than he can be a great saint. Most of us are just indifferent, mixed-up creatures; we muddle through the world without realizing the meaning and the inner sense of things, and, consequently, our wickedness and our goodness are alike second-rate, unimportant."

"And you think the great sinner, then, will be an ascetic, as well as the great saint?"

"Great people of all kinds forsake the imperfect copies and go to the perfect originals. I have no doubt but that many of the very highest among the saints have never done a 'good action' (using the words in their ordinary sense). And, on the other hand, there have been those who have sounded the very depths of sin, who all their lives have never done an 'ill deed.'"

He went out of the room for a moment, and Cotgrave, in high delight, turned to his friend and thanked him for the introduction.

"He's grand," he said. "I never saw that kind of lunatic before."

Ambrose returned with more whisky and helped the two men in a liberal manner. He abused the teetotal sect with ferocity, as he handed the seltzer, and pouring out a glass of water for himself, was about to resume his monologue, when Cotgrave broke in—

"I can't stand it, you know," he said, "your paradoxes are too monstrous. A man may be a great sinner and yet never do anything sinful! Come!"

"You're quite wrong," said Ambrose. "I never make paradoxes; I wish I could. I merely said that a man may have an exquisite taste in Romanée Conti, and yet never have even smelt four ale. That's all, and it's more like a truism than a paradox, isn't it? Your surprise at my remark is due to the fact that you haven't realized what sin is. Oh, yes, there is a sort of connexion between Sin with the capital letter, and actions which are commonly called sinful: with murder, theft, adultery, and so forth. Much the same connexion that there is between the A, B, C and fine literature. But I believe that the misconception—it is all but universal—arises in great measure from our looking at the matter through social spectacles. We think that a man who does evil to *us* and to his neighbours must be very evil. So he is, from a social standpoint; but can't you realize that Evil in its essence is a lonely thing, a passion of the solitary, individual soul? Really, the average murderer, *quâ* murderer, is not by any means a sinner in the true sense of the word. He is simply a wild beast that we have to get rid of to save our own necks from his knife. I should class him rather with tigers than with sinners."

"It seems a little strange."

"I think not. The murderer murders not from positive qualities, but from negative ones; he lacks something which non-murderers possess. Evil, of course, is wholly positive—only it is on the wrong side. You may believe me that sin in its proper sense is very rare; it is probable that there have been far fewer sinners than saints. Yes, your standpoint is all very well for practical, social purposes; we are naturally inclined to think that a person who is very disagreeable to us must be a very great sinner! It is very disagreeable to have one's pocket picked, and we pronounce the thief to be a very great sinner. In truth, he is merely an undeveloped man. He cannot be a saint, of course; but he may be, and often is, an infinitely better creature than thousands who have never broken a single commandment. He is a great nuisance to *us*, I admit, and we very properly lock him up if we catch him; but between his troublesome and unsocial action and evil—Oh, the connexion is of the weakest."

It was getting very late. The man who had brought Cotgrave had probably heard all this before, since he assisted with a bland and judicious smile, but Cotgrave began to think that his "lunatic" was turning into a sage.

"Do you know," he said, "you interest me immensely? You think, then, that we do not understand the real nature of evil?"

"No, I don't think we do. We over-estimate it and we under-estimate it. We take the very numerous infractions of our social 'bye-laws'—the very necessary and very proper regulations which keep the human company together—and we get frightened at the prevalence of 'sin' and 'evil.' But this is really nonsense. Take theft, for example. Have you any *horror* at the thought of Robin Hood, of the Highland caterans of the seventeenth century, of the moss-troopers, of the company promoters of our day?

"Then, on the other hand, we underrate evil. We attach such an enormous importance to the 'sin' of meddling with our pockets (and our wives) that we have quite forgotten the awfulness of real sin."

"And what is sin?" said Cotgrave.

"I think I must reply to your question by another. What would your feelings be, seriously, if your cat or your dog began to talk to you, and to dispute with you in human accents? You would be overwhelmed with horror. I am sure of it. And if the roses in your garden sang a weird song, you would go mad. And suppose the stones in the road began to swell and grow before your eyes, and if the pebble that you noticed at night had shot out stony blossoms in the morning?

"Well, these examples may give you some notion of what sin really is."

"Look here," said the third man, hitherto placid, "you two seem pretty well wound up. But I'm going home. I've missed my tram, and I shall have to walk."

Ambrose and Cotgrave seemed to settle down more profoundly when the other had gone out into the early misty morning and the pale light of the lamps.

"You astonish me," said Cotgrave. "I had never thought of that. If that is really so, one must turn everything upside down. Then the essence of sin really is—"

"In the taking of heaven by storm, it seems to me," said Ambrose. "It appears to me that it is simply an attempt to penetrate into another and higher sphere in a forbidden manner. You can understand why it is so rare. There are few, indeed, who wish to penetrate into other spheres, higher or lower, in ways allowed or forbidden. Men, in the mass, are amply content with life as they find it. Therefore there are few saints, and sinners (in the proper sense) are fewer still, and men of genius, who partake sometimes of each character, are rare also. Yes; on the whole, it is, perhaps, harder to be a great sinner than a great saint."

"There is something profoundly unnatural about Sin? Is that what you mean?"

"Exactly. Holiness requires as great, or almost as great, an effort; but holiness works on lines that *were* natural once; it is an effort to recover the ecstasy that was before the Fall. But sin is an effort to gain the ecstasy and the knowledge that pertain alone to angels and in making this effort man becomes a demon. I told you that the mere murderer is not *therefore* a sinner; that is true, but the sinner is sometimes a murderer. Gilles de Raiz is an instance. So you see that while the good and the evil are unnatural to man as he now is—to man the social, civilized being—evil is unnatural in a much deeper sense than good. The saint endeavours to recover a gift which he has lost; the sinner tries to obtain something which was never his. In brief, he repeats the Fall."

"But are you a Catholic?" said Cotgrave.

"Yes; I am a member of the persecuted Anglican Church."

"Then, how about those texts which seem to reckon as sin that which you would set down as a mere trivial dereliction?"

"Yes; but in one place the word 'sorcerers' comes in the same sentence, doesn't it? That seems to me to give the key-note. Consider: can you imagine for a moment that a false statement which saves an innocent man's life is a sin? No; very good, then, it is not the mere liar who is excluded by those words; it is, above all, the 'sorcerers' who use the material life, who use the failings incidental to material life as instruments to obtain their infinitely wicked ends. And let me tell you this: our higher senses are so blunted, we are so drenched with materialism, that we should probably fail to recognize real wickedness if we encountered it."

"But shouldn't we experience a certain horror—a terror such as you hinted we would experience if a rose tree sang—in the mere presence of an evil man?"

"We should if we were natural: children and women feel this horror you speak of, even animals experience it. But with most of us convention and civilization and education have blinded and deafened and obscured the natural reason. No, sometimes we may recognize evil by its hatred of the good—one doesn't need much penetration to guess at the influence which dictated, quite unconsciously, the 'Blackwood' review of Keats—but this is purely incidental; and, as a rule, I suspect that the Hierarchs of Tophet pass quite unnoticed, or, perhaps, in certain cases, as good but mistaken men."

"But you used the word 'unconscious' just now, of Keats' reviewers. Is wickedness ever unconscious?"

"Always. It must be so. It is like holiness and genius in this as in other points; it is a certain rapture or ecstasy of the soul; a transcendent effort to surpass the ordinary bounds. So, surpassing these, it surpasses also the understanding, the faculty that takes note of that which comes before it. No, a man may be infinitely and horribly wicked and never suspect it. But I tell you, evil in this, its certain and true sense, is rare, and I think it is growing rarer."

"I am trying to get hold of it all," said Cotgrave. "From what you say, I gather that the true evil differs generically from that which we call evil?"

"Quite so. There is, no doubt, an analogy between the two; a resemblance such as enables us to use, quite legitimately, such terms as the 'foot of the mountain' and the 'leg of the table.' And, sometimes, of course, the two speak, as it were, in the same language. The rough miner, or 'puddler,' the untrained, undeveloped 'tiger-man,' heated by a quart or two above his usual measure, comes home and kicks his irritating and injudicious wife to death. He is a murderer. And Gilles de Raiz was a murderer. But you see the gulf that separates the two? The 'word,' if I may so speak, is accidentally the same in each case, but the 'meaning' is utterly different. It is flagrant 'Hobson Jobson' to confuse the two, or rather, it is as if one supposed that Juggernaut and the Argonauts had something to do etymologically with one another. And no doubt the same weak likeness, or analogy, runs between all the 'social' sins and the real spiritual sins, and in some cases, perhaps, the lesser may be 'schoolmasters' to lead one on to the greater—from the shadow to the reality. If you are anything of a Theologian, you will see the importance of all this."

"I am sorry to say," remarked Cotgrave, "that I have devoted very little of my time to theology. Indeed, I have often wondered on what grounds theologians have claimed the title of Science of Sciences for their favourite study; since the 'theological' books I have looked into have always seemed to me to be concerned with feeble and obvious pieties, or with the kings of Israel and Judah. I do not care to hear about those kings."

Ambrose grinned.

"We must try to avoid theological discussion," he said. "I perceive that you would be a bitter disputant. But perhaps the 'dates of the kings' have as much to do with theology as the hobnails of the murderous puddler with evil."

"Then, to return to our main subject, you think that sin is an esoteric, occult thing?"

"Yes. It is the infernal miracle as holiness is the supernal. Now and then it is raised to such a pitch that we entirely fail to suspect its existence; it is like the note of the great pedal pipes of the organ, which is so deep that we cannot hear it. In other cases it may lead to the lunatic asylum, or to still stranger issues. But you must never confuse it with mere social misdoing. Remember how the Apostle, speaking of the 'other side,' distinguishes between 'charitable' actions and charity. And as one may give all one's goods to the poor, and yet lack charity; so, remember, one may avoid every crime and yet be a sinner."

"Your psychology is very strange to me," said Cotgrave, "but I confess I like it, and I suppose that one might fairly deduce from your premisses the conclusion that the real sinner might very possibly strike the observer as a harmless personage enough?"

"Certainly, because the true evil has nothing to do with social life or social laws, or if it has, only incidentally and accidentally. It is a lonely passion of the soul—or a passion of the lonely soul—whichever you like. If, by chance, we understand it, and grasp its full significance, then, indeed, it will fill us with horror and with awe. But this emotion is widely distinguished from the fear and the disgust with which we regard the ordinary criminal, since this latter is largely or entirely founded on the regard which we have for our own skins or purses. We hate a murder, because we know that we should hate to be murdered, or to have anyone that we like murdered. So, on the 'other side,' we venerate the saints, but we don't 'like' them as well as our friends. Can you persuade yourself that you would have 'enjoyed' St. Paul's company? Do you think that you and I would have 'got on' with Sir Galahad?

"So with the sinners, as with the saints. If you met a very evil man, and recognized his evil; he would, no doubt, fill you with horror and awe; but there is no reason why you should 'dislike' him. On the contrary, it is quite possible that if you could succeed in putting the sin out of your mind you might find the sinner capital company, and in a little while you might have to reason yourself back into horror. Still, how awful it is. If the roses and the lilies suddenly sang on this coming morning; if the furniture began to move in procession, as in De Maupassant's tale!"

"I am glad you have come back to that comparison," said Cotgrave, "because I wanted to ask you what it is that corresponds in humanity to these imaginary feats of inanimate things. In a word—what is sin?

You have given me, I know, an abstract definition, but I should like a concrete example."

"I told you it was very rare," said Ambrose, who appeared willing to avoid the giving of a direct answer. "The materialism of the age, which has done a good deal to suppress sanctity, has done perhaps more to suppress evil. We find the earth so very comfortable that we have no inclination either for ascents or descents. It would seem as if the scholar who decided to 'specialize' in Tophet, would be reduced to purely antiquarian researches. No palaeontologist could show you a *live* pterodactyl."

"And yet you, I think, have 'specialized,' and I believe that your researches have descended to our modern times."

"You are really interested, I see. Well, I confess, that I have dabbled a little, and if you like I can show you something that bears on the very curious subject we have been discussing."

Ambrose took a candle and went away to a far, dim corner of the room. Cotgrave saw him open a venerable bureau that stood there, and from some secret recess he drew out a parcel, and came back to the window where they had been sitting.

Ambrose undid a wrapping of paper, and produced a green pocket-book.

"You will take care of it?" he said. "Don't leave it lying about. It is one of the choicer pieces in my collection, and I should be very sorry if it were lost."

He fondled the faded binding.

"I knew the girl who wrote this," he said. "When you read it, you will see how it illustrates the talk we have had tonight. There is a sequel, too, but I won't talk of that.

"There was an odd article in one of the reviews some months ago," he began again, with the air of a man who changes the subject. "It was written by a doctor—Dr. Coryn, I think, was the name. He says that a lady, watching her little girl playing at the drawing-room window, suddenly saw the heavy sash give way and fall on the child's fingers. The lady fainted, I think, but at any rate the doctor was summoned, and when he had dressed the child's wounded and maimed fingers he was summoned to the mother. She was groaning with pain, and it was found that three fingers of her hand, corresponding with those that had been injured on the child's hand, were swollen and inflamed, and later, in the doctor's language, purulent sloughing set in."

Ambrose still handled delicately the green volume.

"Well, here it is," he said at last, parting with difficulty, it seemed, from his treasure.

"You will bring it back as soon as you have read it," he said, as they went out into the hall, into the old garden, faint with the odour of white lilies.

There was a broad red band in the east as Cotgrave turned to go, and from the high ground where he stood he saw that awful spectacle of London in a dream.

The Green Book

The morocco binding of the book was faded, and the colour had grown faint, but there were no stains nor bruises nor marks of usage. The book looked as if it had been bought "on a visit to London" some seventy or eighty years ago, and had somehow been forgotten and suffered to lie away out of sight. There was an old, delicate, lingering odour about it, such an odour as sometimes haunts an ancient piece of furniture for a century or more. The end-papers, inside the binding, were oddly decorated with coloured patterns and faded gold. It looked small, but the paper was fine, and there were many leaves, closely covered with minute, painfully formed characters.

I found this book (the manuscript began) in a drawer in the old bureau that stands on the landing. It was a very rainy day and I could not go out, so in the afternoon I got a candle and rummaged in the bureau. Nearly all the drawers were full of old dresses, but one of the small ones looked empty, and I found this book hidden right at the back. I wanted a book like this, so I took it to write in. It is full of secrets. I have a great many other books of secrets I have written, hidden in a safe place, and I am going to write here many of the old secrets and some new ones; but there are some I shall not put down at all. I must not write down the real names of the days and months which I found out a year ago, nor the way to make the Aklo letters, or the Chian language, or the great beautiful Circles, nor the Mao Games, nor the chief songs. I may write something about all these things but not the way to do them, for peculiar reasons. And I must not say who the Nymphs are, or the Dôls, or Jeelo, or what voolas mean. All these are most secret secrets, and I am glad when I remember what they are, and how many wonderful languages I know, but there are somethings that I call the secrets of the secrets of the secrets that I dare not think of unless I am quite alone, and then I shut my eyes, and put my hands over them and whisper the word, and the Alala comes. I only do this at night in my room or in certain woods that I know, but I must not describe them, as they are secret woods. Then there are the Ceremonies, which are all of them important, but some are more delightful than others—there are the White Ceremonies, and the Green Ceremonies, and the Scarlet Ceremonies. The Scarlet Ceremonies are the best, but there is only one place where they can be performed properly, though there is a very nice imitation which I have done in other places. Besides these, I have the dances, and the Comedy, and I have done the Comedy sometimes when the others were looking, and they didn't understand anything about it. I was very little when I first knew about these things.

When I was very small, and mother was alive, I can remember remembering things before that, only it has all got confused. But I remember when I was five or six I heard them talking about me when they thought I was not noticing. They were saying how queer I was a year or two before, and how nurse had called my mother to come and listen to me talking all to myself, and I was saying words that nobody could understand. I was speaking the Xu language, but I only remember a very few of the words, as it was about the little white faces that used to look at me when I was lying in my cradle. They used to talk to me, and I learnt their language and talked to them in it about some great white place where they lived, where the trees and the grass were all white, and there were white hills as high up as the moon, and a cold wind. I have often dreamed of it afterwards, but the faces went away when I was very little. But a wonderful thing happened when I was about five. My nurse was carrying me on her shoulder; there was a field of yellow corn, and we went through it, it was very hot. Then we came to a path through a wood, and a tall man came after us, and went with us till we came to a place where there was a deep pool, and it was very dark and shady. Nurse put me down on the soft moss under a tree, and she said: "She can't get to the pond now." So they left me there, and I sat quite still and watched, and out of the water and out of the wood came two wonderful white people, and they began to play and dance and sing. They were a kind of creamy white like the old ivory figure in the drawing-room; one was a beautiful lady with kind dark eyes, and a grave face, and long black hair, and she smiled such a strange sad smile at the other, who laughed and came to her. They played together, and danced round and round the pool, and they sang a song till I fell asleep. Nurse woke me up when she came back, and she was looking something like the lady had looked, so I told her all about it, and asked her why she looked like that. At first she cried, and then she looked very frightened, and turned quite pale. She put me down on the grass and stared at me, and I could see she was shaking all over. Then she said I had been dreaming, but I knew I hadn't. Then she made me promise not to say a word about it to anybody, and if I did I should be thrown into the black pit. I was not frightened at all, though nurse was, and I never forgot about it, because

ARTHUR MACHEN

when I shut my eyes and it was quite quiet, and I was all alone, I could see them again, very faint and far away, but very splendid; and little bits of the song they sang came into my head, but I couldn't sing it.

I was thirteen, nearly fourteen, when I had a very singular adventure, so strange that the day on which it happened is always called the White Day. My mother had been dead for more than a year, and in the morning I had lessons, but they let me go out for walks in the afternoon. And this afternoon I walked a new way, and a little brook led me into a new country, but I tore my frock getting through some of the difficult places, as the way was through many bushes, and beneath the low branches of trees, and up thorny thickets on the hills, and by dark woods full of creeping thorns. And it was a long, long way. It seemed as if I was going on forever and ever, and I had to creep by a place like a tunnel where a brook must have been, but all the water had dried up, and the floor was rocky, and the bushes had grown overhead till they met, so that it was quite dark. And I went on and on through that dark place; it was a long, long way. And I came to a hill that I never saw before. I was in a dismal thicket full of black twisted boughs that tore me as I went through them, and I cried out because I was smarting all over, and then I found that I was climbing, and I went up and up a long way, till at last the thicket stopped and I came out crying just under the top of a big bare place, where there were ugly grey stones lying all about on the grass, and here and there a little twisted, stunted tree came out from under a stone, like a snake. And I went up, right to the top, a long way. I never saw such big ugly stones before; they came out of the earth some of them, and some looked as if they had been rolled to where they were, and they went on and on as far as I could see, a long, long way. I looked out from them and saw the country, but it was strange. It was winter time, and there were black terrible woods hanging from the hills all round; it was like seeing a large room hung with black curtains, and the shape of the trees seemed quite different from any I had ever seen before. I was afraid. Then beyond the woods there were other hills round in a great ring, but I had never seen any of them; it all looked black, and everything had a voor over it. It was all so still and silent, and the sky was heavy and grey and sad, like a wicked voorish dome in Deep Dendo. I went on into the dreadful rocks. There were hundreds and hundreds of them. Some were like horrid-grinning men; I could see their faces as if they would jump at me out of the stone, and catch hold of me, and drag me with them back into the rock, so that I should always be there. And there were other rocks that were like animals, creeping, horrible animals, putting out their tongues, and others were like words that I could not say, and others like dead people lying on the grass. I went on among them, though they frightened me, and my heart was full of wicked songs that they put into it; and I wanted to make faces and twist myself about in the way they did, and I went on and on a long way till at last I liked the rocks, and they didn't frighten me anymore. I sang the songs I thought of; songs full of words that must not be spoken or written down. Then I made faces like the faces on the rocks, and I twisted myself about like the twisted ones, and I lay down flat on the ground like the dead ones, and I went up to one that was grinning, and put my arms round him and hugged him. And so I went on and on through the rocks till I came to a round mound in the middle of them. It was higher than a mound, it was nearly as high as our house, and it was like a great basin turned upside down, all smooth and round and green, with one stone, like a post, sticking up at the top. I climbed up the sides, but they were so steep I had to stop or I should have rolled all the way down again, and I should have knocked against the stones at the bottom, and perhaps been killed. But I wanted to get up to the very top of the big round mound, so I lay down flat on my face, and took hold of the grass with my hands and drew myself up, bit by bit, till I was at the top. Then I sat down on the stone in the middle, and looked all round about. I felt I had come such a long, long way, just as if I were a hundred miles from home, or in some other country, or in one of the strange places I had read about in the "Tales of the Genie" and the "Arabian Nights," or as if I had gone across the sea, far away, for years and I had found another world that nobody had ever seen or heard of before, or as if I had somehow flown through the sky and fallen on one of the stars I had read about where everything is dead and cold and grey, and there is no air, and the wind doesn't blow. I sat on the stone and looked all round and down and round about me. It was just as if I was sitting on a tower in the middle of a great empty town, because I could see nothing all around but the grey rocks on the ground. I couldn't make out their shapes anymore, but I could see them on and on for a long way, and I looked at them, and they seemed as if they had been arranged into patterns, and shapes, and figures. I knew they couldn't be, because I had seen a lot of them coming right out of the earth, joined to the deep rocks below, so I looked again, but still I saw nothing but circles, and small circles inside big ones, and pyramids, and domes, and spires, and

ARTHUR MACHEN

they seemed all to go round and round the place where I was sitting, and the more I looked, the more I saw great big rings of rocks, getting bigger and bigger, and I stared so long that it felt as if they were all moving and turning, like a great wheel, and I was turning, too, in the middle. I got quite dizzy and queer in the head, and everything began to be hazy and not clear, and I saw little sparks of blue light, and the stones looked as if they were springing and dancing and twisting as they went round and round and round. I was frightened again, and I cried out loud, and jumped up from the stone I was sitting on, and fell down. When I got up I was so glad they all looked still, and I sat down on the top and slid down the mound, and went on again. I danced as I went in the peculiar way the rocks had danced when I got giddy, and I was so glad I could do it quite well, and I danced and danced along, and sang extraordinary songs that came into my head. At last I came to the edge of that great flat hill, and there were no more rocks, and the way went again through a dark thicket in a hollow. It was just as bad as the other one I went through climbing up, but I didn't mind this one, because I was so glad I had seen those singular dances and could imitate them. I went down, creeping through the bushes, and a tall nettle stung me on my leg, and made me burn, but I didn't mind it, and I tingled with the boughs and the thorns, but I only laughed and sang. Then I got out of the thicket into a close valley, a little secret place like a dark passage that nobody ever knows of, because it was so narrow and deep and the woods were so thick round it. There is a steep bank with trees hanging over it, and there the ferns keep green all through the winter, when they are dead and brown upon the hill, and the ferns there have a sweet, rich smell like what oozes out of fir trees. There was a little stream of water running down this valley, so small that I could easily step across it. I drank the water with my hand, and it tasted like bright, yellow wine, and it sparkled and bubbled as it ran down over beautiful red and yellow and green stones, so that it seemed alive and all colours at once. I drank it, and I drank more with my hand, but I couldn't drink enough, so I lay down and bent my head and sucked the water up with my lips. It tasted much better, drinking it that way, and a ripple would come up to my mouth and give me a kiss, and I laughed, and drank again, and pretended there was a nymph, like the one in the old picture at home, who lived in the water and was kissing me. So I bent low down to the water, and put my lips softly to it, and whispered to the nymph that I would come again. I felt sure it could not be common water, I was so glad when I got up and went on; and I danced again and went up and up the valley, under hanging hills. And when I came to the top, the ground rose up in front of me, tall and steep as a wall, and there was nothing but the green wall and the sky. I thought of "forever and forever, world without end, Amen"; and I thought I must have really found the end of the world, because it was like the end of everything, as if there could be nothing at all beyond, except the kingdom of Voor, where the light goes when it is put out, and the water goes when the sun takes it away. I began to think of all the long, long way I had journeyed, how I had found a brook and followed it, and followed it on, and gone through bushes and thorny thickets, and dark woods full of creeping thorns. Then I had crept up a tunnel under trees, and climbed a thicket, and seen all the grey rocks, and sat in the middle of them when they turned round, and then I had gone on through the grey rocks and come down the hill through the stinging thicket and up the dark valley, all a long, long way. I wondered how I should get home again, if I could ever find the way, and if my home was there anymore, or if it were turned and everybody in it into grey rocks, as in the *Arabian Nights*. So I sat down on the grass and thought what I should do next. I was tired, and my feet were hot with walking, and as I looked about I saw there was a wonderful well just under the high, steep wall of grass. All the ground round it was covered with bright, green, dripping moss; there was every kind of moss there, moss like beautiful little ferns, and like palms and fir trees, and it was all green as jewellery, and drops of water hung on it like diamonds. And in the middle was the great well, deep and shining and beautiful, so clear that it looked as if I could touch the red sand at the bottom, but it was far below. I stood by it and looked in, as if I were looking in a glass. At the bottom of the well, in the middle of it, the red grains of sand were moving and stirring all the time, and I saw how the water bubbled up, but at the top it was quite smooth, and full and brimming. It was a great well, large like a bath, and with the shining, glittering green moss about it, it looked like a great white jewel, with green jewels all round. My feet were so hot and tired that I took off my boots and stockings, and let my feet down into the water, and the water was soft and cold, and when I got up I wasn't tired anymore, and I felt I must go on, farther and farther, and see what was on the other side of the wall. I climbed up it very slowly, going sideways all the time, and when I got to the top and looked over, I was in the queerest country I had seen, stranger even than the hill of the grey rocks. It looked as if earth-children had been playing there with their spades, as it was all hills and hollows, and castles and walls made of earth and covered with grass. There were two mounds like big beehives, round and great and solemn, and then hollow basins, and then a steep mounting wall like the ones I saw once by the seaside where the big guns and the soldiers were. I nearly fell into one of the round hollows, it went away from under my feet so suddenly, and I ran fast down the side and stood at the bottom and looked up. It was strange and solemn to look up. There was nothing but the grey, heavy sky and the sides of the hollow; everything else had gone away, and the hollow was the whole world, and I thought that at night it must be full of ghosts and moving shadows and pale things when the moon shone down to the bottom at the dead of the night, and the wind wailed up above. It was so strange and solemn and lonely, like a hollow temple of dead heathen gods. It reminded me of a tale my nurse had told me when I was quite little; it was the same nurse that took me into the wood where I saw the beautiful white people. And I remembered how nurse had told me the story one winter night, when the wind was beating the trees against the wall, and crying and moaning in the nursery chimney. She said there was, somewhere or other, a hollow pit, just like the one I was standing in, everybody was afraid to go into it or near it, it was such a bad place. But once upon a time there was a poor girl who said she would go into the hollow pit, and everybody tried to stop her, but she would go. And she went down into the pit and came back laughing, and said there was nothing there at all, except green grass and red stones, and white stones and yellow flowers. And soon after people saw she had most beautiful emerald earrings, and they asked how she got them, as she and her mother were quite poor. But she laughed, and said her earrings were not made of emeralds at all, but only of green grass. Then, one day, she wore on her breast the reddest ruby that anyone had ever seen, and it was as big as a hen's egg, and glowed and sparkled like a hot burning coal of fire. And they asked how she got it, as she and her mother were quite poor. But she laughed, and said it was not a ruby at all, but only a red stone. Then one day she wore round her neck the loveliest necklace that anyone had ever seen, much finer than the queen's finest, and it was made of great bright diamonds, hundreds of them, and they shone like all the stars on a night in June. So they asked her how she got it, as she and her mother were quite poor. But she laughed, and said they were not diamonds at all, but only white stones. And one day she went to the Court, and she wore on her head a crown of pure angel-gold, so nurse said, and it shone like the sun, and it was much more splendid than the crown the king was wearing himself, and in her ears she wore the emeralds, and the big ruby was the brooch on her breast, and the great diamond necklace was sparkling on her neck. And the king and queen thought she was some great princess from a long way off, and got down from their thrones and went to meet her, but somebody told the king and queen who she was, and that she was quite poor. So the king asked why she wore a gold crown, and how she got it, as she and her mother were so poor. And she laughed, and said it wasn't a gold crown at all, but only some yellow flowers she had put in her hair. And the king thought it was very strange, and said she should stay at the Court, and they would see what would happen next. And she was so lovely that everybody said that her eyes were greener than the emeralds, that her lips were redder than the ruby, that her skin was whiter than the diamonds, and that her hair was brighter than the golden crown. So the king's son said he would marry her, and the king said he might. And the bishop married them, and there was a great supper, and afterwards the king's son went to his wife's room. But just when he had his hand on the door, he saw a tall, black man, with a dreadful face, standing in front of the door, and a voice said—

Venture not upon your life,
This is mine own wedded wife.

Then the king's son fell down on the ground in a fit. And they came and tried to get into the room, but they couldn't, and they hacked at the door with hatchets, but the wood had turned hard as iron, and at last everybody ran away, they were so frightened at the screaming and laughing and shrieking and crying that came out of the room. But next day they went in, and found there was nothing in the room but thick black smoke, because the black man had come and taken her away. And on the bed there were two knots of faded grass and a red stone, and some white stones, and some faded yellow flowers. I remembered this tale of nurse's while I was standing at the bottom of the deep hollow; it was so strange and solitary there, and I felt afraid. I could not see any stones or flowers, but I was afraid of bringing them away without knowing, and I thought I would do a charm that came into my head to keep the black man away. So I stood right in the very middle of the hollow, and I made sure that I had none of those things on me, and then I walked round the place, and touched my eyes, and my lips, and my hair in a peculiar manner, and whispered some queer words that nurse taught me to keep bad things away. Then I felt safe and climbed up out of the hollow, and went on through all those mounds and hollows and walls, till I came to the end, which was high above all the rest, and I could see that all the different shapes of the earth were arranged in patterns, something like the grey rocks, only the pattern was different. It was getting late, and the air was indistinct, but it looked from where I was standing something like two great figures of people lying on the grass. And I went on, and at last I found a certain wood, which is too secret to be described, and nobody knows of the passage into it, which I found out in a very curious manner, by seeing some little animal run into the wood through it. So I went after the animal by a very narrow dark way, under thorns and bushes, and it was almost dark when I came to a kind of open place in the middle. And there I saw the most wonderful sight I have ever seen, but it was only for a minute, as I ran away directly, and crept out of the wood by the passage I had come by, and ran and ran as fast as ever I could, because I was afraid, what I had seen was so wonderful and so strange and beautiful. But I wanted to get home and think of it, and I did not know what might not happen if I stayed by the wood. I was hot all over and trembling, and my heart was beating, and strange cries that I could not help came from me as I ran from the wood. I was glad that a great white moon came up from over a round hill and showed me the way, so I went back through the mounds and hollows and down the close valley, and up through the thicket over the place of the grey rocks, and so at last I got home again. My father was busy in his study, and the servants had not told about my not coming home, though they were frightened, and wondered what they ought to do, so I told them I had lost my way, but I did not let them find out the real way I had been. I went to bed and lay awake all through the night, thinking of what I had seen. When I came out of the narrow way, and it looked all shining, though the air was dark, it seemed so certain, and all the way home I was quite sure that I had seen it, and I wanted to be alone in my room, and be glad over it all to myself, and shut my eyes and pretend it was there, and do all the things I would have done if I had not been so afraid. But when I shut my eyes the sight would not come, and I began to think about my adventures all over again, and I remembered how dusky and queer it was at the end, and I was afraid it must be all a mistake, because it seemed impossible it could happen. It seemed like one of nurse's tales, which I didn't really believe in, though I was frightened at the bottom of the hollow; and the stories she told me when I was little came back into my head, and I wondered whether it was really there what I thought I had seen, or whether any of her tales could have happened a long time ago. It was so queer; I lay awake there in my room at the back of the house, and the moon was shining on the other side towards the river, so the bright light did not fall upon the wall. And the house was quite still. I had heard my father come upstairs, and just after the clock struck twelve, and after the house was still and empty, as if there was nobody alive in it. And though it was all dark and indistinct in my room, a pale glimmering kind of light shone in through the white blind, and once I got up and looked out, and there was a great black shadow of the house covering the garden, looking like a prison where men are hanged; and then beyond it was all white; and the wood shone white with black gulfs between the trees. It was still and clear, and there were no clouds on the sky. I wanted to think of what I had seen but I couldn't, and I began to think of all the tales that nurse had told me so long ago that I thought I had forgotten, but they all came back, and mixed up with the thickets and the grey rocks and the hollows in the earth and the secret wood, till I hardly knew what was new and what was old, or whether it was not all dreaming. And then I remembered that hot summer afternoon, so long ago, when nurse left me by myself in the shade, and the white people came out of the water and out of the wood, and played, and danced, and sang, and I began to fancy that nurse told me about something like it before I saw them, only I couldn't recollect exactly what she told me. Then I wondered whether she had been the white lady, as I remembered she was just as white and beautiful, and had the same dark eyes and black hair; and sometimes she smiled and looked like the lady had looked, when she was telling me some of her stories, beginning with "Once on a time," or "In the time of the fairies." But I thought she couldn't be the lady, as she seemed to have gone a different way into the wood, and I didn't think the man who came after us could be the other, or I couldn't have seen that wonderful secret in the secret wood. I thought of the moon: but it was afterwards when I was in the middle of the wild land, where the earth was made into the shape of great figures, and it was all walls, and mysterious hollows, and smooth round mounds, that I saw the great white moon come up over a round hill. I was wondering about all these things, till at last I got quite frightened, because I was afraid something had happened to me, and I remembered nurse's tale of the poor girl who went into the hollow pit, and was carried away at last by the black man. I knew I had gone into a hollow pit too, and perhaps it was the same, and I had done something dreadful. So I did the charm over again, and touched my eyes and my lips and my hair in a peculiar manner, and said the old words from the fairy language, so that I might be sure I had not been carried away. I tried again to see the secret wood, and to creep up the passage and see what I had seen there, but somehow I couldn't, and I kept on thinking of nurse's stories. There was one I remembered about a young man who once upon a time went hunting, and all the day he and his hounds hunted everywhere, and they crossed the rivers and went into all the woods, and went round the marshes, but they couldn't find anything at all, and they hunted all day till the sun sank down and began to set behind the mountain. And the young man was angry because he couldn't find anything, and he was going to turn back, when just as the sun touched the mountain, he saw come out of a brake in front of him a beautiful white stag. And he cheered to his hounds, but they whined and would not follow, and he cheered to his horse, but it shivered and stood stock still, and the young man jumped off the horse and left the hounds and began to follow the white stag all alone. And soon it was quite dark, and the sky was black, without a single star shining in it, and the stag went away into the darkness. And though the man had brought his gun with him he never shot at the stag, because he wanted to catch it, and he was afraid he would lose it in the night. But he never lost it once, though the sky was so black and the air was so dark, and the stag went on and on till the young man didn't know a bit where he was. And they went through enormous woods where the air was full of whispers and a pale, dead light came out from the rotten trunks that were lying on the ground, and just as the man thought he had lost the stag, he would see it all white and shining in front of him, and he would run fast to catch it, but the stag always ran faster, so he did not catch it. And they went through the enormous woods, and they swam across rivers, and they waded through black marshes where the ground bubbled, and the air was full of will-o'-the-wisps, and the stag fled away down into rocky narrow valleys, where the air was like the smell of a vault, and the man went after it. And they went over the great mountains and the man heard the wind come down from the sky, and the stag went on and the man went after. At last the sun rose and the young man found he was in a country that he had never seen before; it was a beautiful valley with a bright stream running through it, and a great, big round hill in the middle. And the stag went down the valley, towards the hill, and it seemed to be getting tired and went slower and slower, and though the man was tired, too, he began to run faster, and he was sure he would catch the stag at last. But just as they got to the bottom of the hill, and the man stretched out his hand to catch the stag, it vanished into the earth, and the man began to cry; he was so sorry that he had lost it after all his long hunting. But as he was crying he saw there was a door in the hill, just in front of him, and he went in, and it was quite dark, but he went on, as he thought he would find the white stag. And all of a sudden it got light, and there was the sky, and the sun shining, and birds singing in the trees, and there was a beautiful fountain. And by the fountain a lovely lady was sitting, who was the queen of the fairies, and she told the man that she had changed herself into a stag to bring him there because she loved him so much. Then she brought out a great gold cup, covered with jewels, from her fairy palace, and she offered him wine in the cup to drink. And he drank, and the more he drank the more he longed to drink, because the wine was enchanted. So he kissed the lovely lady, and she became his wife, and he stayed all that day and all that night in the hill where she lived, and when he woke he found he was lying on the ground, close to where he had seen the stag first, and his horse was there and his hounds were there waiting, and he looked up, and the sun sank behind the mountain. And he went home and lived a long time, but he would never kiss any other lady because he had kissed the queen of the fairies, and he would never drink common wine anymore, because he had drunk enchanted wine. And sometimes nurse told me tales that she had heard from her great-grandmother, who was very old, and lived in a cottage on the mountain all alone, and most of these tales were about a hill where people used to meet at night long ago, and they used to play all sorts of strange games and do queer things that nurse told me of, but I couldn't understand, and now, she said, everybody but her great-grandmother had forgotten all about it, and nobody knew where the hill was, not even her great-grandmother. But she told me one very strange story about the hill, and I trembled when I remembered it. She said that people always went there in summer, when it was very hot, and they had to dance a good deal. It would be all dark at first, and there were trees there, which made it much darker, and people would come, one by one, from all directions, by a secret path which nobody

ARTHUR MACHEN

else knew, and two persons would keep the gate, and everyone as they came up had to give a very curious sign, which nurse showed me as well as she could, but she said she couldn't show me properly. And all kinds of people would come; there would be gentle folks and village folks, and some old people and boys and girls, and quite small children, who sat and watched. And it would all be dark as they came in, except in one corner where someone was burning something that smelt strong and sweet, and made them laugh, and there one would see a glaring of coals, and the smoke mounting up red. So they would all come in, and when the last had come there was no door anymore, so that no one else could get in, even if they knew there was anything beyond. And once a gentleman who was a stranger and had ridden a long way, lost his path at night, and his horse took him into the very middle of the wild country, where everything was upside down, and there were dreadful marshes and great stones everywhere, and holes underfoot, and the trees looked like gibbet-posts, because they had great black arms that stretched out across the way. And this strange gentleman was very frightened, and his horse began to shiver all over, and at last it stopped and wouldn't go any farther, and the gentleman got down and tried to lead the horse, but it wouldn't move, and it was all covered with a sweat, like death. So the gentleman went on all alone, going farther and farther into the wild country, till at last he came to a dark place, where he heard shouting and singing and crying, like nothing he had ever heard before. It all sounded quite close to him, but he couldn't get in, and so he began to call, and while he was calling, something came behind him, and in a minute his mouth and arms and legs were all bound up, and he fell into a swoon. And when he came to himself, he was lying by the roadside, just where he had first lost his way, under a blasted oak with a black trunk, and his horse was tied beside him. So he rode on to the town and told the people there what had happened, and some of them were amazed; but others knew. So when once everybody had come, there was no door at all for anybody else to pass in by. And when they were all inside, round in a ring, touching each other, someone began to sing in the darkness, and someone else would make a noise like thunder with a thing they had on purpose, and on still nights people would hear the thundering noise far, far away beyond the wild land, and some of them, who thought they knew what it was, used to make a sign on their breasts when they woke up in their beds at dead of night and heard that terrible deep noise, like thunder on the mountains. And the noise and the singing would go on and on for a long time, and the people who were in a ring swayed a little to and fro; and the song was in an old, old language that nobody knows now, and the tune was queer. Nurse said her great-grandmother had known someone who remembered a little of it, when she was quite a little girl, and nurse tried to sing some of it to me, and it was so strange a tune that I turned all cold and my flesh crept as if I had put my hand on something dead. Sometimes it was a man that sang and sometimes it was a woman, and sometimes the one who sang it did it so well that two or three of the people who were there fell to the ground shrieking and tearing with their hands. The singing went on, and the people in the ring kept swaying to and fro for a long time, and at last the moon would rise over a place they called the Tole Deol, and came up and showed them swinging and swaying from side to side, with the sweet thick smoke curling up from the burning coals, and floating in circles all around them. Then they had their supper. A boy and a girl brought it to them; the boy carried a great cup of wine, and the girl carried a cake of bread, and they passed the bread and the wine round and round, but they tasted quite different from common bread and common wine, and changed everybody that tasted them. Then they all rose up and danced, and secret things were brought out of some hiding place, and they played extraordinary games, and danced round and round and round in the moonlight, and sometimes people would suddenly disappear and never be heard of afterwards, and nobody knew what had happened to them. And they drank more of that curious wine, and they made images and worshipped them, and nurse showed me how the images were made one day when we were out for a walk, and we passed by a place where there was a lot of wet clay. So nurse asked me if I would like to know what those things were like that they made on the hill, and I said yes. Then she asked me if I would promise never to tell a living soul a word about it, and if I did I was to be thrown into the black pit with the dead people, and I said I wouldn't tell anybody, and she said the same thing again and again, and I promised. So she took my wooden spade and dug a big lump of clay and put it in my tin bucket, and told me to say if anyone met us that I was going to make pies when I went home. Then we went on a little way till we came to a little brake growing right down into the road, and nurse stopped, and looked up the road and down it, and then peeped through the hedge into the field on the other side, and then she said, "Quick!" and we ran into the brake, and crept in and out among the bushes till we had gone a good way from the road. Then we sat down under a bush, and I wanted so much to know what nurse was going to make with the clay, but before she would begin she made me promise again not to say a word about it, and she went again and peeped through the bushes on every side, though the lane was so small and deep that hardly anybody ever went there. So we sat down, and nurse took the clay out of the bucket, and began to knead it with her hands, and do queer things with it, and turn it about. And she hid it under a big dock-leaf for a minute or two and then she brought it out again, and then she stood up and sat down, and walked round the clay in a peculiar manner, and all the time she was softly singing a sort of rhyme, and her face got very red. Then she sat down again, and took the clay in her hands and began to shape it into a doll, but not like the dolls I have at home, and she made the queerest doll I had ever seen, all out of the wet clay, and hid it under a bush to get dry and hard, and all the time she was making it she was singing these rhymes to herself, and her face got redder and redder. So we left the doll there, hidden away in the bushes where nobody would ever find it. And a few days later we went the same walk, and when we came to that narrow, dark part of the lane where the brake runs down to the bank, nurse made me promise all over again, and she looked about, just as she had done before, and we crept into the bushes till we got the green place where the little clay man was hidden. I remember it all so well, though I was only eight, and it is eight years ago now as I am writing it down, but the sky was a deep violet blue, and in the middle of the brake where we were sitting there was a great elder tree covered with blossoms, and on the other side there was a clump of meadowsweet, and when I think of that day the smell of the meadowsweet and elder blossom seems to fill the room, and if I shut my eyes I can see the glaring blue sky, with little clouds very white floating across it, and nurse who went away long ago sitting opposite me and looking like the beautiful white lady in the wood. So we sat down and nurse took out the clay doll from the secret place where she had hidden it, and she said we must "pay our respects," and she would show me what to do, and I must watch her all the time. So she did all sorts of queer things with the little clay man, and I noticed she was all streaming with perspiration, though we had walked so slowly, and then she told me to "pay my respects," and I did everything she did because I liked her, and it was such an odd game. And she said that if one loved very much, the clay man was very good, if one did certain things with it, and if one hated very much, it was just as good, only one had to do different things, and we played with it a long time, and pretended all sorts of things. Nurse said her great-grandmother had told her all about these images, but what we did was no harm at all, only a game. But she told me a story about these images that frightened me very much, and that was what I remembered that night when I was lying awake in my room in the pale, empty darkness, thinking of what I had seen and the secret wood. Nurse said there was once a young lady of the high gentry, who lived in a great castle. And she was so beautiful that all the gentlemen wanted to marry her, because she was the loveliest lady that anybody had ever seen, and she was kind to everybody, and everybody thought she was very good. But though she was polite to all the gentlemen who wished to marry her, she put them off, and said she couldn't make up her mind, and she wasn't sure she wanted to marry anybody at all. And her father, who was a very great lord, was angry, though he was so fond of her, and he asked her why she wouldn't choose a bachelor out of all the handsome young men who came to the castle. But she only said she didn't love any of them very much, and she must wait, and if they pestered her, she said she would go and be a nun in a nunnery. So all the gentlemen said they would go away and wait for a year and a day, and when a year and a day were gone, they would come back again and ask her to say which one she would marry. So the day was appointed and they all went away; and the lady had promised that in a year and a day it would be her wedding day with one of them. But the truth was, that she was the queen of the people who danced on the hill on summer nights, and on the proper nights she would lock the door of her room, and she and her maid would steal out of the castle by a secret passage that only they knew of, and go away up to the hill in the wild land. And she knew more of the secret things than anyone else, and more than anyone knew before or after, because she would not tell anybody the most secret secrets. She knew how to do all the awful things, how to destroy young men, and how to put a curse on people, and other things that I could not understand. And her real name was the Lady Avelin, but the dancing people called her Cassap, which meant somebody very wise, in the old language. And she was whiter than any of them and taller, and her eyes shone in the dark like burning rubies; and she could sing songs that none of the others could sing, and when she sang they all fell down on their faces and worshipped her. And she could do what they called shib-show, which was a very wonderful enchantment. She

ARTHUR MACHEN

would tell the great lord, her father, that she wanted to go into the woods to gather flowers, so he let her go, and she and her maid went into the woods where nobody came, and the maid would keep watch. Then the lady would lie down under the trees and begin to sing a particular song, and she stretched out her arms, and from every part of the wood great serpents would come, hissing and gliding in and out among the trees, and shooting out their forked tongues as they crawled up to the lady. And they all came to her, and twisted round her, round her body, and her arms, and her neck, till she was covered with writhing serpents, and there was only her head to be seen. And she whispered to them, and she sang to them, and they writhed round and round, faster and faster, till she told them to go. And they all went away directly, back to their holes, and on the lady's breast there would be a most curious, beautiful stone, shaped something like an egg, and coloured dark blue and yellow, and red, and green, marked like a serpent's scales. It was called a glame stone, and with it one could do all sorts of wonderful things, and nurse said her great-grandmother had seen a glame stone with her own eyes, and it was for all the world shiny and scaly like a snake. And the lady could do a lot of other things as well, but she was quite fixed that she would not be married. And there were a great many gentlemen who wanted to marry her, but there were five of them who were chief, and their names were Sir Simon, Sir John, Sir Oliver, Sir Richard, and Sir Rowland. All the others believed she spoke the truth, and that she would choose one of them to be her man when a year and a day was done; it was only Sir Simon, who was very crafty, who thought she was deceiving them all, and he vowed he would watch and try if he could find out anything. And though he was very wise he was very young, and he had a smooth, soft face like a girl's, and he pretended, as the rest did, that he would not come to the castle for a year and a day, and he said he was going away beyond the sea to foreign parts. But he really only went a very little way, and came back dressed like a servant girl, and so he got a place in the castle to wash the dishes. And he waited and watched, and he listened and said nothing, and he hid in dark places, and woke up at night and looked out, and he heard things and he saw things that he thought were very strange. And he was so sly that he told the girl that waited on the lady that he was really a young man, and that he had dressed up as a girl because he loved her so very much and wanted to be in the same house with her, and the girl was so pleased that she told him many things, and he was more than ever certain that the Lady Avelin was deceiving him and the others. And he was so clever, and told the servant so many lies, that one night he managed to hide in the Lady Avelin's room behind the curtains. And he stayed quite still and never moved, and at last the lady came. And she bent down under the bed, and raised up a stone, and there was a hollow place underneath, and out of it she took a waxen image, just like the clay one that I and nurse had made in the brake. And all the time her eyes were burning like rubies. And she took the little wax doll up in her arms and held it to her breast, and she whispered and she murmured, and she took it up and she laid it down again, and she held it high, and she held it low, and she laid it down again. And she said, "Happy is he that begat the bishop, that ordered the clerk, that married the man, that had the wife, that fashioned the hive, that harboured the bee, that gathered the wax that my own true love was made of." And she brought out of an aumbry a great golden bowl, and she brought out of a closet a great jar of wine, and she poured some of the wine into the bowl, and she laid her mannikin very gently in the wine, and washed it in the wine all over. Then she went to a cupboard and took a small round cake and laid it on the image's mouth, and then she bore it softly and covered it up. And Sir Simon, who was watching all the time, though he was terribly frightened, saw the lady bend down and stretch out her arms and whisper and sing, and then Sir Simon saw beside her a handsome young man, who kissed her on the lips. And they drank wine out of the golden bowl together, and they ate the cake together. But when the sun rose there was only the little wax doll, and the lady hid it again under the bed in the hollow place. So Sir Simon knew quite well what the lady was, and he waited and he watched, till the time she had said was nearly over, and in a week the year and a day would be done. And one night, when he was watching behind the curtains in her room, he saw her making more wax dolls. And she made five, and hid them away. And the next night she took one out, and held it up, and filled the golden bowl with water, and took the doll by the neck and held it under the water. Then she said—

> *Sir Dickon, Sir Dickon, your day is done,*
> *You shall be drowned in the water wan.*

And the next day news came to the castle that Sir Richard had been drowned at the ford. And at night she took another doll and tied a violet cord round its neck and hung it up on a nail. Then she said—

ARTHUR MACHEN

> *Sir Rowland, your life has ended its span,*
> *High on a tree I see you hang.*

And the next day news came to the castle that Sir Rowland had been hanged by robbers in the wood. And at night she took another doll, and drove her bodkin right into its heart. Then she said—

> *Sir Noll, Sir Noll, so cease your life,*
> *Your heart is piercèd with the knife.*

And the next day news came to the castle that Sir Oliver had fought in a tavern, and a stranger had stabbed him to the heart. And at night she took another doll, and held it to a fire of charcoal till it was melted. Then she said—

> *Sir John, return, and turn to clay,*
> *In fire of fever you waste away.*

And the next day news came to the castle that Sir John had died in a burning fever. So then Sir Simon went out of the castle and mounted his horse and rode away to the bishop and told him everything. And the bishop sent his men, and they took the Lady Avelin, and everything she had done was found out. So on the day after the year and a day, when she was to have been married, they carried her through the town in her smock, and they tied her to a great stake in the market-place, and burned her alive before the bishop with her wax image hung round her neck. And people said the wax man screamed in the burning of the flames. And I thought of this story again and again as I was lying awake in my bed, and I seemed to see the Lady Avelin in the market-place, with the yellow flames eating up her beautiful white body. And I thought of it so much that I seemed to get into the story myself, and I fancied I was the lady, and that they were coming to take me to be burnt with fire, with all the people in the town looking at me. And I wondered whether she cared, after all the strange things she had done, and whether it hurt very much to be burned at the stake. I tried again and again to forget nurse's stories, and to remember the secret I had seen that afternoon, and what was in the secret wood, but I could only see the dark and a glimmering in the dark, and then it went away, and I only saw myself running, and then a great moon came up white over a dark round hill. Then all the old stories came back again, and the queer rhymes that nurse used to sing to me; and there was one beginning "Halsy cumsy Helen musty," that she used to sing very softly when she wanted me to go to sleep. And I began to sing it to myself inside of my head, and I went to sleep.

The next morning I was very tired and sleepy, and could hardly do my lessons, and I was very glad when they were over and I had had my dinner, as I wanted to go out and be alone. It was a warm day, and I went to a nice turfy hill by the river, and sat down on my mother's old shawl that I had brought with me on purpose. The sky was grey, like the day before, but there was a kind of white gleam behind it, and from where I was sitting I could look down on the town, and it was all still and quiet and white, like a picture. I remembered that it was on that hill that nurse taught me to play an old game called "Troy Town," in which one had to dance, and wind in and out on a pattern in the grass, and then when one had danced and turned long enough the other person asks you questions, and you can't help answering whether you want to or not, and whatever you are told to do you feel you have to do it. Nurse said there used to be a lot of games like that that some people knew of, and there was one by which people could be turned into anything you liked and an old man her great-grandmother had seen had known a girl who had been turned into a large snake. And there was another very ancient game of dancing and winding and turning, by which you could take a person out of himself and hide him away as long as you liked, and his body went walking about quite empty, without any sense in it. But I came to that hill because I wanted to think of what had happened the day before, and of the secret of the wood. From the place where I was sitting I could see beyond the town, into the opening I had found, where a little brook had led me into an unknown country. And I pretended I was following the brook over again, and I went all the way in my mind, and at last I found the wood, and crept into it under the bushes, and then in the dusk I saw something that made me feel as if I were filled with fire, as if I wanted to dance and sing and fly up into the air, because I was changed and wonderful. But what I saw was not changed at all, and had not grown old, and I wondered again and again how such things could happen, and whether nurse's stories were really true, because in the daytime in the open air everything seemed quite different from what it was at night, when I was frightened, and thought I was to be burned alive. I once told my father one of her little tales, which was about a ghost, and asked him if it was true, and he told me it was not true at all, and that only common, ignorant people believed in such rubbish. He was very angry with nurse for telling me the story, and scolded her, and after that I promised her I would never whisper a word of what she told me, and if I did I should be bitten by the great black snake that lived in the pool in the wood. And all alone on the hill I wondered what was true. I had seen something very amazing and very lovely, and I knew a story, and if I had really seen it, and not made it up out of the dark, and the black bough, and the bright shining that was mounting up to the sky from over the great round hill, but had really seen it in truth, then there were all kinds of wonderful and lovely and terrible things to think of, so I longed and trembled, and I burned and got cold. And I looked down on the town, so quiet and still, like a little white picture, and I thought over and over if it could be true. I was a long time before I could make up my mind to anything; there was such a strange fluttering at my heart that seemed to whisper to me all the time that I had not made it up out of my head, and yet it seemed quite impossible, and I knew my father and everybody would say it was dreadful rubbish. I never dreamed of telling him or anybody else a word about it, because I knew it would be of no use, and I should only get laughed at or scolded, so for a long time I was very quiet, and went about thinking and wondering; and at night I used to dream of amazing things, and sometimes I woke up in the early morning and held out my arms with a cry. And I was frightened, too, because there were dangers, and some awful thing would happen to me, unless I took great care, if the story were true. These old tales were always in my head, night and morning, and I went over them and told them to myself over and over again, and went for walks in the places where nurse had told them to me; and when I sat in the nursery by the fire in the evenings I used to fancy nurse was sitting in the other chair, and telling me some wonderful story in a low voice, for fear anybody should be listening. But she used to like best to tell me about things when we were right out in the country, far from the house, because she said she was telling me such secrets, and walls have ears. And if it was something more than ever secret, we had to hide in brakes or woods; and I used to think it was such fun creeping along a hedge, and going very softly, and then we would get behind the bushes or run into the wood all of a sudden, when we were sure that none was watching us; so we knew that we had our secrets quite all to ourselves, and nobody else at all knew anything about them. Now and then, when we had hidden ourselves as I have described, she used to show me all sorts of odd things. One day, I remember, we were in a hazel brake, overlooking the brook, and we were so snug and warm, as though it was April; the sun was quite hot, and the leaves were just coming out. Nurse said she would show me something funny that would make me laugh, and then she showed me, as she said, how one could turn a whole house upside down, without anybody being able to find out, and the pots and pans would jump about, and the china would be broken, and the chairs would tumble over of themselves. I tried it one day in the kitchen, and I found I could do it quite well, and a whole row of plates on the dresser fell off it, and cook's little work-table tilted up and turned right over "before her eyes," as she said, but she was so frightened and turned so white that I didn't do it again, as I liked her. And afterwards, in the hazel copse, when she had shown me how to make things tumble about, she showed me how to make rapping noises, and I learnt how to do that, too. Then she taught me rhymes to say on certain occasions, and peculiar marks to make on other occasions, and other things that her great-grandmother had taught her when she was a little girl herself. And these were all the things I was thinking about in those days after the strange walk when I thought I had seen a great secret, and I wished nurse were there for me to ask her about it, but she had gone away more than two years before, and nobody seemed to know what had become of her, or where she had gone. But I shall always remember those days if I live to be quite old, because all the time I felt so strange, wondering and doubting, and feeling quite sure at one time, and making up my mind, and then I would feel quite sure that such things couldn't happen really, and it began all over again. But I took great care not to do certain things that might be very dangerous. So I waited and wondered for a long time, and though I was not sure at all, I never dared to try to find out. But one day I became sure that all that nurse said was quite true, and I was all alone when I found it out. I trembled all over with joy and terror, and as fast as I could I ran into one of the old brakes where we used to go—it was the one by the lane, where nurse made the little clay man—and I ran into it, and I crept into it; and when I came to the place where the elder was, I covered up my face with my hands and lay down flat on the grass, and I stayed there for two hours without moving, whispering to myself delicious, terrible things, and saying some words over and over again. It was all true and wonderful and splendid, and when I remembered the story I knew and thought of what I had really seen, I got hot and I got cold, and the air seemed full of scent, and flowers, and singing. And first I wanted to make a little clay man, like the one nurse had made so long ago, and I had to invent plans and stratagems, and to look about, and to think of things beforehand, because nobody must dream of anything that I was doing or going to do, and I was too old to carry clay about in a tin bucket. At last I thought of a plan, and I brought the wet clay to the brake, and did everything that nurse had done, only I made a much finer image than the one she had made; and when it was finished I did everything that I could imagine and much more than she did, because it was the likeness of something far better. And a few days later, when I had done my lessons early, I went for the second time by the way of the little brook that had led me into a strange country. And I followed the brook, and went through the bushes, and beneath the low branches of trees, and up thorny thickets on the hill, and by dark woods full of creeping thorns, a long, long way. Then I crept through the dark tunnel where the brook had been and the ground was stony, till at last I came to the thicket that climbed up the hill, and though the leaves were coming out upon the trees, everything looked almost as black as it was on the first day that I went there. And the thicket was just the same, and I went up slowly till I came out on the big bare hill, and began to walk among the wonderful rocks. I saw the terrible voor again on everything, for though the sky was brighter, the ring of wild hills all around was still dark, and the hanging woods looked dark and dreadful, and the strange rocks were as grey as ever; and when I looked down on them from the great mound, sitting on the stone, I saw all their amazing circles and rounds within rounds, and I had to sit quite still and watch them as they began to turn about me, and each stone danced in its place, and they seemed to go round and round in a great whirl, as if one were in the middle of all the stars and heard them rushing through the air. So I went down among the rocks to dance with them and to sing extraordinary songs; and I went down through the other thicket, and drank from the bright stream in the close and secret valley, putting my lips down to the bubbling water; and then I went on till I came to the deep, brimming well among the glittering moss, and I sat down. I looked before me into the secret darkness of the valley, and behind me was the great high wall of grass, and all around me there were the hanging woods that made the valley such a secret place. I knew there was nobody here at all besides myself, and that no one could see me. So

I took off my boots and stockings, and let my feet down into the water, saying the words that I knew. And it was not cold at all, as I expected, but warm and very pleasant, and when my feet were in it I felt as if they were in silk, or as if the nymph were kissing them. So when I had done, I said the other words and made the signs, and then I dried my feet with a towel I had brought on purpose, and put on my stockings and boots. Then I climbed up the steep wall, and went into the place where there are the hollows, and the two beautiful mounds, and the round ridges of land, and all the strange shapes. I did not go down into the hollow this time, but I turned at the end, and made out the figures quite plainly, as it was lighter, and I had remembered the story I had quite forgotten before, and in the story the two figures are called Adam and Eve, and only those who know the story understand what they mean. So I went on and on till I came to the secret wood which must not be described, and I crept into it by the way I had found. And when I had gone about halfway I stopped, and turned round, and got ready, and I bound the handkerchief tightly round my eyes, and made quite sure that I could not see at all, not a twig, nor the end of a leaf, nor the light of the sky, as it was an old red silk handkerchief with large yellow spots, that went round twice and covered my eyes, so that I could see nothing. Then I began to go on, step by step, very slowly. My heart beat faster and faster, and something rose in my throat that choked me and made me want to cry out, but I shut my lips, and went on. Boughs caught in my hair as I went, and great thorns tore me; but I went on to the end of the path. Then I stopped, and held out my arms and bowed, and I went round the first time, feeling with my hands, and there was nothing. I went round the second time, feeling with my hands, and there was nothing. Then I went round the third time, feeling with my hands, and the story was all true, and I wished that the years were gone by, and that I had not so long a time to wait before I was happy forever and ever.

Nurse must have been a prophet like those we read of in the Bible. Everything that she said began to come true, and since then other things that she told me of have happened. That was how I came to know that her stories were true and that I had not made up the secret myself out of my own head. But there was another thing that happened that day. I went a second time to the secret place. It was at the deep brimming well, and when I was standing on the moss I bent over and looked in, and then I knew who the white lady was that I had seen come out of the water in the wood long ago when I was quite little. And I trembled all over, because that told me other things. Then I remembered how sometime after I had seen the white people in the wood, nurse asked me more about them, and I told her all over again, and she listened, and said nothing for a long, long time, and at last she said, "You will see her again." So I understood what had happened and what was to happen. And I understood about the nymphs; how I might meet them in all kinds of places, and they would always help me, and I must always look for them, and find them in all sorts of strange shapes and appearances. And without the nymphs I could never have found the secret, and without them none of the other things could happen. Nurse had told me all about them long ago, but she called them by another name, and I did not know what she meant, or what her tales of them were about, only that they were very queer. And there were two kinds, the bright and the dark, and both were very lovely and very wonderful, and some people saw only one kind, and some only the other, but some saw them both. But usually the dark appeared first, and the bright ones came afterwards, and there were extraordinary tales about them. It was a day or two after I had come home from the secret place that I first really knew the nymphs. Nurse had shown me how to call them, and I had tried, but I did not know what she meant, and so I thought it was all nonsense. But I made up my mind I would try again, so I went to the wood where the pool was, where I saw the white people, and I tried again. The dark nymph, Alanna, came, and she turned the pool of water into a pool of fire. . .

Epilogue

"That's a very queer story," said Cotgrave, handing back the green book to the recluse, Ambrose. "I see the drift of a good deal, but there are many things that I do not grasp at all. On the last page, for example, what does she mean by 'nymphs'?"

"Well, I think there are references throughout the manuscript to certain 'processes' which have been handed down by tradition from age to age. Some of these processes are just beginning to come within the purview of science, which has arrived at them—or rather at the steps which lead to them—by quite different paths. I have interpreted the reference to 'nymphs' as a reference to one of these processes."

"And you believe that there are such things?"

"Oh, I think so. Yes, I believe I could give you convincing evidence on that point. I am afraid you have neglected the study of alchemy? It is a pity, for the symbolism, at all events, is very beautiful, and moreover if you were acquainted with certain books on the subject, I could recall to your mind phrases which might explain a good deal in the manuscript that you have been reading."

"Yes; but I want to know whether you seriously think that there is any foundation of fact beneath these fancies. Is it not all a department of poetry; a curious dream with which man has indulged himself?"

"I can only say that it is no doubt better for the great mass of people to dismiss it all as a dream. But if you ask my veritable belief—that goes quite the other way. No; I should not say belief, but rather knowledge. I may tell you that I have known cases in which men have stumbled quite by accident on certain of these 'processes,' and have been astonished by wholly unexpected results. In the cases I am thinking of there could have been no possibility of 'suggestion' or sub-conscious action of any kind. One might as well suppose a schoolboy 'suggesting' the existence of Æschylus to himself, while he plods mechanically through the declensions.

"But you have noticed the obscurity," Ambrose went on, "and in this particular case it must have been dictated by instinct, since the writer never thought that her manuscripts would fall into other hands. But the practice is universal, and for most excellent reasons. Powerful and sovereign medicines, which are, of necessity, virulent poisons also, are kept in a locked cabinet. The child may find the key by chance, and

ARTHUR MACHEN

drink herself dead; but in most cases the search is educational, and the phials contain precious elixirs for him who has patiently fashioned the key for himself."

"You do not care to go into details?"

"No, frankly, I do not. No, you must remain unconvinced. But you saw how the manuscript illustrates the talk we had last week?"

"Is this girl still alive?"

"No. I was one of those who found her. I knew the father well; he was a lawyer, and had always left her very much to herself. He thought of nothing but deeds and leases, and the news came to him as an awful surprise. She was missing one morning; I suppose it was about a year after she had written what you have read. The servants were called, and they told things, and put the only natural interpretation on them—a perfectly erroneous one.

"They discovered that green book somewhere in her room, and I found her in the place that she described with so much dread, lying on the ground before the image."

"It was an image?"

"Yes, it was hidden by the thorns and the thick undergrowth that had surrounded it. It was a wild, lonely country; but you know what it was like by her description, though of course you will understand that the colours have been heightened. A child's imagination always makes the heights higher and the depths deeper than they really are; and she had, unfortunately for herself, something more than imagination. One might say, perhaps, that the picture in her mind which she succeeded in a measure in putting into words, was the scene as it would have appeared to an imaginative artist. But it is a strange, desolate land."

"And she was dead?"

"Yes. She had poisoned herself—in time. No; there was not a word to be said against her in the ordinary sense. You may recollect a story I told you the other night about a lady who saw her child's fingers crushed by a window?"

"And what was this statue?"

"Well, it was of Roman workmanship, of a stone that with the centuries had not blackened, but had become white and luminous. The thicket had grown up about it and concealed it, and in the Middle Ages the followers of a very old tradition had known how to use it for their own purposes. In fact it had been incorporated into the monstrous mythology of the Sabbath. You will have noted that those to whom a sight of that shining whiteness had been vouchsafed by chance, or rather, perhaps, by apparent chance, were required to blindfold themselves on their second approach. That is very significant."

"And is it there still?"

"I sent for tools, and we hammered it into dust and fragments."

"The persistence of tradition never surprises me," Ambrose went on after a pause. "I could name many an English parish where such traditions as that girl had listened to in her childhood are still existent in occult but unabated vigour. No, for me, it is the 'story' not the 'sequel,' which is strange and awful, for I have always believed that wonder is of the soul."

THE END

THE TERROR

I

THE COMING OF THE TERROR

After two years we are turning once more to the morning's news with a sense of appetite and glad expectation. There were thrills at the beginning of the war; the thrill of horror and of a doom that seemed at once incredible and certain; this was when Namur fell and the German host swelled like a flood over the French fields, and drew very near to the walls of Paris. Then we felt the thrill of exultation when the good news came that the awful tide had been turned back, that Paris and the world were safe; for awhile at all events.

Then for days we hoped for more news as good as this or better. Has Von Kluck been surrounded? Not today, but perhaps he will be surrounded tomorrow. But the days became weeks, the weeks drew out to months; the battle in the West seemed frozen. Now and again things were done that seemed hopeful, with promise of events still better. But Neuve Chapelle and Loos dwindled into disappointments as their tale was told fully; the lines in the West remained, for all practical purposes of victory, immobile. Nothing seemed to happen; there was nothing to read save the record of operations that were clearly trifling and insignificant. People speculated as to the reason of this inaction; the hopeful said that Joffre had a plan, that he was "nibbling," others declared that we were short of munitions, others again that the new levies were not yet ripe for battle. So the months went by, and almost two years of war had been completed before the motionless English line began to stir and quiver as if it awoke from a long sleep, and began to roll onward, overwhelming the enemy.

The secret of the long inaction of the British Armies has been well kept. On the one hand it was rigorously protected by the censorship, which severe, and sometimes severe to the point of absurdity—"the captains and the. . . depart," for instance—became in this particular matter ferocious. As soon as the real significance of that which was happening, or beginning to happen, was perceived by the authorities, an underlined circular was issued to the newspaper proprietors of Great Britain and Ireland. It warned each proprietor that he might impart the contents of this circular to one other person only, such person being the responsible editor of his paper, who was to keep the communication secret under the severest penalties. The circular forbade any mention of certain events that had taken place, that might take place; it forbade any kind of allusion to these events or any hint of their existence, or of the possibility of their existence, not only in the Press, but in any form whatever. The subject was not to be alluded to in conversation, it was not to be hinted at, however obscurely, in letters; the very existence of the circular, its subject apart, was to be a dead secret.

These measures were successful. A wealthy newspaper proprietor of the North, warmed a little at the end of the Throwsters' Feast (which was held as usual, it will be remembered), ventured to say to the man next to him: "How awful it would be, wouldn't it, if. . ." His words were repeated, as proof, one regrets to say, that it was time for "old Arnold" to "pull himself together"; and he was fined a thousand pounds. Then, there was the case of an obscure weekly paper published in the county town of an agricultural district in Wales. The *Meiros Observer* (we will call it) was issued from a stationer's back premises, and filled its four pages with accounts of local flower shows, fancy fairs at vicarages, reports of parish councils, and rare bathing fatalities. It also issued a visitors' list, which has been known to contain six names.

This enlightened organ printed a paragraph, which nobody noticed, which was very like paragraphs that small country newspapers have long been in the habit of printing, which could hardly give so much as a hint to anyone—to anyone, that is, who was not fully instructed in the secret. As a matter of fact, this piece of intelligence got into the paper because the proprietor, who was also the editor, incautiously left the last processes of this particular issue to the staff, who was the Lord-High-Every-thing-Else of the establishment; and the staff put in a bit of gossip he had heard in the market to fill up two inches on the back page. But the result was that the *Meiros Observer* ceased to appear, owing to "untoward circumstances" as the proprietor said; and he would say no more. No more, that is, by way of explanation, but a great deal more by way of execration of "damned, prying busybodies."

Now a censorship that is sufficiently minute and utterly remorseless can do amazing things in the way of hiding. . . what it wants to hide. Before the war, one would have thought otherwise; one would have said that, censor or no censor, the fact of the murder at X or the fact of the bank robbery at Y would certainly become known; if not through the Press, at all events through rumor and the passage of the news from mouth to mouth. And this would be true—of England three hundred years ago, and of savage tribelands of today. But we have grown of late to such a reverence for the printed word and such a reliance on it, that the old faculty of disseminating news by word of mouth has become atrophied. Forbid the Press to mention the fact that Jones has been murdered, and it is marvelous how few people will hear of it, and of those who hear how few will credit the story that they have heard. You meet a man in the train who remarks that he has been told something about a murder in Southwark; there is all the difference in the world between the impression you receive from such a chance communication and that given by half a dozen lines of print with name, and street and date and all the facts of the case. People in trains repeat all sorts of tales, many of them false; newspapers do not print accounts of murders that have not been committed.

Then another consideration that has made for secrecy. I may have seemed to say that the old office of rumor no longer exists; I shall be reminded of the strange legend of "the Russians" and the mythology of the "Angels of Mons." But let me point out, in the first place, that both these absurdities depended on the papers for their wide dissemination. If there had been no newspapers or magazines Russians and Angels would have made but a brief, vague appearance of the most shadowy kind—a few would have heard of them, fewer still would have believed in them, they would have been gossiped about for a bare week or two, and so they would have vanished away.

And, then, again, the very fact of these vain rumors and fantastic tales having been so widely believed for a time was fatal to the credit of any stray mutterings that may have got abroad. People had been taken in twice; they had seen how grave persons, men of credit, had preached and lectured about the shining forms that had saved the British Army at Mons, or had testified to the trains, packed with gray-coated Muscovites, rushing through the land at dead of night: and now there was a hint of something more amazing than either of the discredited legends. But this time there was no word of confirmation to be found in daily paper, or weekly review, or parish magazine, and so the few that heard either laughed, or, being serious, went home and jotted down notes for essays on "War-time Psychology: Collective Delusions."

I FOLLOWED NEITHER OF THESE courses. For before the secret circular had been issued my curiosity had somehow been aroused by certain paragraphs concerning a "Fatal Accident to Well-known Airman." The propeller of the airplane had been shattered, apparently by a collision with a flight of pigeons; the blades had been broken and the machine had fallen like lead to the earth. And soon after I had seen this account, I heard of some very odd circumstances relating to an explosion in a great munition factory in the Midlands. I thought I saw the possibility of a connection between two very different events.

IT HAS BEEN POINTED OUT to me by friends who have been good enough to read this record, that certain phrases I have used may give the impression that I ascribe all the delays of the war on the Western front to the extraordinary circumstances which occasioned the issue of the Secret Circular. Of course this is not the case, there were many reasons for the immobility of our lines from October 1914 to July 1916. These causes have been evident enough and have been openly discussed and deplored. But behind them was something of infinitely greater moment. We lacked men, but men were pouring into the new army; we were short of shells, but when the shortage was proclaimed the nation set itself to mend this matter with all its energy. We could undertake to supply the defects of our army both in men and munitions—*if* the new and incredible danger could be overcome. It has been overcome; rather, perhaps, it has ceased to exist; and the secret may now be told.

I have said my attention was attracted by an account of the death of a well-known airman. I have not the habit of preserving cuttings, I am sorry to say, so that I cannot be precise as to the date of this event. To the best of my belief it was either towards the end of May or the beginning of June 1915. The newspaper paragraph announcing the death of Flight-Lieutenant Western-Reynolds was brief enough; accidents, and fatal accidents, to the men who are storming the air for us are, unfortunately, by no means so rare as to demand an elaborated notice. But the manner in which Western-Reynolds met his death struck me as extraordinary, inasmuch as it revealed a new danger in the element that we have lately conquered. He was brought down, as I said, by a flight of birds; of pigeons, as appeared by what was found on the bloodstained and shattered blades of the propeller. An eye-witness of the accident, a fellow-officer, described how Western-Reynolds set out from the aerodrome on a fine afternoon, there being hardly any wind. He was going to France; he had made the journey to and fro half a dozen times or more, and felt perfectly secure and at ease.

"'Wester' rose to a great height at once, and we could scarcely see the machine. I was turning to go when one of the fellows called out, 'I say! What's this?' He pointed up, and we saw what looked like a black cloud coming from the south at a tremendous rate. I saw at once it wasn't a cloud; it came with a swirl and a rush quite different from any cloud I've ever seen. But for a second I couldn't make out exactly what it was. It altered its shape and turned into a great crescent, and wheeled and veered about as if it was looking for something. The man who had called out had got his glasses, and was staring for all he was worth. Then he shouted that it was a tremendous flight of birds, 'thousands of them.' They went on wheeling and beating about high up in the air, and we were watching them, thinking it was interesting, but not supposing that they would make any difference to 'Wester,' who was just about out of sight. His machine was just a speck. Then the two arms of the crescent drew in as quick as lightning, and these thousands of birds shot in a solid mass right up there across the sky, and flew away somewhere about nor'-nor'-by-west. Then Henley, the man with the glasses, called out, 'He's down!' and started running, and I went after him. We got a car and as we were going along Henley told me that he'd seen the machine drop dead, as if it came out of that cloud of birds. He thought then that they must have mucked up the propeller somehow. That turned out to be the case. We found the propeller blades all broken and covered with blood and pigeon feathers, and carcasses of the birds had got wedged in between the blades, and were sticking to them."

This was the story that the young airman told one evening in a small company. He did not speak "in confidence," so I have no hesitation in reproducing what he said. Naturally, I did not take a verbatim note of his conversation, but I have something of a knack of remembering talk that interests me, and I think my reproduction is very near to the tale that I heard. And let it be noted that the flying man told his story without any sense or indication of a sense that the incredible, or all but the incredible, had happened. So far as he knew, he said, it was the first accident of the kind. Airmen in France had been bothered once or twice by birds—he thought they were eagles—flying viciously at them, but poor old "Wester" had been the first man to come up against a flight of some thousands of pigeons.

"And perhaps I shall be the next," he added, "but why look for trouble? Anyhow, I'm going to see *Toodle-oo* tomorrow afternoon."

WELL, I HEARD THE STORY, as one hears all the varied marvels and terrors of the air; as one heard some years ago of "air pockets," strange gulfs or voids in the atmosphere into which airmen fell with great peril; or as one heard of the experience of the airman who flew over the Cumberland mountains in the burning summer of 1911, and as he swam far above the heights was suddenly and vehemently blown upwards, the hot air from the rocks striking his plane as if it had been a blast from a furnace chimney. We have just begun to navigate a strange region; we must expect to encounter strange adventures, strange perils. And here a new chapter in the chronicles of these perils and adventures had been opened by the death of Western-Reynolds; and no doubt invention and contrivance would presently hit on some way of countering the new danger.

It was, I think, about a week or ten days after the airman's death that my business called me to a northern town, the name of which, perhaps, had better remain unknown. My mission was to inquire into certain charges of extravagance which had been laid against the working people, that is, the munition workers of this especial town. It was said that the men who used to earn £2 10s. a week were now getting from seven to eight pounds, that "bits of girls" were being paid two pounds instead of seven or eight shillings, and that, in consequence, there was an orgy of foolish extravagance. The girls, I was told, were eating chocolates at four, five, and six shillings a pound, the women were ordering thirty-pound pianos which they couldn't play, and the men bought gold chains at ten and twenty guineas apiece.

I dived into the town in question and found, as usual, that there was a mixture of truth and exaggeration in the stories that I had heard. Gramophones, for example: they cannot be called in strictness necessaries, but they were undoubtedly finding a ready sale, even in the more expensive brands. And I thought that there were a great many very spick and span perambulators to be seen on the pavement; smart perambulators, painted in tender shades of color and expensively fitted.

"And how can you be surprised if people will have a bit of a fling?" a worker said to me. "We're seeing money for the first time in our lives, and it's bright. And we work hard for it, and we risk our lives to get it. You've heard of explosion yonder?"

He mentioned certain works on the outskirts of the town. Of course, neither the name of the works nor of the town had been printed; there had been a brief notice of "Explosion at Munition Works in the Northern District: Many Fatalities." The working man told me about it, and added some dreadful details.

"They wouldn't let their folks see bodies; screwed them up in coffins as they found them in shop. The gas had done it."

"Turned their faces black, you mean?"

"Nay. They were all as if they had been bitten to pieces."

This was a strange gas.

I asked the man in the northern town all sorts of questions about the extraordinary explosion of which he had spoken to me. But he had very little more to say. As I have noted already, secrets that may not be printed are often deeply kept; last summer there were very few people outside high official circles who knew anything about the "Tanks," of which we have all been talking lately, though these strange instruments of war were being exercised and tested in a park not far from London. So the man who told me of the explosion in the munition factory was most likely genuine in his profession that he knew nothing more of the disaster. I found out that he was a smelter employed at a furnace on the other side of the town to the ruined factory; he didn't know even what they had been making there; some very dangerous high explosive, he supposed. His information was really nothing more than a bit of gruesome gossip, which he had heard probably at third or fourth or fifth hand. The horrible detail of faces "as if they had been bitten to pieces" had made its violent impression on him, that was all.

I gave him up and took a tram to the district of the disaster; a sort of industrial suburb, five miles from the center of the town. When I asked for the factory, I was told that it was no good my going to it as there was nobody there. But I found it; a raw and hideous shed with a walled yard about it, and a shut gate. I looked for signs of destruction, but there was nothing. The roof was quite undamaged; and again it struck me that this had been a strange accident. There had been an explosion of sufficient violence to kill workpeople in the building, but the building itself showed no wounds or scars.

A man came out of the gate and locked it behind him. I began to ask him some sort of question, or rather, I began to "open" for a question with "A terrible business here, they tell me," or some such phrase of convention. I got no farther. The man asked me if I saw a policeman walking down the street. I said I did, and I was given the choice of getting about my business forthwith or of being instantly given in charge as a spy. "Th'ast better be gone and quick about it," was, I think, his final advice, and I took it.

Well, I had come literally up against a brick wall. Thinking the problem over, I could only suppose that the smelter or his informant had twisted the phrases of the story. The smelter had said the dead men's faces were "bitten to pieces"; this might be an unconscious perversion of "eaten away." That phrase might describe well enough the effect of strong acids, and, for all I knew of the processes of munition-making, such acids might be used and might explode with horrible results in some perilous stage of their admixture.

It was a day or two later that the accident to the airman, Western-Reynolds, came into my mind. For one of those instants which are far shorter than any measure of time there flashed out the possibility of a link between the two disasters. But here was a wild impossibility, and I drove it away. And yet I think that the thought, mad as it seemed, never left me; it was the secret light that at last guided me through a somber grove of enigmas.

It was about this time, so far as the date can be fixed, that a whole district, one might say a whole county, was visited by a series of extraordinary and terrible calamities, which were the more terrible inasmuch as they continued for sometime to be inscrutable mysteries. It is, indeed, doubtful whether these awful events do not still remain mysteries to many of those concerned; for before the inhabitants of this part of the country had time to join one link of evidence to another the circular was issued, and thenceforth no one knew how to distinguish undoubted fact from wild and extravagant surmise.

The district in question is in the far west of Wales; I shall call it, for convenience, Meirion. In it there is one seaside town of some repute with holiday-makers for five or six weeks in the summer, and dotted about the county there are three or four small old towns that seem drooping in a slow decay, sleepy and gray with age and forgetfulness. They remind me of what I have read of towns in the west of Ireland. Grass grows between the uneven stones of the pavements, the signs above the shop windows decline, half the letters of these signs are missing, here and there a house has been pulled down, or has been allowed to slide into ruin, and wild greenery springs up through the fallen stones, and there is silence in all the streets. And, it is to be noted, these are not places that were once magnificent. The Celts have never had the art of building, and so far as I can see, such towns as Towy and Merthyr Tegveth and Meiros must have been always much as they are now, clusters of poorish, meanly-built houses, ill-kept and down at heel.

And these few towns are thinly scattered over a wild country where north is divided from south by a wilder mountain range. One of these places is sixteen miles from any station; the others are doubtfully and deviously connected by single-line railways served by rare trains that pause and stagger and hesitate on their slow journey up mountain passes, or stop for half an hour or more at lonely sheds called stations, situated in the midst of desolate marshes. A few years ago I traveled with an Irishman on one of these queer lines, and he looked to right and saw the bog with its yellow and blue grasses and stagnant pools, and he looked to left and saw a ragged hillside, set with gray stone walls. "I can hardly believe," he said, "that I'm not still in the wilds of Ireland."

Here, then, one sees a wild and divided and scattered region a land of outland hills and secret and hidden valleys. I know white farms on this coast which must be separate by two hours of hard, rough walking from any other habitation, which are invisible from any other house. And inland, again, the farms are often ringed about by thick groves of ash, planted by men of old days to shelter their roof-trees from rude winds of the mountain and stormy winds of the sea; so that these places, too, are hidden away, to be surmised only by the wood smoke that rises from the green surrounding leaves. A Londoner must see them to believe in them; and even then he can scarcely credit their utter isolation.

Such, then in the main is Meirion, and on this land in the early summer of last year terror descended—a terror without shape, such as no man there had ever known.

It began with the tale of a little child who wandered out into the lanes to pick flowers one sunny afternoon, and never came back to the cottage on the hill.

II

Death in the Village

The child who was lost came from a lonely cottage that stands on the slope of a steep hillside called the Allt, or the height. The land about it is wild and ragged; here the growth of gorse and bracken, here a marshy hollow of reeds and rushes, marking the course of the stream from some hidden well, here thickets of dense and tangled undergrowth, the outposts of the wood. Down through this broken and uneven ground a path leads to the lane at the bottom of the valley; then the land rises again and swells up to the cliffs over the sea, about a quarter of a mile away. The little girl, Gertrude Morgan, asked her mother if she might go down to the lane and pick the purple flowers—these were orchids—that grew there, and her mother gave her leave, telling her she must be sure to be back by tea-time, as there was apple-tart for tea.

She never came back. It was supposed that she must have crossed the road and gone to the cliff's edge, possibly in order to pick the sea-pinks that were then in full blossom. She must have slipped, they said, and fallen into the sea, two hundred feet below. And, it may be said at once, that there was no doubt some truth in this conjecture, though it stopped very far short of the whole truth. The child's body must have been carried out by the tide, for it was never found.

The conjecture of a false step or of a fatal slide on the slippery turf that slopes down to the rocks was accepted as being the only explanation possible. People thought the accident a strange one because, as a rule, country children living by the cliffs and the sea become wary at an early age, and Gertrude Morgan was almost ten years old. Still, as the neighbors said, "that's how it must have happened, and it's a great pity, to be sure." But this would not do when in a week's time a strong young laborer failed to come to his cottage after the day's work. His body was found on the rocks six or seven miles from the cliffs where the child was supposed to have fallen; he was going home by a path that he had used every night of his life for eight or nine years, that he used of dark nights in perfect security, knowing every inch of it. The police asked if he drank, but he was a teetotaler; if he were subject to fits, but he wasn't. And he was not murdered for his wealth, since agricultural laborers are not wealthy. It was only possible again to talk of slippery turf and a false step; but people began to be frightened. Then a woman was found with her neck broken at the bottom of a disused quarry near Llanfihangel, in the middle of the county. The "false step" theory was eliminated here, for the quarry was guarded with a natural hedge of gorse bushes. One would have to struggle and fight through sharp thorns to destruction in such a place as this; and indeed the gorse bushes were broken as if someone had rushed furiously through them, just above the place where the woman's body was found. And this was strange: there was a dead sheep lying beside her in the pit, as if the woman and the sheep together had been chased over the brim of the quarry. But chased by whom, or by what? And then there was a new form of terror.

This was in the region of the marshes under the mountain. A man and his son, a lad of fourteen or fifteen, set out early one morning to work and never reached the farm where they were bound. Their way skirted the marsh, but it was broad, firm and well metalled, and it had been raised about two feet above the bog. But when search was made in the evening of the same day Phillips and his son were found dead in the marsh, covered with black slime and pondweed. And they lay some ten yards from the path, which, it would seem, they must have left deliberately. It was useless of course, to look for tracks in the black ooze, for if one threw a big stone into it a few seconds removed all marks of the disturbance. The men who found the two bodies beat about the verges and purlieus of the marsh in hope of finding some trace of the murderers; they went to and fro over the rising ground where the black cattle were grazing, they searched the alder thickets by the brook; but they discovered nothing.

MOST HORRIBLE OF ALL THESE horrors, perhaps, was the affair of the Highway, a lonely and unfrequented by-road that winds for many miles on high and lonely land. Here, a mile from any other dwelling, stands a cottage on the edge of a dark wood. It was inhabited by a laborer named Williams, his wife, and their three children. One hot summer's evening, a man who had been doing a day's gardening at a rectory three or four miles away, passed the cottage, and stopped for a few minutes to chat with Williams, the laborer, who was pottering about his garden, while the children were playing on the path by the door. The two talked of their neighbors and of the potatoes till Mrs. Williams appeared at the doorway and said supper was ready, and

Williams turned to go into the house. This was about eight o'clock, and in the ordinary course the family would have their supper and be in bed by nine, or by half-past nine at latest. At ten o'clock that night the local doctor was driving home along the Highway. His horse shied violently and then stopped dead just opposite the gate to the cottage. The doctor got down, frightened at what he saw; and there on the roadway lay Williams, his wife, and the three children, stone dead, all of them. Their skulls were battered in as if by some heavy iron instrument; their faces were beaten into a pulp.

III

The Doctors Theory

It is not easy to make any picture of the horror that lay dark on the hearts of the people of Meirion. It was no longer possible to believe or to pretend to believe that these men and women and children had met their deaths through strange accidents. The little girl and the young laborer might have slipped and fallen over the cliffs, but the woman who lay dead with the dead sheep at the bottom of the quarry, the two men who had been lured into the ooze of the marsh, the family who were found murdered on the Highway before their own cottage door; in these cases there could be no room for the supposition of accident. It seemed as if it were impossible to frame any conjecture or outline of a conjecture that would account for these hideous and, as it seemed, utterly purposeless crimes. For a time people said that there must be a madman at large, a sort of country variant of Jack the Ripper, some horrible pervert who was possessed by the passion of death, who prowled darkling about that lonely land, hiding in woods and in wild places, always watching and seeking for the victims of his desire.

Indeed, Dr. Lewis, who found poor Williams, his wife and children miserably slaughtered on the Highway, was convinced at first that the presence of a concealed madman in the countryside offered the only possible solution to the difficulty.

"I felt sure," he said to me afterwards, "that the Williams's had been killed by a homicidal maniac. It was the nature of the poor creatures' injuries that convinced me that this was the case. Some years ago thirty-seven or thirty-eight years ago as a matter of fact—I had something to do with a case which on the face of it had a strong likeness to the Highway murder. At that time I had a practice at Usk, in Monmouthshire. A whole family living in a cottage by the roadside were murdered one evening; it was called, I think, the Llangibby murder; the cottage was near the village of that name. The murderer was caught in Newport; he was a Spanish sailor, named Garcia, and it appeared that he had killed father, mother, and the three children for the sake of the brass works of an old Dutch clock, which were found on him when he was arrested.

"Garcia had been serving a month's imprisonment in Usk Jail for some small theft, and on his release he set out to walk to Newport, nine or ten miles away; no doubt to get another ship. He passed the cottage and saw the man working in his garden. Garcia stabbed him with his sailor's knife. The wife rushed out; he stabbed her. Then he went into the cottage and stabbed the three children, tried to set the place on fire, and made off with the clockworks. That looked like the deed of a madman, but Garcia wasn't mad—they hanged him, I may say—he was merely a man of a very low type, a degenerate who hadn't the slightest value for human life. I am not sure, but I think he came from one of the Spanish islands, where the people are said to be degenerates, very likely from too much inter-breeding.

"But my point is that Garcia stabbed to kill and did kill, with one blow in each case. There was no senseless hacking and slashing. Now those poor people on the Highway had their heads smashed to pieces by what must have been a storm of blows. Anyone of them would have been fatal, but the murderer must have gone on raining blows with his iron hammer on people who were already stone dead. And *that* sort of thing is the work of a madman, and nothing but a madman. That's how I argued the matter out to myself just after the event.

"I was utterly wrong, monstrously wrong. But who could have suspected the truth?"

Thus Dr. Lewis, and I quote him, or the substance of him, as representative of most of the educated opinion of the district at the beginnings of the terror. People seized on this theory largely because it offered at least the comfort of an explanation, and any explanation, even the poorest, is better than an intolerable and terrible mystery. Besides, Dr. Lewis's theory was plausible; it explained the lack of purpose that seemed to characterize the murders. And yet—there were difficulties even from the first. It was hardly possible that a strange madman should be able to keep hidden in a countryside where any stranger is instantly noted and noticed; sooner or later he would be seen as he prowled along the lanes or across the wild places. Indeed, a drunken, cheerful, and altogether harmless tramp was arrested by a farmer and his man in the fact and act of sleeping off beer under a hedge; but the vagrant was able to prove complete and undoubted alibis, and was soon allowed to go on his wandering way.

Then another theory, or rather a variant of Dr. Lewis's theory, was started. This was to the effect that the person responsible for the outrages was, indeed, a madman; but a madman only at intervals. It was one of the members of the Porth Club, a certain Mr. Remnant, who was supposed to have originated this more subtle explanation. Mr. Remnant was a middle-aged man, who, having nothing particular to do, read a great many books by way of conquering the hours. He talked to the club—doctors, retired colonels, parsons, lawyers—about "personality," quoted various psychological textbooks in support of his contention that personality was sometimes fluid and unstable, went back to "Dr. Jekyll and Mr. Hyde" as good evidence of this proposition, and laid stress on Dr. Jekyll's speculation that the human soul, so far from being one and indivisible, might, possibly turn out to be a mere polity, a state in which dwelt many strange and incongruous citizens, whose characters were not merely unknown but altogether unsurmised by that form of consciousness which so rashly assumed that it was not only the president of the republic but also its sole citizen.

"The long and the short of it is," Mr. Remnant concluded, "that anyone of us may be the murderer, though he hasn't the faintest notion of the fact. Take Llewelyn there."

Mr. Payne Llewelyn was an elderly lawyer, a rural Tulkinghorn. He was the hereditary solicitor to the Morgans of Pentwyn. This does not sound anything tremendous to the Saxons of London; but the style is far more than noble to the Celts of West Wales; it is immemorial; Teilo Sant was of the collaterals of the first known chief of the race. And Mr. Payne Llewelyn did his best to look like the legal adviser of this ancient house. He was weighty, he was cautious, he was sound, he was secure. I have compared him to Mr. Tulkinghorn of Lincoln's Inn Fields; but Mr. Llewelyn would most certainly never have dreamed of employing his leisure in peering into the cupboards where the family skeletons were hidden. Supposing such cupboards to have existed, Mr. Payne Llewelyn would have risked large out-of-pocket expenses to furnish them with double, triple, impregnable locks. He was a new man, an *advena*, certainly; for he was partly of the Conquest, being descended on one side from Sir Payne Turberville; but he meant to stand by the old stock.

"Take Llewelyn now," said Mr. Remnant. "Look here, Llewelyn, can you produce evidence to show where you were on the night those people were murdered on the Highway? I thought not."

Mr. Llewelyn, an elderly man, as I have said, hesitated before speaking.

"I thought not," Remnant went on. "Now I say that it is perfectly possible that Llewelyn may be dealing death throughout Meirion, although in his present personality he may not have the faintest suspicion that there is another Llewelyn within him, a Llewelyn who follows murder as a fine art."

Mr. Payne Llewelyn did not at all relish Mr. Remnant's suggestion that he might well be a secret murderer, ravening for blood, remorseless as a wild beast. He thought the phrase about his following murder as a fine art was both nonsensical and in the worst taste, and his opinion was not changed when Remnant pointed out that it was used by De Quincey in the title of one of his most famous essays.

"If you had allowed me to speak," he said with some coldness of manner, "I would have told you that on Tuesday last, the night on which those unfortunate people were murdered on the Highway I was staying at the Angel Hotel, Cardiff. I had business in Cardiff, and I was detained till Wednesday afternoon."

Having given this satisfactory alibi, Mr. Payne Llewelyn left the club, and did not go near it for the rest of the week.

Remnant explained to those who stayed in the smoking room that, of course, he had merely used Mr. Llewelyn as a concrete example of his theory, which, he persisted, had the support of a considerable body of evidence.

"There are several cases of double personality on record," he declared. "And I say again that it is quite possible that these murders may have been committed by one of us in his secondary personality. Why, I may be the murderer in my Remnant B. state, though Remnant A. knows nothing whatever about it, and is perfectly convinced that he could not kill a fowl, much less a whole family. Isn't it so, Lewis?"

Dr. Lewis said it was so, in theory, but he thought not in fact.

"Most of the cases of double or multiple personality that have been investigated," he said, "have been in connection with the very dubious experiments of hypnotism, or the still more dubious experiments of spiritualism. All that sort of thing, in my opinion, is like tinkering with the works of a clock—amateur tinkering, I mean. You fumble about with the wheels and cogs and bits of mechanism that you don't really know anything about; and then you find your clock going backwards or striking 240 at tea-time. And I believe it's just the same thing with these psychical research experiments; the secondary personality is very likely the result of the tinkering and fumbling with a very delicate apparatus that we know nothing about. Mind, I can't say that it's impossible for one of us to be the Highway murderer in his B. state, as Remnant puts it. But I think it's extremely improbable. Probability is the guide of life, you know, Remnant," said Dr. Lewis, smiling at that gentleman, as if to say that he also had done a little reading in his day. "And it follows" therefore, that improbability is also the guide of life. When you get a very high degree of probability, that is, you are justified in taking it as a certainty; and on the other hand, if a supposition is highly improbable, you are justified in treating it as an impossible one. That is, in nine hundred and ninety-nine cases out of a thousand."

"How about the thousandth case?" said Remnant. "Supposing these extraordinary crimes constitute the thousandth case?"

The doctor smiled and shrugged his shoulders, being tired of the subject. But for some little time highly respectable members of Porth society would look suspiciously at one another wondering whether, after all, there mightn't be "something in it." However, both Mr. Remnant's somewhat crazy theory and Dr. Lewis's plausible theory became untenable when two more victims of an awful and mysterious death were offered up in, sacrifice, for a man was found dead in the Llanfihangel quarry, where the woman had been discovered. And on the same day a girl of fifteen was found broken on the jagged rocks under the cliffs near Porth. Now, it appeared that these two deaths must have occurred at about the same time, within an hour of one another, certainly; and the distance between the quarry and the cliffs by Black Rock is certainly twenty miles.

"A motor could do it," one man said.

But it was pointed out that there was no high road between the two places; indeed, it might be said that there was no road at all between them. There was a network of deep, narrow, and tortuous lands that wandered into one another at all manner of queer angles for, say, seventeen miles; this in the middle, as it were, between Black Rock and the quarry at Llanfihangel. But to get to the high land of the cliffs one had to take a path that went through two miles of fields; and the quarry lay a mile away from the nearest by-road in the midst of gorse and bracken and broken land. And, finally, there was no track of motor-car or motor-bicycle in the lanes which must have been followed to pass from one place to the other.

"What about an airplane, then?" said the man of the motor-car theory. Well, there was certainly an aerodrome not far from one of the two places of death; but somehow, nobody believed that the Flying Corps harbored a homicidal maniac. It seemed clear, therefore, that there must be more than one person concerned in the terror of Meirion. And Dr. Lewis himself abandoned his own theory.

"As I said to Remnant at the Club," he remarked, "improbability is the guide of life. I can't believe that there are a pack of madmen or even two madmen at large in the country. I give it up."

And now a fresh circumstance or set of circumstances became manifest to confound judgment and to awaken new and wild surmises. For at about this time people realized that none of the dreadful events that were happening all about them was so much as mentioned in the Press. I have already spoken of the fate of the *Meiros Observer*. This paper was suppressed by the authorities because it had inserted a brief paragraph about some person who had been "found dead under mysterious circumstances"; I think that paragraph referred to the first death of Llanfihangel quarry. Thenceforth, horror followed on horror, but no word was printed in any of the local journals. The curious went to the newspaper offices—there were two left in the county—but found nothing save a firm refusal to discuss the matter. And the Cardiff papers were drawn and found blank; and the London Press was apparently ignorant of the fact that crimes that had no parallel were terrorizing a whole countryside. Everybody wondered what could have happened, what was happening; and then it was whispered that the coroner would allow no inquiry to be made as to these deaths of darkness.

"In consequence of instructions received from the Home Office," one coroner was understood to have said, "I have to tell the jury that their business will be to hear the medical evidence and to bring in a verdict immediately in accordance with that evidence. I shall disallow all questions."

One jury protested. The foreman refused to bring in any verdict at all.

"Very good," said the coroner. "Then I beg to inform you, Mr. Foreman and gentlemen of the jury, that under the Defense of the Realm Act, I have power to supersede your functions, and to enter a verdict according to the evidence which has been laid before the Court as if it had been the verdict of you all."

The foreman and jury collapsed and accepted what they could not avoid. But the rumors that got abroad of all this, added to the known fact that the terror was ignored in the Press, no doubt by official command, increased the panic that was now; arising, and gave it a new direction. Clearly, people reasoned, these Government restrictions and prohibitions could only refer to the war, to some great danger in connection with the war. And that being so, it followed that the outrages which must be kept so secret were the work of the enemy, that is of concealed German agents.

The Spread of the Terror

It is time, I think, for me to make one point clear. I began this history with certain references to an extraordinary accident to an airman whose machine fell to the ground after collision with a huge flock of pigeons; and then to an explosion in a northern munition factory, an explosion, as I noted, of a very singular kind. Then I deserted the neighborhood of London, and the northern district, and dwelt on a mysterious and terrible series of events which occurred in the summer of 1915 in a Welsh county, which I have named, for convenience, Meirion.

Well, let it be understood at once that all this detail that I have given about the occurrences in Meirion does not imply that the county in the far west was alone or especially afflicted by the terror that was over the land. They tell me that in the villages about Dartmoor the stout Devonshire hearts sank as men's hearts used to sink in the time of plague and pestilence. There was horror, too, about the Norfolk Broads, and far up by Perth no one would venture on the path that leads by Scone to the wooded heights above the Tay. And in the industrial districts: I met a man by chance one day in an odd London corner who spoke with horror of what a friend had told him.

"'Ask no questions, Ned,' he says to me, 'but I tell yow a' was in Bairnigan t'other day, and a' met a pal who'd seen three hundred coffins going out of a works not far from there.'"

And then the ship that hovered outside the mouth of the Thames with all sails set and beat to and fro in the wind, and never answered any hail, and showed no light! The forts shot at her and brought down one of the masts, but she went suddenly about with a change of wind under what sail still stood, and then veered down Channel, and drove ashore at last on the sandbanks and pinewoods of Arcachon, and not a man alive on her, but only rattling heaps of bones! That last voyage of the *Semiramis* would be something horribly worth telling; but I only heard it at a distance as a yarn, and only believed it because it squared with other things that I knew for certain.

This, then, is my point; I have written of the terror as it fell on Meirion, simply because I have had opportunities of getting close there to what really happened. Third or fourth or fifth hand in the other places; but round about Porth and Merthyr Tegveth I have spoken with people who have seen the tracks of the terror with their own eyes.

Well, I have said that the people of that far western county realized, not only that death was abroad in their quiet lanes and on their peaceful hills, but that for some reason it was to be kept all secret. Newspapers might not print any news of it, the very juries summoned to investigate it were allowed to investigate nothing. And so they concluded that this veil of secrecy must somehow be connected with the war; and from this position it was not a long way to a further inference: that the murderers of innocent men and women and children were either Germans or agents of Germany. It would be just like the Huns, everybody agreed, to think out such a devilish scheme as this; and they always thought out their schemes beforehand. They hoped to seize Paris in a few weeks, but when they were beaten on the Marne they had their trenches on the Aisne ready to fall back on: it had all been prepared years before the war. And so, no doubt, they had devised this terrible plan against England in case they could not beat us in open fight: there were people ready, very likely, all over the country, who were prepared to murder and destroy everywhere as soon as they got the word. In this way the Germans intended to sow terror throughout England and fill our hearts with panic and dismay, hoping so to weaken their enemy at home that he would lose all heart over the war abroad. It was the Zeppelin notion, in another form; they were committing these horrible and mysterious outrages thinking that we should be frightened out of our wits.

It all seemed plausible enough; Germany had by this time perpetrated so many horrors and had so excelled in devilish ingenuities that no abomination seemed too abominable to be probable, or too ingeniously wicked to be beyond the tortuous malice of the Hun. But then came the questions as to who the agents of this terrible design were, as to where they lived, as to how they contrived to move unseen from field to field, from lane to lane. All sorts of fantastic attempts were made to answer these questions; but it was felt that they remained unanswered. Some suggested that the murderers landed from submarines, or flew from hiding places on the West Coast of Ireland, coming and going by night; but there were seen to be flagrant impossibilities in both these suggestions. Everybody agreed that the evil work was no doubt the work of Germany; but nobody could begin to guess how it was done. Somebody at the Club asked Remnant for his theory.

"My theory," said that ingenious person, "is that human progress is simply a long march from one inconceivable to another. Look at that airship of ours that came over Porth yesterday: ten years ago that would have been an inconceivable sight. Take the steam engine, stake printing, take the theory of gravitation: they were all inconceivable till somebody thought of them. So it is, no doubt, with this infernal dodgery that we're talking about: the Huns have found it out, and we haven't; and there you are. We can't conceive how these poor people have been murdered, because the method's inconceivable to us."

The club listened with some awe to this high argument. After Remnant had gone, one member said:

"Wonderful man, that." "Yes," said Dr. Lewis. "He was asked whether he knew something. And his reply really amounted to 'No, I don't,' But I have never heard it better put."

It was, I suppose, at about this time when the people were puzzling their heads as to the secret methods used by the Germans or their agents to accomplish their crimes that a very singular circumstance became known to a few of the Porth people. It related to the murder of the Williams family on the Highway in front of their cottage door. I do not know that I have made it plain that the old Roman road called the Highway follows the course of a long, steep hill that goes steadily westward till it slants down and droops towards the sea. On either side of the road the ground falls away, here into deep shadowy woods, here to high pastures, now and again into a field of corn, but for the most part into the wild and broken land that is characteristic of Arfon. The fields are long and narrow, stretching up the steep hillside; they fall into sudden dips and hollows, a well springs up in the midst of one and a grove of ash and thorn bends over it, shading it; and beneath it the ground is thick with reeds and rushes. And then may come on either side of such a field territories glistening with the deep growth of bracken, and rough with gorse and rugged with thickets of blackthorn, green lichen hanging strangely from the branches; such are the lands on either side of the Highway.

Now on the lower slopes of it, beneath the Williams's cottage, some three or four fields down the hill, there is a military camp. The place has been used as a camp for many years, and lately the site has been extended and huts have been erected. But a considerable number of the men were under canvas here in the summer of 1915.

On the night of the Highway murder this camp, as it appeared afterwards, was the scene of the extraordinary panic of the horses.

A GOOD MANY MEN IN the camp were asleep in their tents soon after 9:30, when the Last Post was sounded. They woke up in panic. There was a thundering sound on the steep hillside above them, and down upon the tents came half a dozen horses, mad with fright, trampling the canvas, trampling the men, bruising dozens of them and killing two.

Everything was in wild confusion, men groaning and screaming in the darkness, struggling with the canvas and the twisted ropes, shouting out, some of them, raw lads enough, that the Germans had landed, others wiping the blood from their eyes, a few, roused suddenly from heavy sleep, hitting out at one another, officers coming up at the double roaring out orders to the sergeants, a party of soldiers who were just returning to camp from the village seized with fright at what they could scarcely see or distinguish, at the wildness of the shouting and cursing and groaning that they could not understand, bolting out of the camp again and racing for their lives back to the village: everything in the maddest confusion of wild disorder.

Some of the men had seen the horses galloping down the hill as if terror itself was driving them. They scattered off into the darkness, and somehow or another found their way back in the night to their pasture above the camp. They were grazing there peacefully in the morning, and the only sign of the panic of the night before was the mud they had scattered all over themselves as they pelted through a patch of wet ground. The farmer said they were as quiet a lot as any in Meirion; he could make nothing of it.

"Indeed," he said, "I believe they must have seen the devil himself to be in such a fright as that: save the people!"

Now all this was kept as quiet as might be at the time when it happened; it became known to the men of the Porth Club in the days when they were discussing the difficult question of the German outrages, as the murders were commonly called. And this wild stampede of the farm horses was held by some to be evidence of the extraordinary and unheard of character of the dreadful agency that was at work. One of the members of the club had been told by an officer who was in the camp at the time of the panic that the horses that came charging down were in a perfect fury of fright, that he had never seen horses in such a state, and so there was endless speculation as to the nature of the sight or the sound that had driven half a dozen quiet beasts into raging madness.

Then, in the middle of this talk, two or three other incidents, quite as odd and incomprehensible, came to be known, borne on chance trickles of gossip that came into the towns from outland farms, or were carried by cottagers tramping into Porth on market day with a fowl or two and eggs and garden stuff; scraps and fragments of talk gathered by servants from the country folk and repeated—to their mistresses. And in such ways it came out that up at Plas Newydd there had been a terrible business over swarming the bees; they had turned as wild as wasps and much more savage. They had come about the people who were taking the swarms like a cloud. They settled on one man's face so that you could not see the flesh for the bees crawling all over it, and they had stung him so badly that the doctor did not know whether he would get over it, and they had chased a girl who had come out to see the swarming, and settled on her and stung her to death. Then they had gone off to a brake below the farm and got into a hollow tree there, and it was not safe to go near it, for they would come out at you by day or by night.

And much the same thing had happened, it seemed, at three or four farms and cottages where bees were kept. And there were stories, hardly so clear or so credible, of sheep dogs, mild and trusted beasts, turning as savage as wolves and injuring the farm boys in a horrible manner—in one case it was said with fatal results. It was certainly true that old Mrs. Owen's favorite Brahma-Dorking cock had gone mad; she came into Porth one Saturday morning with her face and her neck all bound up and plastered. She had gone out to her bit of a field to feed the poultry the night before, and the bird had flown at her and attacked her most savagely, inflicting some very nasty wounds before she could beat it off.

"There was a stake handy, lucky for me," she said, "and I did beat him and beat him till the life was out of him. But what is come to the world, whatever?"

Now Remnant, the man of theories, was also a man of extreme leisure. It was understood that he had succeeded to ample means when he was quite a young man, and after tasting the savors of the law, as it were, for half a dozen terms at the board of the Middle Temple, he had decided that it would be senseless to bother himself with passing examinations for a profession which he had not the faintest intention of practising. So he turned a deaf ear to the call of "Manger" ringing through the Temple Courts, and set himself out to potter amiably through the world. He had pottered all over Europe, he had looked at Africa, and had even put his head in at the door of the East, on a trip which included the Greek isles and Constantinople. Now getting into the middle fifties, he had settled at Porth for the sake, as he said, of the Gulf Stream and the fuchsia hedges, and pottered over his books and his theories and the local gossip. He was no more brutal than the general public, which revels in the details of mysterious crime; but it must be said that the terror, black though it was, was a boon to him. He peered and investigated and poked about with the relish of a man to whose life a new zest has been added. He listened attentively to the strange tales of bees and dogs and poultry that came into Porth with the country baskets of butter, rabbits, and green peas; and he evolved at last a most extraordinary theory.

Full of this discovery, as he thought it, he went one night to see Dr. Lewis and take his view of the matter.

"I want to talk to you," said Remnant to the doctor, "about what I have called provisionally, the Z Ray."

V

The Incident of the Unknown Tree

Dr. Lewis, smiling indulgently, and quite prepared for some monstrous piece of theorizing, led Remnant into the room that overlooked the terraced garden and the sea.

The doctor's house, though it was only a ten minutes' walk from the center of the town, seemed remote from all other habitations. The drive to it from the road came through a deep grove of trees and a dense shrubbery, trees were about the house on either side, mingling with neighboring groves, and below, the garden fell down, terrace by green terrace, to wild growth, a twisted path amongst red rocks, and at last to the yellow sand of a little cove. The room to which the doctor took Remnant looked over these terraces and across the water to the dim boundaries of the bay. It had French windows that were thrown wide open, and the two men sat in the soft light of the lamp—this was before the days of severe lighting regulations in the Far West—and enjoyed the sweet odors and the sweet vision of the summer evening. Then Remnant began:

"I suppose, Lewis, you've heard these extraordinary stories of bees and dogs and things that have been going about lately?"

"Certainly I have heard them. I was called in at Plas Newydd, and treated Thomas Trevor, who's only just out of danger, by the way. I certified for the poor child, Mary Trevor. She was dying when I got to the place. There was no doubt she was stung to death by bees, and I believe there were other very similar cases at Llantarnam and Morwen; none fatal, I think. What about them?"

"Well: then there are the stories of good-tempered old sheepdogs turning wicked and 'savaging' children?"

"Quite so. I haven't seen any of these cases professionally; but I believe the stories are accurate enough."

"And the old woman assaulted by her own poultry?"

"That's perfectly true. Her daughter put some stuff of their own concoction on her face and neck, and then she came to me. The wounds seemed going all right, so I told her to continue the treatment, whatever it might be."

"Very good," said Mr. Remnant. He spoke now with an italic impressiveness. *"Don't you see the link between all this and the horrible things that have been happening about here for the last month?"*

Lewis stared at Remnant in amazement. He lifted his red eyebrows and lowered them in a kind of scowl. His speech showed traces of his native accent.

"Great burning!" he exclaimed. "What on earth are you getting at now? It is madness. Do you mean to tell me that you think there is some connection between a swarm or two of bees that have turned nasty, a cross dog, and a wicked old barn-door cock and these poor people that have been pitched over the cliffs and hammered to death on the road? There's no sense in it, you know."

"I am strongly inclined to believe that there is a great deal of sense in it," replied Remnant, with extreme calmness. "Look here, Lewis, I saw you grinning the other day at the club when I was telling the fellows that in my opinion all these outrages had been committed, certainly by the Germans, but by some method of which we have no conception. But what I meant to say when I talked about inconceivables was just this: that the Williams's and the rest of them have been killed in some way that's not in theory at all, not in our theory, at all events, some way we've not contemplated, not thought of for an instant. Do you see my point?"

"Well, in a sort of way. You mean there's an absolute originality in the method? I suppose that is so. But what next?"

Remnant seemed to hesitate, partly from a sense of the portentous nature of what he was about to say, partly from a sort of half-unwillingness to part with so profound a secret.

"Well," he said, "you will allow that we have two sets of phenomena of a very extraordinary kind occurring at the same time. Don't you think that it's only reasonable to connect the two sets with one another."

"So the philosopher of Tenterden steeple and the Goodwin Sands thought, certainly," said Lewis. "But what is the connection? Those poor folks on the Highway weren't stung by bees or worried by a dog. And horses don't throw people over cliffs or stifle them in marshes."

"No; I never meant to suggest anything so absurd. It is evident to me that in all these cases of animals turning suddenly savage the cause has been terror, panic, fear. The horses that went charging into the camp were mad with fright, we know. And I say that in the other instances we have been discussing the cause was the same. The creatures were exposed to an infection of fear, and a frightened beast or bird or insect uses its weapons, whatever they may be. If, for example, there had been anybody with those horses when they took their panic they would have lashed out at him with their heels."

"Yes, I dare say that that is so. Well."

"Well; my belief is that the Germans have made an extraordinary discovery. I have called it the Z Ray. You know that the ether is merely an hypothesis; we have to suppose that it's there to account for the passage of the Marconi current from one place to another. Now, suppose that there is a psychic ether as well as a material ether, suppose that it is possible to direct irresistible impulses across this medium, suppose that these impulses are towards murder or suicide; then I think that you have an explanation of the terrible series of events that have been happening in Meirion for the last few weeks. And it is quite clear to my mind that the horses and the other creatures have been exposed to this Z Ray, and that it has produced on them the effect of terror, with ferocity as the result of terror. Now what do you say to that? Telepathy, you know, is well established; so is hypnotic suggestion. You have only to look in the Encyclopædia Britannica' to see that, and suggestion is so strong in some cases as to be an irresistible imperative. Now don't you feel that putting telepathy and suggestion together, as it were, you have more than the elements of what I call the Z Ray? I feel myself that I have more to go on in making my hypothesis than the inventor of the steam engine had in making his hypothesis when he saw the lid of the kettle bobbing up and down. What do you say?"

Dr. Lewis made no answer. He was watching the growth of a new, unknown tree in his garden.

THE DOCTOR MADE NO ANSWER to Remnant's question. For one thing, Remnant was profuse in his eloquence—he has been rigidly condensed in this history—and Lewis was tired of the sound of his voice. For another thing, he found the Z Ray theory almost too extravagant to be bearable, wild enough to tear patience to tatters. And then as the tedious argument continued Lewis became conscious that there was something strange about the night.

It was a dark summer night. The moon was old and faint, above the Dragon's Head across the bay, and the air was very still. It was so still that Lewis had noted that not a leaf stirred on the very tip of a high tree that stood out against the sky; and yet he knew that he was listening to some sound that he could not determine or define. It was not the wind in the leaves, it was not the gentle wash of the water of the sea against the rocks; that latter sound he could distinguish quite easily. But there was something else. It was scarcely a sound; it was as if the air itself trembled and fluttered, as the air trembles in a church when they open the great pedal pipes of the organ.

The doctor listened intently. It was not an illusion, the sound was not in his own head, as he had suspected for a moment; but for the life of him he could not make out whence it came or what it was. He gazed down into the night over the terraces of his garden, now sweet with the scent of the flowers of the night; tried to peer over the tree-tops across the sea towards the Dragon's Head. It struck him suddenly that this strange fluttering vibration of the air might be the noise of a distant aeroplane or airship; there was not the usual droning hum, but this sound might be caused by a new type of engine. A new type of engine? Possibly it was an enemy airship; their range, it had been said, was getting longer; and Lewis was just going to call Remnant's attention to the sound, to its possible cause, and to the possible danger that might be hovering over them, when he saw something that caught his breath and his heart with wild amazement and a touch of terror.

He had been staring upward into the sky, and, about to speak to Remnant, he had let his eyes drop for an instant. He looked down towards the trees in the garden, and saw with utter astonishment that one had changed its shape in the few hours that had passed since the setting of the sun. There was a thick grove of ilexes bordering the lowest terrace, and above them rose one tall pine, spreading its head of sparse, dark branches dark against the sky.

As Lewis glanced down over the terraces he saw that the tall pine tree was no longer there. In its place there rose above the ilexes what might have been a greater ilex; there was the blackness of a dense growth of foliage rising like a broad and far-spreading and rounded cloud over the lesser trees.

Here, then was a sight wholly incredible, impossible. It is doubtful whether the process of the human mind in such a case has ever been analyzed and registered; it is doubtful whether it ever can be registered. It is hardly fair to bring in the mathematician, since he deals with absolute truth (so far as mortality can conceive absolute truth); but how would a mathematician feel if he were suddenly confronted with a two-sided triangle? I suppose he would instantly become a raging madman;

and Lewis, staring wide-eyed and wild-eyed at a dark and spreading tree which his own experience informed him was not there, felt for an instant that shock which should affront us all when we first realize the intolerable antinomy of Achilles and the Tortoise. Common sense tells us that Achilles will flash past the tortoise almost with the speed of the lightning; the inflexible truth of mathematics assures us that till the earth boils and the heavens cease to endure the Tortoise must still be in advance; and thereupon we should, in common decency, go mad. We do not go mad, because, by special grace, we are certified that, in the final: court of appeal, all science is a lie, even the highest science of all; and so we simply grin at Achilles and the Tortoise, as we grin at Darwin, deride Huxley, and laugh at Herbert Spencer.

Dr. Lewis did not grin. He glared into the dimness of the night, at the great spreading tree that he knew could not be there. And as he gazed he saw that what at first appeared the dense blackness of foliage was fretted and starred with wonderful appearances of lights and colors.

Afterwards he said to me: "I remember thinking to myself: 'Look here, I am not delirious; my temperature is perfectly normal. I am not drunk; I only had a pint of Graves with my dinner, over three hours ago. I have not eaten any poisonous fungus; I have not taken *Anhelonium Lewinii* experimentally. So, now then! What is happening?'"

The night had gloomed over; clouds obscured the faint moon and the misty stars. Lewis rose, with some kind of warning and inhibiting gesture to Remnant, who, he was conscious was gaping at him in astonishment. He walked to the open French window, and took a pace forward on to the path outside, and looked, very intently, at the dark shape of the tree, down below the sloping garden, above the washing of the waves. He shaded the light of the lamp behind him by holding his hands on each side of his eyes.

The mass of the tree—the tree that couldn't be there—stood out against the sky, but not so clearly, now that the clouds had rolled up. Its edges, the limits of its leafage, were not so distinct. Lewis thought that he could detect some sort of quivering movement in it; though the air was at a dead calm. It was a night on which one might hold up a lighted match and watch it burn without any wavering or inclination of the flame.

"You know," said Lewis, "how a bit of burnt paper will sometimes hang over the coals before it goes up the chimney, and little worms of fire will shoot through it. It was like that, if you should be standing some distance away. Just threads and hairs of yellow light I saw, and specks and sparks of fire, and then a twinkling of a ruby no bigger than a pin point, and a green wandering in the black, as if an emerald were crawling, and then little veins of deep blue. 'Woe is me!' I said to myself in Welsh, 'What is all this color and burning?'

"And, then, at that very moment there came a thundering rap at the door of the room inside, and there was my man telling me that I was wanted directly up at the Garth, as old Mr. Trevor Williams had been taken very bad. I knew his heart was not worth much, so I had to go off directly, and leave Remnant to make what he could of it all."

VI

Mr. Remnant's Z Ray

D r. Lewis was kept sometime at the Garth. It was past twelve when he got back to his house.

He went quickly to the room that overlooked the garden and the sea and threw open the French window and peered into the darkness. There, dim indeed against the dim sky but unmistakable, was the tall pine with its sparse branches, high above the dense growth of the ilex trees. The strange boughs which had amazed him had vanished; there was no appearance now of colors or of fires.

He drew his chair up to the open window and sat there gazing and wondering far into the night, till brightness came upon the sea and sky, and the forms of the trees in the garden grew clear and evident. He went up to his bed at last filled with a great perplexity, still asking questions to which there was no answer.

The doctor did not say anything about the strange tree to Remnant. When they next met, Lewis said that he had thought there was a man hiding amongst the bushes—this in explanation of that warning gesture he had used, and of his going out into the garden and staring into the night. He concealed the truth because he dreaded the Remnant doctrine that would undoubtedly be produced; indeed, he hoped that he had heard the last of the theory of the Z Ray. But Remnant firmly reopened this subject.

"We were interrupted just as I was putting my case to you," he said. "And to sum it all up, it amounts to this: that the Huns have made one of the great leaps of science. They are sending 'suggestions' (which amount to irresistible commands) over here, and the persons affected are seized with suicidal or homicidal mania. The people who were killed by falling over the cliffs or into the quarry probably committed suicide; and so with the man and boy who were found in the bog. As to the Highway case, you remember that Thomas Evans said that he stopped and talked to Williams on the night of the murder. In my opinion Evans was the murderer. He came under the influence of the Ray, became a homicidal maniac in an instant, snatched Williams's spade from his hand and killed him and the others."

"The bodies were found by me on the road."

"It is possible that the first impact of the Ray produces violent nervous excitement, which would manifest itself externally. Williams might have called to his wife to come and see what was the matter with Evans. The children would naturally follow their mother. It seems to me simple. And as for the animals—the horses, dogs, and so forth, they as I say, were no doubt panic stricken by the Ray, and hence driven to frenzy."

"Why should Evans have murdered Williams instead of Williams murdering Evans? Why should the impact of the Ray affect one and not the other?"

"Why does one man react violently to a certain drug, while it makes no impression on another man? Why is A able to drink a bottle of whisky and remain sober, while B is turned into something very like a lunatic after he has drunk three glasses?"

"It is a question of idiosyncrasy," said the doctor.

"Is idiosyncrasy Greek for 'I don't know'?" asked Remnant.

"Not at all," said Lewis, smiling blandly. "I mean that in some diatheses whisky—as you have mentioned whisky—appears not to be pathogenic, or at all events not immediately pathogenic. In other cases, as you very justly observed, there seems to be a very marked cachexia associated with the exhibition of the spirit in question, even in comparatively small doses."

Under this cloud of professional verbiage Lewis escaped from the Club and from Remnant. He did not want to hear anymore about that Dreadful Ray, because he felt sure that the Ray was all nonsense. But asking himself why he felt this certitude in the matter he had to confess that he didn't know. An aeroplane, he reflected, was all nonsense before it was made; and he remembered talking in the early nineties to a friend of his about the newly discovered X Rays. The friend laughed incredulously, evidently didn't believe a word of it, till Lewis told him that there was an article on the subject in the current number of the *Saturday Review*; whereupon the unbeliever said, "Oh, is that so? Oh, really. I *see*," and was converted on the X Ray faith on the spot. Lewis, remembering this talk, marveled at the strange processes of the human mind, its illogical and yet all-compelling *ergos*, and wondered whether he himself was only waiting for an article on the Z Ray in the *Saturday Review* to become a devout believer in the doctrine of Remnant.

But he wondered with far more fervor as to the extraordinary thing he had seen in his own garden with his own eyes. The tree that changed all its shape for an hour or two of the night, the growth of strange boughs, the apparition of secret fires among them, the sparkling of emerald and ruby lights: how could one fail to be afraid with great amazement at the thought of such a mystery?

DR. LEWIS'S THOUGHTS WERE DISTRACTED FROM the incredible adventure of the tree by the visit of his sister and her husband. Mr. and Mrs. Merritt lived in a well-known manufacturing town of the Midlands, which was now, of course, a center of munition work. On the day of their arrival at Porth, Mrs. Merritt, who was tired after the long, hot journey, went to bed early, and Merritt and Lewis went into the room by the garden for their talk and tobacco. They spoke of the year that had passed since their last meeting, of the weary dragging of the war, of friends that had perished in it, of the hopelessness of an early ending of all this misery. Lewis said nothing of the terror that was on the land. One does not greet a tired man who is come to a quiet, sunny place for relief from black smoke and work and worry with a tale of horror. Indeed, the doctor saw that his brother-in-law looked far from well. And he seemed "jumpy"; there was an occasional twitch of his mouth that Lewis did not like at all.

"Well," said the doctor, after an interval of silence and port wine, "I am glad to see you here again. Porth always suits you. I don't think you're looking quite up to your usual form. But three weeks of Meirion air will do wonders."

"Well, I hope it will," said the other. "I am not up to the mark. Things are not going well at Midlingham."

"Business is all right, isn't it?"

"Yes. Business is all right. But there are other things that are all wrong. We are living under a reign of terror. It comes to that."

"What on earth do you mean?"

"Well, I suppose I may tell you what I know. It's not much. I didn't dare write it. But do you know that at everyone of the munition works in Midlingham and all about it there's a guard of soldiers with drawn bayonets and loaded rifles day and night? Men with bombs, too. And machine-guns at the big factories."

"German spies?"

"You don't want Lewis guns to fight spies with. Nor bombs. Nor a platoon of men. I woke up last night. It was the machine-gun at Benington's Army Motor Works. Firing like fury. And then bang! bang! bang! That was the hand bombs."

"But what against?"

"Nobody knows."

"Nobody knows what is happening," Merritt repeated, and he went on to describe the bewilderment and terror that hung like a cloud over the great industrial city in the Midlands, how the feeling of concealment, of some intolerable secret danger that must not be named, was worst of all.

"A young fellow I know," he said, "was on short leave the other day from the front, and he spent it with his people at Belmont—that's about four miles out of Midlingham, you know. 'Thank God,' he said to me, 'I am going back tomorrow. It's no good saying that the Wipers salient is nice, because it isn't. But it's a damned sight better than this. At the front you know what you're up against anyhow.' At Midlingham everybody has the feeling that we're up against something awful and we don't know what; it's that that makes people inclined to whisper. There's terror in the air."

Merritt made a sort of picture of the great town cowering in its fear of an unknown danger.

"People are afraid to go about alone at nights in the outskirts. They make up parties at the stations to go home together if it's anything like dark, or if there are any lonely bits on their way."

"But why? I don't understand. What are they afraid of?"

"Well, I told you about my being awakened up the other night with the machine-guns at the motor works rattling away, and the bombs exploding and making the most terrible noise. That sort of thing alarms one, you know. It's only natural."

"Indeed, it must be very terrifying. You mean, then, there is a general nervousness about, a vague sort of apprehension that makes people inclined to herd together?"

"There's that, and there's more. People have gone out that have never come back. There were a couple of men in the train to Holme, arguing about the quickest way to get to Northend, a sort of outlying part of Holme where they both lived. They argued all the way out of Midlingham, one saying that the high road was the quickest though it was the longest way. 'It's the quickest going because it's the cleanest going,' he said."

"The other chap fancied a short cut across the fields, by the canal. 'It's half the distance,' he kept on. 'Yes, if you don't lose your way,' said the other. Well, it appears they put an even half-crown on it, and each was to try his own way when they got out of the train. It was arranged that they were to meet at the 'Wagon' in Northend. 'I shall be at the "Wagon" first,' said the man who believed in the short cut, and with that he climbed over the stile and made off across the fields. It wasn't late enough to be really dark, and a lot of them thought he might win the stakes. But he never turned up at the Wagon—or anywhere else for the matter of that."

"What happened to him?"

"He was found lying on his back in the middle of a field—some way from the path. He was dead. The doctors said he'd been suffocated. Nobody knows how. Then there have been other cases. We whisper about them at Midlingham, but we're afraid to speak out."

Lewis was ruminating all this profoundly. Terror in Meirion and terror far away in the heart of England; but at Midlingham, so far as he could gather from these stories of soldiers on guard, of crackling machine-guns, it was a case of an organized attack on the munitioning of the army. He felt that he did not know enough to warrant his deciding that the terror of Meirion and of Stratfordshire were one.

Then Merritt began again:

"There's a queer story going about, when the door's shut and the curtain's drawn, that is, as to a place right out in the country over the other side of Midlingham; on the opposite side to Dunwich. They've built one of the new factories out there, a great red brick town of sheds they tell me it is, with a tremendous chimney. It's not been finished more than a month or six weeks. They plumped it down right in the middle of the fields, by the line, and they're building huts for the workers as fast as they can but up to the present the men are billeted all about, up and down the line.

"About two hundred yards from this place there's an old footpath, leading from the station and the main road up to a small hamlet on the hillside. Part of the way this path goes by a pretty large wood, most of it thick undergrowth. I should think there must be twenty acres of wood, more or less. As it happens, I used this path once long ago; and I can tell you it's a black place of nights.

"A man had to go this way one night. He got along all right till he came to the wood. And then he said his heart dropped out of his body.

ARTHUR MACHEN

It was awful to hear the noises in that wood. Thousands of men were in it, he swears that. It was full of rustling, and pattering of feet trying to go dainty, and the crack of dead boughs lying on the ground as someone trod on them, and swishing of the grass, and some sort of chattering speech going on, that sounded, so he said, as if the dead sat in their bones and talked! He ran for his life, anyhow; across fields, over hedges, through brooks. He must have run, by his tale, ten miles out of his way before he got home to his wife, and beat at the door, and broke in, and bolted it behind him."

"There is something rather alarming about any wood at night," said Dr. Lewis.

Merritt shrugged his shoulders.

"People say that the Germans have landed, and that they are hiding in underground places all over the country."

VII

The Case of the Hidden Germans

Lewis gasped for a moment, silent in contemplation of the magnificence of rumor. The Germans already landed, hiding underground, striking by night, secretly, terribly, at the power of England! Here was a conception which made the myth of "The Russians" a paltry fable; before which the Legend of Mons was an ineffectual thing.

It was monstrous. And yet—

He looked steadily at Merritt; a square-headed, black-haired, solid sort of man. He had symptoms of nerves about him for the moment, certainly, but one could not wonder at that, whether the tales he told were true, or whether he merely believed them to be true. Lewis had known his brother-in-law for twenty years or more, and had always found him a sure man in his own small world. "But then," said the doctor to himself, "those men, if they once get out of the ring of that little world of theirs, they are lost. Those are the men that believed in Madame Blavatsky."

"Well," he said, "what do you think yourself? The Germans landed and hiding somewhere about the country: there's something extravagant in the notion, isn't there?"

"I don't know what to think. You can't get over the facts. There are the soldiers with their rifles and their guns at the works all over Stratfordshire, and those guns go off. I told you I'd heard them. Then who are the soldiers shooting at? That's what we ask ourselves at Midlingham."

"Quite so; I quite understand. It's an extraordinary state of things."

"It's more than extraordinary; it's an awful state of things. It's terror in the dark, and there's nothing worse than that. As that young fellow I was telling you about said, 'At the front you do know what you're up against.'"

"And people really believe that a number of Germans have somehow got over to England and have hid themselves underground?"

"People say they've got a new kind of poison-gas. Some think that they dig underground places and make the gas there, and lead it by secret pipes into the shops; others say that they throw gas bombs into the factories. It must be worse than anything they've used in France, from what the authorities say."

"The authorities? Do *they* admit that there are Germans in hiding about Midlingham?"

"No. They call it 'explosions.' But we know it isn't explosions. We know in the Midlands what an explosion sounds like and looks like. And we know that the people killed in these 'explosions' are put into their coffins in the works. Their own relations are not allowed to see them."

"And so you believe in the German theory?"

"If I do, it's because one must believe in something. Some say they've seen the gas. I heard that a man living in Dunwich saw it one night like a black cloud with sparks of fire in it floating over the tops of the trees by Dunwich Common."

The light of an ineffable amazement came into Lewis's eyes. The night of Remnant's visit, the trembling vibration of the air, the dark tree that had grown in his garden since the setting of the sun, the strange leafage that was starred with burning, with emerald and ruby fires, and all vanished away when he returned from his visit to the Garth; and such a leafage had appeared as a burning cloud far in the heart of England: what intolerable mystery, what tremendous doom was signified in this? But one thing was clear and certain: that the terror of Meirion was also the terror of the Midlands.

Lewis made up his mind most firmly that if possible all this should be kept from his brother-in-law. Merritt had come to Porth as to a city of refuge from the horrors of Midlingham; if it could be managed he should be spared the knowledge that the cloud of terror had gone before him and hung black over the western land. Lewis passed the port and said in an even voice:

"Very strange, indeed; a black cloud with sparks of fire?"

"I can't answer for it, you know; it's only a rumor."

"Just so; and you think or you're inclined to think that this and all the rest you've told me is to be put down to the hidden Germans?"

"As I say; because one must think something."

"I quite see your point. No doubt, if it's true, it's the most awful blow that has ever been dealt at any nation in the whole history of man. The enemy established in our vitals! But is it possible, after all? How could it have been worked?"

Merritt told Lewis how it had been worked, or rather, how people said it had been worked. The idea, he said, was that this was a part, and a most important part, of the great German plot to destroy England and the British Empire.

The scheme had been prepared years ago, some thought soon after the Franco-Prussian War. Moltke had seen that the invasion of England (in the ordinary sense of the term invasion) presented very great difficulties. The matter was constantly in discussion in the inner military and high political circles, and the general trend of opinion in these quarters was that at the best, the invasion of England would involve Germany in the gravest difficulties, and leave France in the position of the *tertius gaudens*. This was the state of affairs when a very high Prussian personage was approached by the Swedish professor, Huvelius.

Thus Merritt, and here I would say in parenthesis that this Huvelius was by all accounts an extraordinary man. Considered personally and apart from his writings he would appear to have been a most amiable individual. He was richer than the generality of Swedes, certainly far richer than the average university professor in Sweden. But his shabby, green frock-coat, and his battered, furry hat were notorious in the university town where he lived. No one laughed, because it was well known that Professor Huvelius spent every penny of his private means and a large portion of his official stipend on works of kindness and charity. He hid his head in a garret, someone said, in order that others might be able to swell on the first floor. It was told of him that he restricted himself to a diet of dry bread and coffee for a month in order that a poor woman of the streets, dying of consumption, might enjoy luxuries in hospital.

And this was the man who wrote the treatise "De Facinore Humano"; to prove the infinite corruption of the human race.

Oddly enough, Professor Huvelius wrote the most cynical book in the world—Hobbes preaches rosy sentimentalism in comparison— with the very highest motives. He held that a very large part of human misery, misadventure, and sorrow was due to the false convention that the heart of man was naturally and in the main well disposed and kindly, if not exactly righteous. "Murderers, thieves, assassins, violators, and all the host of the abominable," he says in one passage, "are created by the false pretense and foolish credence of human virtue. A lion in a cage is a fierce beast, indeed; but what will he be if we declare him to be a lamb and open the doors of his den? Who will be guilty of the deaths of the men, women and children whom he will surely devour, save those who unlocked the cage?" And he goes on to show that kings and the rulers of the peoples could decrease the sum of human misery to a vast extent by acting on the doctrine of human wickedness. "War," he declares, "which is one of the worst of evils, will always continue to exist. But a wise king will desire a brief war rather than a lengthy one, a short evil rather than a long evil. And this not from the benignity of his heart towards his enemies, for we have seen that the human heart is naturally malignant, but because he desires to conquer, and to conquer easily, without a great expenditure of men or of treasure, knowing that if he can accomplish this feat his people will love him and his crown will be secure. So he will wage brief victorious wars, and not only spare his own nation, but the nation of the enemy, since in a short war the loss is less on both sides than in a long war. And so from evil will come good."

And how, asks Huvelius, are such wars to be waged? The wise prince, he replies, will begin by assuming the enemy to be infinitely corruptible and infinitely stupid, since stupidity and corruption are the chief characteristics of man. So the prince will make himself friends in the very councils of his enemy, and also amongst the populace, bribing the wealthy by proffering to them the opportunity of still greater wealth, and winning the poor by swelling words. "For, contrary to the common opinion, it is the wealthy who are greedy of wealth; while the populace are to be gained by talking to them about liberty, their unknown god. And so much are they enchanted by the words liberty, freedom, and such like, that the wise can go to the poor, rob them of what little they have, dismiss them with a hearty kick, and win their hearts and their votes forever, if only they will assure them that the treatment which they have received is called liberty."

Guided by these principles, says Huvelius, the wise prince will entrench himself in the country that he desires to conquer; "nay, with but little trouble, he may actually and literally throw his garrisons into the heart of the enemy country before war has begun."

This is a long and tiresome parenthesis; but it is necessary as explaining the long tale which Merritt told his brother-in-law, he having received it from some magnate of the Midlands, who had traveled in Germany. It is probable that the story was suggested in the first place by the passage from Huvelius which I have just quoted.

Merritt knew nothing of the real Huvelius, who was all but a saint; he thought of the Swedish professor as a monster of iniquity, "worse," as he said, "than Neech"—meaning, no doubt, Nietzsche.

So he told the story of how Huvelius had sold his plan to the Germans; a plan for filling England with German soldiers. Land was to be bought in certain suitable and well-considered places, Englishmen were to be bought as the apparent owners of such land, and secret excavations were to be made, till the country was literally undermined. A subterranean Germany, in fact, was to be dug under selected districts of England; there were to be great caverns, underground cities, well drained, well ventilated, supplied with water, and in these places vast stores both of food and of munitions were to be accumulated, year after year, till "the Day" dawned. And then, warned in time, the secret garrison would leave shops, hotels, offices, villas, and vanish underground, ready to begin their work of bleeding England at the heart.

"That's what Henson told me," said Merritt at the end of his long story. "Henson, head of the Buckley Iron and Steel Syndicate. He has been a lot in Germany."

"Well," said Lewis, "of course, it may be so. If it is so, it is terrible beyond words."

Indeed, he found something horribly plausible in the story. It was an extraordinary plan, of course; an unheard of scheme; but it did not seem impossible. It was the Trojan Horse on a gigantic scale; indeed, he reflected, the story of the horse with the warriors concealed within it which was dragged into the heart of Troy by the deluded Trojans themselves might be taken as a prophetic parable of what had happened to England—if Henson's theory were well founded. And this theory certainly squared with what one had heard of German preparations in Belgium and in France: emplacements for guns ready for the invader, German manufactories which were really German forts on Belgian soil, the caverns by the Aisne made ready for the cannon; indeed, Lewis thought he remembered something about suspicious concrete tennis-courts on the heights commanding London. But a German army hidden under English ground! It was a thought to chill the stoutest heart.

And it seemed from that wonder of the burning tree, that the enemy mysteriously and terribly present at Midlingham, was present also in Meirion. Lewis, thinking of the country as he knew it, of its wild and desolate hillsides, its deep woods, its wastes and solitary places, could not but confess that no more fit region could be found for the deadly enterprise of secret men. Yet, he thought again, there was but little harm to be done in Meirion to the armies of England or to their munitionment. They were working for panic terror? Possibly that might be so; but the camp under the Highway? That should be their first object, and no harm had been done there.

Lewis did not know that since the panic of the horses men had died terribly in that camp; that it was now a fortified place, with a deep, broad trench, a thick tangle of savage barbed wire about it, and a machine-gun planted at each corner.

VIII

What Mr. Merritt Found

M r. Merritt began to pick up his health and spirits a good deal. For the first morning or two of his stay at the doctor's he contented himself with a very comfortable deck chair close to the house, where he sat under the shade of an old mulberry tree beside his wife and watched the bright sunshine on the green lawns, on the creamy crests of the waves, on the headlands of that glorious coast, purple even from afar with the imperial glow of the heather, on the white farmhouses gleaming in the sunlight, high over the sea, far from any turmoil, from any troubling of men.

The sun was hot, but the wind breathed all the while gently, incessantly, from the east, and Merritt, who had come to this quiet place, not only from dismay, but from the stifling and oily airs of the smoky Midland town, said that that east wind, pure and clear and like well water from the rock, was new life to him. He ate a capital dinner, at the end of his first day at Porth and took rosy views. As to what they had been talking about the night before, he said to Lewis, no doubt there must be trouble of some sort, and perhaps bad trouble; still, Kitchener would soon put it all right.

So things went on very well. Merritt began to stroll about the garden, which was full of the comfortable spaces, groves, and surprises that only country gardens know. To the right of one of the terraces he found an arbor or summer-house covered with white roses, and he was as pleased as if he had discovered the Pole. He spent a whole day there, smoking and lounging and reading a rubbishy sensational story, and declared that the Devonshire roses had taken many years off his age. Then on the other side of the garden there was a filbert grove that he had never explored on any of his former visits; and again there was a find. Deep in the shadow of the filberts was a bubbling well, issuing from rocks, and all manner of green, dewy ferns growing about it and above it, and an angelica springing beside it. Merritt knelt on his knees, and hollowed his hand and drank the well water. He said (over his port) that night that if all water were like the water of the filbert well the world would turn to teetotalism. It takes a townsman to relish the manifold and exquisite joys of the country.

ARTHUR MACHEN

It was not till he began to venture abroad that Merritt found that something was lacking of the old rich peace that used to dwell in Meirion. He had a favorite walk which he never neglected, year after year. This walk led along the cliffs towards Meiros, and then one could turn inland and return to Porth by deep winding lanes that went over the Allt. So Merritt set out early one morning and got as far as a sentry-box at the foot of the path that led up to the cliff. There was a sentry pacing up and down in front of the box, and he called on Merritt to produce his pass, or to turn back to the main road. Merritt was a good deal put out, and asked the doctor about this strict guard. And the doctor was surprised.

"I didn't know they had put their bar up there," he said. "I suppose it's wise. We are certainly in the far West here; still, the Germans might slip round and raid us and do a lot of damage just because Meirion is the last place we should expect them to go for."

"But there are no fortifications, surely, on the cliff?"

"Oh, no; I never heard of anything of the kind there."

"Well, what's the point of forbidding the public to go on the cliff, then? I can quite understand putting a sentry on the top to keep a look-out for the enemy. What I don't understand is a sentry at the bottom who can't keep a look-out for anything, as he can't see the sea. And why warn the public off the cliffs? I couldn't facilitate a German landing by standing on Pengareg, even if I wanted to."

"It is curious," the doctor agreed. "Some military reasons, I suppose."

He let the matter drop, perhaps because the matter did not affect him. People who live in the country all the year round, country doctors certainly, are little given to desultory walking in search of the picturesque.

Lewis had no suspicion that sentries whose object was equally obscure were being dotted all over the country. There was a sentry, for example, by the quarry at Llanfihangel, where the dead woman and the dead sheep had been found some weeks before. The path by the quarry was used a good deal, and its closing would have inconvenienced the people of the neighborhood very considerably. But the sentry had his box by the side of the track and had his orders to keep everybody strictly to the path, as if the quarry were a secret fort.

It was not known till a month or two ago that one of these sentries was himself a victim of the terror. The men on duty at this place were given certain very strict orders, which from the nature of the case, must have seemed to them unreasonable. For old soldiers, orders are orders;

but here was a young bank clerk, scarcely in training for a couple of months, who had not begun to appreciate the necessity of hard, literal obedience to an order which seemed to him meaningless. He found himself on a remote and lonely hillside, he had not the faintest notion that his every movement was watched; and he disobeyed a certain instruction that had been given him. The post was found deserted by the relief; the sentry's dead body was found at the bottom of the quarry.

This by the way; but Mr. Merritt discovered again and again that things happened to hamper his walks and his wanderings. Two or three miles from Porth there is a great marsh made by the Afon river before it falls into the sea, and here Merritt had been accustomed to botanize mildly. He had learned pretty accurately the causeways of solid ground that lead through the sea of swamp and ooze and soft yielding soil, and he set out one hot afternoon determined to make a thorough exploration of the marsh, and this time to find that rare Bog Bean, that he felt sure, must grow somewhere in its wide extent.

He got into the by-road that skirts the marsh, and to the gate which he had always used for entrance.

There was the scene as he had known it always, the rich growth of reeds and flags and rushes, the mild black cattle grazing on the "islands" of firm turf, the scented procession of the meadowsweet, the royal glory of the loosestrife, flaming pennons, crimson and golden, of the giant dock.

But they were bringing out a dead man's body through the gate.

A laboring man was holding open the gate on the marsh. Merritt, horrified, spoke to him and asked who it was, and how it had happened.

"They do say he was a visitor at Porth. Somehow he has been drowned in the marsh, whatever."

"But it's perfectly safe. I've been all over it a dozen times."

"Well, indeed, we did always think so. If you did slip by accident, like, and fall into the water, it was not so deep; it was easy enough to climb out again. And this gentleman was quite young, to look at him, poor man; and he has come to Meirion for his pleasure and holiday and found his death in it!"

"Did he do it on purpose? Is it suicide?"

"They say he had no reasons to do that."

Here the sergeant of police in charge of the party interposed, according to orders, which he himself did not understand.

"A terrible thing, sir, to be sure, and a sad pity; and I am sure this is not the sort of sight you have come to see down in Meirion this beautiful summer. So don't you think, sir, that it would be more pleasant like, if you would leave us to this sad business of ours? I have heard many gentlemen staying in Porth say that there is nothing to beat the view from the hill over there, not in the whole of Wales."

Everyone is polite in Meirion, but somehow Merritt understood that, in English, this speech meant "move on."

MERRITT MOVED BACK TO PORTH—HE was not in the humor for any idle, pleasurable strolling after so dreadful a meeting with death. He made some inquiries in the town about the dead man, but nothing seemed known of him. It was said that he had been on his honeymoon, that he had been staying at the Porth Castle Hotel; but the people of the hotel declared that they had never heard of such a person. Merritt got the local paper at the end of the week; there was not a word in it of any fatal accident in the marsh. He met the sergeant of police in the street. That officer touched his helmet with the utmost politeness and a "hope you are enjoying yourself, sir; indeed you do look a lot better already"; but as to the poor man who was found drowned or stifled in the marsh, he knew nothing.

The next day Merritt made up his mind to go to the marsh to see whether he could find anything to account for so strange a death. What he found was a man with an armlet standing by the gate. The armlet had the letters "C.W." on it, which are understood to mean Coast Watcher. The Watcher "said he had strict instructions to keep everybody away from the marsh. Why? He didn't know, but some said that the river was changing its course since the new railway embankment was built, and the marsh had become dangerous to people who didn't know it thoroughly.

"Indeed, sir," he added, "it is part of my orders not to set foot on the other side of that gate myself, not for one scrag-end of a minute."

Merritt glanced over the gate incredulously. The marsh looked as it had always looked; there was plenty of sound, hard ground to walk on; he could see the track that he used to follow as firm as ever. He did not believe in the story of the changing course of the river, and Lewis said he had never heard of anything of the kind. But Merritt had put the question in the middle of general conversation; he had not led up to it from any discussion of the death in the marsh, and so the doctor was taken unawares. If he had known of the connection in

Merritt's mind between the alleged changing of the Afon's course and the tragical event in the marsh, no doubt he would have confirmed the official explanation. He was, above all things, anxious to prevent his sister and her husband from finding out that the invisible hand of terror that ruled at Midlingham was ruling also in Meirion.

Lewis himself had little doubt that the man who was found dead in the marsh had been struck down by the secret agency, whatever it was, that had already accomplished so much of evil; but it was a chief part of the terror that no one knew for certain that this or that particular event was to be ascribed to it. People do occasionally fall over cliffs through their own carelessness, and as the case of Garcia, the Spanish sailor, showed, cottagers and their wives and children are now and then the victims of savage and purposeless violence. Lewis had never wandered about the marsh himself; but Remnant had pottered round it and about it, and declared that the man who met his death there—his name was never known, in Porth at all events—must either have committed suicide by deliberately lying prone in the ooze and stifling himself, or else must have been held down in it. There were no details available, so it was clear that the authorities had classified this death with the others; still, the man might have committed suicide, or he might have had a sudden seizure and fallen in the slimy water face-downwards. And so on: it was possible to believe that case A *or* B *or* C was in the category of ordinary accidents or ordinary crimes. But it was not possible to believe that A *and* B *and* C were all in that category. And thus it was to the end, and thus it is now. We know that the terror reigned, and how it reigned, but there were many dreadful events ascribed to its rule about which there must always be room for doubt.

For example, there was the case of the *Mary Ann*, the rowing-boat which came to grief in so strange a manner, almost under Merritt's eyes. In my opinion he was quite wrong in associating the sorry fate of the boat and her occupants with a system of signaling by flashlights which he detected or thought that he detected, on the afternoon in which the *Mary Ann* was capsized. I believe his signaling theory to be all nonsense, in spite of the naturalized German governess who was lodging with her employers in the suspected house. But, on the other hand, there is no doubt in my own mind that the boat was overturned and those in it drowned by the work of the terror.

IX

The Light on the Water

Let it be noted carefully that so far Merritt had not the slightest suspicion that the terror of Midlingham was quick over. Meirion. Lewis had watched and shepherded him carefully. He had let out no suspicion of what had happened in Meirion, and before taking his brother-in-law to the club he had passed round a hint among the members. He did not tell the truth about Midlingham—and here again is a point of interest, that as the terror deepened the general public cooperated voluntarily, and, one would say, almost subconsciously, with the authorities in concealing what they knew from one another—but he gave out a desirable portion of the truth: that his brother-in-law was "nervy," not by any means up to the mark, and that it was therefore desirable that he should be spared the knowledge of the intolerable and tragic mysteries which were being enacted all about them.

"He knows about that poor fellow who was found in the marsh," said Lewis, "and he has a kind of vague suspicion that there is something out of the common about the case; but no more than that."

"A clear case of suggested, or rather commanded suicide," said Remnant. "I regard it as a strong confirmation of my theory."

"Perhaps so," said the doctor, dreading lest he might have to hear about the Z Ray all over again. "But please don't let anything out to him; I want him to get built up thoroughly before he goes back to Midlingham."

Then, on the other hand, Merritt was as still as death about the doings of the Midlands; he hated to think of them, much more to speak of them; and thus, as I say, he and the men at the Porth Club kept their secrets from one another; and thus, from the beginning to the end of the terror, the links were not drawn together. In many cases, no doubt, A and B met everyday and talked familiarly, it may be confidentially, on other matters of all sorts, each having in his possession half of the truth, which he concealed from the other. So the two halves were never put together to make a whole.

Merritt, as the doctor guessed, had a kind of uneasy feeling—it scarcely amounted to a suspicion—as to the business of the marsh; chiefly because he thought the official talk about the railway embankment and the course of the river rank nonsense. But finding that nothing more happened, he let the matter drop from his mind, and settled himself down to enjoy his holiday.

He found to his delight that there were no sentries or watchers to hinder him from the approach to Larnac Bay, a delicious cove, a place where the ashgrove and the green meadow and the glistening bracken sloped gently down to red rocks and firm yellow sands. Merritt remembered a rock that formed a comfortable seat, and here he established himself of a golden afternoon, and gazed at the blue of the sea and the crimson bastions and bays of the coast as it bent inward to Sarnau and swept out again southward to the odd-shaped promontory called the Dragon's Head. Merritt gazed on, amused by the antics of the porpoises who were tumbling and splashing and gamboling a little way out at sea, charmed by the pure and radiant air that was so different from the oily smoke that often stood for heaven at Midlingham, and charmed, too, by the white farmhouses dotted here and there on the heights of the curving coast.

Then he noticed a little row-boat at about two hundred yards from the shore. There were two or three people aboard, he could not quite make out how many, and they seemed to be doing something with a line; they were no doubt fishing, and Merritt (who disliked fish) wondered how people could spoil such an afternoon, such a sea, such pellucid and radiant air by trying to catch white, flabby, offensive, evil-smelling creatures that would be excessively nasty when cooked. He puzzled over this problem and turned away from it to the contemplation of the crimson headlands. And then he says that he noticed that signaling was going on. Flashing lights of intense brilliance, he declares, were coming from one of those farms on the heights of the coast; it was as if white fire was spouting from it. Merritt was certain, as the light appeared and disappeared, that some message was being sent, and he regretted that he knew nothing of heliography. Three short flashes, a long and very brilliant flash, then two short flashes. Merritt fumbled in his pocket for pencil and paper so that he might record these signals, and, bringing his eyes down to the sea level, he became aware, with amazement and horror, that the boat had disappeared. All that he could see was some vague, dark object far to westward, running out with the tide.

Now it is certain, unfortunately, that the *Mary Ann* was capsized and that two schoolboys and the sailor in charge were drowned. The bones of the boat were found amongst the rocks far along the coast, and the three bodies were also washed ashore. The sailor could not swim at all, the boys only a little, and it needs an exceptionally fine swimmer to fight against the outward suck of the tide as it rushes past Pengareg Point.

But I have no belief whatever in Merritt's theory. He held (and still holds, for all I know), that the flashes of light which he saw coming from Penyrhaul, the farmhouse oh the height, had some connection with the disaster to the *Mary Ann*. When it was ascertained that a family were spending their summer at the farm, and that the governess was a German, though a long naturalized German, Merritt could not see that there was anything left to argue about, though there might be many details to discover. But, in my opinion, all this was a mere mare's nest; the flashes of brilliant light were caused, no doubt, by the sun lighting up one window of the farmhouse after the other.

Still, Merritt was convinced from the very first, even before the damning circumstance of the German governess was brought to light; and on the evening of the disaster, as Lewis and he sat together after dinner, he was endeavoring to put what he called the common sense of the matter to the doctor.

"If you hear a shot," said Merritt, "and you see a man fall, you know pretty well what killed him."

There was a flutter of wild wings in the room. A great moth beat to and fro and dashed itself madly against the ceiling, the walls, the glass bookcase. Then a sputtering sound, a momentary dimming of the lamp. The moth had succeeded in its mysterious quest.

"Can you tell me," said Lewis as if he were answering Merritt, "why moths rush into the flame?"

LEWIS HAD PUT HIS QUESTION as to the strange habits of the common moth to Merritt with the deliberate intent of closing the debate on death by heliograph. The query was suggested, of course, by the incident of the moth in the lamp, and Lewis thought that he had said, "Oh, shut up!" in a somewhat elegant manner. And, in fact Merritt looked dignified, remained silent, and helped himself to port.

That was the end that the doctor had desired. He had no doubt in his own mind that the affair of the *Mary Ann* was but one more item in the long account of horrors that grew larger almost with everyday; and he was in no humor to listen to wild and futile theories as to the manner in which the disaster had been accomplished. Here was a proof that the terror that was upon them was mighty not only on the land but on the waters; for Lewis could not see that the boat could have been attacked by any ordinary means of destruction. From Merritt's story, it must have been in shallow water. The shore of Larnac Bay shelves very gradually, and the Admiralty charts showed the depth of water two hundred yards out to be only two fathoms; this would be too shallow for a submarine. And it could not have been shelled, and it could not have been torpedoed; there was no explosion. The disaster might have been due to carelessness; boys, he considered, will play the fool anywhere, even in a boat; but he did not think so; the sailor would have stopped them. And, it may be mentioned, that the two boys were as a matter of fact extremely steady, sensible young fellows, not in the least likely to play foolish tricks of any kind.

Lewis was immersed in these reflections, having successfully silenced his brother-in-law; he was trying in vain to find some clue to the horrible enigma. The Midlingham theory of a concealed German force, hiding in places under the earth, was extravagant enough, and yet it seemed the only solution that approached plausibility; but then again even a subterranean German host would hardly account for this wreckage of a boat, floating on a calm sea. And then what of the tree with the burning in it that had appeared in the garden there a few weeks ago, and the cloud with a burning in it that had shown over the trees of the Midland village?

I think I have, already written something of the probable emotions of the mathematician confronted suddenly with an undoubted two-sided triangle. I said, if I remember, that he would be forced, in decency, to go mad; and I believe that Lewis was very near to this point. He felt himself confronted with an intolerable problem that most instantly demanded solution, and yet, with the same breath, as it were, denied the possibility of there being any solution. People were being killed in an inscrutable manner by some inscrutable means, day after day, and one asked "why" and "how"; and there seemed no answer. In the Midlands, where every kind of munitionment was manufactured, the explanation of German agency was plausible; and even if the subterranean notion was to be rejected as savoring altogether too much of the fairytale, or rather of the sensational romance, yet it was possible that the backbone of the theory was true; the Germans might have planted their agents in some way or another in the midst of our factories. But here in Meirion, what serious effect could be produced by the casual and indiscriminate slaughter of a couple of schoolboys in a boat, of a harmless holiday-maker in a marsh? The creation of an atmosphere of terror and dismay? It was possible, of course, but it hardly seemed tolerable, in spite of the enormities of Louvain and of the *Lusitania*.

Into these meditations, and into the still dignified silence of Merritt broke the rap on the door of Lewis's man, and those words which harass the ease of the country doctor when he tries to take any ease: "You're wanted in the surgery, if you please, sir." Lewis bustled out, and appeared no more that night.

The doctor had been summoned to a little hamlet on the outskirts of Porth, separated from it by half a mile or three-quarters of road. One dignifies, indeed, this settlement without a name in calling it a hamlet; it was a mere row of four cottages, built about a hundred years ago for the accommodation of the workers in a quarry long since disused. In one of these cottages the doctor found a father and mother weeping and crying out to "doctor bach, doctor bach," and two frightened children, and one little body, still and dead. It was the youngest of the three, little Johnnie, and he was dead.

The doctor found that the child had been asphyxiated. He felt the clothes; they were dry; it was not a case of drowning. He looked at the neck; there was no mark of strangling. He asked the father how it had happened, and father and mother, weeping most lamentably, declared they had no knowledge of how their child had been killed: "unless it was the People that had done it." The Celtic fairies are still malignant. Lewis asked what had happened that evening; where had the child been?

"Was he with his brother and sister? Don't they know anything about it?"

Reduced into some sort of order from its original piteous confusion, this is the story that the doctor gathered.

All three children had been well and happy through the day. They had walked in with the mother, Mrs. Roberts, to Porth on a marketing expedition in the afternoon; they had returned to the cottage, had had their tea, and afterwards played about on the road in front of the house. John Roberts had come home somewhat late from his work, and it was after dusk when the family sat down to supper. Supper over, the three children went out again to play with other children from the cottage next door, Mrs. Roberts telling them that they might have half an hour before going to bed.

The two mothers came to the cottage gates at the same moment and called out to their children to come along and be quick about it. The two small families had been playing on the strip of turf across the road, just by the stile into the fields. The children ran across the road; all of them except Johnnie Roberts. His brother Willie said that just as their mother called them he heard Johnnie cry out:

"Oh, what is that beautiful shiny thing over the stile?"

X

The Child and the Moth

The little Roberts's ran across the road, up the path, and into the lighted room. Then they noticed that Johnnie had not followed them. Mrs. Roberts was doing something in the back kitchen, and Mr. Roberts had gone out to the shed to bring in some sticks for the next morning's fire. Mrs. Roberts heard the children run in and went on with her work. The children whispered to one another that Johnnie would "catch it" when their mother came out of the back room and found him missing; but they expected he would run in through the open door any minute. But six or seven, perhaps ten, minutes passed, and there was no Johnnie. Then the father and mother came into the kitchen together, and saw that their little boy was not there.

They thought it was some small piece of mischief—that the two other children had hidden the boy somewhere in the room: in the big cupboard perhaps.

"What have you done with him then?" said Mrs. Roberts. "Come out, you little rascal, directly in a minute."

There was no little rascal to come out, and Margaret Roberts, the girl, said that Johnnie had not come across the road with them: he must be still playing all by himself by the hedge.

"What did you let him stay like that for?" said Mrs. Roberts. "Can't I trust you for two minutes together? Indeed to goodness, you are all of you more trouble than you are worth." She went to the open door:

"Johnnie! Come you in directly, or you will be sorry for it. Johnnie!"

The poor woman called at the door. She went out to the gate and called there:

"Come you, little Johnnie. Come you, bachgen, there's a good boy. I do see you hiding there."

She thought he must be hiding in the shadow of the hedge, and that he would come running and laughing—"he was always such a happy little fellow"—to her across the road. But no little merry figure danced out of the gloom of the still, dark night; it was all silence.

It was then, as the mother's heart began to chill, though she still called cheerfully to the missing child, that the elder boy told how

Johnnie had said there was something beautiful by the stile: "and perhaps he did climb over, and he is running now about the meadow, and has lost his way."

The father got his lantern then, and the whole family went crying and calling about the meadow, promising cakes and sweets and a fine toy to poor Johnnie if he would come to them.

They found the little body, under the ashgrove in the middle of the field. He was quite still and dead, so still that a great moth had settled on his forehead, fluttering away when they lifted him up.

Dr. Lewis heard this story. There was nothing to be done; little to be said to these most unhappy people.

"Take care of the two that you have left to you," said the doctor as he went away. "Don't let them out of your sight if you can help it. It is dreadful times that we are living in."

It is curious to record, that all through these dreadful times the simple little "season" went through its accustomed course at Porth. The war and its consequences had somewhat thinned the numbers of the summer visitors; still a very fair contingent of them occupied the hotels and boarding-houses and lodging-houses and bathed from the old-fashioned machines on one beach, or from the new-fashioned tents on the other, and sauntered in the sun, or lay stretched out in the shade under the trees that grow down almost to the water's edge. Porth never tolerated Ethiopians or shows of any kind on its sands, but "The Rockets" did very well during that summer in their garden entertainment, given in the castle grounds, and the fit-up companies that came to the Assembly Rooms are said to have paid their bills to a woman and to a man.

Porth depends very largely on its midland and northern custom, custom of a prosperous, well-established sort. People who think Llandudno overcrowded and Colwyn Bay too raw and red and new, come year after year to the placid old town in the southwest and delight in its peace; and as I say, they enjoyed themselves much as usual there in the summer of 1915. Now and then they became conscious, as Mr. Merritt became conscious, that they could not wander about quite in the old way; but they accepted sentries and coast-watchers and people who politely pointed out the advantages of seeing the view from this point rather than from that as very necessary consequences of the dreadful war that was being waged; nay, as a Manchester man said, after having been turned back from his favorite walk to Castell Coch, it was gratifying to think that they were so well looked after.

"So far as I can see," he added, "there's nothing to prevent a submarine from standing out there by Ynys Sant and landing half a dozen men in a collapsible boat in any of these little coves. And pretty fools we should look, shouldn't we, with our throats cut on the sands; or carried back to Germany in the submarine?" He tipped the coast-watcher half-a-crown.

"That's right, lad," he said, "you give us the tip."

Now here was a strange thing. The north-countryman had his thoughts on elusive submarines and German raiders; the watcher had simply received instructions to keep people off the Castell Coch fields, without reason assigned. And there can be no doubt that the authorities themselves, while they marked out the fields as in the "terror zone," gave their orders in the dark and were themselves profoundly in the dark as to the manner of the slaughter that had been done there; for if they had understood what had happened, they would have understood also that their restrictions were useless.

The Manchester man was warned off his walk about ten days after Johnnie Roberts's death. The Watcher had been placed at his post because, the night before, a young farmer had been found by his wife lying in the grass close to the Castle, with no scar on him, nor any mark of violence, but stone dead.

The wife of the dead man, Joseph Cradock, finding her husband lying motionless on the dewy turf, went white and stricken up the path to the village and got two men who bore the body to the farm. Lewis was sent for, and knew, at once when he saw the dead man that he had perished in the way that the little Roberts boy had perished—whatever that awful way might be. Cradock had been asphyxiated; and here again there was no mark of a grip on the throat. It might have been a piece of work by Burke and Hare, the doctor reflected; a pitch plaster might have been clapped over the man's mouth and nostrils and held there.

Then a thought struck him; his brother-in-law had talked of a new kind of poison gas that was said to be used against the munition workers in the Midlands: was it possible that the deaths of the man and the boy were due to some such instrument? He applied his tests but could find no trace of any gas having been employed. Carbonic acid gas? A man could not be killed with that in the open air; to be fatal that required a confined space, such a position as the bottom of a huge vat or of a well.

He did not know how Cradock had been killed; he confessed it to himself. He had been suffocated; that was all he could say.

It seemed that the man had gone out at about half-past nine to look after some beasts. The field in which they were was about five minutes' walk from the house. He told his wife he would be back in a quarter of an hour or twenty minutes. He did not return, and when he had been gone for three-quarters of an hour Mrs. Cradock went out to look for him. She went into the field where the beasts were, and everything seemed all right, but there was no trace of Cradock. She called out; there was no answer.

Now the meadow in which the cattle were pastured is high ground; a hedge divides it from the fields which fall gently down to the castle and the sea. Mrs. Cradock hardly seemed able to say why, having failed to find her husband among his beasts, she turned to the path which led to Castell Coch. She said at first that she had thought that one of the oxen might have broken through the hedge and strayed, and that Cradock had perhaps gone after it. And then, correcting herself, she said:

"There was that; and then there was something else that I could not make out at all. It seemed to me that the hedge did look different from usual. To be sure, things do look different at night, and there was a bit of sea mist about, but somehow it did look odd to me, and I said to myself, 'have I lost my way, then?'"

She declared that the shape of the trees in the hedge appeared to have changed, and besides, it had a look "as if it was lighted up, somehow," and so she went on towards the stile to see what all this could be, and when she came near everything was as usual. She looked over the stile and called and hoped to see her husband coming towards her or to hear his voice; but there was no answer, and glancing down the path she saw, or thought she saw, some sort of brightness on the ground, a dim sort of light like a bunch of glow-worms in a hedge-bank.

"And so I climbed over the stile and went down the path, and the light seemed to melt away; and there was my poor husband lying on his back, saying not a word to me when I spoke to him and touched him."

So FOR LEWIS THE TERROR blackened and became altogether intolerable, and others, he perceived, felt as he did. He did not know, he never asked whether the men at the club had heard of these deaths of the child and the young farmer; but no one spoke of them. Indeed, the change was evident; at the beginning of the terror men spoke of nothing else; now it had become all too awful for ingenious chatter or labored and grotesque theories. And Lewis had received a letter from his brother-in-law at Midlingham; it contained the sentence, "I am afraid Fanny's health has not greatly benefited by her visit to Porth; there are still several symptoms I don't at all like." And this told him, in a phraseology that the doctor and Merritt had agreed upon, that the terror remained heavy in the Midland town.

It was soon after the death of Cradock that people began to tell strange tales of a sound that was to be heard of nights about the hills and valleys to the northward of Porth. A man who had missed the last train from Meiros and had been forced to tramp the ten miles between Meiros and Porth seems to have been the first to hear it. He said he had got to the top of the hill by Tredonoc, somewhere between half-past ten and eleven, when he first noticed an odd noise that he could not make out at all; it was like a shout, a long, drawn-out, dismal wail coming from a great way off, faint with distance. He stopped to listen, thinking at first that it might be owls hooting in the woods; but it was different, he said, from that: it was a long cry, and then there was silence and then it began over again. He could make nothing of it, and feeling frightened, he did not quite know of what, he walked on briskly and was glad to see the lights of Porth station.

He told his wife of this dismal sound that night, and she told the neighbors, and most of them thought that it was "all fancy"—or drink, or the owls after all. But the night after, two or three people, who had been to some small merrymaking in a cottage just off the Meiros road, heard the sound as they were going home, soon after ten. They, too, described it as a long, wailing cry, indescribably dismal in the stillness of the autumn night; "like the ghost of a voice," said one; "as if it came up from the bottom of the earth," said another.

XI

AT TREFF LOYNE FARM

Let it be remembered, again and again, that, all the while that the terror lasted, there was no common stock of information as to the dreadful things that were being done. The press had not said one word upon it, there was no criterion by which the mass of the people could separate fact from mere vague rumor, no test by which ordinary misadventure or disaster could be distinguished from the achievements of the secret and awful force that was at work.

And so with every event of the passing day. A harmless commercial traveler might show himself in the course of his business in the tumbledown main street of Meiros and find himself regarded with looks of fear and suspicion as a possible worker of murder, while it is likely enough that the true agents of the terror went quite unnoticed. And since the real nature of all this mystery of death was unknown, it followed easily that the signs and warnings and omens of it were all the more unknown. Here was horror, there was horror; but there was no links to join one horror with another; no common basis of knowledge from which the connection between this horror and that horror might be inferred.

So there was no one who suspected at all that this dismal and hollow sound that was now heard of nights in the region to the north of Porth, had any relation at all to the case of the little girl who went out one afternoon to pick purple flowers and never returned, or to the case of the man whose body was taken out of the peaty slime of the marsh, or to the case of Cradock, dead in his fields, with a strange glimmering of light about his body, as his wife reported. And it is a question as to how far the rumor of this melancholy, nocturnal summons got abroad at all. Lewis heard of it, as a country doctor hears of most things, driving up and down the lanes, but he heard of it without much interest, with no sense that it was in any sort of relation to the terror. Remnant had been given the story of the hollow and echoing voice of the darkness in a colored and picturesque form; he employed a Tredonoc man to work in his garden once a week. The gardener had not heard the summons himself, but he knew a man who had done so.

"Thomas Jenkins, Pentoppin, he did put his head out late last night to see what the weather was like, as he was cutting a field of corn the next day, and he did tell me that when he was with the Methodists in Cardigan he did never hear no singing eloquence in the chapels that was like to it. He did declare it was like a wailing of Judgment Day."

Remnant considered the matter, and was inclined to think that the sound must be caused by a subterranean inlet of the sea; there might be, he supposed, an imperfect or half-opened or tortuous blow-hole in the Tredonoc woods, and the noise of the tide, surging up below, might very well produce that effect of a hollow wailing, far away. But neither he nor anyone else paid much attention to the matter; save the few who heard the call at dead of night, as it echoed awfully over the black hills.

The sound had been heard for three or perhaps four nights, when the people coming out of Tredonoc church after morning service on Sunday noticed that there was a big yellow sheepdog in the churchyard. The dog, it appeared, had been waiting for the congregation; for it at once attached itself to them, at first to the whole body, and then to a group of half a dozen who took the turning to the right. Two of these presently went off over the fields to their respective houses, and four strolled on in the leisurely Sunday-morning manner of the country, and these the dog followed, keeping to heel all the time. The men were talking hay, corn and markets and paid no attention to the animal, and so they strolled along the autumn lane till they came to a gate in the hedge, whence a roughly made farm road went through the fields, and dipped down into the woods and to Treff Loyne farm.

Then the dog became like a possessed creature. He barked furiously. He ran up to one of the men and looked up at him, "as if he were begging for his life," as the man said, and then rushed to the gate and stood by it, wagging his tail and barking at intervals. The men stared and laughed.

"Whose dog will that be?" said one of them.

"It will be Thomas Griffith's, Treff Loyne," said another.

"Well, then, why doesn't he go home? Go home then!" He went through the gesture of picking up a stone from the road and throwing it at the dog. "Go home, then! Over the gate with you."

But the dog never stirred. He barked and whined and ran up to the men and then back to the gate. At last he came to one of them, and crawled and abased himself on the ground and then took hold of the man's coat and tried to pull him in the direction of the gate. The farmer shook the dog off, and the four went on their way; and the dog stood in the road and watched them and then put up its head and uttered a long and dismal howl that was despair.

The four farmers thought nothing of it; sheepdogs in the country are dogs to look after sheep, and their whims and fancies are not studied. But the yellow dog—he was a kind of degenerate collie—haunted the Tredonoc lanes from that day. He came to a cottage door one night and scratched at it, and when it was opened lay down, and then, barking, ran to the garden gate and waited, entreating, as it seemed, the cottager to follow him. They drove him away and again he gave that long howl of anguish. It was almost as bad, they said, as the noise that they had heard a few nights before. And then it occurred to somebody, so far as I can make out with no particular reference to the odd conduct of the Treff Loyne sheepdog, that Thomas Griffith had not been seen for sometime past. He had missed market day at Porth, he had not been at Tredonoc church, where he was a pretty regular attendant on Sunday; and then, as heads were put together, it appeared that nobody had seen any of the Griffith family for days and days.

Now in a town, even in a small town, this process of putting heads together is a pretty quick business. In the country, especially in a countryside of wild lands and scattered and lonely farms and cottages, the affair takes time. Harvest was going on, everybody was busy in his own fields, and after the long day's hard work neither the farmer nor his men felt inclined to stroll about in search of news or gossip. A harvester at the day's end is ready for supper and sleep and for nothing else.

And so it was late in that week when it was discovered that Thomas Griffith and all his house had vanished from this world.

I have often been reproached for my curiosity over questions which are apparently of slight importance, or of no importance at all. I love to inquire, for instance, into the question of the visibility of a lighted candle at a distance. Suppose, that is, a candle lighted on a still, dark night in the country; what is the greatest distance at which you can see that there is a light at all? And then as to the human voice; what is its carrying distance, under good conditions, as a mere sound, apart from any matter of making out words that may be uttered?

They are trivial questions, no doubt, but they have always interested me, and the latter point has its application to the strange business of Treff Loyne. That melancholy and hollow sound, that wailing summons that appalled the hearts of those who heard it was, indeed, a human voice, produced in a very exceptional manner; and it seems to have been heard at points varying from a mile and a half to two miles from the farm. I do not know whether this is anything extraordinary; I do not know whether the peculiar method of production was calculated to increase or to diminish the carrying power of the sound.

Again and again I have laid emphasis in this story of the terror on the strange isolation of many of the farms and cottages in Meirion. I have done so in the effort to convince the townsman of something that he has never known. To the Londoner a house a quarter of a mile from the outlying suburban lamp, with no other dwelling within two hundred yards, is a lonely house, a place to fit with ghosts and mysteries and terrors. How can he understand then, the true loneliness of the white farmhouses of Meirion, dotted here and there, for the most part not even on the little lanes and deep winding byways, but set in the very heart of the fields, or alone on huge bastioned headlands facing the sea, and whether on the high verge of the sea or on the hills or in the hollows of the inner country, hidden from the sight of men, far from the sound of any common call. There is Penyrhaul, for example, the farm from which the foolish Merritt thought he saw signals of light being made: from seaward it is of course, widely visible; but from landward, owing partly to the curving and indented configuration of the bay, I doubt whether any other habitation views it from a nearer distance than three miles.

And of all these hidden and remote places, I doubt if any is so deeply buried as Treff Loyne. I have little or no Welsh, I am sorry to say, but I suppose that the name is corrupted from Trellwyn, or Tref-y-llwyn, "the place in the grove," and, indeed, it lies in the very heart of dark, overhanging woods. A deep, narrow valley runs down from the high lands of the Allt, through these woods, through steep hillsides of bracken and gorse, right down to the great marsh, whence Merritt saw the dead man being carried. The valley lies away from any road, even from that by-road, little better than a bridlepath, where the four farmers, returning from church were perplexed by the strange antics of the sheepdog. One cannot say that the valley is overlooked, even from a distance, for so narrow is it that the ashgroves that rim it on either side seem to meet and shut it in. I, at all events, have never found any high place from which Treff Loyne is visible; though, looking down from the Allt, I have seen blue wood-smoke rising from its hidden chimneys.

Such was the place, then, to which one September afternoon a party went up to discover what had happened to Griffith and his family. There were half a dozen farmers, a couple of policemen, and four soldiers, carrying their arms; those last had been lent by the officer commanding at the camp. Lewis, too, was of the party; he had heard by chance that no one knew what had become of Griffith and his family; and he was anxious about a young fellow, a painter, of his acquaintance, who had been lodging at Treff Loyne all the summer.

They all met by the gate of Tredonoc churchyard, and tramped solemnly along the narrow lane; all of them, I think, with some vague discomfort of mind, with a certain shadowy fear, as of men who do not quite know what they may encounter. Lewis heard the corporal and the three soldiers arguing over their orders.

"The Captain says to me," muttered the corporal, "'Don't hesitate to shoot if there's any trouble.' 'Shoot what, sir,' I says. 'The trouble,' says he, and that's all I could get out of him."

The men grumbled in reply; Lewis thought he heard some obscure reference to ratpoison, and wondered what they were talking about.

They came to the gate in the hedge, where the farm road led down to Treff Loyne. They followed this track, roughly made, with grass growing up between its loosely laid stones, down by the hedge from field to wood, till at last they came to the sudden walls of the valley, and the sheltering groves of the ash trees. Here the way curved down the steep hillside, and bent southward, and followed henceforward the hidden hollow of the valley, under the shadow of the trees.

Here was the farm enclosure; the outlying walls of the yard and the barns and sheds and outhouses. One of the farmers threw open the gate and walked into the yard, and forthwith began bellowing at the top of his voice:

"Thomas Griffith! Thomas Griffith! Where be you, Thomas Griffith?"

The rest followed him. The corporal snapped out an order over his shoulder, and there was a rattling metallic noise as the men fixed their bayonets and became in an instant dreadful dealers out of death, in place of harmless fellows with a feeling for beer.

"Thomas Griffith!" again bellowed the farmer.

There was no answer to this summons. But they found poor Griffith lying on his face at the edge of the pond in the middle of the yard. There was a ghastly wound in his side, as if a sharp stake had been driven into his body.

XII

The Letter of Wrath

It was a still September afternoon. No wind stirred in the hanging woods that were dark all about the ancient house of Treff Loyne; the only sound in the dim air was the lowing of the cattle; they had wandered, it seemed, from the fields and had come in by the gate of the farmyard and stood there melancholy, as if they mourned for their dead master. And the horses; four great, heavy, patient-looking beasts they were there too, and in the lower field the sheep were standing, as if they waited to be fed.

"You would think they all knew there was something wrong," one of the soldiers muttered to another. A pale sun showed for a moment and glittered on their bayonets. They were standing about the body of poor, dead Griffith, with a certain grimness growing on their faces and hardening there. Their corporal snapped something at them again; they were quite ready. Lewis knelt down by the dead man and looked closely at the great gaping wound in his side.

"He's been dead a long time," he said. "A week, two weeks, perhaps. He was killed by some sharp pointed weapon. How about the family? How many are there of them? I never attended them."

"There was Griffith, and his wife, and his son Thomas and Mary Griffith, his daughter. And I do think there was a gentleman lodging with them this summer."

That was from one of the farmers. They all looked at one another, this party of rescue, who knew nothing of the danger that had smitten this house of quiet people, nothing of the peril which had brought them to this pass of a farmyard with a dead man in it, and his beasts standing patiently about him, as if they waited for the farmer to rise up and give them their food. Then the party turned to the house. It was an old, sixteenth century building, with the singular round, "Flemish" chimney that is characteristic of Meirion. The walls were snowy with whitewash, the windows were deeply set and stone mullioned, and a solid, stone-tiled porch sheltered the doorway from any winds that might penetrate to the hollow of that hidden valley. The windows were shut tight. There was no sign of any life or movement about the place. The party of men looked at one another, and the churchwarden amongst the farmers, the sergeant of police, Lewis, and the corporal drew together.

"What is it to goodness, doctor?" said the churchwarden.

"I can tell you nothing at all—except that that poor man there has been pierced to the heart," said Lewis.

"Do you think they are inside and they will shoot us?" said another farmer. He had no notion of what he meant by "they," and no one of them knew better than he. They did not know what the danger was, or where it might strike them, or whether it was from without or from within. They stared at the murdered man, and gazed dismally at one another.

"Come!" said Lewis, "we must do something. We must get into the house and see what is wrong."

"Yes, but suppose they are at us while we are getting in," said the sergeant. "Where shall we be then, Doctor Lewis?"

The corporal put one of his men by the gate at the top of the farmyard, another at the gate by the bottom of the farmyard, and told them to challenge and shoot. The doctor and the rest opened the little gate of the front garden and went up to the porch and stood listening by the door. It was all dead silence. Lewis took an ash stick from one of the farmers and beat heavily three times on the old, black, oaken door studded with antique nails.

He struck three thundering blows, and then they all waited. There was no answer from within. He beat again, and still silence. He shouted to the people within, but there was no answer. They all turned and looked at one another, that party of quest and rescue who knew not what they sought, what enemy they were to encounter. There was an iron ring on the door. Lewis turned it but the door stood fast; it was evidently barred and bolted. The sergeant of police called out to open, but again there was no answer.

They consulted together. There was nothing for it but to blow the door open, and someone of them called in a loud voice to anybody that might be within to stand away from the door, or they would be killed. And at this very moment the yellow sheepdog came bounding up the yard from the woods and licked their hands and fawned on them and barked joyfully.

"Indeed now," said one of the farmers; "he did know that there was something amiss. A pity it was, Thomas Williams, that we did not follow him when he implored us last Sunday."

The corporal motioned the rest of the party back, and they stood looking fearfully about them at the entrance to the porch. The corporal disengaged his bayonet and shot into the keyhole, calling out once more before he fired. He shot and shot again; so heavy and firm was the ancient door, so stout its bolts and fastenings. At last he had to fire at the massive hinges, and then they all pushed together and the door lurched open and fell forward. The corporal raised his left hand and stepped back a few paces. He hailed his two men at the top and bottom of the farmyard. They were all right, they said. And so the party climbed and struggled over the fallen door into the passage, and into the kitchen of the farmhouse.

Young Griffith was lying dead before the hearth, before a dead fire of white wood ashes. They went on towards the "parlor," and in the doorway of the room was the body of the artist, Secretan, as if he had fallen in trying to get to the kitchen. Upstairs the two women, Mrs. Griffith and her daughter, a girl of eighteen, were lying together on the bed in the big bedroom, clasped in each others' arms.

They went about the house, searched the pantries, the back kitchen and the cellars; there was no life in it.

"Look!" said Dr. Lewis, when they came back to the big kitchen, "look! It is as if they had been besieged. Do you see that piece of bacon, half gnawed through?"

Then they found these pieces of bacon, cut from the sides on the kitchen wall, here and there about the house. There was no bread in the place, no milk, no water.

"And," said one of the farmers, "they had the best water here in all Meirion. The well is down there in the wood; it is most famous water. The old people did use to call it Ffynnon Teilo; it was Saint Teilo's Well, they did say."

"They must have died of thirst," said Lewis. "They have been dead for days and days."

The group of men stood in the big kitchen and stared at one another, a dreadful perplexity in their eyes. The dead were all about them, within the house and without it; and it was in vain to ask why they had died thus. The old man had been killed with the piercing thrust of some sharp weapon; the rest had perished, it seemed probable, of thirst; but what possible enemy was this that besieged the farm and shut in its inhabitants? There was no answer.

The sergeant of police spoke of getting a cart and taking the bodies into Porth, and Dr. Lewis went into the parlor that Secretan had used as a sitting-room, intending to gather any possessions or effects of the dead artist that he might find there. Half a dozen portfolios were piled up in one corner, there were some books on a side table, a fishing-rod and basket behind the door—that seemed all. No doubt there would be clothes and such matters upstairs, and Lewis was about to rejoin the rest of the party in the kitchen, when he looked down at some scattered papers lying with the books on the side table. On one of the sheets he read to his astonishment the words: "Dr. James Lewis, Porth." This was written in a staggering trembling scrawl, and examining the other leaves he saw that they were covered with writing.

The table stood in a dark corner of the room, and Lewis gathered up the sheets of paper and took them to the window-ledge and began to read, amazed at certain phrases that had caught his eye. But the manuscript was in disorder; as if the dead man who had written it had not been equal to the task of gathering the leaves into their proper sequence; it was sometime before the doctor had each page in its place. This was the statement that he read, with ever-growing wonder, while a couple of the farmers were harnessing one of the horses in the yard to a cart, and the others were bringing down the dead women.

"I DO NOT THINK THAT I can last much longer. We shared out the last drops of water a long time ago. I do not know how many days ago. We fall asleep and dream and walk about the house in our dreams, and I am often not sure whether I am awake or still dreaming, and so the days and nights are confused in my mind. I awoke not long ago, at least I suppose I awoke and found I was lying in the passage. I had a confused feeling that I had had an awful dream which seemed horribly real, and I thought for a moment what a relief it was to know that it wasn't true, whatever it might have been. I made up my mind to have a good long walk to freshen myself up, and then I looked round and found that I had been lying on the stones of the passage; and it all came back to me. There was no walk for me.

"I have not seen Mrs. Griffith or her daughter for a long while. They said they were going upstairs to have a rest. I heard them moving about the room at first, now I can hear nothing. Young Griffith is lying in the kitchen, before the hearth. He was talking to himself about the harvest and the weather when I last went into the kitchen. He didn't seem to know I was there, as he went gabbling on in a low voice very fast, and then he began to call the dog, Tiger.

"There seems no hope for any of us. We are in the dream of death. . ."

Here the manuscript became unintelligible for half a dozen lines. Secretan had written the words "dream of death" three or four times over. He had begun a fresh word and had scratched it out and then followed strange, unmeaning characters, the script, as Lewis thought, of a terrible language. And then the writing became clear, clearer than it was at the beginning of the manuscript, and the sentences flowed more easily, as if the cloud on Secretan's mind had lifted for a while. There was a fresh start, as it were, and the writer began again, in ordinary letter-form:

DEAR LEWIS,

"I hope you will excuse all this confusion and wandering. I intended to begin a proper letter to you, and now I find all that stuff that you have been reading—if this ever gets into your hands. I have not the energy even to tear it up. If you read it you will know to what a sad pass I had come when it was written. It looks like delirium or a bad dream, and even now, though my mind seems to have cleared up a good deal, I have to hold myself in tightly to be sure that the experiences of the last days in this awful place are true, real things, not a long nightmare from which I shall wake up presently and find myself in my rooms at Chelsea.

"I have said of what I am writing, 'if it ever gets into your hands,' and I am not at all sure that it ever will. If what is happening here is happening everywhere else, then I suppose, the world is coming to an end. I cannot understand it, even now I can hardly believe it. I know that I dream such wild dreams and walk in such mad fancies that I have to look out and look about me to make sure that I am not still dreaming.

"Do you remember that talk we had about two months ago when I dined with you? We got on, somehow or other, to space and time, and I think we agreed that as soon as one tried to reason about space and time one was landed in a maze of contradictions. You said something to the effect that it was very curious but this was just like a dream. 'A man will sometimes wake himself from his crazy dream,' you said, 'by realizing that he is thinking nonsense.' And we both wondered whether these contradictions that one can't avoid if one begins to think of time and space may not really be proofs that the whole of life is a dream, and the moon and the stars bits of nightmare. I have often thought over that lately. I kick at the walls as Dr. Johnson kicked at the stone, to make sure that the things about me are there. And then that other question gets into my mind—is the world really coming to an end, the world as we have always known it; and what on earth will this new world be like? I can't imagine it; it's a story like Noah's Ark and the Flood. People used to talk about the end of the world and fire, but no one ever thought of anything like this.

"And then there's another thing that bothers me. Now and then I wonder whether we are not all mad together in this house. In spite of what I see and know, or, perhaps, I should say, because what I see and know is so impossible, I wonder whether we are not all suffering from a delusion. Perhaps we are our own gaolers, and we are really free to go out and live. Perhaps what we think we see is not there at all. I believe I have heard of whole families going mad together, and I may have come under the influence of the house, having lived in it for the last four months. I know there have been people who have been kept alive by their keepers forcing food down their throats, because they are quite sure that their throats are closed, so that they feel they are unable to swallow a morsel. I wonder now and then whether we are all like this in Treff Loyne; yet in my heart I feel sure that it is not so.

"Still, I do not want to leave a madman's letter behind me, and so I will not tell you the full story of what I have seen, or believe I have seen. If I am a sane man you will be able to fill in the blanks for yourself from your own knowledge. If I am mad, burn the letter and say nothing about it. Or perhaps—and indeed, I am not quite sure—I may wake up and hear Mary Griffith calling to me in her cheerful sing-song that breakfast will be ready 'directly, in a minute,' and I shall enjoy it and walk over to Porth and tell you the queerest, most horrible dream that a man ever had, and ask what I had better take.

"I think that it was on a Tuesday that we first noticed that there was something queer about, only at the time we didn't know that there was anything really queer in what we noticed. I had been out since nine o'clock in the morning trying to paint the marsh, and I found it a very tough job. I came home about five or six o'clock and found the family at Treff Loyne laughing at old Tiger, the sheepdog. He was making short runs from the farmyard to the door of the house, barking, with quick, short yelps. Mrs. Griffith and Miss Griffith were standing by the porch, and the dog would go to them, look in their faces, and then run up the farmyard to the gate, and then look back with that eager yelping bark, as if he were waiting for the women to follow him. Then, again and again, he ran up to them and tugged at their skirts as if he would pull them by main force away from the house.

"Then the men came home from the fields and he repeated this performance. The dog was running all up and down the farmyard, in and out of the barn and sheds yelping, barking; and always with that eager run to the person he addressed, and running away directly, and looking back as, if to see whether we were following him. When the house door was shut and they all sat down to supper, he would give them no peace, till at last they turned him out of doors. And then he sat in the porch and scratched at the door with his claws, barking all the while. When the daughter brought in my meal, she said: 'We can't think what is come to old Tiger, and indeed, he has always been a good dog, too.'

"The dog barked and yelped and whined and scratched at the door all through the evening. They let him in once, but he seemed to have become quite frantic. He ran up to one member of the family after another; his eyes were bloodshot and his mouth was foaming, and he tore at their clothes till they drove him out again into the darkness. Then he broke into a long, lamentable howl of anguish, and we heard no more of him."

XIII

The Last Words of Mr. Secretan

I slept ill that night I awoke again and again from uneasy M dreams, and I seemed in my sleep to hear strange calls and noises and a sound of murmurs and beatings on the door. There were deep, hollow voices, too, that echoed in my sleep, and when I woke I could hear the autumn wind, mournful, on the hills above us. I started up once with a dreadful scream in my ears; but then the house was all still, and I fell again into uneasy sleep.

"It was soon after dawn when I finally roused myself. The people in the house were talking to each other in high voices, arguing about something that I did not understand.

"'It is those damned gipsies, I tell you,' said old Griffith.

"'What would they do a thing like that for?' asked Mrs. Griffith. 'If it was stealing now—'"

"'It is more likely that John Jenkins has done it out of spite,' said the son. 'He said that he would remember you when we did catch him poaching.'"

"They seemed puzzled and angry, so far as I could make out, but not at all frightened. I got up and began to dress. I don't think I looked out of the window. The glass on my dressing-table is high and broad, and the window is small; one would have to poke one's head round the glass to see anything.

"The voices were still arguing downstairs. I heard the old man say, 'Well, here's for a beginning anyhow,' and then the door slammed.

"A minute later the old man shouted, I think, to his son. Then there was a great noise which I will not describe more particularly, and a dreadful screaming and crying inside the house and a sound of rushing feet. They all cried out at once to each other. I heard the daughter crying, 'it is no good, mother, he is dead, indeed they have killed him,' and Mrs. Griffith screaming to the girl to let her go. And then one of them rushed out of the kitchen and shot the great bolts of oak across the door, just as something beat against it with a thundering crash.

"I ran downstairs. I found them all in wild confusion, in an agony of grief and horror and amazement. They were like people who had seen something so awful that they had gone mad.

"I went to the window looking out on the farmyard. I won't tell you all that I saw. But I saw poor old Griffith lying by the pond, with the blood pouring out of his side.

"I wanted to go out to him and bring him in. But they told me that he must be stone dead, and such things also that it was quite plain that anyone who went out of the house would not live more than a moment. We could not believe it, even as we gazed at the body of the dead man; but it was there. I used to wonder sometimes what one would feel like if one saw an apple drop from the tree and shoot up into the air and disappear. I think I know now how one would feel.

"Even then we couldn't believe that it would last. We were not seriously afraid for ourselves. We spoke of getting out in an hour or two, before dinner anyhow. It couldn't last, because it was impossible. Indeed, at twelve o'clock young Griffith said he would go down to the well by the back way and draw another pail of water. I went to the door and stood by it. He had not gone a dozen yards before they were on him. He ran for his life, and we had all we could do to bar the door in time. And then I began to get frightened.

"Still we could not believe in it. Somebody would come along shouting in an hour or two and it would all melt away and vanish. There could not be any real danger. There was plenty of bacon in the house, and half the weekly baking of loaves and some beer in the cellar and a pound or so of tea, and a whole pitcher of water that had been drawn from the well the night before. We could do all right for the day and in the morning it would have all gone away.

"But day followed day and it was still there. I knew Treff Loyne was a lonely place—that was why I had gone there, to have a long rest from all the jangle and rattle and turmoil of London, that makes a man alive and kills him too. I went to Treff Loyne because it was buried in the narrow valley under the ash trees, far away from any track. There was not so much as a footpath that was near it; no one ever came that way. Young Griffith had told me that it was a mile and a half to the nearest house, and the thought of the silent peace and retirement of the farm used to be a delight to me.

"And now this thought came back without delight, with terror. Griffith thought that a shout might be heard on a still night up away on the Allt, 'if a man was listening for it,' he added, doubtfully. My voice was clearer and stronger than his, and on the second night I said I would go up to my bedroom and call for help through the open window.

I waited till it was all dark and still, and looked out through the window before opening it. And then I saw over the ridge of the long barn across the yard what looked like a tree, though I knew there was no tree there. It was a dark mass against the sky, with wide-spread boughs, a tree of thick, dense growth. I wondered what this could be, and I threw open the window, not only because I was going to call for help, but because I wanted to see more clearly what the dark growth over the barn really was.

"I saw in the depth of the dark of it points of fire, and colors in light, all glowing and moving, and the air trembled. I stared out into the night, and the dark tree lifted over the roof of the barn and rose up in the air and floated towards me. I did not move till at the last moment when it was close to the house; and then I saw what it was and banged the window down only just in time. I had to fight, and I saw the tree that was like a burning cloud rise up in the night and sink again and settle over the barn.

"I told them downstairs of this. They sat with white faces, and Mrs. Griffith said that ancient devils were let loose and had come out of the trees and out of the old hills because of the wickedness that was on the earth. She began to, murmur something to herself, something that sounded to me like broken-down Latin.

"I went up to my room again an hour later, but the dark tree swelled over the barn. Another day went by, and at dusk I looked out, but the eyes of fire were watching me. I dared not open the window.

"And then I thought of another plan. There was the great old fireplace, with the round Flemish chimney going high above the house. If I stood beneath it and shouted I thought perhaps the sound might be carried better than if I called out of the window; for all I knew the round chimney might act as a sort of megaphone. Night after night, then, I stood in the hearth and called for help from nine o'clock to eleven. I thought of the lonely place, deep in the valley of the ashtrees, of the lonely hills and lands about it. I thought of the little cottages far away and hoped that my voice might reach to those within them. I thought of the winding lane high on the Allt, and of the few men that came there of nights; but I hoped that my cry might come to one of them.

"But we had drunk up the beer, and we would only let ourselves have water by little drops, and on the fourth night my throat was dry, and I began to feel strange and weak; I knew that all the voice I had in my lungs would hardly reach the length of the field by the farm.

ARTHUR MACHEN

"It was then we began to dream of wells and fountains, and water coming very cold, in little drops, out of rocky places in the middle of a cool wood. We had given up all meals; now and then one would cut a lump from the sides of bacon on the kitchen wall and chew a bit of it, but the saltness was like fire.

"There was a great shower of rain one night. The girl said we might open a window and hold out bowls and basins and catch the rain. I spoke of the cloud with burning eyes. She said 'we will go to the window in the dairy at the back, and one of us can get some water at all events,' She stood up with her basin on the stone slab in the dairy and looked out and heard the plashing of the rain, falling very fast. And she unfastened the catch of the window and had just opened it gently with one hand, for about an inch, and had her basin in the other hand. 'And then,' said she, 'there was something that began to tremble and shudder and shake as it did when we went to the Choral Festival at St. Teilo's, and the organ played, and there was the cloud and the burning close before me.'

"And then we began to dream, as I say. I woke up in my sitting-room one hot afternoon when the sun was shining, and I had been looking and searching in my dream all through the house, and I had gone down to the old cellar that wasn't used, the cellar with the pillars and the vaulted room, with an iron pike in my hand. Something said to me that there was water there, and in my dream I went to a heavy stone by the middle pillar and raised it up, and there beneath was a bubbling well of cold, clear water, and I had just hollowed my hand to drink it when I woke. I went into the kitchen and told young Griffith. I said I was sure there was water there. He shook his head, but he took up the great kitchen poker and we went down to the old cellar. I showed him the stone by the pillar, and he raised it up. But there was no well.

"Do you know, I reminded myself of many people whom I have met in life? I would not be convinced. I was sure that, after all, there was a well there. They had a butcher's cleaver in the kitchen and I took it down to the old cellar and hacked at the ground with it. The others didn't interfere with me. We were getting past that. We hardly ever spoke to one another. Each one would be wandering about the house, upstairs and downstairs, each one of us, I suppose, bent on his own foolish plan and mad design, but we hardly ever spoke. Years ago, I was an actor for a bit, and I remember how it was on first nights; the actors treading softly up and down the wings, by their entrance, their lips moving and muttering over the words of their parts, but without a word for one another. So it was with us. I came upon young Griffith one evening evidently trying to make a subterranean passage under one of the walls of the house. I knew he was mad, as he knew I was mad when he saw me digging for a well in the cellar; but neither said anything to the other.

"Now we are past all this. We are too weak. We dream when we are awake and when we dream we think we wake. Night and day come and go and we mistake one for another; I hear Griffith murmuring to himself about the stars when the sun is high at noonday, and at midnight I have found myself thinking that I walked in bright sunlit meadows beside cold, rushing streams that flowed from high rocks.

"Then at the dawn figures in black robes, carrying lighted tapers in their hands pass slowly about and about; and I hear great rolling organ music that sounds as if some tremendous rite were to begin, and voices crying in an ancient song shrill from the depths of the earth.

"Only a little while ago I heard a voice which sounded as if it were at my very ears, but rang and echoed and resounded as if it were rolling and reverberated from the vault of some cathedral, chanting in terrible modulations. I heard the words quite clearly.

"*INCIPIT LIBER IRÆ DOMINI DEI nostri.* (Here beginneth The Book of the Wrath of the Lord our God.)

"And then the voice sang the word *Aleph*, prolonging it, it seemed through ages, and a light was extinguished as it began the chapter:

"*In that day, saith the Lord, there shall be a cloud over the land, and in the cloud a burning and a shape of fire, and out of the cloud shall issue forth my messengers; they shall run all together, they shall not turn aside; this shall be a day of exceeding bitterness, without salvation. And on every high hill, saith the Lord of Hosts, I will set my sentinels, and my armies shall encamp in the place of every valley; in the house that is amongst rushes I will execute judgment, and in vain shall they fly for refuge to the munitions of the rocks. In the groves of the woods, in the places where the leaves are as a tent above them, they shall find the sword of the slayer; and they that put their trust in walled cities shall be confounded. Woe unto the armed man, woe unto him that taketh pleasure in the strength of his artillery, for a little thing shall smite him, and by one that hath no might shall he be brought down into the dust. That which is low shall be set on high; I will make the lamb and the young sheep to be as the lion from the swellings of Jordan; they shall not spare, saith the Lord, and the doves shall be as eagles on the hill Engedi; none shall be found that may abide the onset of their battle.*

"Even now I can hear the voice rolling far away, as if it came from the altar of a great church and I stood at the door. There are lights very far away in the hollow of a vast darkness, and one by one they are put out. I hear a voice chanting again with that endless modulation that climbs and aspires to the stars, and shines there, and rushes down to the dark depths of the earth, again to ascend; the word is *Zain*."

Here the manuscript lapsed again, and finally into utter, lamentable confusion. There were scrawled lines wavering across the page on which Secretan seemed to have been trying to note the unearthly music that swelled in his dying ears. As the scrapes and scratches of ink showed, he had tried hard to begin a new sentence. The pen had dropped at last out of his hand upon the paper, leaving a blot and a smear upon it.

Lewis heard the tramp of feet along the passage; they were carrying out the dead to the cart.

XIV

The End of the Terror

Dr. Lewis maintained that we should never begin to understand the real significance of life until we began to study just those aspects of it which we now dismiss and overlook as utterly inexplicable, and therefore, unimportant.

We were discussing a few months ago the awful shadow of the terror which at length had passed away from the land. I had formed my opinion, partly from observation, partly from certain facts which had been communicated to me, and the pass-words having been exchanged, I found that Lewis had come by very different ways to the same end.

"And yet," he said, "it is not a true end, or rather, it is like all the ends of human inquiry, it leads one to a great mystery. We must confess that what has happened might have happened at anytime in the history of the world. It did not happen till a year ago as a matter of fact, and therefore we made up our minds that it never could happen; or, one would better say, it was outside the range even of imagination. But this is our way. Most people are quite sure that the Black Death—otherwise the Plague—will never invade Europe again. They have made up their complacent minds that it was due to dirt and bad drainage. As a matter of fact the Plague had nothing to do with dirt or with drains; and there is nothing to prevent its ravaging England tomorrow. But if you tell people so, they won't believe you. They won't believe in anything that isn't there at the particular moment when you are talking to them. As with the Plague, so with the Terror. We could not believe that such a thing could ever happen. Remnant said, truly enough, that whatever it was, it was outside theory, outside our theory. Flatland cannot believe in the cube or the sphere."

I agreed with all this. I added that sometimes the world was incapable of seeing, much less believing, that which was before its own eyes.

"Look," I said, "at any eighteenth century print of a Gothic cathedral. You will find that the trained artistic eye even could not behold in any true sense the building that was before it. I have seen an old print of Peterborough Cathedral that looks as if the artist had drawn it from a clumsy model, constructed of bent wire and children's bricks."

"Exactly; because Gothic was outside the aesthetic theory (and therefore vision) of the time. You can't believe what you don't see: rather, you can't see what you don't believe. It was so during the time of the Terror. All this bears out what Coleridge said as to the necessity of having the idea before the facts could be of any service to one. Of course, he was right; mere facts, without the correlating idea, are nothing and lead to no conclusion. We had plenty of facts, but we could make nothing of them. I went home at the tail of that dreadful procession from Treff Loyne in a state of mind very near to madness. I heard one of the soldiers saying to the other: 'There's no rat that'll spike a man to the heart, Bill.' I don't know why, but I felt that if I heard anymore of such talk as that I should go crazy; it seemed to me that the anchors of reason were parting. I left the party and took the short cut across the fields into Porth. I looked up Davies in the High Street and arranged with him that he should take on any cases I might have that evening, and then I went home and gave my man his instructions to send people on. And then I shut myself up to think it all out—if I could.

"You must not suppose that my experiences of that afternoon had afforded me the slightest illumination. Indeed, if it had not been that I had seen poor old Griffith's body lying pierced in his own farmyard, I think I should have been inclined to accept one of Secretan's hints, and to believe that the whole family had fallen a victim to a collective delusion or hallucination, and had shut themselves up and died of thirst through sheer madness. I think there have been such cases. It's the insanity of inhibition, the belief that you can't do something which you are really perfectly capable of doing. But; I had seen the body of the murdered man and the wound that had killed him.

"Did the manuscript left by Secretan give me no hint? Well, it seemed to me to make confusion worse confounded. You have seen it; you know that in certain places it is evidently mere delirium, the wanderings of a dying mind. How was I to separate the facts from the phantasms—lacking the key to the whole enigma. Delirium is often a sort of cloud-castle, a sort of magnified and distorted shadow of actualities, but it is a very difficult thing, almost an impossible thing, to reconstruct the real house from the distortion of it, thrown on the clouds of the patient's brain. You see, Secretan in writing that extraordinary document almost insisted on the fact that he was not in his proper sense; that for days he had been part asleep, part awake, part delirious. How was one to judge his statement, to separate delirium from fact? In one thing he stood confirmed; you remember he speaks of calling for help up the old chimney of Treff Loyne; that did seem to fit in with the tales of a hollow, moaning cry that had been heard upon the Allt: so far one could take him as a recorder of actual experiences. And I looked in the old cellars of the farm and found a frantic sort of rabbit-hole dug by one of the pillars; again he was confirmed. But what was one to make of that story of the chanting voice, and the letters of the Hebrew alphabet, and the chapter out of some unknown Minor Prophet? When one has the key it is easy enough to sort out the facts, or the hints of facts from the delusions; but I hadn't the key on that September evening. I was forgetting the 'tree' with lights and fires in it; that, I think, impressed me more than anything with the feeling that Secretan's story was, in the main, a true story. I had seen a like appearance down there in my own garden; but what was it?

"Now, I was saying that, paradoxically, it is only by the inexplicable things that life can be explained. We are apt to say, you know, 'a very odd coincidence' and pass the matter by, as if there were no more to be said, or as if that were the end of it. Well, I believe that the only real path lies through the blind alleys."

"How do you mean?"

"Well, this is an instance of what I mean. I told you about Merritt, my brother-in-law, and the capsizing of that boat, the *Mary Ann*. He had seen, he said, signal lights flashing from one of the farms on the coast, and he was quite certain that the two things were intimately connected as cause and effect. I thought it all nonsense, and I was wondering how I was going to shut him up when a big moth flew into the room through that window, fluttered about, and succeeded in burning itself alive in the lamp. That gave me my cue; I asked Merritt if he knew why moths made for lamps or something of the kind; I thought it would be a hint to him that I was sick of his flashlights and his half-baked theories. So it was—he looked sulky and held his tongue.

"But a few minutes later I was called out by a man who had found his little boy dead in a field near his cottage about an hour before. The child was so still, they said, that a great moth had settled on his forehead and only fluttered away when they lifted up the body. It was absolutely illogical; but it was this odd 'coincidence' of the moth in my lamp and the moth on the dead boy's forehead that first set me on the track. I can't say that it guided me in any real sense; it was more like a great flare of red paint on a wall; it rang up my attention, if I may say so; it was a

ARTHUR MACHEN

sort of shock like a bang on the big drum. No doubt Merritt was talking great nonsense that evening so far as his particular instance went; the flashes of light from the farm had nothing to do with the wreck of the boat. But his general principle was sound; when you hear a gun go off and see a man fall it is idle to talk of 'a mere coincidence.' I think a very interesting book might be written on this question: I would call it 'A Grammar of Coincidence.'

"But as you will remember, from having read my notes on the matter, I was called in about ten days later to see a man named Cradock, who had been found in a field near his farm quite dead. This also was at night. His wife found him, and there were some very queer things in her story. She said that the hedge of the field looked as if it were changed; she began to be afraid that she had lost her way and got into the wrong field. Then she said the hedge was lighted up as if there were a lot of glow-worms in it, and when she peered over the stile there seemed to be some kind of glimmering upon the ground, and then the glimmering melted away, and she found her husband's body near where this light had been. Now this man Cradock had been suffocated just as the little boy Roberts had been suffocated, and as that man in the Midlands who took a short cut one night had been suffocated. Then I remembered that poor Johnnie Roberts had called out about 'something shiny' over the stile just before he played truant. Then, on my part, I had to contribute the very remarkable sight I witnessed here, as I looked down over the garden; the appearance as of a spreading tree where I knew there was no such tree, and then the shining and burning of lights and moving colors. Like the poor child and Mrs. Cradock, I had seen something shiny, just as some man in Stratfordshire had seen a dark cloud with points of fire in it floating over the trees. And Mrs. Cradock thought that the shape of the trees in the hedge had changed.

"My mind almost uttered the word that was wanted; but you see the difficulties. This set of circumstances could not, so far as I could see, have any relation with the other circumstances of the Terror. How could I connect all this with the bombs and machine-guns of the Midlands, with the armed men who kept watch about the munition shops by day and night. Then there was the long list of people here who had fallen over the cliffs or into the quarry; there were the cases of the men stifled in the slime of the marshes; there was the affair of the family murdered in front of their cottage on the Highway; there was the capsized *Mary Ann*. I could not see any thread that could bring all these incidents together; they seemed to me to be hopelessly disconnected. I could not make out any relation between the agency that beat out the brains of the Williams's and the agency, that overturned the boat. I don't know, but I think it's very likely if nothing more had happened that I should have put the whole thing down as an unaccountable series of crimes and accidents which chanced to occur in Meirion in the summer of 1915. Well, of course, that would have been an impossible standpoint in view of certain incidents in Merritt's story. Still, if one is confronted by the insoluble, one lets it go at last. If the mystery is inexplicable, one pretends that there isn't any mystery. That is the justification for what is called free thinking.

"Then came that extraordinary business of Treff Loyne. I couldn't put that on one side. I couldn't pretend that nothing strange or out of the way had happened. There was no getting over it or getting round it. I had seen with my eyes that there was a mystery, and a most horrible mystery. I have forgotten my logic, but one might say that Treff Loyne demonstrated the existence of a mystery in the figure of Death.

"I took it all home, as I have told you, and sat down for the evening before it. It appalled me, not only by its horror, but here again by the discrepancy between its terms. Old Griffith, so far as I could judge, had been killed by the thrust of a pike or perhaps of a sharpened stake: how could one relate this to the burning tree that had floated over the ridge of the barn. It was as if I said to you: 'here is a man drowned, and here is a man burned alive: show that each death was caused by the same agency!' And the moment that I left this particular case of Treff Loyne, and tried to get some light on it from other instances of the Terror, I would think of the man in the midlands who heard the feet of a thousand men rustling in the wood, and their voices as if dead men sat up in their bones and talked. And then I would say to myself, 'and how about that boat overturned in a calm sea?' There seemed no end to it, no hope of any solution.

"It was, I believe, a sudden leap of the mind that liberated me from the tangle. It was quite beyond logic. I went back to that evening when Merritt was boring me with his flashlights, to the moth in the candle, and to the moth on the forehead of poor Johnnie Roberts. There was no sense in it; but I suddenly determined that the child and Joseph Cradock the farmer, and that unnamed Stratfordshire man, all found at night, all asphyxiated, had been choked by vast swarms of moths. I don't pretend even now that this is demonstrated, but I'm sure it's true.

"Now suppose you encounter a swarm of these creatures in the dark. Suppose the smaller ones fly up your nostrils. You will gasp for breath and open your mouth. Then, suppose some hundreds of them fly into your mouth, into your gullet, into your windpipe, what will happen to you? You will be dead in a very short time, choked, asphyxiated."

"But the moths would be dead too. They would be found in the bodies."

"The moths? Do you know that it is extremely difficult to kill a moth with cyanide of potassium? Take a frog, kill it, open its stomach. There you will find its dinner of moths and small beetles, and the 'dinner' will shake itself and walk off cheerily, to resume an entirely active existence. No; that is no difficulty.

"Well, now I came to this. I was shutting out all the other cases. I was confining myself to those that came under the one formula. I got to the assumption or conclusion, whichever you like, that certain people had been asphyxiated by the action of moths. I had accounted for that extraordinary appearance of burning or colored lights that I had witnessed myself, when I saw the growth of that strange tree in my garden. That was clearly the cloud with points of fire in it that the Stratfordshire man took for a new and terrible kind of poison gas, that was the shiny something that poor little Johnnie Roberts had seen over the stile, that was the glimmering light that had led Mrs. Cradock to her husband's dead body, that was the assemblage of terrible eyes that had watched over Treff Loyne by night. Once on the right track I understood all this, for coming into this room in the dark, I have been amazed by the wonderful burning and the strange fiery colors of the eyes of a single moth, as it crept up the pane of glass, outside. Imagine the effect of myriads of such eyes, of the movement of these lights and fires in a vast swarm of moths, each insect being in constant motion while it kept its place in the mass: I felt that all this was clear and certain.

"Then the next step. Of course, we know nothing really about moths; rather, we know nothing of moth reality. For all I know there may be hundreds of books which treat of moth and nothing but moth. But these are scientific books, and science only deals with surfaces; it has nothing to do with realities—it is impertinent if it attempts to do with realities. To take a very minor matter; we don't even know why the moth desires the flame. But we do know what the moth does not do; it does not gather itself into swarms with the object of destroying human life. But here, by the hypothesis, were cases in which the moth had done this very thing; the moth race had entered, it seemed, into a malignant conspiracy against the human race. It was quite impossible, no doubt—that is to say, it had never happened before—but I could see no escape from this conclusion.

"These insects, then, were definitely hostile to man; and then I stopped, for I could not see the next step, obvious though it seems to me now. I believe that the soldiers' scraps of talk on the way to Treff Loyne and back flung the next plank over the gulf. They had spoken of 'rat poison,' of no rat being able to spike a man through the heart; and then, suddenly, I saw my way clear. If the moths were infected with hatred of men, and possessed the design and the power of combining against him; why not suppose this hatred, this design, this power shared by other non-human creatures.

"The secret of the Terror might be condensed into a sentence: the animals had revolted against men.

"Now, the puzzle became easy enough; one had only to classify. Take the cases of the people who met their deaths by falling over cliffs or over the edge of quarries. We think of sheep as timid creatures, who always ran away. But suppose sheep that don't run away; and, after all, in reason why should they run away? Quarry or no quarry, cliff or no cliff; what would happen to you if a hundred sheep ran after you instead of running from you? There would be no help for it; they would have you down and beat you to death or stifle you. Then suppose man, woman, or child near a cliff's edge or a quarry-side, and a sudden rush of sheep. Clearly there is no help; there is nothing for it but to go over. There can be no doubt that that, is what happened in all these cases.

"And again; you know the country and you know how a herd of cattle will sometimes pursue people through the fields in a solemn, stolid sort of way. They behave as if they wanted to close in on you. Townspeople sometimes get frightened and scream and run; you or I would take no notice, or at the utmost, wave our sticks at the herd, which will stop dead or lumber off. But suppose they don't lumber off. The mildest old cow, remember, is stronger than any man. What can one man or half a dozen men do against half a hundred of these beasts no longer restrained by that mysterious inhibition, which has made for ages the strong the humble slaves of the weak? But if you are botanizing in the marsh, like that poor fellow who was staying at Porth, and forty or fifty young cattle gradually close round you, and refuse to move when you shout and wave your stick, but get closer and closer instead, and get you into the slime. Again, where is your help? If you haven't got an automatic pistol, you must go down and stay down, while the beasts lie quietly on you for five minutes. It was a quicker death for poor Griffith of Treff Loyne—one of his own beasts gored him to death with one sharp thrust of its horn into his heart. And from that morning those within the house were closely besieged by their own cattle and horses and sheep; and when those unhappy people within opened a window to call for help or to catch a few drops of rain water to relieve their burning thirst, the cloud waited for them with its myriad eyes of fire. Can you wonder that Secretan's statement reads in places like mania? You perceive the horrible position of those people in Treff Loyne; not only did they see death advancing on them, but advancing with incredible steps, as if one were to die not only in nightmare but by nightmare. But no one in his wildest, most fiery dreams had ever imagined such a fate. I am not astonished that Secretan at one moment suspected the evidence of his own senses, at another surmised that the world's end had come."

"And how about the Williams's who were murdered on the Highway near here?"

"The horses were the murderers; the horses that afterwards stampeded the camp below. By some means which is still obscure to me they lured that family into the road and beat their brains out; their shod hoofs were the instruments of execution. And, as for the *Mary Ann*, the boat that was capsized, I have no doubt that it was overturned by a sudden rush of the porpoises that were gamboling about in the water of Larnac Bay. A porpoise is a heavy beast—half a dozen of them could easily upset a light rowing-boat. The munition works? Their enemy was rats. I believe that it has been calculated that in 'greater London' the number of rats is about equal to the number of human beings, that is, there are about seven millions of them. The proportion would be about the same in all the great centers of population; and the rat, moreover, is, on occasion, migratory in its habits. You can understand now that story of the *Semiramis*, beating about the mouth of the Thames, and at last cast away by Arcachon, her only crew dry heaps of bones. The rat is an expert boarder of ships. And so one can understand the tale told by the frightened man who took the path by the wood that led up from the new munition works. He thought he heard a thousand men treading softly through the wood and chattering to one another in some horrible tongue; what he did hear was the marshaling of an army of rats—their array before the battle.

"And conceive the terror of such an attack. Even one rat in a fury is said to be an ugly customer to meet; conceive then, the irruption of these terrible, swarming myriads, rushing upon the helpless, unprepared, astonished workers in the munition shops."

THERE CAN BE NO DOUBT, I think, that Dr. Lewis was entirely justified in these extraordinary conclusions. As I say, I had arrived at pretty much the same end, by different ways; but this rather as to the general situation, while Lewis had made his own particular study of those circumstances of the Terror that were within his immediate purview, as a physician in large practice in the southern part of Meirion. Of some of the cases which he reviewed he had, no doubt, no immediate or first-hand knowledge; but he judged these instances by their similarity to the facts which had come under his personal notice. He spoke of the affairs of the quarry at Llanfihangel on the analogy of the people who were found dead at the bottom of the cliffs near Porth, and he was no doubt justified in doing so. He told me that, thinking the whole matter over, he was hardly more astonished by the Terror in itself than by the strange way in which he had arrived at his conclusions.

"You know," he said, "those certain evidences of animal malevolence which we knew of, the bees that stung the child to death, the trusted sheepdog's turning savage, and so forth. Well, I got no light whatever from all this; it suggested nothing to me—simply because I had not got that 'idea' which Coleridge rightly holds necessary in all inquiry; facts *qua* facts, as we said, mean nothing and, come to nothing. You do not believe, therefore you cannot see.

"And then, when the truth at last appeared it was through the whimsical 'coincidence' as we call such signs, of the moth in my lamp and the moth on the dead child's forehead. This, I think, is very extraordinary."

"And there seems to have been one beast that remained faithful; the dog at Treff Loyne. That is strange."

"That remains a mystery."

IT WOULD NOT BE WISE, even now, to describe too closely the terrible scenes that were to be seen in the munition areas of the north and the midlands during the black months of the Terror. Out of the factories

ARTHUR MACHEN

issued at black midnight the shrouded dead in their coffins, and their very kinsfolk did not know how they had come by their deaths. All the towns were full of houses of mourning, were full of dark and terrible rumors; incredible, as the incredible reality. There were things done and suffered that perhaps never will be brought to light, memories and secret traditions of these things will be whispered in families, delivered from father to son, growing wilder with the passage of the years, but never growing wilder than the truth.

It is enough to say that the cause of the Allies was for awhile in deadly peril. The men at the front called in their extremity for guns and shells. No one told them what was happening in the places where these munitions were made.

At first the position was nothing less than desperate; men in high places were almost ready to cry "mercy" to the enemy. But, after the first panic, measures were taken such as those described by Merritt in his account of the matter. The workers were armed with special weapons, guards were mounted, machine-guns were placed in position, bombs and liquid flame were ready against the obscene hordes of the enemy, and the "burning clouds" found a fire fiercer than their own. Many deaths occurred amongst the airmen; but they, too, were given special guns, arms that scattered shot broadcast, and so drove away the dark flights that threatened the airplanes.

And, then, in the winter of 1915–16, the Terror ended suddenly as it had begun. Once more a sheep was a frightened beast that ran instinctively from a little child; the cattle were again solemn, stupid creatures, void of harm; the spirit and the convention of malignant design passed out of the hearts of all the animals. The chains that they had cast off for awhile were thrown again about them.

And, finally, there comes the inevitable "why?" Why did the beasts who had been humbly and patiently subject to man, or affrighted by his presence, suddenly know their strength and learn how to league together, and declare bitter war against their ancient master?

It is a most difficult and obscure question. I give what explanation I have to give with very great diffidence, and an eminent disposition to be corrected, if a clearer light can be found.

Some friends of mine, for whose judgment I have very great respect, are inclined to think that there was a certain contagion of hate. They hold that the fury of the whole world at war, the great passion of death that seems driving all humanity to destruction, infected at last these lower creatures, and in place of their native instinct of submission, gave them rage and wrath and ravening.

This may be the explanation. I cannot say that it is not so, because I do not profess to understand the working of the universe. But I confess that the theory strikes me as fanciful. There may be a contagion of hate as there is a contagion of smallpox; I do not know, but I hardly believe it.

In my opinion, and it is only an opinion, the source of the great revolt of the beasts is to be sought in a much subtler region of inquiry. I believe that the subjects revolted because the king abdicated. Man has dominated the beasts throughout the ages, the spiritual has reigned over the rational through the peculiar quality and grace of spirituality that men possess, that makes a man to be that which he is. And when he maintained this power and grace, I think it is pretty clear that between him and the animals there was a certain treaty and alliance. There was supremacy on the one hand, and submission on the other; but at the same time there was between the two that cordiality which exists between lords and subjects in a well-organized state. I know a socialist who maintains that Chaucer's "Canterbury Tales" give a picture of true democracy. I do not know about that, but I see that knight and miller were able to get on quite pleasantly together, just because the knight knew that he was a knight and the miller knew that he was a miller. If the knight had had conscientious objections to his knightly grade, while the miller saw no reason why he should not be a knight, I am sure that their intercourse would have been difficult, unpleasant, and perhaps murderous.

So with man. I believe in the strength and truth of tradition. A learned man said to me a few weeks ago: "When I have to choose between the evidence of tradition and the evidence of a document, I always believe the evidence of tradition. Documents may be falsified, and often are falsified; tradition is never falsified." This is true; and, therefore, I think, one may put trust in the vast body of folklore which asserts that there was once a worthy and friendly alliance between man and the beasts. Our popular tale of Dick Whittington and his Cat no doubt represents the adaptation of a very ancient legend to a comparatively modern personage, but we may go back into the ages and find the popular tradition asserting that not only are the animals the subjects, but also the friends of man.

All that was in virtue of that singular spiritual element in man which the rational animals do not possess. Spiritual does not mean respectable, it does not even mean moral, it does not mean "good" in the ordinary acceptation of the word. It signifies the royal prerogative of man, differentiating him from the beasts.

For long ages he has been putting off this royal robe, he has been wiping the balm of consecration from his own breast. He has declared, again and again, that he is not spiritual, but rational, that is, the equal of the beasts over whom he was once sovereign. He has vowed that he is not Orpheus but Caliban.

But the beasts also have within them something which corresponds to the spiritual quality in men—we are content to call it instinct. They perceived that the throne was vacant—not even friendship was possible between them and the self-deposed monarch. If he were not king he was a sham, an imposter, a thing to be destroyed.

Hence, I think, the Terror. They have risen once—they may rise again.

THE END

OUT OF THE EARTH

There was some sort of confused complaint during last August of the ill behaviour of the children at certain Welsh watering-places. Such reports and vague rumours are most difficult to trace to their heads and fountains; none has better reason to know that than myself. I need not go over the old ground here, but I am afraid that many people are wishing by this time that they had never heard my name; again, a considerable number of estimable persons are concerning themselves gloomily enough, from my point of view, with my everlasting welfare. They write me letters, some in kindly remonstrance, begging me not to deprive poor, sick-hearted souls of what little comfort they possess amidst their sorrows. Others send me tracts and pink leaflets with allusions to "the daughter of a well-known canon"; others again are violently and anonymously abusive. And then in open print, in fair book form, Mr. Begbie has dealt with me righteously but harshly, as I cannot but think.

Yet, it was all so entirely innocent, nay casual, on my part. A poor linnet of prose, I did but perform my indifferent piping in the Evening News because I wanted to do so, because I felt that the story of "The Bowmen" ought to be told. An inventor of fantasies is a poor creature, heaven knows, when all the world is at war; but I thought that no harm would be done, at any rate, if I bore witness, after the fashion of the fantastic craft, to my belief in the heroic glory of the English host who went back from Mons fighting and triumphing.

And then, somehow or other, it was as if I had touched a button and set in action a terrific, complicated mechanism of rumours that pretended to be sworn truth, of gossip that posed as evidence, of wild tarradiddles that good men most firmly believed. The supposed testimony of that "daughter of a well-known canon" took parish magazines by storm, and equally enjoyed the faith of dissenting divines. The "daughter" denied all knowledge of the matter, but people still quoted her supposed sure word; and the issues were confused with tales, probably true, of painful hallucinations and deliriums of our retreating soldiers, men fatigued and shattered to the very verge of death. It all became worse than the Russian myths, and as in the fable of the Russians, it seemed impossible to follow the streams of delusion to their fountain-head—or heads. Who was it who said that "Miss M. knew two officers who, etc., etc."? I suppose we shall never know his lying, deluding name.

And so, I dare say, it will be with this strange affair of the troublesome children of the Welsh seaside town, or rather of a group of small towns and villages lying within a certain section or zone, which I am not going to indicate more precisely than I can help, since I love that country, and my recent experience with "The Bowmen" have taught me that no tale is too idle to be believed. And, of course, to begin with, nobody knew how this odd and malicious piece of gossip originated. So far as I know, it was more akin to the Russian myth than to the tale of "The Angels of Mons." That is, rumour preceded print; the thing was talked of here and there and passed from letter to letter long before the papers were aware of its existence. And—here it resembles rather the Mons affair—London and Manchester, Leeds and Birmingham were muttering vague unpleasant things while the little villages concerned basked innocently in the sunshine of an unusual prosperity.

In this last circumstance, as some believe, is to be sought the root of the whole matter. It is well known that certain east coast towns suffered from the dread of air-raids, and that a good many of their usual visitors went westward for the first time. So there is a theory that the east coast was mean enough to circulate reports against the west coast out of pure malice and envy. It may be so; I do not pretend to know. But here is a personal experience, such as it is, which illustrated the way in which the rumour was circulated. I was lunching one day at my Fleet Street tavern—this was early in July—and a friend of mine, a solicitor, of Serjeants' Inn, came in and sat at the same table. We began to talk of holidays and my friend Eddis asked me where I was going. "To the same old place," I said. "Manavon. You know we always go there." "Are you really?" said the lawyer; "I thought that coast had gone off a lot. My wife has a friend who's heard that it's not at all that it was."

I was astonished to hear this, not seeing how a little village like Manavon could have "gone off." I had known it for ten years as having accommodation for about twenty visitors, and I could not believe that rows of lodging houses had sprung up since the August of 1914. Still I put the question to Eddis: "Trippers?" I asked, knowing firstly that trippers hate the solitudes of the country and the sea; secondly, that there are no industrial towns within cheap and easy distance, and thirdly, that the railways were issuing no excursion tickets during the war.

"No, not exactly trippers," the lawyer replied. "But my wife's friend knows a clergyman who says that the beach at Tremaen is not at all pleasant now, and Tremaen's only a few miles from Manavon, isn't it?"

"In what way not pleasant?" I carried on my examination. "Pierrots and shows, and that sort of thing?" I felt that it could not be so, for the solemn rocks of Tremaen would have turned the liveliest Pierrot to stone. He would have frozen into a crag on the beach, and the seagulls would carry away his song and make it a lament by lonely, booming caverns that look on Avalon. Eddis said he had heard nothing about showmen; but he understood that since the war the children of the whole district had gone quite out of hand.

"Bad language, you know," he said, "and all that sort of thing, worse than London slum children. One doesn't want one's wife and children to hear foul talk at anytime, much less on their holiday. And they say that Castell Coch is quite impossible; no decent woman would be seen there!"

I said: "Really, that's a great pity," and changed the subject. But I could not make it out at all. I knew Castell Coch well—a little bay bastioned by dunes and red sandstone cliffs, rich with greenery. A stream of cold water runs down there to the sea; there is the ruined Norman Castle, the ancient church and the scattered village; it is altogether a place of peace and quiet and great beauty. The people there, children and grown-ups alike, were not merely decent but courteous folk: if one thanked a child for opening a gate, there would come the inevitable response: "And welcome kindly, sir." I could not make it out at all. I didn't believe the lawyer's tales; for the life of me I could not see what he could be driving at. And, for the avoidance of all unnecessary mystery, I may as well say that my wife and child and myself went down to Manavon last August and had a most delightful holiday. At the time we were certainly conscious of no annoyance or unpleasantness of any kind. Afterwards, I confess, I heard a story that puzzled and still puzzles me, and this story, if it be received, might give its own interpretation to one or two circumstances which seemed in themselves quite insignificant.

But all through July I came upon traces of evil rumours affecting this most gracious corner of the earth. Some of these rumours were repetitions of Eddis's gossip; others amplified his vague story and made it more definite. Of course, no first-hand evidence was available. There never is any first-hand evidence in these cases. But A knew B who had heard from C that her second cousin's little girl had been set upon and beaten by a pack of young Welsh savages. Then people quoted "a doctor in large practice in a well-known town in the Midlands," to the effect that Tremaen was a sink of juvenile depravity. They said that a responsible medical man's evidence was final and convincing; but they didn't bother to find out who the doctor was, or whether there was any doctor at all—or any doctor relevant to the issue. Then the thing began to get into the papers in a sort of oblique, by-the-way sort of manner. People cited the case of these imaginary bad children in support of their educational views. One side said that "these unfortunate little ones" would have been quite well behaved if they had had no education at all; the opposition declared that continuation schools would speedily reform them and make them into admirable citizens. Then the poor Arfonshire children seemed to become involved in quarrels about Welsh disestablishment and in the question of the miners; and all the while they were going about behaving politely and admirably as they always do behave. I knew all the time that it was all nonsense, but I couldn't understand in the least what it meant, or who was pulling the wires of rumour, or their purpose in so pulling. I began to wonder whether the pressure and anxiety and suspense of a terrible war had unhinged the public mind, so that it was ready to believe any fable, to debate the reasons for happenings which had never happened. At last, quite incredible things began to be whispered: visitors' children had not only been beaten, they had been tortured; a little boy had been found impaled on a stake in a lonely field near Manavon; another child had been lured to destruction over the cliffs at Castell Coch. A London paper sent a good man down quietly to Arfon to investigate. He was away for a week, and at the end of that period returned to his office and in his own phrase, "threw the whole story down." There was not a word of truth, he said, in any of these rumours; no vestige of a foundation for the mildest forms of all this gossip. He had never seen such a beautiful country; he had never met pleasanter men, women or children; there was not a single case of anyone having been annoyed or troubled in any sort or fashion.

Yet all the while the story grew, and grew more monstrous and incredible. I was too much occupied in watching the progress of my own mythological monster to pay much attention. The town clerk of Tremaen, to which the legend had at length penetrated, wrote a brief letter to the press indignantly denying that there was the slightest foundation for "the unsavoury rumours" which, he understood, were being circulated; and about this time we went down to Manavon and, as I say, enjoyed ourselves extremely. The weather was perfect: blues of paradise in the skies, the seas all a shimmering wonder, olive greens and emeralds, rich purples, glassy sapphires changing by the rocks; far away a haze of magic lights and colours at the meeting of sea and sky. Work and anxiety had harried me; I found nothing better than to rest on the thymy banks by the shore, finding an infinite balm and refreshment in the great sea before me, in the tiny flowers beside me. Or we would rest all the summer afternoon on a "shelf" high on the grey cliffs and watch the tide creaming and surging about the rocks, and listen to it booming in the hollows and caverns below. Afterwards, as I say, there were one or two things that struck cold. But at the time those were nothing. You see a man in an odd white hat pass by and think little or nothing about it. Afterwards, when you hear that a man wearing just such a hat had committed murder in the next street five minutes before, then you find in that hat a certain interest and significance. "Funny children," was the phrase my little boy used; and I began to think they were "funny" indeed.

If there be a key at all to this queer business, I think it is to be found in a talk I had not long ago with a friend of mine named Morgan. He is a Welshman and a dreamer, and some people say he is like a child who has grown up and yet has not grown up like other children of men. Though I did not know it, while I was at Manavon, he was spending his holiday time at Castell Coch. He was a lonely man and he liked lonely places, and when we met in the autumn he told me how, day after day, he would carry his bread and cheese and beer in a basket to a remote headland on that coast known as the Old Camp. Here, far above the waters, are solemn, mighty walls, turf-grown; circumvallations rounded and smooth with the passing of many thousand years. At one end of this most ancient place there is a tumulus, a tower of observation, perhaps, and underneath it slinks the green, deceiving ditch that seems to wind into the heart of the camp, but in reality rushes down to sheer rock and a precipice over the waters.

Here came Morgan daily, as he said, to dream of Avalon, to purge himself from the fuming corruption of the streets.

And so, as he told me, it was with singular horror that one afternoon as he dozed and dreamed and opened his eyes now and again to watch the miracle and magic of the sea, as he listened to the myriad murmurs of the waves, his meditation was broken by a sudden burst of horrible raucous cries—and the cries of children, too, but children of the lowest type. Morgan says that the very tones made him shudder—"They were to the ear what slime is to the touch," and then the words: every foulness, every filthy abomination of speech; blasphemies that struck like blows at the sky, that sank down into the pure, shining depths, defiling them! He was amazed. He peered over the green wall of the fort, and there in the ditch he saw a swarm of noisome children, horrible little stunted creatures with old men's faces, with bloated faces, with little sunken eyes, with leering eyes. It was worse than uncovering a brood of snakes or a nest of worms.

No; he would not describe what they were about. "Read about Belgium," said Morgan, "and think they couldn't have been more than five or six years old." There was no infamy, he said, that they did not perpetrate; they spared no horror of cruelty. "I saw blood running in streams, as they shrieked with laughter, but I could not find the mark of it on the grass afterwards."

Morgan said he watched them and could not utter a word; it was as if a hand held his mouth tight. But at last he found his voice and shrieked at them, and they burst into a yell of obscene laughter and shrieked back at him, and scattered out of sight. He could not trace them; he supposes that they hid in the deep bracken behind the Old Camp.

"Sometimes I can't understand my landlord at Castell Coch," Morgan went on. "He's the village postmaster and has a little farm of his own—a decent, pleasant, ordinary sort of chap. But now and again he will talk oddly. I was telling him about these beastly children and wondering who they could be when he broke into Welsh, something like 'the battle that is for age unto ages; and the People take delight in it.'"

So far Morgan, and it was evident that he did not understand at all. But this strange tale of his brought back an odd circumstance or two that I recollected: a matter of our little boy straying away more than once, and getting lost among the sand dunes and coming back screaming, evidently frightened horribly, and babbling about "funny children." We took no notice; did not trouble, I think, to look whether there were any children wandering about the dunes or not. We were accustomed to his small imaginations.

But after hearing Morgan's story I was interested and I wrote an account of the matter to my friend, old Doctor Duthoit, of Hereford. And he:

"They were only visible, only audible to children and the childlike. Hence the explanation of what puzzled you at first; the rumours, how did they arise? They arose from nursery gossip, from scraps and odds and ends of half-articulate children's talk of horrors that they didn't understand, of words that shamed their nurses and their mothers.

　　　　　　　　　　　　　　　ARTHUR MACHEN

"These little people of the earth rise up and rejoice in these times of ours. For they are glad, as the Welshman said, when they know that men follow their ways."

THE END

ORNAMENTS IN JADE

The Rose Garden

And afterwards she went very softly, and opened the window and looked out. Behind her, the room was in a mystical semi-darkness; chairs and tables were hovering, ill-defined shapes; there was but the faintest illusory glitter from the talc moons in the rich Indian curtain which she had drawn across the door. The yellow silk draperies of the bed were but suggestions of colour, and the pillow and the white sheets glimmered as a white cloud in a far sky at twilight.

She turned from the dusky room, and with dewy tender eyes gazed out across the garden towards the lake. She could not rest nor lay herself down to sleep; though it was late, and half the night had passed, she could not rest. A sickle moon was slowly drawing upwards through certain filmy clouds that stretched in a long band from east to west, and a pallid light began to flow from the dark water, as if there also some vague planet were rising. She looked with eyes insatiable for wonder; and she found a strange eastern effect in the bordering of reeds, in their spearlike shapes, in the liquid ebony that they shadowed, in the fine inlay of pearl and silver as the moon shone free; a bright symbol in the steadfast calm of the sky.

There were faint stirring sounds heard from the fringe of reeds, and now and then the drowsy, broken cry of the waterfowl, for they knew that the dawn was not far off. In the centre of the lake was a carved white pedestal, and on it shone a white boy, holding the double flute to his lips.

Beyond the lake the park began, and sloped gently to the verge of the wood, now but a dark cloud beneath the sickle moon. And then beyond, and farther still, undiscovered hills, grey bands of cloud, and the steep pale height of the heaven. She gazed on with her tender eyes, bathing herself, as it were, in the deep rest of the night, veiling her soul with the half-light and the half-shadow, stretching out her delicate hands into the coolness of the misty silvered air, wondering at her hands.

And then she turned from the window, and made herself a divan of cushions on the Persian carpet, and half sat, half lay there, as motionless, as ecstatic as a poet dreaming under roses, far in Ispahan. She had gazed out, after all, to assure herself that sight and the eyes showed nothing but a glimmering veil, a gauze of curious lights and figures: that in it there was no reality nor substance. He had always told her that there was only one existence, one science, one religion, that the external world was but a variegated shadow which might either conceal or reveal the truth; and now she believed.

He had shewn her that bodily rapture might be the ritual and expression of the ineffable mysteries, of the world beyond sense, that must be entered by the way of sense; and now she believed. She had never much doubted any of his words, from the moment of their meeting a month before. She had looked up as she sat in the arbour, and her father was walking down through the avenue of roses, bringing to her the stranger, thin and dark, with a pointed beard and melancholy eyes. He murmured something to himself as they shook hands; she heard the rich, unknown words that sounded as the echo of far music. Afterwards he had told her what those words signified:

> *"How say ye that I was lost? I wandered among roses.*
> *Can he go astray that enters the rose garden?*
> *The Lover in the house of the Beloved is not forlorn.*
> *I wandered among roses. How say ye that I was lost?"*

His voice, murmuring the strange words, had persuaded her, and now she had the rapture of the perfect knowledge. She had looked out into the silvery uncertain night in order that she might experience the sense that for her these things no longer existed. She was not anymore a part of the garden, or of the lake, or of the wood, or of the life that she had led hitherto. Another line that he had quoted came to her:

> *"The kingdom of I and We forsake and your home*
> *in annihilation make."*

It had seemed at first almost nonsense—if it had been possible for him to talk nonsense; but now she was filled and thrilled with the meaning of it. Herself was annihilated; at his bidding she had destroyed all her old feelings and emotions, her likes and dislikes, all the inherited loves and hates that her father and mother had given her; the old life had been thrown utterly away.

It grew light, and when the dawn burned she fell asleep, murmuring:

> *"How say ye that I was lost?"*

The Turanians

The smoke of the tinkers' camp rose a thin pale blue from the heart of the wood.

Mary had left her mother at work on "things," and had gone out with a pale and languid face into the hot afternoon. She had talked of walking across the fields to the Green, and of having a chat with the doctor's daughter, but she had taken the other path that crept down towards the hollow and the dark thickets of the wood.

After all, she had felt too lazy to rouse herself, to make the effort of conversation, and the sunlight scorched the path that was ruled straight from stile to stile across the brown August fields, and she could see, even from far away, how the white dust clouds were smoking on the road by the Green. She hesitated, and at last went down under the far-spreading oak-trees, by a winding way of grass that cooled her feet.

Her mother, who was very kind and good, used to talk to her sometimes on the evils of "exaggeration," on the necessity of avoiding phrases violently expressed, words of too fierce an energy. She remembered how she had run into the house a few days before and had called her mother to look at a rose in the garden that "burnt like a flame." Her mother had said the rose was very pretty, and a little later had hinted her doubts as to the wisdom of "such very strong expressions."

"I know, my dear Mary," she had said, "that in your case it isn't affectation. You really *feel* what you say, don't you? Yes; but is it nice to feel like that? Do you think that it's quite *right*, even?"

The mother had looked at the girl with a curious wistfulness, almost as if she would say something more, and sought for the fit words, but could not find them. And then she merely remarked:

"You haven't seen Alfred Moorhouse since the tennis party, have you? I must ask him to come next Tuesday; you like him?"

The daughter could not quite see the link between her fault of "exaggeration" and the charming young barrister, but her mother's warning recurred to her as she strayed down the shadowed path, and felt the long dark grass cool and refreshing about her feet. She would not have put this sensation into words, but she thought it was as though her ankles were gently, sweetly kissed as the rich grass touched them, and her mother would have said it was not right to think such things.

And what a delight there was in the colours all about her! It was as though she walked in a green cloud; the strong sunlight was filtered through the leaves, reflected from the grass, and made all visible things, the tree-stems, the flowers, and her own hands seem new, transformed into another likeness. She had walked by the wood-path over and over again, but today it had become full of mystery and hinting, and every turn brought a surprise.

Today the mere sense of being alone under the trees was an acute secret joy, and as she went down deeper and the wood grew dark about her, she loosened her brown hair, and when the sun shone over the fallen tree she saw her hair was not brown but bronze and golden, glowing on her pure white dress.

She stayed by the well in the rock, and dared to make the dark water her mirror, looking to right and left with shy glances and listening for the rustle of parted boughs, before she would match her gold with luminous ivory. She saw wonders in a glass as she leaned over the shadowed mysterious pool, and smiled at the smiling nymph, whose lips parted as if to whisper secrets.

As she went on her way, the thin blue smoke rose from a gap in the trees, and she remembered her childish dread of "the gipsies." She walked a little farther, and laid herself to rest on a smooth patch of turf, and listened to the strange intonations that sounded from the camp. "Those horrible people" she had heard the yellow folk called, but she found now a pleasure in voices that sang and, indistinctly heard, were almost chanting, with a rise and fall of notes and a wild wail, and the solemnity of unknown speech. It seemed a fit music for the unknown woodland, in harmony with the drip of the well, and the birds' sharp notes, and the rustle and hurry of the wood creatures.

She rose again and went on till she could see the red fire between the boughs; and the voices thrilled into an incantation. She longed to summon up courage, and talk to these strange wood-folk, but she was afraid to burst into the camp. So she sat down under a tree and waited, hoping that one of them might happen to come her way.

There were six or seven men, as many women, and a swarm of fantastic children, lolling and squatting about the fire, gabbling to one another in their singsong speech. They were people of curious aspect, short and squat, high-cheekboned, with dingy yellow skin and long almond eyes; only in one or two of the younger men there was a suggestion of a wild, almost faunlike grace, as of creatures who always moved between the red fire and the green leaf. Though everybody called them gipsies, they were in reality Turanian metal-workers, degenerated into wandering tinkers; their ancestors had fashioned the bronze battle-axes, and they mended pots and kettles. Mary waited under the tree, sure that she had nothing to fear, and resolved not to run away if one of them appeared.

The sun sank into a mass of clouds and the air grew close and heavy; a mist steamed up about the trees, a blue mist like the smoke of a wood-fire. A strange smiling face peered out from between the leaves, and the girl knew that her heart leapt as the young man walked towards her.

The Turanians moved their camp that night. There was a red glint, like fire, in the vast shadowy west, and then a burning paten floated up from a wild hill. A procession of weird bowed figures passed across the crimson disk, one stumbling after another in long single file, each bending down beneath his huge shapeless pack, and the children crawled last, goblinlike, fantastic.

The girl was lying in her white room, caressing a small green stone, a curious thing cut with strange devices, awful with age. She held it close to the luminous ivory, and the gold poured upon it.

She laughed for joy, and murmured and whispered to herself, asking herself questions in the bewilderment of her delight. She was afraid to say anything to her mother.

The Idealist

"Did you notice Symonds while Beever was telling that story just now?" said one clerk to the other.

"No. Why? Didn't he like it?"

The second clerk had been putting away his papers and closing his desk in a grave and business-like manner, but when Beever's story was recalled to him he began to bubble anew, tasting the relish of the tale for a second time.

"He's a fair scorcher, old Beever," he remarked between little gasps of mirth. "But didn't Symonds like it?"

"Like it? He looked disgusted, I can tell you. Made a face, something in this style": and the man drew his features into a design of sour disapproval, as he gave his hat the last polish with his coatsleeve.

"Well, I'm off now," he said. "I want to get home early, as there's tart for tea," and he fashioned another grimace, an imitation of his favourite actor's favourite contortion.

"Well, goodbye," said his friend. "You are a hot 'un, you are. You're worse than Beever. See you on Monday. What will Symonds say?" and he shouted after him as the door swung to and fro.

Charles Symonds, who had failed to see the humour of Mr. Beever's tale, had left the office a few minutes earlier and was now pacing slowly westward, mounting Fleet Street. His fellow clerk had not been much amiss in his observation. Symonds had heard the last phrases of Beever's story, and unconsciously had looked half round towards the group, angry and disgusted at their gross and stupid merriment. Beever and his friends seemed to him guilty of sacrilege; he likened them to plough-boys pawing and deriding an exquisite painted panel, blaring out their contempt and brutal ignorance. He could not control his features; in spite of himself he looked loathing at the three yahoos. He would have given anything if he could have found words and told them what he thought, but even to look displeasure was difficult. His shyness was a perpetual amusement to the other clerks, who often did little things to annoy him, and enjoyed the spectacle of Symonds inwardly raging and burning like Etna, but too hopelessly diffident to say a word. He would turn dead man's white, and grind his teeth at an insult, and pretend to join in the laugh, and pass it off as a joke. When he was a boy his mother was puzzled by him, not knowing whether he were sullen or insensible, or perhaps very good-tempered.

He climbed Fleet Street, still raw with irritation, partly from a real disgust at the profane coarseness of the clerks, and partly from a feeling that they talked so because they knew he hated such gross farces and novels. It was hideous to live and work with such foul creatures, and he glanced back fury at the City, the place of the stupid, the blatant, the intolerable.

He passed into the rush and flood of the Strand, into the full tide of a Saturday afternoon, still meditating the outrage, and constructing a cutting sentence for future use, heaping up words which should make Beever tremble. He was quite aware that he would never utter one of those biting phrases, but the pretence soothed him, and he began to remember other things. It was in late November and the clouds were already gathering for the bright solemnity of the sunset, flying to their places before the wind. They curled into fantastic shapes, high up there in the wind's whirlpool, and Symonds, looking towards the sky, was attarcted by two grey writhing clouds that drew together in the west, in the far perspective of the Strand. He saw them as if they had been living creatures, noting every change and movement and transformation, till the shaking winds made them one and drove a vague form away to the south.

The curious interest he had taken in the cloud shapes had driven away the thought of the office, of the fetid talk which he so often heard. Beever and his friends ceased to exist, and Symonds escaped to his occult and private world which no one had ever divined. He lived far away down in Fulham, but he let the buses rock past him, and walked slowly, endeavouring to prolong the joys of anticipation. Almost with a visible gesture he drew himself apart, and went solitary, his eyes downcast, and gazing not on the pavement but on certain clear imagined pictures.

He quickened his steps as he passed along the northern pavement of Leicester Square, hurrying to escape the sight of the enamelled strange spectra who were already beginning to walk and stir abroad, issuing from their caves and waiting for the gas-light. He scowled as he looked up and chanced to see on a hoarding an icon with raddled cheeks and grinning teeth, at which some young men were leering; and one was recalling this creature's great song:

"And that's the way they do it.
How d'ye fink it's done?

> *Oh,* that's *the way they do it.*
> Doesn't *it taike the bun?"*

Symonds scowled at the picture of her, remembering how Beever had voted her "good goods," how the boys bellowed the chorus under his windows of Saturday nights. Once he had opened the window as they passed by, and had sworn at them and cursed them, in a whisper, lest he should be overheard.

He peered curiously at the books in a Piccadilly shop; now and then when he could save a few pounds he had made purchases there, but the wares which the bookseller dealt in were expensive, and he was obliged to be rather neatly dressed at the office, and he had other esoteric expenses. He had made up his mind to learn Persian and he hesitated as to whether he should turn back now, and see if he could pick up a grammar in Great Russell Street at a reasonable price. But it was growing dark, and the mists and shadows that he loved were gathering and inviting him onwards to those silent streets near the river.

When he at last diverged from the main road he made his way by a devious and eccentric track, threading an intricate maze of streets which to most people would have been dull and gloomy and devoid of interest. But to Symonds these backwaters of London were as bizarre and glowing as a cabinet of Japanese curios; he found here his delicately chased bronzes, work in jade, the flush and flame of extraordinary colours. He delayed at a corner, watching a shadow on a lighted blind, watching it fade and blacken and fade, conjecturing its secrets, inventing dialogue for this drama in *Ombres Chinoises.* He glanced up at another window, and saw a room vivid, in a hard yellow light of flaming gas, and lurked in the shelter of an old elm till he was perceived and the curtains were drawn hastily. On the way he had chosen, it was his fortune to pass many well-ordered decent streets, by villas detached and semi-detached, half hidden behind flowering-shrubs and evergreens. At this hour, on a Saturday in November, few were abroad, and Symonds was often able, crouching down by the fence, to peer into a lighted room, to watch persons who thought themselves utterly unobserved. As he came near to his home he went through meaner streets, and he stopped at a corner, observing two children at play, regarding them with the minute scrutiny of an entomologist at the microscope. A woman who had been out shopping crossed the road and drove the children home, and Symonds moved on, hastily, but with a long sigh of enjoyment.

His breath came quick, in gusts, as he drew out his latch-key. He lived in an old Georgian house, and he raced up the stairs, and locked the door of the great lofty room in which he lived. The evening was damp and chilly, but the sweat streamed down his face. He struck a match, and there was a strange momentary vision of the vast room, almost empty of furniture, a hollow space bordered by grave walls and the white glimmer of the corniced ceiling.

He lit a candle, opened a large box that stood in a corner, and set to work. He seemed to be fitting together some sort of lay figure; a vague hint of the human shape increased under his hands. The candle sparkled at the other end of the room, and Symonds was sweating over his task in a cavern of dark shadow. His nervous shaking fingers fumbled over that uncertain figure, and then he began to draw out incongruous monstrous things. In the dusk, white silk shimmered, laces and delicate frills hovered for a moment, as he bungled over the tying of knots, the fastening of bands. The old room grew rich, heavy, vaporous with subtle scents; the garments that were passing through his hands had been drenched with fragrance. Passion had contorted his face; he grinned stark in the candlelight.

When he had finished the work he drew it with him to the window, and lighted three more candles. In his excitement, for that night he forgot the effect of *Ombres Chinoises,* and those who passed and happened to look up at the white staring blind found singular matter for speculation.

R ather left the others behind, haven't we, Miss Custance?" said the captain, looking back to the gate and the larchwood.

"I'm afraid we have, Captain Knight. I hope you don't mind very much, do you?"

"Mind? Delighted, you know. Sure this damp air isn't bad for you, Miss Custance?"

"Oh, d'you think it's damp? I like it. Ever since I can remember I've enjoyed these quiet autumn days. I won't hear of father's going anywhere else."

"Charmin' place, the Grange. Don't wonder you like comin' down here."

Captain Knight glanced back again and suddenly chuckled.

"I say, Miss Custance," he said, "I believe the whole lot's lost their way. Don't see a sign of them. Didn't we pass another path on the left?"

"Yes, and don't you remember you wanted to turn off?"

"Yes, of course. I thought it looked more possible, don't you know. That's where they must have gone. Where does it lead?"

"Oh, nowhere exactly. It dwindles and twists about a lot, and I'm afraid the ground is rather marshy."

"You don't say so?" The captain laughed out loud. "How awfully sick Ferris will be. He hates crossing Piccadilly if there's a bit of mud about."

"Poor Mr. Ferris!" And the two went on, picking their way on the rough path, till they came in sight of a little old cottage sunken alone in a hollow amongst the woods.

"Oh, you must come and see Mrs. Wise," said Miss Custance. "She's such a dear old thing, I'm sure you'd fall in love with her. And she'd never forgive me if she heard afterwards that we'd passed so close without coming in. Only for five minutes, you know."

"Certainly, Miss Custance. Is that the old lady there at the door?"

"Yes. She's always been so good to us children, and I know she'll talk of our coming to see her for months. You don't mind, do you?"

"I shall be charmed, I'm sure," and he looked back once more to see if there were any appearance of Ferris and his party.

"Sit down, Miss Ethel, sit down, please, miss," said the old woman when they went in. "And please to sit down here, sir, will you be so kind?"

She dusted the chairs, and Miss Custance enquired after the rheumatism and the bronchitis, and promised to send something from the Grange. The old woman had good country manners, and spoke well, and now and then politely tried to include Captain Knight in the conversation. But all the time she was quietly looking at him.

"Yes, sir, I be a bit lonely at times," she said when her visitors rose. "I do miss Nathan sorely; you can hardly remember my husband, can you, Miss Ethel? But I have the Book, sir, and good friends too."

A COUPLE OF DAYS LATER Miss Custance came alone to the cottage. Her hand trembled as she knocked at the door.

"Is it done?" she asked, when the old woman appeared.

"Come in, miss," said Mrs. Wise, and she shut the door, and put up the wooden bolt. Then she crept to the hearth, and drew out something from a hiding-place in the stones.

"Look at that," she said, showing it to the young lady. "Isn't it a picture?"

Miss Custance took the object into her fine delicate hands, and glanced at it, and then flushed scarlet.

"How horrible!" she exclaimed. "What did you do that for? You never told me."

"It's the only way, miss, to get what you want."

"It's a loathsome thing. I wonder you're not ashamed of yourself."

"I be as much ashamed as you be, I think," said Mrs. Wise, and she leered at the pretty, shy-faced girl. Their eyes met and their eyes laughed at one another.

"Cover it up, please, Mrs. Wise; I needn't look at it now, at all events. But are you sure?"

"There's never been a mishap since old Mrs. Cradoc taught me, and she's been dead for sixty year and more. She used to tell of her grandmother's days when there were meetings in the wood over there."

"And you're quite sure?"

"You do as I tell you. You must take it like this"; and the old woman whispered her instructions, and would have put out a hand in illustration, but the girl pushed it away.

"I understand now, Mrs. Wise. No, don't do that. I quite see what you mean. Here's the money."

"And whatever you do, don't you forget the ointment as I told you," said Mrs. Wise.

"I've been to read to poor old Mrs. Wise," Ethel said that evening to Captain Knight. "She's over eighty and her eyesight is getting very bad."

"Very good of you, Miss Custance, I'm sure," said Captain Knight, and he moved away to the other end of the drawing-room, and began to talk to a girl in yellow, with whom he had been exchanging smiles at a distance, ever since the men came in from the dining-room.

That night, when she was alone in her room, Ethel followed Mrs. Wise's instructions. She had hidden the object in a drawer, and as she drew it out, she looked about her, though the curtains were drawn close.

She forgot nothing, and when it was done she listened.

The Ceremony

From her childhood, from those early and misty days which began to seem unreal, she recollected the grey stone in the wood.

It was something between the pillar and the pyramid in shape, and its grey solemnity amidst the leaves and the grass shone and shone from those early years, always with some hint of wonder. She remembered how, when she was quite a little girl, she had strayed one day, on a hot afternoon, from her nurse's side, and only a little way in the wood the grey stone rose from the grass, and she cried out and ran back in panic terror.

"What a silly little girl," the nurse had said. "It's only the. . . stone." She had quite forgotten the name that the servant had given, and she was always ashamed to ask as she grew older.

But always that hot day, that burning afternoon of her childhood when she had first looked consciously on the grey image in the wood, remained not a memory but a sensation. The wide wood swelling like the sea, the tossing of the bright boughs in the sunshine, the sweet smell of the grass and flowers, the beating of the summer wind upon her cheek, the gloom of the underglade rich, indistinct, gorgeous, significant as old tapestry; she could feel it and see it all, and the scent of it was in her nostrils. And in the midst of the picture, where the strange plants grew gross in shadow, was the old grey shape of the stone.

But there were in her mind broken remnants of another and far earlier impression. It was all uncertain, the shadow of a shadow, so vague that it might well have been a dream that had mingled with the confused waking thoughts of a little child. She did not know that she remembered, she rather remembered the memory. But again it was a summer day, and a woman, perhaps the same nurse, held her in her arms, and went through the wood. The woman carried bright flowers in one hand; the dream had in it a glow of bright red, and the perfume of cottage roses. Then she saw herself put down for a moment on the grass, and the red colour stained the grim stone, and there was nothing else—except that one night she woke up and heard the nurse sobbing.

She often used to think of the strangeness of very early life; one came, it seemed, from a dark cloud, there was a glow of light, but for a moment, and afterwards the night. It was as if one gazed at a velvet curtain, heavy, mysterious, impenetrable blackness, and then, for the twinkling of an eye, one spied through a pin-hole a storied town that flamed, with fire about its walls and pinnacles. And then again the folding darkness, so that sight became illusion, almost in the seeing. So to her was that earliest, doubtful vision of the grey stone, of the red colour spilled upon it, with the incongruous episode of the nursemaid, who wept at night.

But the later memory was clear; she could feel, even now, the inconsequent terror that sent her away shrieking, running to the nurse's skirts. Afterwards, through the days of girlhood, the stone had taken its place amongst the vast array of unintelligible things which haunt every child's imagination. It was part of life, to be accepted and not questioned; her elders spoke of many things which she could not understand, she opened books and was dimly amazed, and in the Bible there were many phrases which seemed strange. Indeed, she was often puzzled by her parents' conduct, by their looks at one another, by their half-words, and amongst all these problems which she hardly recognized as problems, was the grey ancient figure rising from dark grass.

Some semi-conscious impulse made her haunt the wood where shadow enshrined the stone. One thing was noticeable; that all through the summer months the passersby dropped flowers there. Withered blossoms were always on the ground, amongst the grass, and on the stone fresh blooms constantly appeared. From the daffodil to the Michaelmas daisy there was marked the calendar of the cottage gardens, and in the winter she had seen sprays of juniper and box, mistletoe and holly. Once she had been drawn through the bushes by a red glow, as if there had been a fire in the wood, and when she came to the place, all the stone shone and all the ground about it was bright with roses.

In her eighteenth year she went one day into the wood, carrying with her a book that she was reading. She hid herself in a nook of hazel, and her soul was full of poetry, when there was a rustling, the rapping of parted boughs returning to their place. Her concealment was but a little way from the stone, and she peered through the net of boughs, and saw a girl timidly approaching. She knew her quite well; it was Annie Dolben, the daughter of a labourer, lately a promising pupil at Sunday school. Annie was a nice-mannered girl, never failing in her curtsy, wonderful for her knowledge of the Jewish Kings. Her face had taken an expression that whispered, that hinted strange things; there was a light and a glow behind the veil of flesh. And in her hand she bore lilies.

ARTHUR MACHEN

The lady hidden in hazels watched Annie come close to the grey image; for a moment her whole body palpitated with expectation, almost the sense of what was to happen dawned upon her. She watched Annie crown the stone with flowers, she watched the amazing ceremony that followed.

And yet, in spite of all her blushing shame, she herself bore blossoms to the wood a few months later. She laid white hothouse lilies upon the stone, and orchids of dying purple, and crimson exotic flowers. Having kissed the grey image with devout passion, she performed there all the antique immemorial rite.

Psychology

M r. Dale, who had quiet rooms in a western part of London, was very busily occupied one day with a pencil and little scraps of paper. He would stop in the middle of his writing, of his monotonous tramp from door to window, jot down a line of hieroglyphics, and turn again to his work. At lunch he kept his instruments on the table beside him, and a little notebook accompanied him on his evening walk about the Green. Sometimes he seemed to experience a certain difficulty in the act of writing, as if the heat of shame or even incredulous surprise held his hand, but one by one the fragments of paper fell into the drawer, and a full feast awaited him at the day's close.

As he lit his pipe at dusk, he was standing by the window and looking out into the street. In the distance cab-lights flashed to and fro, up and down the hill, on the main road. Across the way he saw the long line of sober grey houses, cheerfully lit up for the most part, displaying against the night the dining-room and the evening meal. In one house, just opposite, there was brighter illumination, and the open windows showed a modest dinner-party in progress, and here and there a drawing-room on the first floor glowed ruddy, as the tall shaded lamp was lit. Everywhere Dale saw a quiet and comfortable respectability; if there were no gaiety there was no riot, and he thought himself fortunate to have got "rooms" in so sane and meritorious a street.

The pavement was almost deserted. Now and again a servant would dart out from a side door and scurry off in the direction of the shops, returning in a few minutes in equal haste. But foot passengers were rare, and only at long intervals a stranger would drift from the highway and wander with slow speculation down Abingdon Road, as if he had passed its entrance a thousand times and had at last been piqued with curiosity and the desire of exploring the unknown. All the inhabitants of the quarter prided themselves on their quiet and seclusion, and many of them did not so much as dream that if one went far enough the road degenerated and became abominable, the home of the hideous, the mouth of a black purlieu. Indeed stories, ill and malodorous, were told of the streets parallel, to east and west, which perhaps communicated with the terrible sink beyond, but those who lived at the good end of Abingdon Road knew nothing of their neighbours.

Dale leant far out of his window. The pale London sky deepened

ARTHUR MACHEN

to violet as the lamps were lit, and in the twilight the little gardens before the houses shone, seemed as if they grew more clear. The golden laburnum but reflected the last bright yellow veil that had fallen over the sky after sunset, the white hawthorn was a gleaming splendour, the red may a flameless fire in the dusk. From the open window, Dale could note the increasing cheerfulness of the diners opposite, as the moderate cups were filled and emptied; blinds in the higher stories brightened up and down the street when the nurses came up with the children. A gentle breeze that smelt of grass and woods and flowers, fanned away the day's heat from the pavement stones, rustled through the blossoming boughs, and sank again, leaving the road to calm.

All the scene breathed the gentle domestic peace of the stories; there were regular lives, dull duties done, sober and common thoughts on every side. He felt that he needed not to listen at the windows, for he could divine all the talk, and guess the placid and usual channels in which the conversation flowed. Here there were no spasms, nor raptures, nor the red storms of romance, but a safe rest; marriage and birth and begetting were no more here than breakfast and lunch and afternoon tea.

And then he turned away from the placid transparency of the street, and sat down before his lamp and the papers he had so studiously noted. A friend of his, an "impossible" man named Jenyns, had been to see him the night before, and they had talked about the psychology of the novelists, discussing their insight, and the depth of their probe.

"It is all very well as far as it goes," said Jenyns. "Yes, it is perfectly accurate. Guardsmen do like chorus-girls, the doctor's daughter is fond of the curate, the grocer's assistant of the Baptist persuasion has sometimes religious difficulties, 'smart' people no doubt think a great deal about social events and complications: the Tragic Comedians felt and wrote all that stuff, I dare say. But do you think that is all? Do you call a description of the gilt tools on the morocco here an exhaustive essay on Shakespeare?"

"But what more is there?" said Dale. "Don't you think, then, that human nature has been fairly laid open? What more?"

"Songs of the frantic lupanar delirium of the mad-house. Not extreme wickedness, but the insensate, the unintelligible, the lunatic passion and idea, the desire that must come from some other sphere that we cannot even faintly imagine. Look for yourself; it is easy."

Dale looked now at the ends and scraps of paper. On them he had carefully registered all the secret thoughts of the day, the crazy lusts, the senseless furies, the foul monsters that his heart had borne, the maniac phantasies that he had harboured. In every note he found a rampant madness, the equivalents in thought of mathematical absurdity, of two-sided triangles, of parallel straight lines which met.

"And we talk of absurd dreams," he said to himself. "And these are wilder than the wildest visions. And our sins; but these are the sins of nightmare.

"And everyday," he went on, "we lead two lives, and the half of our soul is madness, and half heaven is lit by a black sun. I say I am a man, but who is the other that hides in me?"

Torture

I really do not know what to do with him," said the father. "He seems absolutely stupid."

"Poor boy!" said his mother, "I am afraid he is not well. He doesn't look in good health."

"But what's the matter with him? He eats well enough; he had two helpings of meat, and two of pudding today at dinner, and a quarter of an hour afterwards he was munching some sweet stuff. His appetite's all right, you see, anyhow."

"But he's very pale. He makes me feel anxious."

"And he makes me feel anxious. Look at this letter from Wells, the head master. Here you see he says: 'It seems almost impossible to get him to play games; he has had two or three thrashings, as I hear, for shirking cricket. And his form master gives me a very bad account of his work during the term, so that I fear the school is doing him little if any good.' And you see, Mary, it isn't as if he were a little boy; he was fifteen last April. It's getting serious, you know."

"What d'you think we had better do?"

"I wish I knew. Look at him here. He's only been home for a week, and you'd think he'd be in the best of spirits, enjoying himself with the squire's boys, and singing and racketing about all over the place. And you know the way he has been going on, almost from the day he came back; lounging and crawling from the house to the garden and back again, staying in bed half the day, and coming down with his eyes half open. I must insist on that being put a stop to, at all events. I shall trust to you to get him up at a proper time."

"Very well, dear. I thought he looked so tired."

"But he does nothing to make him tired! I wouldn't mind so much if the fellow were bookish, but you see what Wells says on that score. Why, I can't even get him to read a story-book. I declare his face is enough to make one angry. One can see he's totally devoid of any interest in anything."

"I am afraid he's unhappy, Robert."

"Unhappy! A schoolboy unhappy! Well, I wish you'd see what you can do. I find it perfectly useless to talk to him myself."

It was curious, but the father was quite right in laughing at the notion of his son's unhappiness. Harry was, in his quiet way, in the best of spirits. It was perfectly true that he hated cricket, and, the head master might have added, he hated other boys. He cared nothing for printed matter of any kind, whether fact or fiction, and he found *Treasure Island* as dull as Cicero. But all through the past term he had been pondering an idea; it had been with him in the early mornings in the dormitory, in schooltime and in playtime, and he watched with it at night, long after the other boys had gone to sleep. Before the coming of the idea he had found his existence unhappy enough. He had a puffy, unwholesome face and sandy hair, and his great wide mouth was made the subject of many jests. He was unpopular because he did not like games, and because he would not bathe unless he were flung into the water, and he was always in trouble over his lessons, which he could not understand. He burst out crying one night in the middle of preparation, and of course he would not say what was the matter. The fact was that he had been trying to extract the meaning from some weary nonsense about triangles, known by the absurd name of Euclid, and he had found it utterly impossible to learn the rabid stuff by heart. The impossibility of it, and the hopeless cloud in his mind, and the terror of the thrashing he would get in the morning, broke him down; the "blubbering idiot," as they said.

Those were unhappy times, but that very night his idea came to him, and the holidays became indeed desirable, and ten times desirable. Everyday and all the day he elaborated and re-elaborated his great thought, and though he was as stupid, unpopular, and unprofitable as ever, he was no longer wretched.

When he got home at the end of term he lost no time in setting about his task. It was true that he was sleepy and heavy in the mornings, but that was because he worked till late at night. He found it impossible to do much in the day-time; his parents spied out his ways, and he knew that he was much too dull to invent lies and explanations. The day after his return his father had come across him as he slunk into a dark corner of the shrubbery with something hidden under his coat. He could only stand and look hopeless, idiotic, when an empty beer bottle was drawn forth; he could not say what he was doing or what he wanted with a green glass bottle. His father had left him, telling him not to play the fool, and he felt that he was always watched. When he took the cord from the back-kitchen one of the maids was peering after him down the passage, and his mother found him trying to bind a large log of wood to the trunk of one of the trees. She wanted to know what he was doing, and whether he could not find some more sensible amusement, and he stared at her with his heavy white face. He knew that he was under observation, and so he worked at night. The two servant girls who slept in the next room often awoke, fancying they heard a queer sort of noise, a "chink-chink," as one of them described the sensation, but they could not make out what it was.

And at last he was ready. He was "loafing about" one afternoon, and he happened to meet Charlotte Emery, a little girl of twelve, the daughter of a neighbour. Harry flushed to a dull burning red.

"Come for a walk with me to the Beeches?" he said. "I wish you would."

"Oh, I mustn't, Harry. Mother wouldn't like it."

"Do come. I've got a new game; grand fun."

"Is it really? What sort of game is it?"

"I can't show you here. Just walk on towards the Beeches, and I'll follow you directly. I knew you would."

Harry ran full tilt to the hiding-place where he had bestowed his apparatus. He soon overtook Charlotte, and the two went off together towards the Beeches, a lonely wooded hill, a mile away. The boy's father would have been astonished if he could have seen him; Harry was glowing and burning with that dull red colour, but he laughed as he walked beside Charlotte.

When they were alone together in the wood, Charlotte said:

"Now you must show me the game. You promised."

"I know. But you must do just as I tell you."

"Yes, I will."

"Even if it hurts?"

"Yes. But you wouldn't hurt me, Harry. I like you."

The boy stared at her, gazed with his dull, fishy, light blue eyes; his white, unwholesome face glared at her almost in terror. She was a dark girl, olive-skinned, with black eyes and black hair, and the scent of her hair had already half-intoxicated him, as they walked close together.

"You like me," he said at last, stuttering.

"Yes, I like you very much. I love you, Harry dear. Won't you give me a kiss?" And she put her arm round his neck, round the neck of the ugly, pasty schoolboy. The leaden marks under his eyes seemed to grow darker.

He dropped the parcel that he held under one arm. It broke open and the contents fell to the ground. There were three or four fantastic instruments, ugly little knives made of green bottle-glass, clumsily set into wooden handles. He had stolen a broom for this purpose. And there were some lengths of rope, fitted with running nooses. It was the idea that he had so long cherished.

But he threw himself full length upon the grass, and burst into tears—the "blubbering idiot."

Midsummer

The old farm-house on the hill flushed rose in the afterglow, and then, as the dusk began to mount from the brook, faded and yet grew brighter, its whitewashed walls gleaming as though light flowed from them, as the moon gleams when the red clouds turn to grey.

The ancient hawthorn tree at the barn-end became a tall black stem and its leaves and boughs a black mass against the pale uncertain blue of the twilight sky. Leonard looked up with a great sigh of relief. He was perched on the stile by the bridge, and as the wind fell, the ripple of the water swelled into a sweeter song, and there was no other sound to be heard. His pipe was finished, and though he knew that his rooms up at the farm looked out on the red rose and the white, he could not make up his mind to leave the view of the shimmering unearthly walls, and the melody of clear running water.

The contrast of it all with London was almost too immense, hardly realized or credible. A few hours before, and his ears seemed bursting with the terrible battle of the streets, with the clangour and jangle of great waggons thundering over the stones, with the sharp rattle of hansoms, the heavy rumble of swaying omnibuses. And during the journey his eyes still saw the thronging crowds, the turbid, furious streams of men that pushed eastward and westward, hurrying and jostling one another, wearying the brain with their constant movement, the everlasting flux and reflux of white faces. And the air, a hot smoke, a faint sick breath as though from a fever-stricken city; the sky, all grey heat that beat upon weary men, as they looked up through the cloud of dust that went before and followed them.

And now he was soothed in the deep silence and soothed by the chanting water, his eyes saw the valley melting into soft shadow, and in his nostrils was the ineffable incense of a summer night, that as a medicine allayed all the trouble and pain of body and mind. He wet his hands in the dew of the long grass and bathed his forehead, as if all the defilement and anguish of the streets should thus be washed utterly away.

He tried to analyse the scent of the night. The green leaves that overshadowed the brook and made the water dark at noon, gave out their odour, and the deep meadow grass was fragrant, a gale of scent breathed from the huge elder-bush that lit up the vague hillside, hanging above the well. But the meadow-sweet was bursting into blossom at his feet, and ah! the wild red roses drooped down from dreamland.

At last he began to climb the hillside towards those white magic walls that had charmed him. His two rooms were at the end of the long low farm-house, and though there was a passage leading to the big kitchen, Leonard's sitting-room opened immediately on the garden, on the crimson roses. He could go and come as he pleased without disturbing the household, or as the pleasant farmer had expressed it, he had a home of his own. He entered and locked the door, and lit the two candles that stood in bright brass candlesticks on the mantelpiece. The room had a low ceiling crossed by a whitewashed beam, the walls were bulging and uneven, decked with samplers, with faded prints, and in a corner stood a glass cupboard, displaying quaint flowery china of some forgotten local pattern.

The room was as quiet, as full of peace, as the air and the night, and Leonard knew that here, at the old bureau, he would find the treasure he had been long vainly seeking. He was tired, but he did not feel inclined to go to bed. He lit his pipe again, and began to arrange his papers, and idly sat down at the bureau, thinking of the task, or rather of the delight, before him. An idea flashed suddenly into his mind, and he began to write hurriedly, in an ecstasy, afraid lest he should lose what he had so happily found.

At midnight his window was still bright on the hill, and he laid down his pen with a sigh of pleasure at the accomplished work. And now he could not go to bed; he felt he must wander into the night, and summon sleep from the velvet air, from the scent of darkness, from the dew. He gently unlocked and locked the door, and walked slowly between the Persian roses, and climbed the stone stile in the garden wall. The moon was mounting to a throne, in full splendour; below, at a little distance, there seemed the painted scene of a village, and higher, beyond the farm-house, a great wood began. And as he thought of the green retreats he had glanced at in the sunlit evening, he was filled with a longing for the wood-world at night, with a desire for its darkness, for the mystery of it beneath the moon. He followed the path he had noted, till on the wood's verge he looked back and found that the shape of the farm-house had fallen into the night and vanished.

He entered the shadow, treading softly, and let the track lead him away from the world. The night became full of whisperings, of dry murmuring noises; it seemed soon as if a stealthy host were beneath the trees, every man tracking another. Leonard quite forgot his work, and its triumph, and felt as though his soul were astray in a new dark sphere that dreams had foretold. He had come to a place remote, without form or colour, made alone of shadow and overhanging gloom. Unconsciously he wandered from the path, and for a time he fought his way through the undergrowth, struggling with interlacing boughs and brambles that dragged back his feet.

At last he got free, and found that he had penetrated into a broad avenue, piercing, it seemed, through the heart of the wood. The moon shone bright from above the tree-tops, and gave a faint green colour to the track which ascended to an open glade; a great amphitheatre amidst the trees. He was tired, and lay down in the darkness beside the turfy road, and wondered whether he had lit on some forgotten way, on some great path that the legions had trodden. And as he lay there watching, gazing at the pale moonlight, he saw a shadow advancing on the grass before him.

"A breath of wind must be stirring some bough behind me," he thought, but in the instant a woman went by, and then the shadows and white women followed thick.

Leonard gripped hard at a stick he was carrying, and drove his nails into the flesh. He saw the farmer's daughter, the girl who had waited on him a few hours before, and behind her came girls with like faces, no doubt the quiet modest girls of the English village, of the English farm-house.

For a moment they fronted him, shameless, unabashed before one another, and then they had passed.

He had seen their smiles, he had seen their gestures, and things that he had thought the world had long forgotten.

The white writhing figures passed up towards the glade, and the boughs hid them, but he never doubted as to what he had seen.

Nature

A nd there was a broad level by the river," Julian went on, telling the story of his holiday. "A broad level of misty meadows, divided by low banks, between the hills and the river. They say the Roman world is lost beneath the turf, that a whole city sleeps there, gold and marble and amber all buried forever."

"You did not see anything?"

"No, I suppose not. I used to get up early, and go out, and leave the little modern village behind me, hidden in the hot haze. And then I would stand in the misty meadows, and watch the green turf shimmer and lighten, as the grey halo rolled away. Oh! the silence. There was no sound except the lapping of the river, the wash of the water on the reeds.

"The banks are yellow mud," he went on, "but in the early morning, as the sun began to shine in the mist, they pearled and grew like silver. There was a low mound that hid something, and on it an old thorn tree bent towards the east; it was a little way from the tide's brim. I stood there and saw the woods swell out of the haze in the early morning, and that white sun seemed to encompass the town with gleaming walls. If I had stayed still, I think I should have seen the glittering legion and the eagles, I should have heard the sonorous trumpets pealing from the walls."

"I expect you have seen and heard more than that," said his friend. "I always told you that the earth too, and the hills, and even the old walls are a language, hard to translate."

"And I came upon a place that made me think of that," said Julian. "It was far from the town; I lost my way amongst those rolling hills, and strayed by footpaths from field to wood, and all that I saw of man was here and there a blue smoke that crawled up from the earth, from the tree, it might be, or the brook, for I could see no house. I went on, always with the sense that I was following an unknown object, and, suddenly, a shape rose from forgotten dreams. An old farm-house, built of grey, silvering stones; a long barn wavering and dipping down to a black pool, pine trees overhanging the roof. It was all dim, as if it had been seen reflected in water. I went a little nearer, and I found that I was lifted free of the maze of hills. I fronted the mountain, looking across a deep broad valley, and all the year the mountain winds must blow upon the porch; they look from their deep windows and see the fleeting of

ARTHUR MACHEN

the clouds and the sun, on that vast green hillside. Yellow flowers were shaking in the garden, for even on that still day the mountain wind swept across the valley. But those grey glistening walls! Alight flowed from them, and they spoke of something beyond thought.

"I visited, too, the river valley, passing out to the north. The town was soon hidden behind trees, behind a curtain of Lombardy poplars, whispering of Italy, of the vine, the olive garden. The curving lane led me beneath orchards, their under-boughs dark-green, almost black, in the shadow, and the road winding between orchard and river led me into the long valley, where the forest is as a cloud upon the hill. I watched the yellow tide cease, and the water flow dear, and the breath of the wind was unearthly. It was there that I saw the burning pools."

"You stayed for the sunset?"

"Yes, I stayed all day within the valley. The sky was grey, but not cloudy; rather it was a glowing of silver light that made the earth seem dim and yet shining. Indeed, I say that though the sun was hidden, you would have dreamed that white moons were floating through the air, for now and again I saw the misty hillside pale and lighten, and a tree would appear suddenly in mid-forest, and glitter as if it blossomed. Yes, and in the calm meadows by the riverside there were little points of brightness, as if tongues of white fire sparkled in the grey grass."

"And the river itself?"

"It was all the day a hieroglyphic, winding in esses beneath those haunting banks, colourless, and yet alight like all the world around. At last, in the evening, I sat down beneath a wych-elm on the slope, where I breathed the scent and knew the heavy stillness of the wood. Then a strong wind blew, high up in heaven, and the grey veil vanished. The sky was clear pale blue; in the west there was exhibited an opal burning green, and beneath a purple wall. Then, in the middle of the purple, a rent opened; there was a red glint, and red momentary rays, as if rose-hot metal were beaten and dinted on the anvil, and the sparks fled abroad. So the sun sank.

"I thought I would wait and see all the valley, the river, and the level, and the woods sink into twilight, become sombre, formless. The light went out from the river, the water paled as it flowed between the sad reeds and grasses. I heard a harsh melancholy cry, and above, in the dusky air, a flight of great birds passed seaward in changing, hieroglyphic order. The keen line of the hills by sunset home seemed to melt away, to become vague.

"Then I saw the sky was blossoming in the north. Rose gardens appeared there, with golden hedges, and bronze gates, and the great purple wall caught fire as it grew leaden. The earth was lit again, but with unnatural jewelled colours; the palest light was sardonyx, the darkness was amethyst. And then the valley was aflame. Fire in the wood, the fire of a sacrifice beneath the oaks. Fire in the level fields, a great burning in the north, and vehement flame to the south, above the town. And in the still river the very splendour of fire, yes, as if all precious things were cast into its furnace pools, as if gold and roses and jewels became flame."

"And then?"

"Then, the shining of the evening star."

"And you," said his friend, "perhaps without knowing, have told me the story of a wonderful and incredible passion."

Julian stared at him, in amazement.

"You are quite right," he said at length.

The Holy Things

The sky was blue above Holborn, and only one little cloud, half white, half golden, floated on the wind's way from west to east. The long aisle of the street was splendid in the full light of the summer, and away in the west, where the houses seemed to meet and join, it was as a rich tabernacle, mysterious, the carven house of holy things.

A man came into the great highway from a quiet court. He had been sitting under plane-tree shade for an hour or more, his mind racked with perplexities and doubts, with the sense that all was without meaning or purpose, a tangle of senseless joys and empty sorrows. He had stirred in it and fought and striven, and now disappointment and success were alike tasteless. To struggle was weariness, to attain was weariness, to do nothing was weariness. He had felt, a little while before, that from the highest to the lowest things of life there was no choice, there was not one thing that was better than another: the savour of the cinders was no sweeter than the savour of the ashes. He had done work which some men liked and others disliked, and liking and disliking were equally tiresome to him. His poetry or his pictures or whatever it was that he worked at had utterly ceased to interest him, and he had tried to be idle, and found idleness as impossible as work. He had lost the faculty for making and he had lost the power of resting; he dozed in the day-time and started up and cried at night. Even that morning he had doubted and hesitated, wondering whether to stay indoors or to go out, sure that in either plan there was an infinite weariness and disgust.

When he at last went abroad he let the crowd push him into the quiet court, and at the same time cursed them in a low voice for doing so; he tried to persuade himself that he had meant to go somewhere else. When he sat down he desperately endeavoured to rouse himself, and as he knew that all the strong interests are egotistic, he made an effort to grow warm over the work he had done, to find a glow of satisfaction in the thought that he had accomplished something. It was nonsense; he had found out a clever trick and had made the most of it, and it was over. Besides, how would it interest him if afterwards he was praised when he was dead? And what was the use of trying to invent some new tricks? It was folly; and he ground his teeth as a new idea came into his mind and was rejected. To get drunk always made him so horribly ill, and other things were more foolish and tiresome than poesy or painting, whichever it was.

He could not even rest on the uncomfortable bench, beneath the dank, stinking plane tree. A young man and a girl came up and sat next to him, and the girl said, "Oh, isn't it beautiful today?" and then they began to jabber to one another—the blasted fools! He flung himself from the seat and went out into Holborn.

As far as one could see, there were two processions of omnibuses, cabs, and vans that went east and west and west and east. Now the long line would move on briskly, now it stopped. The horses' feet rattled and pattered on the asphalt, the wheels ground and jarred, a bicyclist wavered in and out between the serried ranks, jangling his bell. The foot passengers went to and fro on the pavement, with an endless change of unknown faces; there was an incessant hum and murmur of voices. In the safety of a blind passage an Italian whirled round the handle of his piano-organ; the sound of it swelled and sank as the traffic surged and paused, and now and then one heard the shrill voices of the children who danced and shrieked in time to the music. Close to the pavement a coster pushed his barrow, and proclaimed flowers in an odd intonation, reminding one of the Gregorian chant. The cyclist went by again with his jangling insistent bell, and a man who stood by the lamp-post set fire to his pastille ribbon, and let the faint blue smoke rise into the sun. Away in the west, where the houses seemed to meet, the play of sunlight on the haze made, as it were, golden mighty shapes that paused and advanced, and paused again.

He had viewed the scene hundreds of times, and for a long while had found it a nuisance and a weariness. But now as he walked stupidly, slowly, along the southern side of Holborn, a change fell. He did not in the least know what it was, but there seemed to be a strange air, and a new charm that soothed his mind.

When the traffic was stopped, to his soul there was a solemn hush that summoned remnants of a far-off memory. The voices of the passengers sank away, the street was endued with a grave and reverent expectation. A shop that he passed had a row of electric lamps burning above the door, and the golden glow of them in the sunlight was, he felt, significant. The grind and jar of the wheels, as the procession moved on again, gave out a chord of music, the opening of some high service that was to be done, and now, in an ecstasy, he was sure that he heard the roll and swell and triumph of the organ, and shrill sweet choristers began to sing. So the music sank and swelled and echoed in the vast aisle—in Holborn.

What could these lamps mean, burning in the bright sunlight? The music was hushed in a grave close, and in the rattle of traffic he heard the last deep sonorous notes shake against the choir walls—he had passed beyond the range of the Italian's instrument. But then a rich voice began alone, rising and falling in monotonous but awful modulations, singing a longing triumphant song, bidding the faithful lift up their hearts, be joined in heart with the Angels and Archangels, with the Thrones and Dominations. He could see no longer, he could not see the man who passed close beside him, pushing his barrow, and calling flowers.

Ah! He could not be mistaken, he was sure now. The air was blue with incense, he smelt the adorable fragrance. The time had almost come. And then the silvery, reiterated, instant summons of a bell; and again, and again.

The tears fell from his eyes, in his weeping the tears poured a rain upon his cheeks. But he saw in the distance, in the far distance, the carven tabernacle, golden mighty figures moving slowly, imploring arms stretched forth.

There was a noise of a great shout; the choir sang in the tongue of his boyhood that he had forgotten:

SANT. . . SANT. . . SANT

Then the silvery bell tinkled anew; and again, and again. He looked and saw the Holy, White, and Shining Mysteries exhibited—in Holborn.

FINIS

A Note About the Author

Arthur Machen (1863–1947) was a Welsh mystic and author. Born Arthur Llewellyn Jones, he was raised in Monmouthshire in a prominent family of clergymen. He developed an early interest in alchemy and other occult matters, and obtained a classical education at Hereford Cathedral School. He moved to London, where he failed to gain admittance to medical school and soon focused on his literary interests. Working as a tutor, he wrote in the evening and published his first poem, "Eleusinia," in 1881. A novel, *The Anatomy of Tobacco* (1884), soon followed, launching his career as a professional writer. Machen made a name for himself as a frequent contributor to London literary magazines and achieved his first major success with the 1894 novella *The Great God Pan*. Following his wife's death from cancer in 1899, he briefly joined the Hermetic Order of the Golden Dawn and began conducting research on Celtic Christianity, the legend of the Holy Grail, and the stories of King Arthur. In 1922, after a decade of working as a journalist for the *Evening News*, he published *The Secret Glory*—a story of the Grail—to popular and critical acclaim. This marked the highpoint of his career as a pioneering author of fantasy, horror, and supernatural fiction whose work has been admired and praised by William Butler Yeats, Arthur Conan Doyle, and Stephen King.

A Note from the Publisher

Spanning many genres, from non-fiction essays to literature classics to children's books and lyric poetry, Mint Edition books showcase the master works of our time in a modern new package. The text is freshly typeset, is clean and easy to read, and features a new note about the author in each volume. Many books also include exclusive new introductory material. Every book boasts a striking new cover, which makes it as appropriate for collecting as it is for gift giving. Mint Edition books are only printed when a reader orders them, so natural resources are not wasted. We're proud that our books are never manufactured in excess and exist only in the exact quantity they need to be read and enjoyed. To learn more and view our library, go to minteditionbooks.com

bookfinity & MINT EDITIONS

Enjoy more of your favorite classics with Bookfinity,
a new search and discovery experience for readers.
With Bookfinity, you can discover more vintage
literature for your collection, find your Reader Type,
track books you've read or want to read,
and add reviews to your favorite books.
Visit www.bookfinity.com, and click on
Take the Quiz to get started.

Don't forget to follow us
@bookfinityofficial and @mint_editions

CPSIA information can be obtained
at www.ICGtesting.com
Printed in the USA
JSHW050751060822
28969JS00003B/4

9 781513 218311